About the Author

Sadie King was born in No............ raised in Lancashire. After graduating with a degree in history from Lancaster University, she moved to West Lothian, Scotland, where she now lives with her husband and children. When she's not writing, Sadie loves long country walks, romantic ruins, Thai food and travelling with her family. She also writes historical fiction and contemporary mysteries as Sarah L King.

Regency Whispers

Regency Whispers:

A Secret Past

SADIE KING

MILLS & BOON

First Published in Great Britain 2024
By Mills & Boon, an imprint of HarperCollins*Publishers* Ltd,
1 London Bridge Street, London, SE1 9GF

www.harpercollins.co.uk

HarperCollins*Publishers*
Macken House, 39/40 Mayor Street Upper,
Dublin 1, D01 C9W8, Ireland

Regency Whispers: A Secret Past © 2024 Harlequin Enterprises ULC.

Spinster with a Scandalous Past © 2024 Sarah Louise King
Rescuing the Runaway Heiress © 2024 Sarah Louise King

ISBN: 978-0-263-32487-7

SPINSTER WITH A SCANDALOUS PAST

For my family

Chapter One

June 1818

As the carriage rattled along the road towards Lowhaven, Louisa Conrad wondered what on earth she had been thinking. The sound of braying horses rang in her ears, and if she closed her eyes she could still feel herself tumbling down, could still feel her body thud against the coach's solid wood as it landed on its side and took her with it.

In her lap, her hands tremored. She clasped them together and pressed her lips into a tight smile, forcing calm where there was none to be found. Her gaze moved between the two brothers sitting before her, but only one of them returned her smile. The other did not even look at her, apparently preferring the country views offered through the small carriage window.

Briefly she furrowed her brow at him, before giving her full attention to his sibling as he struck up a conversation once again.

'I'm sure that you will find Juniper Street to your liking,' Mr Liddell said.

'I'm sure I shall, sir,' she replied crisply. 'And I believe that after the journey we've had I will appreciate it all the more.'

'Indeed, indeed. A wholesome meal and a good night's repose cures most ills, I find.' His eyes shone, almost teasing. 'You have both had quite an adventure.'

Beside her, Nan shifted, gripping the cushioned seat so hard that her knuckles turned white. Louisa couldn't decide what was distressing her maid more. The terror of the stagecoach accident, or everything that had happened since.

'I'm not sure I would describe it quite like that,' Louisa answered him. 'Those poor horses were dreadfully frightened after the coach turned over. I'm quite sure that the coachman was beside himself with concern for their welfare.'

'Of course—well, until the next time he's whipping them relentlessly so that he might travel at a dangerous speed,' Mr Liddell countered, a smile playing on his lips.

Louisa gave him a small nod, suppressing her own smile but finding that she could not, in earnest, disagree. Nan, meanwhile, chose that moment to clear her throat, no doubt to remind Louisa of the impropriety of their situation. They would have words later, that was for certain. Strong words about getting into the carriage of some unknown gentlemen, about reckless decisions and their consequences, about the manifold horrors which might have occurred.

Louisa had already prepared her defences. What else could they have done when they were stranded in the middle of nowhere, miles from the nearest inn? Were they not fortunate that the gentlemen happened upon them just moments after the coach had overturned?

Her hands trembled again, reminding her that she was not certain of her own argument. After all, Nan's undoubted reservations would be more than justified. Shaken and disorientated, the coach stricken and their luggage scattered on the ground, she could hardly claim to have been thinking clearly. No, instead she had allowed them to be swept along, embracing the notion of rescue without reservation. In those few moments she had been utterly unguarded. And Louisa, more than most, ought to remember the dangers inherent in letting down one's guard.

'Forgive me, Miss Conrad, I am making light of a difficult day, but you might have been seriously injured. I would urge you to consult a doctor once you are settled at your aunt's house. I can ask our physician to pay a visit to you, if you wish?'

'That's very kind of you, sir,' she replied, 'but I'm sure there's no need. We are, as you see, unharmed.'

She forced a smile, ignoring the ache in her ribs which served to remind her that she was not being entirely truthful.

'My brother is right.'

Louisa blinked, startled by the low timbre of the voice which had interjected. The other brother looked at her now, fixing his deep blue eyes upon her so intently that she almost wished he'd return to looking out of the window. Sir Isaac, Mr Liddell had called him during their fraught introductions earlier. Sir Isaac Liddell of Hayton Hall. As she stared back at him now, Louisa realised that this was the first time Sir Isaac had spoken to her in the several hours they'd been travelling together.

'My brother is right,' he repeated. 'We will send our physician.'

Louisa nodded her assent, sensing it was not worth her while to disagree. This appeared to satisfy him, as he said nothing more, but continued to look at her for a little longer than would be deemed polite. Louisa dropped her gaze, and after a moment she sensed him resume his interest in the scenery outside.

'What did you say your aunt's name was, Miss Conrad?' Mr Liddell asked, apparently keen to break the awkward silence which had descended in the carriage.

'I'm not sure that I did, but it is Miss Clarissa Howarth.'

'Miss Clarissa Howarth,' he repeated. 'I know that name. Is your aunt the rector's daughter from Hayton?'

Reluctantly Louisa nodded, feeling immediately guarded at this new line of questioning. 'That's correct, sir.'

Mr Liddell nudged his brother. 'Do you remember Reverend Howarth, Isaac?'

'Of course,' Sir Isaac muttered, not troubling himself to tear his gaze from the window.

From across the carriage Louisa found herself observing him, both offended by and grateful for his apparent lack of interest. With his striking blue gaze safely averted, she felt able to note his other features: near-black hair, a strong, angular jawline, and a sun-kissed complexion which hinted at time spent outdoors. He was dressed from head to toe in black, apart from the white shirt which she glimpsed beneath his coat, and it struck Louisa that he would not look out of place as a character in one of Mrs Radcliffe's gothic romances.

He was handsome, she concluded, but disagreeable. Not that either aspect of Sir Isaac Liddell mattered to her.

'It must be some time now since Reverend Howarth's passing?' Mr Liddell continued.

She nodded, returning her attention once more to the talkative brother. Unlike Sir Isaac, his features were fair, his hair the colour of sand and his eyes a pale blue-grey. In both looks and demeanour, it was hard to believe that they were related.

'Yes,' she replied, 'almost fifteen years.'

'And now your aunt lives on Juniper Street,' he said, in a way which seemed to be neither a statement nor a question.

'She does, yes.'

Now it was Louisa who turned to look out of the window, emulating Sir Isaac's aloof posture in the hope that it would signal an end to the conversation about her family history. Answering questions about Aunt Clarissa was all very well, but she was not keen to see where Mr Liddell's enquiries might lead. He'd already discovered where she'd come from, not long after they'd settled into the carriage.

'Berkshire…?' he'd pondered, before remarking upon how far she'd travelled and recounting a tale of some arduous journey south he'd previously undertaken.

She'd only half listened, and after a while he'd seemed to sense her weariness, smiling an apology and insisting that she needed to rest. Now, so close to her destination, she was determined that they would not revisit the subject. Louisa Conrad was a stranger here, and that was how it was going to remain.

Fortunately, it appeared she wouldn't have to deflect his attempts at conversation for much longer. Outside the carriage window, the wild Cumberland countryside had given way to a gentle townscape of smart grey and white buildings, and the streets were alive with coaches, carts and crowds, as people went about their business.

Her first glimpse of Lowhaven was a reassuring one, and she recalled the excitement she'd first felt when her parents had proposed this sojourn to her. A change of scenery, they'd called it. An opportunity to travel, just as she'd always wished.

She suspected there was more to their desire to send her away than mere broadened horizons, but she didn't care, and had loved the idea from the very first moment. Her eagerness had been dampened somewhat by the travails of the journey, but now, as it reached its welcome conclusion, it returned with renewed vigour. Even Nan looked happier, staring wide-eyed out of the window, her mouth agape at the town as it unravelled in front of her.

'Juniper Street is not far from the port,' Mr Liddell informed them. 'I do hope you won't find the noise and traffic too disturbing.'

Louisa thought about her family's estate, enveloped in rolling green fields and an almost unendurable silence. About the large country house, containing too few people and too many opportunities to ruminate on what might have been. Without doubt, she'd had her fill of living quietly in recent years.

'If it's near to the port then it is near to the sea, which will do very well for me,' she countered cheerfully. 'Besides, lively places can be very diverting.'

Mr Liddell let out a soft laugh. 'If diversion is what you seek, Miss Conrad, then I do believe you will find it in Lowhaven.'

The carriage drew to a halt on a dusty street, lined on either side by rather humble-looking stone townhouses, uniformly built, but with little embellishment. After a moment the coachman opened the door and Mr Liddell exited, offering Louisa his hand as she descended the steps, with Nan following closely behind her.

Louisa smoothed her palms over the crumpled, muddied skirt of her day dress as she took her first breath of Lowhaven's fresh sea air. *Yes,* she thought, *this will do very well indeed.*

'Our driver will fetch your luggage to the door for you, Miss Conrad,' Mr Liddell said.

Louisa turned to face him, realising then that Sir Isaac had not followed them out of the carriage. Instead he remained within, his sombre countenance visible through the little window to which he'd given so much of his attention throughout the journey. Briefly Louisa shook her head at his rudeness, before regarding Mr Liddell once more. There might have been two gentlemen in the carriage today, she thought, but really only one of them could be regarded as their rescuer.

'Mr Liddell, I must thank you most sincerely for coming to our aid today. Truly, you are a good Samaritan. I only hope we have not caused any significant delay to your own journey.'

The gentleman shook his head. 'None whatsoever. Our home is merely a few miles up the road. It was a pleasure to escort you, and to see you safely to your destination, and I will see to it that our physician calls upon you later. I hope that your stay in Lowhaven is agreeable. It is not comparable with the fashionable resorts of the south coast, but nonetheless it has its charms.'

'I'm obliged to you, sir. Will you not stay for some

tea? I'm sure my aunt would be glad to welcome you both,' she added, glancing warily once more towards the carriage.

'You're very kind, Miss Conrad, but I'm afraid we must take our leave,' he replied, tipping his hat briefly. 'Perhaps our paths will cross again, while you are here.'

Before Louisa could respond, Mr Liddell had climbed back into the carriage and closed the door behind him. Through the window he gave her one last broad smile, before his coachman cracked his whip once more and they were off.

For a moment Louisa just stood there, staring after that handsome carriage, surrounded by the luggage which Nan was frantically trying to put into order. After the ordeal of their journey, it seemed miraculous that they had finally arrived. In fact, it almost didn't seem real: the accident, the rescue, the kind gentleman, the rude gentleman—all of it.

Louisa let out a weary sigh. What a long and strange day it had been.

Then, behind her, a door opened and a voice she hadn't heard for years rang out in delight.

'Louisa! Oh, my dear Louisa! Is it really you?'

Louisa turned around and walked straight into the outstretched arms of her Aunt Clarissa, who embraced her quickly before stepping back to regard her niece. The woman looked older than Louisa remembered, her face heavily lined, her once blonde hair now silver and peering wildly from beneath a lace cap. Thinner, too, Louisa thought. She could compete with the minuscule Nan in terms of slenderness.

'You look well, my dear, all things considered,' her aunt said carefully, and Louisa couldn't help but suspect that she was referring to more than just the long journey. 'Your mother was right; you've grown into quite a beautiful young lady.'

Louisa laughed aloud, gesturing at her mud-spattered travelling clothes. 'I look far from beautiful right now, Aunt! And I don't believe I merit being described as "young" any more, either.'

Clarissa raised a curious eyebrow. 'Oh, nonsense—you're barely five-and-twenty; you're not allowed to deny your youth for a few years yet!' She placed a gentle hand on Louisa's arm and steered her towards the door. 'However, you do look as though you've become acquainted with our Cumberland countryside already. Come, let's get your luggage brought in, then we can have some tea and you can tell me all about it.'

'Tell you all about what, Aunt?'

'Your journey, of course—I'd say it's quite a story, judging by the state of your dress.' Clarissa smiled, a look of amusement sparkling in her keen blue eyes. 'But above all you must tell me—how on earth did you come to be accompanied here by Samuel Liddell of Hayton Hall?'

Chapter Two

Samuel Liddell patted his older brother on the back as they walked through the grand wooden door of Hayton Hall. 'I'd say that was a very successful trip,' he declared. 'A number of business matters put to bed, and we rescued a fair maiden in distress on the way home.'

Isaac grunted as he loosened his cravat and threw off his coat, wearied both by the long journey and his brother's endlessly cheerful disposition.

It had been only a short stay in Penrith, and that had been quite long enough. With every passing hour Isaac had found himself yearning to return to the peace and tranquillity of Hayton Hall. The bustle of towns had never suited him and, after spending so long away from them, he now found that he disliked them all the more. He'd never felt so relieved when they'd finally left the coaching inn that morning and begun the final part of their journey home.

A journey which had taken far longer than it should have, thanks to a stagecoach accident on the road and Samuel's insistence that they deliver that young woman and her maid to her aunt in Lowhaven.

'Related to the old rector, Howarth, and coming all the way from an estate in Berkshire,' Samuel remarked, mulling over the details he'd managed to prise from their unexpected carriage guest. 'A gentleman's daughter, to be sure.'

'The very reckless daughter of a gentleman,' Isaac countered as he marched towards his library. 'Getting into a carriage with us—we could have been anyone.'

Samuel followed, his amused chuckle seeming to echo down the hall. 'Well, fortunately for her, we were perfect gentlemen. Or at least I was. You barely looked at her.'

Isaac grunted again as he collapsed into his favourite armchair. Samuel was wrong about that: he had looked at her. Had observed the deep brown of her eyes, her pink pursed lips, and the way her striking blonde curls peered from the edges of her damaged bonnet. He'd noted the mud on her dress, and the way she'd winced and put her hand against her ribs every time the carriage met a bump on the road. He'd caught her frowning at him, more than once, and sensed that his aloofness displeased her. Not that any of it mattered to him.

He slumped back in his chair and closed his eyes as Samuel rang for some tea. No, he thought. Fair maidens and their opinions of him were of no consequence.

'You'd better make sure that you do send the physician to attend to her,' Isaac said. 'Despite her protestations, I do believe that she was injured.'

'Ah, so you are taking an interest in her?' Samuel teased.

Isaac's eyes flew open and he sat up straight. 'I'm merely concerned for her welfare after being in such a bad accident. And might I remind you that it was you who invited the lady and her maid into our carriage?'

'And you'd have left them stranded on the road?' Samuel scoffed.

'Of course not,' Isaac snapped. 'I am many things, but I am not heartless.'

Isaac watched as his brother sat down in the armchair opposite him, sighing heavily as he resigned himself to a lecture. It had been like this ever since Samuel had returned from his European travels, apparently determined to atone for his lengthy absence by seeing to it that his grieving recluse of a brother got his life in order.

Sometimes he was glad of it, content to have his morose moods offset by a dose of his brother's buoyancy and relieved to have the large rooms of his ancestral home filled with lively chatter once more. At other times Samuel's good intentions grated on him—largely because he no longer felt he needed to be looked after. And because his brother had not been there when he really had needed his care…during those darkest days when he'd wallowed, unwashed and undressed, drinking himself into oblivion.

Samuel must have seen something in his brother's expression to dissuade him from pursuing the matter of Isaac's heart, as when he finally spoke it was to change the subject.

'I'm glad you decided to come with me to Penrith. I know you have much to attend to on the estate, but I do believe it's done you the world of good.'

Isaac grunted, the temptation to offer one of his usual cutting retorts thwarted by the earnest look on Samuel's face. 'I suppose it did end up being something of an adventure,' he confessed, surprised to find himself thinking about the lady with the brown eyes and fair curls once more.

'Ah—you see!' Samuel declared, clapping his hands together. 'Even Sir Isaac Liddell is not immune to a bit of chivalry.'

'I wouldn't go that far,' Isaac retorted. 'As you said yourself, I barely acknowledged the lady.'

And he hadn't—not really. Noticing a pretty face was one thing, but his days of being a knight in shining armour to a fair maiden were long past. He was alone now; that was the cruel hand fate had dealt him, and that was how it was going to remain.

After being plied with tea, copious amounts of cake, and a conversation which bordered on an interrogation, it was with some relief and a very full stomach that Louisa made her way to her bedroom later that afternoon.

Aunt Clarissa had been horrified by the stagecoach accident, expressing her consternation that Louisa's parents had not seen fit to escort her on the long journey north. Louisa had protested mildly, informing her aunt that her family were all presently in London, and doing her best to ignore her nagging suspicions about exactly why her parents had left her to fend for herself. Why they were so keen for her to spend the summer here. What they thought it might teach her.

Her aunt's mood had mercifully lightened when the conversation had turned to Louisa's rescuers—or at least, the one she had seen.

'Mr Samuel Liddell,' she said, beaming. 'He has been away for some time, travelling in Europe, and has only recently returned to Hayton Hall. The Liddells are a distinguished family in this part of the country. You will recall that your grandfather was the rector of Hayton? He knew the family very well.'

'Yes, Mr Liddell spoke of my grandfather during the journey,' Louisa had replied. 'He said that he remembered him.'

'Mr Samuel would have been quite young back then. Your grandfather knew his father better. He passed away suddenly, years ago, before Mr Samuel came of age. I recall his mother followed not long afterwards. Mr Samuel's older brother inherited the baronetcy.'

The mention of Mr Liddell's brother had caused Louisa's stomach to lurch quite unexpectedly. Doubtless it was the memory of his sombre disposition and curt indifference which had vexed her.

'Sir Isaac Liddell was also travelling with us this afternoon,' she'd said, feeling duty-bound to report to her guardian the exact details of her rescue.

Her aunt's eyes had widened in surprise. 'Really? I did not see him.'

'He remained in the carriage when we arrived,' she'd explained, trying to suppress a fresh wave of irritation at his rudeness.

'I see. Well, my dear, you have had a rare introduction. Sir Isaac is almost never seen in town. Indeed, it is said that he seldom leaves his estate.'

Louisa had nodded, utterly unsurprised by her aunt's revelation. The gentleman she'd encountered earlier today had been inattentive and unsociable, and clearly had not wished to be in her company, so it was little wonder to her that he did not relish being in anyone else's.

On the other hand, she'd reflected, as she had sipped her tea, there were many good reasons to shut oneself away from society, as she knew only too well.

She'd been about to enquire what Sir Isaac's might be when her aunt had changed the subject.

'I'd suggest you don't mention the stagecoach accident or your subsequent rescue to your mother when you write to her,' she'd advised. 'I'm not sure that she would approve.'

Louisa had furrowed her brow at this. 'I've done nothing I should be ashamed of, surely? Nan was with me—and besides, I'm not sure what else I could have done. Mr Liddell was very kind, and Sir Isaac has insisted that their physician will call upon Nan and me, as a precaution.'

'I mean no criticism, my dear,' her aunt had replied, chuckling at her niece's defensive tone. 'Sometimes in life we find ourselves in difficult situations, and the choices offered to us are less than ideal. In those situations we are forced to trust our instincts. You should be reassured that, as an unmarried woman, you can rely upon yours. That's important—especially if this is the path you're set upon.'

Those words rang in Louisa's ears as she walked into her room to find Nan, still unpacking. The room Clarissa had given her was small, but well-appointed, tucked away at the rear of the house and overlooking a charming little courtyard. Beyond it were more houses, walls and courtyards; wherever she looked, there seemed only stone to be found.

It occurred to Louisa then that it had been a long time since she had looked out of a window and seen anything other than fields. Her last London season had been six years ago, and she'd seen nothing of any town since. Another aspect of the path she had embarked upon.

'Your books are on the table, miss,' Nan said as she bustled about. 'I know you'll be looking for them before you trouble yourself with your dresses.'

Louisa thanked her maid, moving to run her fingers over her most prized possessions as she gazed out of the window. The afternoon was ebbing away towards evening, but the light was still good, the early June sunshine warm and bright and uninhibited by cloud.

She wondered how often the room's previous inhabitant had stood there and enjoyed the view over the town. For years Aunt Clarissa had shared her home with another spinster, Miss Slater, until the woman had quite unexpectedly married at the age of five and fifty. The now Mrs Knight had subsequently relocated to Carlisle, with her husband, leaving Aunt Clarissa alone.

Louisa knew that this was partly what had prompted her mother to send her to Lowhaven—although she was not so naïve that she did not recognise the other motivations her parents were likely to have for wishing to remove her from Berkshire entirely.

'Have you told your aunt about what happened this afternoon?' Nan asked. 'I hope she is not too vexed by it.'

Louisa gave her maid a brisk nod. 'I have, and I must say she was only concerned that we might have been injured. The rest of the tale didn't seem to perturb her in the slightest.'

Nan stared at her mistress, her mouth agape. 'But, miss, your reputation—'

'In these parts I have no reputation, Nan. I am known to no one, so there is no one to discuss whether or not I should have got into that carriage, or to condemn me as silly, naïve or without virtue. And if I have my way that is how it shall remain. I am here to visit my aunt and to enjoy a pleasant summer before returning to Berkshire, and that is all.'

'I'm sorry, miss. I only worry for you, given what happened with your captain—'

Louisa held up a hand in protest and looked her maid directly in the eye. 'Nan, you will not mention any of that while we are here; I forbid it. You do not know who might be listening. I will not have my life become the subject of tittle-tattle between servants.'

Nan nodded meekly. 'Yes, of course, miss.'

Louisa's stern expression dissolved into a fond smile. She couldn't help it; she'd known Nan since she was a girl. At a little more than ten years her senior, her maid was not old enough to be a motherly figure, but nonetheless the pair shared a close bond which had only deepened as Louisa's life had taken increasingly difficult turns. Nan knew all of it, she'd seen everything, and yet she still cared.

Louisa retreated from the window once more, sitting down upon the bed which was situated in the centre of the room. She patted the sheets at her side, indicating that Nan should rest for a moment and join her.

'This is such a beautiful bedroom,' Louisa remarked, surveying her surroundings once more. 'I'm glad my aunt saw fit to put me at the back of the house. I'm not sure how well I would sleep with all the noise from the street outside. It was Miss Slater's room; my aunt told me so at tea.'

Nan's eyes widened at that. 'Well, I daresay that staying in this room is a good omen, miss. If its last occupant managed to find herself a husband in this town, perhaps you will, too.'

Louisa bristled. The words were kindly meant, but they stung her nonetheless. She closed her eyes for a moment, allowing herself the luxury of small remembered glimpses: his chestnut hair, his green eyes, his deep blue frock coat. The delicate feeling of his fingers caressing her face. The way that he always seemed to smell like the ocean, even though he'd been on land for months. The way he'd kissed her at their last meeting. The fearful urgency of it—as though he had already seen that a rising tide was coming and that it would part them for good.

Her thoughts darkened then, wandering to everything that had come after…everything she'd had to face alone. Everything that made finding a husband in a new town utterly impossible.

From beneath her lashes, a tear slipped out. 'You know that is out of the question, Nan. There is no one for me now, and that is an end to it.'

Then, before Nan could say anything further, Louisa fled from the room.

Chapter Three

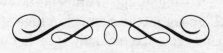

Isaac whipped his horse, pushing the poor beast to gallop as fast as its legs could manage. The weather was as foul as his mood, having turned in these last few days from still and sunlit to blustery and beset with heavy grey cloud. It hadn't begun to rain yet, thank God. Like everyone else, he feared that if it did, it might never stop.

He might have little interaction with the world outside Hayton Hall these days, but he was not immune to its worries. They'd endured two of the worst summers he could remember, cold and endlessly wet, damaging crops and causing many a harvest to fail. What Cumberland and England prayed for was a long, hot summer.

He'd pray, too, if he could bring himself to speak to his maker any more.

Isaac growled, cracking his whip again as he sped towards the cliffs before turning to chart a rough path along their rugged edges. In front of him the land sloped down towards Lowhaven, its orderly buildings and busy port nestled into the bay. He wouldn't go as far as that; it was out of the question. It was difficult enough to slip away from Hayton unnoticed. He was almost guaranteed to be seen in town, to be remarked upon, and he despised being the subject of gossip.

Perhaps he ought to turn back now, before he got too close…

'You're a damnable coward, Isaac Liddell,' he muttered to himself.

Samuel would certainly agree. He'd more or less said it himself, a few nights ago at dinner. The evening had started well enough, with Samuel in high spirits after they'd gallantly rescued that lady from her overturned coach. His good cheer had eventually grown on Isaac, and after a pleasant meal and a few glasses of port he had found himself smiling, too. He'd relaxed, allowing himself to take comfort in his brother's company, to reflect that it was preferable to dining alone.

Samuel must have sensed that his guard was down, or perhaps he'd really been in his cups—either way, his words had not been gentle.

'You should go out more,' he'd said. 'Put on your best clothes. Go to a ball. Go to London! Find yourself a nice wife. Stop hiding yourself away, licking your wounds and hoping the world will forget that you exist.'

Isaac groaned at the memory of it, the pained sound mercifully carried away by the howling wind. The brothers had always been very different men, in both outlook and temperament, but these past couple of years seemed to have placed an unnavigable chasm between them. Samuel had travelled and Isaac had lost; one brother's horizons had expanded, whilst the other's world had shrunk.

Samuel would never understand that Isaac's life could not be repaired by embracing society or getting himself on to the dancing card of a beautiful lady.

'Watch out!'

He'd been so absorbed by his own thoughts that he hadn't seen the woman until the very last moment. In fact, his horse saw her first. The creature reared, letting out a high-pitched whinny as it drew to a sudden halt. Isaac clung hard to the reins; he was a good horseman, but not beyond being unseated by a startled beast.

'Hell and damnation!' he cried out, finally bringing his horse under control.

The woman stared up at him, wide-eyed and apparently frozen to the spot. Her terror was written all over her face, which had turned a ghastly shade of white. Despite the fright she'd given him, immediately he recognised the deep brown gaze, contrasting starkly with the fair curls which sprang at the edges of her bonnet.

The fair maiden they'd welcomed into their carriage on the way home from Penrith. The one travelling from Berkshire with her maid before falling victim to a careless driver and an overturned stagecoach. He watched as she furrowed her brow at him, giving him the same disapproving look he'd spied during that long journey to Lowhaven. Instead of stepping aside, the lady remained in his way, and inexplicably he felt the heat of irritation rise in his chest.

'What the blazes are you doing, walking into the path of my horse?' he snapped.

His accusing tone seemed to bring her to her senses. 'What am I doing?' she repeated. 'I am walking, sir. I might ask what you are doing, riding your horse in such a reckless manner, with no consideration for those whom you might encounter up here.'

Her question was a fair one; he had been riding with little care. With a sigh, he dismounted from his horse. 'I do not expect to see anyone up here. Not on a day like today, at least.' He drew closer to the woman. 'I am very sorry to have frightened you.'

'I wasn't frightened,' she answered him, taking a step back.

If he'd been in a better frame of mind he would have found her indignation amusing. Instead he found himself struck by the petite, pretty, but very stern figure standing in front of him, well turned out in a fetching pale blue dress and matching spencer, steadfastly holding her bonnet in place as the fierce wind threatened to carry it away.

A gentleman's daughter, Samuel had called her, and indeed there was no mistaking the air of gentility about her.

As he considered this, Isaac found himself regretting his coarse words. He gave her a small, belated bow. 'Forgive me,' he said. 'If I am not mistaken, I believe we have met before. My name is Isaac Liddell. We—that is my brother and I—escorted you to Lowhaven after that dreadful stagecoach accident. You may not recall… In fact…' He shook his head at himself, unable to comprehend his sudden lack of ability to speak coherently. 'That is to say, you may remember my brother better, as he made all the arrangements.'

The lady offered him a brisk nod. 'I remember you,' she said simply. 'Sir Isaac Liddell of Hayton Hall.'

He winced at the cool way with which she accorded him his proper title. 'Did our physician attend you? I asked my brother to arrange it.'

'He did, thank you.' For the first time, a small smile played upon her lips. 'I daresay Mr Liddell likes to arrange things.'

Isaac frowned. 'What makes you say that?'

She beheld him with a steely gaze he couldn't read.

'I was merely thinking about the day of the coach accident, and the way he took charge of the situation,' she replied.

Isaac tried not to feel the sting in her observation—tried not to consider the implication that, while Samuel had been something of a hero, he'd done nothing much at all. 'I suppose some people are good at fixing things,' he said. 'Or at least they like to believe that they are.'

'Indeed. But not everything can be fixed, can it?'

Such a knowing remark unsettled him, and he felt his breath catch in his throat. 'Fortunately, rescuing a fair maiden after a stagecoach accident and sending for a physician are skills well within Samuel's repertoire.' He kept his tone light, cheery, almost jovial. Everything he did not feel in that moment.

The woman frowned. 'Excuse me? A fair maiden?'

Isaac suppressed a groan, realising he'd said that aloud. Damn, it had been so long since he had spent time in company, and even longer since he'd spoken to a lady. It seemed that his sense of etiquette was something else he'd lost.

'Forgive me,' he said again. 'It was how my brother described you. He meant it kindly, but it was impolite of me to repeat it.'

'I see.' The woman raised her eyebrows at him, then pursed those pretty pink lips once more before adding, 'I'd wager you cannot even recall my name, sir.'

Such directness took him aback, and he felt an unusual heat rising from beneath his collar and creeping to his face. During their first fraught encounter on the road, some brief and extremely awkward introductions had been made. She had given her name then—of course she had—but he was damned if he could remember it. Ever since then, in his mind she had been the fair maiden. Samuel's name for her had well and truly stuck, and he hadn't needed another when conjuring the memory of her dark gaze or her disapproving glances. A memory, he realised now, that he'd conjured more than once.

'Indeed I do,' he replied, floundering as he grasped at the only name he knew. 'I do recall, Miss… Howarth.'

'Miss Howarth is my aunt,' she replied flatly, although something like amusement flickered across her face. 'My name is Miss Louisa Conrad,' she added, extending a hand towards him.

He accepted the gesture as the olive branch it was clearly intended to be, and took hold of her hand with as much grace as he could muster. Although they both wore gloves, he found himself struck by the feeling of her small, delicate fingers resting briefly in his.

'It's a pleasure to make your acquaintance again, Miss Conrad. Please accept my sincere apology. I meant no disrespect.'

Miss Conrad laughed. 'To be honest, I'm not sure which is worse—being referred to as a fair maiden, or having your name forgotten entirely.'

Isaac winced at her gentle teasing. 'Truly, I am sorry on both counts,' he replied. 'You have my solemn promise that I will never refer to you as a fair maiden ever again.'

'Do not fret, sir. I have been called worse, I'm sure,' she quipped.

'Really?' asked Isaac, disconcerted by the forthright remark. 'That I cannot believe. Although you will have been seen arriving in Lowhaven with my brother and me.

Such an event is certain to set tongues wagging around these parts.'

Isaac had made the observation in jest, but immediately he could see that he'd offended her all over again. The look on her face hardened, and those dark eyes blazed with something he couldn't quite name. Hotter than hurt, but cooler than anger.

He shook his head at himself, unable to believe his own impertinence. Truly, what had become of him?

'I'm sorry, Miss Conrad, I didn't mean—'

'Oh, I'm quite sure you did,' she replied, her tone scathing. She gave a brief, insincere curtsey. 'I think I'd best take my leave of you now, sir. I wouldn't wish my unchaperoned presence here to provide any further fodder for the gossips. Good day.'

She spun round, determinedly marching away from him and back towards Lowhaven. Isaac stared after her for a few moments, dumbstruck at his own stupidity. What on earth had possessed him to talk so loosely to a woman he barely knew?

He sighed, and found himself wondering what Samuel would say if he'd borne witness to all that had just occurred. It was just as well he'd no intention of marrying again. After two years of solitude, it was clear that all his charm had simply withered away.

As she walked back to her aunt's house, Louisa felt that she ought to question her sanity. Aunt Clarissa had expressed reservations about her taking long walks alone, making vague insinuations about the possible dangers to a young woman, and saying how she really ought to accompany her but she feared she could not walk so far. It turned out that her aunt had been right—although perhaps not in the way she would have imagined.

It had only been days since Louisa had arrived in Cumberland. Already she'd got into the carriage of two unknown gentlemen, and now she'd argued with one of them for good measure. She shook her head, berating herself as she hurried in the direction of Juniper Street. Why had she spoken to him in that way, and with such a careless tongue? It was bad enough that her actions on the day of the coach accident had shown her to be a foolish and improper young woman, but to then suggest that there might be some further stain on her character, that people might see fit to besmirch her reputation— that was unforgivable.

It was also true, she reminded herself. She knew well enough what Berkshire society said about her. She had, without doubt, been called far worse than a fair maiden.

'A fair maiden, indeed,' she muttered as she marched along.

She tried not to imagine how the brothers must have made fun of her—how they must have laughed as they talked of the silly southern lady they'd rescued on their journey home. Certainly, Sir Isaac had all but told her what he thought of her, hadn't he? That she was the sort of woman about whom people chattered, and therefore, by implication, the sort of woman whose behaviour was unbecoming of a gentleman's daughter. That had been the point of his impertinent remark, hadn't it?

'Such a rude, disagreeable gentleman,' she said aloud to herself.

He had been rude—there could be no question about that. A man of honour would have kept such thoughts to himself, even if provoked by her own ill-advised commentary. A man of honour would not have cursed in her presence, either, or tried to suggest that she was to blame for his bad horsemanship.

She reflected once more upon the sight of him, his wild hair and thunderous expression as he'd stared down at her from his horse. A man of honour would have concealed such anger, not indulged it.

No, she thought. There was something altogether very disagreeable about Sir Isaac Liddell. Tomorrow she would walk a different route and hope that their paths did not cross again. He was a man whose company ought to be avoided.

Chapter Four

Louisa's return to her aunt's house put a swift end to all thoughts of her unpleasant encounter. She was greeted in the hall by an agitated Nan, who was mumbling about how long she'd been away and where she'd got to, and how she had been beginning to worry. Like Aunt Clarissa, her maid did not approve of the long promenades she'd so quickly established as a habit.

Louisa tried not to show her irritation; she knew that they both had her best interests at heart. She couldn't possibly explain to them how free she felt, able to wander the countryside unburdened by the worry of who might see her and what they might say. She couldn't expect them to understand what these past years had been like for her, confined to her family's estate, unwilling to venture beyond their own land. It had been her choice, she knew that; she'd been her own gaoler. But here she was unknown; Cumberland was indifferent to her, and it was liberating.

She smiled as Nan took her spencer from her and gave her skirts a swift brush with her hand. 'I haven't been away all that long, Nan—and besides, what is the hurry? I have nothing I need to attend to.'

'You do today, miss. Your aunt has visitors in the parlour and you've some mud on the hem of this dress. Do you wish to change first?'

Louisa frowned. 'No, the dress will do. Who are the visitors, Nan?' she asked, curious now. She glanced at the long-case clock in the hall, realising it was past noon. Her long walk had indeed encroached upon calling hours.

'A Mrs Pearson and her daughter. I gather they are fairly new in town and only recently acquainted with your aunt.'

'I see,' she replied. 'Well, then, Nan, I think I'd best be introduced, hadn't I?'

Nan led her mistress to the parlour, where she opened the door for her before briefly bobbing a curtsey and taking her leave. Tentatively, Louisa walked into the room, feeling suddenly self-conscious as her aunt's two guests stared at her from across the table where they were enjoying cake and tea. She was not used to company...not used to making polite conversation. Briefly, the thought of her earlier walk returned to her. She'd already failed in one social encounter today. She hoped she wouldn't give a bad account of herself in another.

'Ah! There you are, my dear,' said Clarissa from her chair. 'Come, sit down and have some tea. I'd like you to meet Mrs Mary Pearson and her daughter, Miss Charlotte Pearson.' She turned back to her guests. 'This is my niece, Miss Louisa Conrad.'

Louisa gave them both a polite nod before taking a seat beside her aunt. 'It's nice to meet you both,' she said, pausing briefly to accept a cup of tea from her aunt's young maid, Cass, who had entered the parlour to wait upon her. 'I apologise for not being here sooner.'

'Oh, not at all, Miss Conrad,' said Mrs Pearson. 'Your aunt was just telling us how much the Lowhaven air is agreeing with you on your daily walks.'

'It is indeed,' Louisa replied. 'The surrounding country is beautiful, and walking by the sea suits me very well.'

'I am glad to hear it. Regrettably, my health doesn't permit me to venture far, but Charlotte likes to promenade—don't you?' Mrs Pearson addressed her daughter, who gave an assenting nod. 'Perhaps you might accompany one another.'

'Ah, that would be wonderful,' Clarissa declared. 'It is better if young ladies walk out together, I think. It is the proper way of things.'

'Yes, indeed,' Mrs Pearson agreed. 'The right and proper way.'

Charlotte gave Louisa a brief look of amusement which said that she had heard such a sentiment expressed at least a hundred times before. Louisa returned it, before allowing herself to make a discreet study of her new acquaintance. Her smooth, freckled face pronounced her youth, and Louisa suspected she could not be much older than twenty. She had the most striking red curls and bright blue eyes, which sat in direct contrast to her mother's ashen complexion, sunken features and greying brown hair. If Mrs Pearson had not already declared herself to be in poor health, Louisa should have easily supposed it.

'Have you ventured far on your walks, Miss Conrad?' Charlotte asked her, clearly determined to make some conversation.

'Just the environs of the town,' Louisa replied. 'Although I did wander a little along the coast today. The cliffs are magnificent.'

Charlotte nodded. 'That is indeed a pleasant walk. There is another I might show you, too, which takes you inland towards a village called Hayton.'

Louisa smiled, glancing at her aunt. 'My grandfather used to be the rector at Hayton. I have heard much about the place, although I confess I have not yet had the opportunity to visit.'

'Ah!' Charlotte exclaimed, clasping her hands together. 'Then we must go! It is very charming, and so quiet. Not at all like Lowhaven. I can show you the church and the rectory, and if time allows we can walk towards Hayton Hall. It is not far from the village, and it is the most spectacular-looking house. Indeed, I think it is the best in all of Cumberland.'

Clarissa smiled at the two young ladies. 'This sounds like a wonderful outing,' she said. 'If I was a younger woman, I might join you. I seldom visit Hayton these days, for all that it is only a few miles along the road. And Charlotte is right; Hayton Hall is very old, you know, and very fine.' Clarissa paused, stirring her tea. 'Although I believe these days it is best viewed from a distance.'

'Oh, Charlotte knows not to venture too close to the house—don't you, Charlotte?' her mother interjected.

Louisa sipped the tea thoughtfully. 'Of course. That is only polite, surely? The family must be afforded their privacy when in residence.'

Clarissa shifted a little in her chair. 'I think it would be fair to say that Hayton Hall has been closed to the outside world for some time.' She patted Louisa's hand. 'It is a sad story, I'm afraid, my dear. Two years ago

Sir Isaac suffered the loss of both his wife and his only child. Since then he has seldom been seen by anyone.'

Louisa felt her heart beat a little faster. 'That is terribly sad,' she said.

Aunt Clarissa nodded her agreement, giving Louisa a conspiratorial look. Neither of them was careless enough to mention that Louisa had met the reclusive baronet and risk revealing the circumstances in which this rare encounter had occurred. And Louisa, for her part, had no intention of telling anyone the sorry tale of their second meeting.

She dropped her gaze, staring into her empty cup and trying not to think of those deep blue eyes staring down at her from the horse. Trying not to think about how she'd failed to spot the sadness lurking behind the near-permanent scowl. A sadness which she, of all people, ought to have seen.

'I hear he has been seen a little more of late,' Mrs Pearson interjected. 'Since his brother returned to Hayton. Hopefully he can bring Sir Isaac some comfort.'

Clarissa gave her friend a grim smile. 'I think we ought to pray for it,' she replied. 'For that is what the poor man deserves—our prayers and our pity.'

Louisa retired to her room early that evening, not long after giving up on the dinner which she had pushed around her plate. She'd brushed off her aunt's professions of concern with an insistence that she was merely tired after an eventful day, explaining away her lack of appetite with the excuse that she'd eaten too heartily at tea that afternoon.

After changing into her bedclothes and dismissing Nan, she'd climbed between the sheets, intent upon reading her book for as long as the remaining daylight and the glow of a single candle would allow.

Hoping she would be able to take her mind somewhere else for a little while, Louisa picked up Mariana Starke's *Letters from Italy*. She might never venture beyond the confines of England, but she could indulge her desire to travel by seeing the continent through another's eyes until she fell asleep.

But, try as she might to fill her head with Mrs Starke's descriptions of vineyards, volcanoes and ancient towns buried by lava, her thoughts kept wandering back to the cliffs above Lowhaven. To the intensity of Sir Isaac's stare, the gentle touch of his gloved hand. To the way his dark hair had been made wild by the wind. To the unpleasant way their brief exchange had ended, and to the cross words she regretted now that she knew the nature of what pained him.

Words she ought to have regretted anyway, she thought as she slammed her book shut. Sir Isaac had been rude, but it shouldn't have been beyond her to meet his rudeness with some grace. Instead she'd been angry—and why? Because he'd spoken the truth, that was why.

She was reckless and improper. She made herself vulnerable to gossip and she bore the taint of scandal. Her reputation might not be known in Cumberland, but it followed her all the same, etching itself on every word she spoke, every decision she made. She was not free of it. She would never be free of it. She was fooling herself if she thought she could be at liberty here, or anywhere. She might as well lock herself away on her family's estate again—this time for good.

Louisa closed her eyes, pressing her lips together tight

as a single tear slipped down her cheek. It seemed she and Sir Isaac had more in common than she could have supposed. They had both loved and lost, and had chosen to shut themselves away, to hide their pain from the world. She wondered if solitude had been a salve for him or if, like her, he had found it only allowed the wounds to fester. She wondered if she would ever see him again, and if she'd find the courage to apologise to him, to acknowledge his suffering without betraying her own.

A knock at the door caused her to sit bolt upright, her eyes wide open now as the unexpected intrusion brushed all thoughts of Sir Isaac Liddell away. After a moment Aunt Clarissa peered round the door.

'I'm sorry to disturb you, dear,' she said, somewhat tentatively.

Louisa gave her a small smile. 'You're not, Aunt. I wasn't yet asleep. Is everything all right? Are you quite well?'

'Oh, yes, nothing is amiss,' Clarissa replied, coming into the room and closing the door behind her. 'It was just that I had meant to tell you at dinner that we have an engagement with the Pearsons on Friday evening.'

'I see. I'm sure that will be lovely. At their home?'

'No, not at their home.' Clarissa paused, seeming to hesitate. 'At the Assembly Rooms. There is to be a ball, it seems. I pay little heed to these events usually, but Mrs Pearson has asked if we will both come.'

Louisa gave a slow shake of her head. 'I'm not sure, Aunt. I...'

Clarissa gave her a pained look. 'I am sorry, my dear, but I have already accepted. Mrs Pearson asked me earlier today, just as she was leaving. In truth, I think she wishes you to attend as a companion for Miss Pearson.

I have not known Mrs Pearson for very long…to have refused her invitation would surely have seemed ungracious, wouldn't it?'

Louisa sighed. 'Indeed, I suppose it would. I regret that I will be rather poor company for Miss Pearson, though, after so long away from society.'

Clarissa reached over and patted her hand. 'You are a charming young lady, and I won't hear anything different said by anyone. Your only flaw is that you are too hard on yourself, my dear. The past is the past. This is a fresh start for you, Louisa. If you want my opinion, a new town, some new friends and a busy social calendar is exactly what you need.'

Louisa gave her aunt a knowing look. 'A friend like Charlotte Pearson, perhaps?'

Clarissa chuckled. 'I cannot deny that I have thought that Miss Pearson would make a suitable companion for you this summer. I simply want you to enjoy your time here, Louisa.'

Louisa shuffled under her sheets, suddenly discomfited. 'That is kind of you, Aunt. You are close to my mother, and I know she has told you much of what occurred several years ago. You have my deepest gratitude for welcoming me into your home in spite of it.'

Her aunt frowned. 'My dear, you speak as though you murdered someone! What happened to you is a tragedy, and if your Berkshire society chose to shun you for it then that reflects poorly on them, not you.'

'But I did not conduct myself as a young lady should…'

'You conducted yourself as many a young woman has and as many young women will continue to do whilst ever there are young men in the world to turn their heads. Your family approved of him, yes? And you were to marry, yes?'

Louisa nodded. 'We had an understanding.'

'Well, then, you were a victim of dreadful circumstance, Louisa, and that is all there is to be said.' Clarissa gave her a tender smile. 'Your mother has told me how these past years have been for you, and I pray that being here in Lowhaven will put an end to all of that. Starting with this ball at the Assembly Rooms on Friday.'

Aunt Clarissa bade her a swift goodnight, leaving Louisa to blow out her candle and settle down beneath her sheets. Oddly, she felt more peaceful now, her aunt's soothing words having replaced the more distressing thoughts she'd entertained earlier. Aunt Clarissa knew about her past and loved her despite it. Perhaps one day she could manage to love herself again, too.

She fell asleep quickly, dreaming not of windswept cliffs and heated conversations, nor of lost sea captains and promises unfulfilled. No, instead thoughts of candlelit rooms, country dances and beautiful gowns spread through her sleeping hours, and when she woke in the morning she wondered if her aunt might be right. Perhaps this truly was a new beginning, after all.

Chapter Five

Isaac gulped down the last of his brandy, wincing as it burned the back of his throat. He seldom took strong drink in the afternoon these days, but today he'd decided to allow himself a single glass. Around him the library was gloomy, the grey day outside providing little by way of either light or solace. With a heavy sigh he hauled himself out of his armchair and set about lighting a candle by which to read. If he could concentrate on a book. If he could concentrate on anything at all.

Beyond the library Hayton Hall was silent, except for the occasional footsteps of a servant going about his duties. Samuel had been out for most of the day, having given no indication as to when he was likely to return. And, although he was loath to admit it, Isaac found himself craving his brother's company, his merry demeanour and even his gentle teasing. Increasingly, it struck him just how much he hated being alone. Just how much he resented the life he'd been condemned to. It was not the sort of life he wanted at all.

Unfortunately for him, it was the only kind of life he was ever going to have. He'd made a vow once, to love and to cherish until death. He'd spoken those words in a church on a fine summer's day, never considering that death would come so soon. Never even contemplating that the years of loving and cherishing would be so painfully brief. Making such a vow again was completely out of the question. His heart had been shattered by his loss, and although it had now mended enough that he felt able to live again, he was not sure he was capable of loving again.

Not the way he'd loved Rosalind. Not how a woman deserved to be loved.

He missed Rosalind as he would miss his own skin. That was how losing her felt—as though someone had flayed the flesh from his bones and he'd been left to walk around raw and bleeding ever since. And the child, too. How he missed his long-awaited, much-beloved son.

In the months after their deaths, with enough darkness and enough drink, he had pretended that they were by his side, his liquor-addled mind conjuring a vision of his wife sitting just across from him, their little boy perched on her lap. He had heard her laughter, seen her brown curls shaking as she teased him about some trivial matter or other.

He'd always been so serious, but she'd been able to counter that with a kind of inherent, light-hearted joy that had made his soul burn for her. He'd loved marriage, loved the companionship of having a wife. He'd loved waking up beside her each day and embracing her before bed each night. Others might be cynical about getting wed, doing it for money or connections, but he had entered into it for neither reason.

He'd married for love.

By God, he had loved her.

'And now look at you…can't even talk properly to a woman, you damn fool,' he muttered to himself.

The incident on the cliffs had been preying on his mind ever since he'd returned home on his horse. He'd left the poor, weary animal with his groom and marched inside, reeling at how Miss Conrad had slighted him, how she'd walked away as though he was the most offensive creature on earth. A few clumsy words—that was all he'd uttered. He wasn't used to conversation any more, or to women, and for some unfathomable reason he had tried to compensate with a loose tongue and ill-judged humour.

She might have been more forgiving.

She might have tried to understand him.

She might have stayed and talked for a little longer.

Inside Hayton Hall he'd poured himself a brandy, just as he'd done today, and inside that glass his indignation had dissolved into regret. He had been rude, he knew that, and a young lady of impeccable character like Miss Louisa Conrad had been quite right to walk away in the face of such insult.

Miss Louisa Conrad… He had rehearsed that name over and over in his mind, so that he might never forget it. He'd promised never to call her a fair maiden again, and yet that was exactly what she was—all dark gaze and honey-coloured curls. Now, a day later, he knew he owed the fair maiden an apology.

This would be no easy task to accomplish. A note simply would not do, but neither could he just turn up on her doorstep. Going to Lowhaven and exposing himself to comment was inconceivable at the best of times, and seeking out a lovely young lady like Miss Conrad was all but guaranteed to send the town's gossips into a frenzy. Perhaps he could ride that same route again and hope to see her. But then he'd be leaving it all too much to chance, and…

'You're a damnable coward, Liddell,' he said, closing his eyes and dragging his fingers down his face.

'Brother, are you quite well?'

Across from him stood Samuel, a look of concern etched upon his face. He'd been so preoccupied with his quandary over the matter of Miss Conrad that he had not even heard his brother return. He looked up now, wondering how long Samuel had been standing there. How much of Isaac's self-critical monologue he'd heard.

'I'm fine,' he replied, forcing a smile. 'Just a little tired, that's all.'

'I see.' Samuel sat down opposite him, and Isaac watched as his brother's gaze shifted warily to the empty glass on the table. 'How many of those have you had?' he asked.

'Only one,' Isaac snapped. 'Why?'

'I'm just making sure you're not falling back into your old ways, brother.'

Isaac flinched at the memory of how he'd lived during those long months he'd spent lost to his grief. Festering in the darkness in his library, surrounded by empty glasses laced with the residue of day-old drink and crumpled newspapers, half-perused and then abandoned. He had tried futilely to numb the pain with so much brandy that it was a minor miracle that he hadn't been struck down with barrel fever.

He was aware that Samuel knew it all—that he'd interviewed the servants almost immediately upon his return to Hayton Hall, ensuring that he had sufficient insight into exactly how his older brother had been faring during his long absence.

'Such bad habits are far behind me,' Isaac replied, glaring at him. 'That was the case even before you dragged yourself home from your continental adventures. I am quite capable of looking after myself these days, Samuel.'

To his surprise, his brother held up his hands in a gesture of surrender. 'I know that. Believe me, I'm not trying to be a nursemaid to you. But I am trying to encourage you to do more, to go out a bit more—for your own good.'

'I do go out,' Isaac countered, sitting back in his chair, arms folded. 'I accompanied you to Penrith at your request, didn't I? And I am out most days on my horse. I went riding just yesterday, if you recall,' he added, his mind wandering immediately to the cliffs, to those dark eyes staring boldly up at him as he spat out his fury.

'I do recall that you went riding alone,' Samuel agreed. 'I recall too that you came back in the most foul temper. A mood which, dare I say, has persisted ever since. A black mood even by your standards, Isaac.'

Isaac curled his lip. 'As I said, I'm just a little tired.'

Samuel, however, was clearly not going to let the matter drop. Instead he sat forward, his elbows pressed against the arms of his chair. 'I regret that I was not here for you, you know. I regret that I did not return home as soon as the news about Rosalind and the baby reached me. I can offer no excuses.'

He drew a deep breath, and instinctively Isaac found himself dreading whatever was coming next.

'But I am here now,' he continued, 'and I think it is time that a few things changed at Hayton Hall.'

Isaac frowned. 'Such as?'

'You are Sir Isaac Liddell, Baronet. It's time you started to act like it again.'

'I do act like it,' Isaac protested. 'I care for my estate and always have. Even when I was at my lowest ebb I did not neglect my duties.'

'That is not all that your position in life involves, and you know it,' Samuel countered. He pointed at the window. 'It involves going out there, visiting your tenants and going into town. It involves being a part of society. You might not spend all day in your robe any more, drinking yourself to death, but you must surely see that you are still living a half-life.'

At this, Isaac groaned. Samuel was right—of course he was. In his widowhood he'd become sullen and reclusive. To such an extent that sometimes he wondered whether he knew how to hold a proper conversation any more. His encounter with Miss Conrad yesterday had shown him just how low he'd sunk. Hot-tempered and impertinent, he had undoubtedly caused great offence.

Rosalind wouldn't have looked at him twice if he'd behaved in such a manner with her. Not that he wanted any woman to look at him the way she had—of course not. But a small, suppressed part of him did desire to see the old Isaac return, to see the man his wife had loved stare back at him in the mirror once more.

'All right,' he said at length. 'I place myself wholly at your disposal, brother. What would you have me do?'

Samuel smiled. 'Quite simply, Isaac, I want you to start venturing into society once again. I want you to show your face in the village, and in Lowhaven, and I want you to go to the events that those in our society would expect you to attend.'

'You really want me to offer myself up as fodder for the gossips?' Isaac scoffed, shaking his head.

'People will simply take it as an indication that you have come out of mourning at last,' Samuel replied flatly. 'They will be glad of it, I am sure. You must stop believing that the world is somehow against you, because truly it is not. We will start by attending a ball at the Assembly Rooms in Lowhaven this Friday.'

'But that is only a few days from now, Samuel.' Isaac stared at him, aghast.

Samuel nodded. 'You must start somewhere, Isaac. Let this be your new beginning.'

'All right,' Isaac conceded with another groan.

'Good,' Samuel replied, rising from his seat. 'Because I am rather looking forward to this ball. A pleasant evening among friends and perhaps a dance or two with some of the young ladies will suit me very well.'

Isaac gave him a wry smile. 'Indeed, brother. I expect you'll find yourself on scores of ladies' dance cards before the night is over.'

'As might you,' Samuel answered him as he made his way to the library door. 'Even you are not immune to the charms of a pretty face.'

Isaac made no attempt to reply, but instead sat back in his chair, exhausted at the mere prospect of what the next few days would hold. Putting on his best clothes and going out in company for the evening was one thing, but dancing with a woman was quite another. Although, he reminded himself, there was one young lady with whom he did wish to speak, and if she happened to be there requesting a dance with her might be his only means of offering an apology.

His stomach churned at the thought of such an interaction, at the possibility of her rebuke. At the small chance of her acceptance and the pleasant prospect of being the recipient of that dark gaze once again.

Samuel was right, it seemed. He was not immune to a pretty woman's charms. Not in the least.

Chapter Six

The sun was still bestowing its pink-orange glow upon Lowhaven when the Pearsons' carriage drew to a halt outside the Assembly Rooms that Friday evening. The Pearsons had arrived to collect Louisa and her aunt a little early, which had thrown the household into brief disarray as Nan hurried to finish dressing her mistress while Aunt Clarissa cajoled them from downstairs.

'It seems that the Pearsons keep to their own time,' she'd said as Louisa had finally emerged, 'and we must keep to it, too, since they are good enough to take us in their carriage.'

Louisa had met the remark with silence. She was not oblivious to her aunt's humble circumstances—no carriage and only two servants in her household—but acknowledging the ageing woman's situation so directly made her uncomfortable. Perhaps, she realised, it was because this was the future that she imagined for herself: independent, but only so far as a small income might allow.

The journey in the carriage had been brief and lively, with the two older women complimenting the younger women's gowns and speculating as to how full both their dance cards might be.

Louisa had felt herself grow anxious at the latter remarks. While she was enjoying having an occasion to wear the pretty rose-pink silk gown that Nan had selected for her, she was nonetheless adamant that dancing was out of the question. Her aunt had asked her to come as Miss Pearson's companion, and she would fulfil her duty, but that was all.

She'd felt relieved when Mr Pearson, a stout man with greying red hair, had changed the subject to ask if she'd found Lowhaven agreeable so far. An easy question, she'd thought, at least for the most part. As long as she did not include clifftop arguments with disagreeable baronets when determining her answer.

The scene which greeted Louisa as she stepped out of the carriage was one of crowds and chaos, as it seemed most of Lowhaven had descended upon the fine white building to enjoy an evening of music and conversation. As she was jostled up the steps and towards the entrance she found herself taking hold of Charlotte's arm, more for her own reassurance than anything else, but Charlotte accepted the gesture warmly.

'We shall be fine if we stay together, I think,' the younger woman whispered to her. 'I promise I shall not leave your side, Louisa.'

Louisa blinked, momentarily taken aback by Charlotte's familiarity in using her first name before deciding to embrace it. By her own admission Aunt Clarissa had identified Charlotte as a suitable companion for her; perhaps during the course of the summer they could become firm friends, too. It had been so long since Louisa had enjoyed a friendship.

She smiled. 'Thank you, Charlotte,' she said.

The two young women made their way inside, trailing behind their older companions as they wove their way through the congregating masses towards the ballroom, from which they could already hear the cheerful sound of violins playing.

Halfway along the corridor Louisa heard Mr Pearson announce his intention to visit the card room and to leave the ladies to their own devices. She smiled, thinking of her own father, who would do much the same thing when out for the evening. Her face grew serious once more as she remembered how long it had been since she had enjoyed such times in the company of her parents.

'Do not worry,' Charlotte said to her, misinterpreting her countenance. 'We shall do quite well without Papa.'

The four ladies settled themselves in a spot at the edge of the ballroom, with Aunt Clarissa and Mrs Pearson fortunate enough to find two seats upon which to make themselves comfortable. Louisa and Charlotte, meanwhile, stood close together, sipping from the small cups of punch they'd each been offered by a passing waiter. The drink was strong, and Louisa resolved to take only a little of it. She would act as an unmarried woman in her position ought to act: with good deal of sense and restraint. She would be a charming and responsible companion to Charlotte, and would give Lowhaven society no reason to gossip on her account.

'Do you know many people here?' Louisa asked Charlotte.

Charlotte shook her head in reply. 'Not so many, no,' she replied. 'I'm afraid we may be standing here like wallflowers for some time.'

Louisa smiled reassuringly. In truth, she did not mind.

It was rather pleasant to stand to one side and watch others as they danced in the warm glow of the candlelight. Her days of hovering beside her mother, trying not to fidget as she waited for some young gentleman to request an introduction and thereafter a dance, were long past. She knew, however, that Charlotte would be experiencing such nervous anticipation right now, and that her hopes for the evening were altogether different from those of a woman settled upon spinsterhood.

'I am sure you will be dancing before too long,' Louisa whispered encouragingly.

At length, Louisa was correct. When one dance ended and before the next began Charlotte was approached by a young man of her acquaintance and swiftly whisked away to dance a lively cotillion. Conscious she was now alone, Louisa stepped back towards her aunt and Mrs Pearson, intent upon looking at ease in their company while standing quietly with her thoughts.

She had managed well so far, she believed, cultivating an air of serenity whilst drawing no attention to herself. Perhaps venturing into society as a stranger was not so bad, after all.

'I'm afraid you may see little of my daughter for the rest of the evening,' Mrs Pearson observed as she approached. 'I usually find that once she secures one dancing partner, she shortly thereafter secures a dozen.'

'I am glad of it,' Louisa replied. 'Although Miss Pearson seemed to suggest that she did not know many of the people here.'

'She knows plenty who are of consequence,' Mrs Pearson answered, giving her a sharp look.

Louisa glanced apologetically at her aunt, fearing she

had unwittingly overstepped the mark. 'Of course,' she replied with a conciliatory nod.

But neither Mrs Pearson nor Aunt Clarissa were paying any further heed to her faux pas, their attention instead captured by something beyond her. Something which had made her aunt's mouth fall open in disbelief.

'Well, I never...' Aunt Clarissa began.

Louisa spun round, watching as the crowd seemed to part like the Red Sea. Standing in the chasm they'd left were two gentlemen—both of them known to her, and both causing her to take a sharp breath, albeit for very different reasons.

The fair-haired gentleman was smiling broadly, his open, friendly expression taking her back to those hours she'd spent in his fine carriage, reeling from the ordeal of the overturned stagecoach. But it was the other gentleman standing by his side who had really captured her attention—and, indeed, the attention of everyone else in the room. The dark, wild-tempered man from the cliffs...the one who'd inflamed her with his insolence and preyed on her thoughts ever since.

She heard herself gasp as he turned and caught her gaze. Then she felt the earlier calm she'd relished simply ebb away.

Isaac ought to have been mortified by the scene his presence had created—by the gawping expressions and unsubtle whispers which welcomed him to his first social outing in more than two years. Indeed, it was exactly this reaction he had dreaded. He had been so reluctant to attend tonight that Samuel had had to all but drag him out of Hayton Hall and into his carriage.

Yet now, standing there, he could think of nothing

but one lady's face, wide-eyed and uncommonly beautiful, just as she had been the last time he'd seen her. He could think of nothing but speaking with her again, of finding some discreet way to deliver the apology which was due to her. The sight of her staring at him with that same aghast look in her eyes that he'd seen when he'd almost trampled her with his horse was enough to make him feel ashamed all over again. How wretched he had been. How uncouth.

'Well, brother, it seems we've caused quite a stir,' Samuel observed, an amused smile playing on his lips.

'Exactly why I did not want to come here,' Isaac replied, although his protest sounded hollow.

Samuel helped himself to a couple of glasses of punch from the tray of a passing waiter, handing one of them to his brother. Isaac took a long sip, savouring its sweetness and the way it warmed his throat, as every pair of eyes in the room seemed to remain intently upon him. At least the drink was strong, he thought. He would need plenty of it if he was going to survive the long evening ahead of him.

'Ah, I see Miss Conrad is here,' Samuel observed, with a polite nod in her direction.

'Miss Conrad?' Isaac asked, feigning ignorance.

'The fair maiden,' Samuel whispered. 'The one whose aid we came to on our way home from Penrith. Surely you cannot have forgotten her, brother?' He nudged Isaac firmly in the ribs, making him wince. 'Come, let us say hello. I am curious to know how she is enjoying her stay in Lowhaven.'

Dutifully, Isaac followed his brother. He hoped he looked sufficiently detached, and that no one would detect his heart hammering in his chest as he walked across the room towards her. As he drew closer, he noted that the two older ladies sitting down behind her had got to their feet. One of them looked familiar, although he could not recall why. He noted, too, how Miss Conrad's eyes seemed to widen even further, her posture so stiff and brittle that she looked as though she might break.

His stomach lurched at the realisation that it was his approach which had provoked such a response.

'Miss Conrad!' Samuel exclaimed, giving her an impeccable bow. 'It is very good to see you again.'

'Mr Liddell.' Miss Conrad met Samuel's enthusiasm with a brisk nod. 'And Sir Isaac, of course,' she added, although she barely lifted her dark eyes to acknowledge him.

Isaac watched as Miss Conrad gestured awkwardly towards her companions and hurriedly undertook the necessary introductions. Isaac bowed politely at the two older ladies, realising that the one with the familiar face was Miss Howarth, the old rector's daughter. The other lady, Mrs Pearson, he did not know, and nor did he warm to her as she stood there, her sharp gaze flitting between them all like a crow choosing its supper.

With the formality of introductions now complete, he found himself watching Miss Conrad once more, his gaze lingering upon her while Samuel gave an account of their meeting Miss Conrad to Mrs Pearson, who had enquired as to how they were acquainted.

He noted that his brother's tale was less than truthful, omitting all mention of taking the young lady and her maid into their carriage. Apparently protecting Miss Conrad's reputation meant more to Samuel than providing evidence of his own gallantry. Guilt surged through him as he compared his brother's gentlemanly behaviour with his own clumsy, brutish tongue that day on the cliffs.

'I daresay that must have been frightening, Miss Conrad,' Mrs Pearson observed. 'Coachmen these days can be so reckless. I am surprised that neither you nor your aunt mentioned it before. It is quite a story,' she added.

Isaac found himself raising an eyebrow at the cutting nature of the remark. It was as though the woman sensed there was a shared secret she was not being made privy to.

'Ah—yes, well, fortunately the coach was able to continue on its way and no harm was done,' Miss Howarth interjected smoothly. 'And my niece is very grateful to you both for stopping to retrieve the fallen luggage,' she added, giving both gentlemen a smile which told them that she appreciated their discretion.

Miss Conrad, however, appeared not to be listening, her eyes cast down, her thoughts elsewhere. Isaac wished he could read them…wished to know what had her so preoccupied. Wished to know if she could stand this latest meeting, or if she wanted to turn and walk away all over again.

Around them the music ceased, and the bustle of men and women changing dancing partners began. Before he could think about what he was doing, Isaac reached out and offered her his hand.

'Would you like to dance, Miss Conrad?' he asked her, and finally she lifted her gaze and those deep brown eyes met his once more.

Chapter Seven

Louisa felt the heat rise in her cheeks as Sir Isaac led her towards the centre of the ballroom. It seemed to her as though every pair of eyes was upon them—as though every person there had the same whispered questions on their lips. Who was this woman? And why had Sir Isaac chosen her for his first dance?

In truth, she desired to know the answer to the latter question herself. After their awful last meeting she had assumed he'd want no further association with her. He'd had to endure his brother's approach and the subsequent conversation—that had been a matter of politeness. But asking her to dance? There had been no requirement for him to do that.

She wished he hadn't asked her. She wished she hadn't felt obliged to accept. It had drawn attention to her, and that was the very last thing she wanted.

They lined up opposite each other and Louisa said a quick prayer, hoping she could remember the steps. She looked up at Sir Isaac, realising she must appear as anxious as she felt when he offered her a small, reassuring smile.

The candlelight seemed to illuminate his face, and her attention was drawn to the gentle creases around his eyes and the smattering of silver in his near-black hair. It struck her that he was older than she'd thought—but then she hadn't thought very much of him at their first or second meeting…at least, not much to his credit. Now, she couldn't seem to take her eyes off him. His countenance—indeed his entire appearance—was very different from that which she had witnessed on the cliffs. Tonight, he looked every inch an elegant gentleman, in his dark tailcoat and contrasting breeches, whilst his windswept hair had been tamed, and apparently so had his rough manners.

Realising she was staring at him, she lowered her gaze, instructing herself to be calm as the music began and they took their first steps towards one another. It was only one dance. It would be over soon enough.

'I fear I have made you uncomfortable, Miss Conrad,' Sir Isaac said in a low voice when they drew close enough to converse. 'I only wish to apologise to you for the way I spoke to you at our last meeting. I was unforgivably rude.'

'Thank you,' she replied softly. 'I appreciate the trouble you have gone to in order to convey your apology.'

'Trouble?'

'Asking me to dance when I am sure there are many others in this room whose company you would find more agreeable. I was not… I was not all that I should have been at our last meeting, either,' she added hesitantly, hoping he would grasp her meaning.

The demands of the dance separated them for a few moments. As she moved with as much grace as she could muster, Louisa found herself feeling impatient.

Why was it that a man and a woman could not have a straightforward conversation in company without any need for the ruse of dancing?

By the time they met again Louisa could barely keep command of her words as they burst forth. 'I was ungracious towards you,' she blurted. 'Truly, I am ashamed of it.'

Sir Isaac caught her gaze, offering her his hand again as the dance required. She accepted it delicately and together they turned, exchanging small smiles which seemed to express a mutual understanding that words could not.

'Then it seems we are both ashamed, Miss Conrad,' Sir Isaac said at last. 'Come, let us start afresh.'

Louisa gave a nod of agreement. Although she very much doubted that any acquaintance between them would be sustained, it eased her conscience to know that there was no animosity between them.

They spent the remainder of the dance largely in silence, punctuated only by Sir Isaac's polite enquiries into the length of her stay in Lowhaven and whether she was enjoying her summer sojourn. She allowed herself to relax, enjoying the dance and the company of a man who, she could not fail to observe, had both charm and handsome looks in abundance.

For this indulgence she chastised herself; her days of admiring a gentleman's appearance were as far behind her as she'd believed her dancing days to be. Occasionally, though, when the steps brought them close together or compelled them to go hand in hand, she felt a long-forgotten warmth spread through her limbs. And when she caught Sir Isaac looking at her, letting his deep blue eyes linger over her face, she remembered why dancing could be preferable to conversation.

Trouble. That was what she'd called it. *Trouble.*

Isaac sat back in the carriage, resting his head against the hard wooden side as he waited for Samuel to join him for their journey back to Hayton Hall. The hour was late and, given the evening's exertions, he knew he ought to be exhausted. But rest could not have been further from his mind. Instead, he found his thoughts revisiting certain memories, again and again.

Her dark eyes staring up at him. The soft feeling of her gloved hand. The arresting sensation of her nearness to him each time the dance commanded them to draw close. The touching sincerity of her apology. It had all caught him unaware and left him so overwrought that he'd managed only the barest amount of conversation. Truly, she must think him the most charmless man she'd ever met.

Trouble? Indeed, he was troubled.

'Well, brother, I do believe that tonight was a success.'

Samuel climbed into the carriage, sitting down opposite him with a satisfied sigh. His eyes were heavy and a little glazed, and Isaac noted the smell of strong liquor emanating from him. His encounter with Miss Conrad had left him feeling distracted for the rest of the night, and he had neither paid attention to his younger sibling's merrymaking nor indulged in the strong punch himself. Now, he found himself wishing he was in his cups, too. Some gentle inebriation might help to distance him from uncomfortable thoughts about a beautiful woman.

'It was not as bad as I feared,' Isaac conceded.

'You see! I was right that you should come,' Samuel declared, with a self-satisfied tap of his knee.

'Indeed... Although I am very weary now,' Isaac replied, suddenly desirous of a quiet journey home.

His brother, however, was not to be dissuaded from his chatter. 'I cannot see how! You barely danced, except with Miss Conrad. That was a surprise, I have to say... you whisking her away like that. I wondered what had come over you.'

'Nothing,' Isaac grunted. 'I merely thought it polite.'

'You were under no obligation. Mind you, she is remarkably handsome. I had thought to ask her myself, but...'

'But what?'

'She's very reserved. Dare I say a little cold, even? I recall thinking as much when we first met her. The way she sat in our carriage, stony-faced and hardly troubling herself to make conversation.'

Isaac felt his fists curl with irritation and he pressed them into the seat. 'She didn't know us, Samuel. She was forced by circumstances to accept our assistance. I think she can be forgiven for being a little wary.'

Samuel let out a wry chuckle. 'You've changed your tune. What was it you called her after we'd left her with her aunt? Reckless?'

'Damn you,' Isaac growled.

Samuel's face grew serious. 'You're quite taken with her, aren't you? I saw the way you were looking at her, you know. I'll bet most of the people in the ballroom did—including her. I've not seen you look at a woman like that since...'

'Don't say her name!' Isaac snapped. 'Don't you dare!' He sighed heavily, composing himself. 'I was not looking at Miss Conrad is any particular way. I was only…'

'Only what?' his brother challenged him, sitting upright now.

'Only—only seeking to apologise to her,' he admitted finally, rubbing his forehead with his hands.

'Apologise?' Samuel frowned. 'What could you possibly need to apologise for?'

'I saw Miss Conrad again—after the day of the stagecoach accident.' Isaac made his admission quietly. 'I was riding up on the cliffs near Lowhaven. Miss Conrad was out for a walk. I nearly trampled the poor woman with my horse. I was in a foul temper and I spoke to her in a way that I had no business to. Asking her to dance with me was the only way I could offer an apology discreetly.'

Samuel raised his eyebrows. 'I see. And when was this?'

Isaac shrugged. 'Less than a week ago. Does it matter?'

'I suppose not.' Samuel slumped back, closing his eyes. 'And that's all there is to it, is there? You've made amends to her and have no intention of seeing her again?'

'Indeed,' Isaac replied. 'Miss Conrad is visiting her aunt for the summer. I doubt that our paths will cross again.'

The only answer Isaac received from his brother was the sound of his loud snores punctuating the air as their carriage rumbled slowly along the road back to Hayton Hall.

Just as well, Isaac thought, settling into his seat. The last thing he wanted was for Samuel to hear how forlorn he sounded, or to realise just how unsettled the evening, the dancing, and above all Miss Louisa Conrad had left him.

* * *

By the time the Pearsons' carriage delivered Louisa and her aunt back to Juniper Street, Louisa could barely keep her eyes open. The short journey home had been quiet, with the older members of the party all dozing and the younger two exchanging only brief whispers about the evening's events.

Charlotte evidently relished her near-constant dancing. Her cheeks were flushed, her face alight with a smile which no amount of weariness could remove. For Charlotte Pearson it had been a very successful night indeed.

Louisa, on the other hand, felt more conflicted about her first foray into Lowhaven society. She hadn't wished to dance at all, and had it not been for Sir Isaac Liddell's invitation she would have succeeded in that regard. Yet, try as she might, she could not bring herself to regret it.

Dancing with Sir Isaac had thrilled and discomfited her in equal measure. She had been pleased to make amends with him, but it was more than that—if she was honest with herself, she had enjoyed his attentions. She'd relished his proximity, and the sensation which had run through her each time he'd taken hold of her hand. She knew she shouldn't feel that way—the dance would have meant little to him, and he'd only asked her so that he could apologise. But still, she decided, there could be nothing wrong with her keeping the memory of it for herself and bringing it out on those occasions when she needed something to make her smile.

'Goodnight, Aunt,' she said, almost as soon as they walked through Clarissa's door, determining to go straight upstairs and to bed.

'Could you perhaps come into the parlour for a moment, my dear?' Clarissa asked her.

Louisa nodded, wordlessly following her aunt into the small room and closing the door. She felt her heart begin to beat faster as she wondered what was amiss. Aunt Clarissa's face was drawn and grey with tiredness; whatever it was must be serious if it could not keep until morning.

'I wanted to speak to you about Mrs Pearson, Louisa.'

'Oh?'

Aunt Clarissa shook her head, clearly troubled. 'Unfortunately I think Mrs Pearson was vexed not to have known that you'd met Sir Isaac and his brother before.'

'I rather think it's none of her business who I am acquainted with, Aunt,' Louisa replied.

'Indeed, but after we'd discussed Sir Isaac at tea…' Clarissa paused, then waved a dismissive hand. 'Oh, never mind about that. I wanted to speak to you about your remark…when you suggested that Miss Pearson did not know many people at the ball.'

'I was merely repeating what Charlotte had told me herself,' Louisa protested mildly.

In truth, her thoughts had been so preoccupied with Sir Isaac that she had quite forgotten the incident altogether.

'I'm sure you were, and I know you spoke in innocence. But I thought I ought to explain to you why I believe Mrs Pearson behaved the way she did.' Clarissa sighed, sitting down on one of the parlour chairs. 'The Pearsons only came to Lowhaven a few months ago. Mrs Pearson is a gentleman's daughter, from Northumberland, but Mr John Pearson's family have made their fortune in trade. From what I have heard, he has squandered it, and the family now find themselves in reduced circumstances. Since coming to town, I believe they've struggled to make good connections. That's what Miss Pearson will have been alluding to when she told you that she had not had all that many introductions.'

Louisa frowned. 'Charlotte seemed to manage well enough this evening. She had sufficient acquaintances to keep her dancing for most of the night.'

'Ah, yes, but I doubt that even one of those young men she danced with will be considered suitable by Mrs Pearson,' Clarissa countered, giving her niece a knowing smile. 'Even though I'm sure she knows well enough that the leading families in the area will want little to do with a hapless tradesman's daughter—especially since I doubt there is even a substantial dowry to tempt them.'

'It cannot be so bad, surely? They manage to keep a carriage and horses of their own.'

'They keep up appearances, my dear, but I believe it is bad enough. Mrs Pearson will want her daughter to marry soon, I think, and as well as possible.'

'I see,' replied Louisa, biting her lip. 'I am sorry, Aunt. I did not mean to offend Mrs Pearson.'

Clarissa got up from her chair, gently patting her niece on the arm. 'I wouldn't worry. I daresay you more than made up for it by securing her an introduction to Sir Isaac and his brother.'

The mention of Sir Isaac made Louisa's face grow warm. 'Oh, yes,' she replied.

Clarissa shook her head. 'I couldn't quite believe my eyes when they walked in together. And then for Sir Isaac to ask you to dance! You did well, my dear. Very well.'

'I'm quite sure Sir Isaac only asked me out of politeness, Aunt.'

At this, Clarissa laughed. 'I might be an old spinster, Louisa, but I know enough about the world to know that a gentleman never asks a lady to dance just to be polite. He did not dance with anyone else all night, you know. And from the way he looked at you, I was quite certain that he'd ask you to take a turn with him a second time.'

Now Louisa felt sure her cheeks must be glowing scarlet. 'Well, I am glad he did not, for I am convinced I could not have borne it,' she replied hotly. 'And now I am tired and must go to bed. Goodnight, Aunt.'

Before Clarissa could say anything further, Louisa opened the door and marched out of the room.

Chapter Eight

'You've done well today, brother.'

Samuel's patronising tone made Isaac flinch, although he knew the remark was well-intended. The day was fine and bright and the two brothers rode side by side, paying visits to the farms and cottages situated across the not inconsiderable swathe of Liddell land.

'I was never so melancholic that I ceased to have any regard for my tenants,' Isaac countered, glancing briefly over his shoulder at his steward, who rode a little further behind. 'Although I will concede that I always had the very best help.'

'I do believe your visits today were appreciated, nonetheless. It means a lot for you to be seen.'

Isaac nodded. 'Indeed. I regret that I have been so absent these past two years. In plentiful times it may have been forgivable, but...'

'You are not responsible for bad harvests, Isaac,' Samuel interjected. 'Only the damnable weather can be blamed for that.'

'No, I know that,' Isaac replied quietly. 'But, as you say, it's important that I'm seen, and while my tenants suffered I was very much invisible.'

Samuel offered his brother a sympathetic smile, and together they rode on in silence. They had one more visit to pay on the edge of the village, before returning to Hayton Hall for luncheon. The mere thought of food made Isaac's stomach growl; they had been out for hours, and he'd barely had time to eat even a small breakfast before meeting his steward at nine o'clock.

Despite his hunger, he had to admit that the busy morning had buoyed his spirits. He'd enjoyed seeing the families, many of whom had lived and worked on his family's land for generations. And, he had to admit, he'd liked having Samuel accompany him as much as he'd appreciated the support of his steward. Samuel's light-hearted, relaxed manner and ability to regale an audience with tales of his European travels had put Isaac at his ease and made him feel less under scrutiny.

Yes, he thought. The morning had been a success.

He'd even managed not to think so much about Miss Conrad.

Isaac sighed, inwardly cursing himself for allowing his thoughts to roam back to that evening once again. Truly, it was ridiculous to think so much about a woman he'd met only a handful of times and danced with once. It was nonsensical to wake in the morning and realise he'd been dreaming about her, twirling in that captivating pink dress she'd worn. It was alarming to realise that the quiet moments of his day were dominated by her—her smile, her large brown eyes, her perfectly curled fair hair.

He supposed this was to be expected—that after so long on his own even the brief company of a woman like Miss Louisa Conrad could prove overpowering. He found the way that she haunted his thoughts unsettling, but at the same time he was forced to admit that he did not want it to stop.

'Almost there,' Samuel called out to him.

Good, he thought. He needed distraction, and thereafter a hearty meal.

'Is it not the most charming little village, Louisa?'

Charlotte took hold of her companion's arm as they made their way along the dusty track which served as the main thoroughfare through Hayton. This was their first outing together since the ball and, as promised, Charlotte had determined that they would walk to Hayton, so that she could show Louisa around the village her family had once called their home.

Louisa found herself easily agreeing with her new friend's opinion—Hayton was indeed as picturesque as it was miniature, with a cluster of low stone cottages forming its centre, framed by trees and hedgerows in full leaf. At its furthest edge was the ancient church where, Charlotte had reliably informed her, the old rectory could be found.

As the two ladies made their way in this direction, Louisa considered what life in Hayton must have been like for her mother and her aunt. Quiet, certainly, with only a handful of neighbours and their parents for company—somewhat different from the life her aunt led now, in a bustling port town.

Rather idly, she wondered which she preferred, and wondered, too, if the isolation of small village life had been the reason she'd never married. For whilst Aunt Clarissa's siblings had sought opportunities in the larger towns or, in her own mother's case, been removed to London by benevolent relatives, Clarissa had remained faithfully at the rectory, at her parents' side. She wondered how much that had been of her own choosing, or whether it had simply been the only option left.

'It is very lovely,' Louisa agreed at last.

'When I marry, I should count myself very fortunate if I was able to live in a place like this,' Charlotte gushed. 'Life in a small country cottage would suit me very well indeed.'

'Perhaps you ought to marry a rector, then. A man with a rural parish to tend to. That should assure you of the quiet life you seek,' Louisa said, a note of gentle teasing in her voice.

Charlotte wrinkled her nose. 'I doubt that would do for Mama.'

'What? Your mother would not approve of a match with a man of the cloth? To a gentleman with a steady income? I do believe most mothers would seek exactly such marriages for their daughters,' Louisa replied.

'Alas, my mother is not "most mothers",' Charlotte countered quietly. 'She is most particular on the subject of whom I might marry.'

Louisa gave her friend's arm a sympathetic squeeze, but made no further remark. She reflected briefly on Aunt Clarissa's words about Mrs Pearson, and the high aspirations she believed she had for her daughter. High indeed, Louisa thought, if she would not give her over to marriage with a clergyman.

'Well, here we are, Louisa,' Charlotte said as they arrived at the gates to the church. 'Here is where your grandfather used to minister to his congregation, and over there is the rectory.'

Louisa stood still at length, admiring the old stone church, its spire reaching far above the humble dwellings of the village. She looked, too, at the rectory, finding it to be a pleasing white house of considerable size. She found herself thinking again about the years both her mother and her aunt had spent here, and how little she knew of it.

'It's strange to see it,' Louisa observed, speaking some of her thoughts aloud. 'I cannot claim to have really known my grandparents. They sent my mother to London to stay with relatives not long before she came of age. I knew her family in the south far better.'

'But you are here now, with your aunt,' Charlotte replied. 'You must know her well enough to want to come all this way to visit?'

'I had not seen Aunt Clarissa since I was a girl, but it is true that we have written often.'

'And after all these years you wished to see her and spend the summer here?' Charlotte asked.

Louisa gave a hesitant smile. 'Yes.'

'I wish you would not leave so soon...' Charlotte groaned. 'I fear I will have only just got to know you and you will be going back to Berkshire. Perhaps you will find a reason to stay?' she added, her expression brightening once more. 'Perhaps you will find a husband here.'

'Oh, no, I shall never marry,' Louisa replied, the instinctive response rolling from her tongue before she could think about it.

'Never?' Charlotte exclaimed. 'But how can you say so?'

Louisa sighed, taking Charlotte's arm again as they turned away from the church and began their return journey through the village. Quietly she cursed herself for being so careless with her words. Such a forthright statement demanded some form of explanation.

'I was engaged once, to a captain in the navy. He died at sea during the war...before we were able to wed. I swore then that I would not marry.' She tried her best to sound matter-of-fact, not to betray her emotions. Not to betray all that she had left out.

'Oh, Louisa, that is very sad. I am sorry for you. But you are still young. I do not think your captain would wish for you to remain alone. Surely if he loved you as you loved him, he would not?'

Louisa offered her friend a small smile, wishing she could explain, but knowing she could not. If Charlotte knew the whole story she would understand. But if Charlotte knew the whole story she would not want to be associated with her at all.

'I'm sure he would not. But it is my wish, and I am very much settled upon it.'

'Mama says the life of a spinster is one that no woman should desire. I have to bite my tongue to stop myself from pointing out that one acquaintance she's made in Lowhaven is just such an unmarried woman, and that she seems to do perfectly well by herself.'

Louisa laughed at this. 'Indeed, my aunt is an example to us all.'

'I suppose that while you are here you might learn something from her about managing alone?'

'Yes, I suppose I might,' Louisa replied, wondering, not for the first time, if such motivation had informed her parents' enthusiasm for sending her here. Wondering, too, if they'd hoped seeing her aunt's life for herself might put her off spinsterhood entirely.

'Mama hopes I will learn from you,' Charlotte continued. 'She says you will be a welcome influence upon me…that you are a gentleman's daughter of good repute and great sensibility.'

But Louisa was no longer listening—which was just as well as she might have reddened at Mrs Pearson's overly generous characterisation of her. Instead, she was staring straight ahead, her eyes wide, at the two approaching men on horseback—both of whom she recognised, and one of whom she had not wished to see so soon.

She had barely managed to collect herself following that evening at the ball, never mind recover from that ill-tempered conversation with her aunt on the subject of her dancing. Truly, she was not sure she could face him again. And yet, she realised as he continued his approach, it seemed she must.

Isaac had known it was her from the moment he saw her in the distance, standing in front of the old church. He hadn't been able to see her clearly, or to recognise her pretty features with any precision, but he'd known. He'd known instinctively from the way his heart beat faster and his empty stomach seemed to tie itself in knots.

For a moment he'd thought about turning his horse around and galloping in the other direction, to put some distance between himself and Miss Louisa Conrad and how she flustered him. However, he'd known that would only cause more problems than it would solve—notably in the form of questions from his brother, who still rode at his side. Besides, he was beginning to suspect that mere miles would not be enough to stem the tide which threatened to overwhelm him when he so much as dared to think about her.

'Ah, look—there is Miss Conrad,' Samuel called. 'And who is that with her? A friend? I wonder what she is doing in Hayton. We should stop to say hello.'

'Huh…' Isaac grunted, trying his best to look uninterested.

He wished he could be uninterested. But as he drew closer and saw her looking up at him, those dark, inquisitive eyes staring into his, he realised his folly. This lady—who'd clambered into his carriage, who'd berated him on the clifftops, who'd danced with him—interested him. Now fate had put her in his path once more, and Isaac found himself feeling unfathomably anxious about speaking to her, about giving a good account of himself.

He swallowed hard. His mouth was as dry as a desert, and his mind seemed barren like one, too.

He dismounted his horse, trying to find the right words.

Damn you, Liddell, he said to himself. *What is the matter with you?*

Chapter Nine

'Good day, Miss Conrad. What a pleasant surprise to see you in Hayton.'

Samuel spoke first—of course he did—finding exactly the words which Isaac lacked. Isaac forced a smile and a courteous nod at the two young women, ignoring the prickle of resentment he felt at his brother's friendly, easy manner. Rosalind had always been better in social situations, too, but she'd been his helpmeet. He'd felt gratitude and admiration for her grace and charm. The superior qualities of a younger brother, by contrast, could only ever be irritating.

Samuel dismounted his horse and Isaac watched as Miss Conrad dropped her gaze and gave them both a polite curtsey.

'Sir Isaac, Mr Liddell…may I introduce my friend, Miss Charlotte Pearson?' she said, raising her eyes to meet his once more.

Realising he was staring, Isaac turned quickly to regard her companion, whose acquaintance Samuel was already making, going to great pains to stress his delight. She was a striking young lady, her fair complexion contrasting with the bright red curls which peered wildly from the edges of her bonnet. She seemed younger than Miss Conrad, and both her appearance and manner betrayed a giddiness over which she didn't seem to have mastered complete control.

He wondered then how old Miss Conrad was. Younger than him, certainly—he was nine-and-thirty, and she looked ten years his junior, at least. Yet there was something in those dark eyes of hers, something about the seriousness of her countenance, which suggested a maturity beyond her years. He ruminated on this observation for a moment, before a nudge from his brother forced him to return his mind to the conversation.

'We would be delighted to accompany you back through the village. It would be our pleasure—wouldn't it, Isaac?' Samuel was saying.

'Yes. Indeed—yes,' Isaac replied hastily, realising he'd missed much of the discussion.

He watched with a mix of delight and anxiety as Samuel and Miss Pearson led the way, leaving him in the company of Miss Conrad. Giving her another nod, he took hold of his horse and together they began to walk, slowly and silently at first, as though each one did not know what to say to the other.

'You have enjoyed your walk to Hayton, I hope?' Isaac began, settling upon what he believed would be an easy topic.

There were so many things he wished to say to her, so many things he wished to know—too much to convey and to discover in a short promenade through the tiny village. He would have to content himself with more mundane subjects.

'Yes, thank you,' she replied. 'As you know, my family used to live in the village. Miss Pearson offered to accompany me while I explored the area. She has been very kind.'

'Miss Pearson is related to the Mrs Pearson you were with at the Assembly Rooms?' Isaac asked.

She nodded. 'Yes, they are mother and daughter. They live in Lowhaven. Mrs Pearson is acquainted with my aunt.'

Isaac furrowed his brow a little. 'I do not think I know any Pearsons from Lowhaven.'

'They are fairly new in town, much like myself,' she replied. 'Although they reside now in Lowhaven, whereas I am only visiting.'

'For the summer,' Isaac said, the temporary nature of their acquaintance striking him again.

Miss Conrad smiled. 'Yes, as I think I told you when we danced. I am here only for the summer.'

He nodded briskly, hoping she wouldn't be able to detect the heat that had risen within him when she had made reference to their dancing. God, how his mind had lingered upon the memory of that night. She spoke of it so matter-of-factly; he knew he never could.

'And you enjoyed the ball?' he asked her, wilfully ignoring the way his instincts were crying out at him to avoid the subject altogether.

'Yes, very much. I confess that I was somewhat out of practice when it came to dancing. I hope I did not miss too many of the steps.'

'You were perfect, from what I could see,' he answered her, a little too forthrightly. Reining in his feelings, he added, 'Although I am no expert, since I am more than a little out of practice myself. In truth, I hadn't danced in a long time until I danced with you.'

She smiled again. 'Then I hope I was a worthy partner.'

Damn, he thought. Worthy? She had no idea.

They were approaching the end of the village, and ahead he could see Miss Pearson and his brother had stopped to wait for them. He felt his heart begin to beat faster; they were almost out of time together and all he'd managed was a conversation about trivialities.

'I don't see a lot of people,' he blurted out. 'Other than my brother, of course. What I mean to say is I don't venture much into society. But I do like to walk, and to ride. I often ride out to the cliffs where we met that time. If—if I was ever to see you there again, I should be very glad to continue our conversation.'

He glanced at her, wondering if she had understood his meaning—nay, hoping she had. She turned to meet his gaze, and for a moment he believed he might lose himself in the depths of those eyes.

'Thank you, Sir Isaac,' she replied demurely. 'On the next fine afternoon, after calling hours, I believe I will walk that way again, too.'

What had come over her? What had she done?

Those same two questions circled around Louisa's mind all the way back to Lowhaven. She barely absorbed a word of anything Charlotte said to her, peppering their very one-sided conversation with 'yes' and 'indeed' in the right places as her friend gushed excitedly about her encounter with Mr Liddell.

She could think of nothing else but Sir Isaac's words to her. The way he'd complimented her dancing, the way he'd made sure she knew the significance of it for him— his first dance in a long time. The way he'd asked to see her again, to meet with her…alone. That *was* what he'd meant, wasn't it? She hadn't imagined that, had she? She hadn't misinterpreted his meaning? No, she wasn't so naïve as to have misunderstood him. But she had been foolish enough to answer in the affirmative.

She had said she would meet him, even though she knew she should not.

She'd been reckless—again.

In truth, she'd felt so flustered throughout their conversation she'd hardly known what to say to him. One look into those bright blue eyes had been enough to render her mind utterly incapable of conjuring any suitable conversation. Thank goodness he had taken the lead, in the end. Their encounter, though polite, had been thick with undertones—layer upon layer of words and thoughts unexpressed. She'd felt it, and she sensed he had, too. She hadn't felt this way in the company of a man since…

No. She would not think of him now. It would not do any good.

'Are you all right, Louisa?' Charlotte asked her, apparently finally running out of things to say about the charming Mr Liddell.

'Yes, I am well…just a little tired,' she replied, offering her friend a small smile of reassurance and hoping it would be sufficient.

'You haven't said much about your promenade with Sir Isaac,' Charlotte remarked. 'I observed you dancing with him at the ball, you know. And Mama told me that you were already acquainted with both Sir Isaac and Mr Liddell.'

'Yes, I met them both on my journey to Lowhaven, and, yes, I did dance with Sir Isaac,' she said. 'Both seem to be very agreeable gentlemen,' she added.

'Agreeable—and handsome,' Charlotte said with a giggle.

'Charlotte!'

'Oh, Louisa, surely even a committed spinster like you can see all that both gentlemen have to recommend them. Good looks and a good deal of wealth, I should say. Especially Sir Isaac, given his rank.'

Louisa flinched, not enjoying the brazen tone Charlotte had adopted. 'These are not the only qualities a woman ought to consider in making a marriage, Charlotte,' she tried to advise her.

'Tell that to my mother,' Charlotte retorted. 'For her, they are the only qualities worth noting. Anyway, you have not yet told me—what did you and Sir Isaac discuss?'

'Nothing of any import,' Louisa replied with a small shrug. 'He asked if I had enjoyed seeing Hayton, and we spoke a little about the ball.'

Charlotte's eyes widened. 'About dancing together?'

'Not really,' Louisa lied, wanting to put an end to this conversation.

'Oh. Well, still… It is fortunate that we saw them here today. Mama has been disappointed that I missed out on an introduction at the ball. Mr Liddell said it was quite by chance that they were riding through the village today, as they had been visiting Sir Isaac's tenants.'

'I see,' Louisa replied, realising with a pang of guilt that she had neglected to enquire as to the reason for their visit to the village. In fact, she hadn't asked Sir Isaac any questions at all.

She wondered then what he must think of her. Reserved—aloof, even? Or merely dull and uninterested? On the other hand, he'd made it plain he wanted to see her again, so she couldn't have done so badly. She bit her lip, resolving to be a better conversationalist next time they met. After all, there would be a next time. In a moment of madness she'd agreed to it. She could hardly go back on her word.

Isaac couldn't recall when he'd last been this hungry. As he tucked in to his plate of bread and cold meat, washing it down with a small glass of wine, he smiled, reflecting upon how well he felt. It had been good to spend the morning outside, to be with his brother and to ride in the warm summer air. It had been good, too, to see his tenants. It had been another step along the road out of mourning, and another way in which he had signalled to the world that he was ready to re-join society. And he was—truly, he was.

But none of that was the reason he felt so exhilarated.

He'd behaved boldly with Miss Conrad—had been far bolder than he'd thought himself capable of being. It was hard to comprehend what had come over him, but ever since that day on the cliffs that woman had been on his mind. Today's encounter had been a co-incidence, but even as they'd walked together he'd felt keenly that he did not want to leave the next time they saw each other to chance. He wanted to talk to her, to get to know her. He wanted to see her alone.

God, he had all but asked her to come alone.

And she'd all but said that she would.

'Well, that was quite an unexpected pleasure,' Samuel said between mouthfuls of food.

Isaac had been so absorbed in his thoughts that he'd almost forgotten his younger brother was sitting opposite. 'What was?'

'Seeing Miss Conrad today. And meeting her friend, the lovely Miss Pearson. A charming girl...very lively.'

Isaac nodded. 'Indeed, she gave that impression. I'm not sure she ever stopped smiling.'

Samuel buttered another slice of bread. 'I found her very agreeable.'

'She seemed very...young,' Isaac remarked, searching for the right words to describe the lady who had clearly caught his brother's attention.

'Not so much younger than me, I don't think,' Samuel retorted. 'Twenty, perhaps? I doubt I have more than ten years on her. Remember, I am much younger than you,' he added, with a grin.

'Huh...' Isaac grunted, occupying himself with his food once more. 'We know nothing of the girl's family other than that they are new to Lowhaven. Miss Conrad told me so.'

'Ah, yes. And how *was* the stoic Miss Conrad?'

'Well, I believe. I wish you would not mock her simply because she seems to be immune to your charms,' Isaac bit back, his tone sounding harsher than he'd intended.

'I don't think you're immune to hers, though,' Samuel replied, giving him a pointed look.

'Nonsense.'

Samuel sighed. 'There is no shame in it, Isaac. Rosalind would want you to be happy.'

Isaac felt the heat of anger flash through him. 'Don't you dare to presume what Rosalind would or would not have wanted!' he snapped.

His ire was directed at Samuel, but Isaac knew that in truth the only person he was frustrated with was himself. He was no naïve youth, ignorant of his growing infatuation with Miss Conrad. But neither was he deaf to that inner voice which niggled at him, suggesting that his preoccupation with her amounted to a betrayal of his dead wife, that it was utterly contrary to his commitment to remaining alone.

A mere two years had passed since Rosalind's death; how could he possibly contemplate moving on? How could he even think of allowing himself to love again when he knew only too well the pain it had brought him? That was if he was even capable of love, he reminded himself. Surely his heart bore too many scars for that.

'All right, all right,' Samuel said, holding his hands up. 'All I'm trying to say is if you like Miss Conrad then you should pursue her. Just be cautious. The last thing you need is some disappointment with a woman to send you back into hiding with a bottle of brandy.'

'Then you have nothing to fear. Because I have no intentions towards Miss Conrad, or any other woman of my acquaintance.'

Damn, how that lie stung his lips. He gave his brother a hard stare, hoping he would not manage to see through the façade. In truth, he barely understood his own intentions. Barely knew what he wanted. All he did know was that he was tired of grief and tired of being alone. He wanted companionship and conversation and joy. He wanted to sit beside a beautiful woman and make her smile, even if it was only for the summer.

He could only hope he would find some of those things next time he rode out to the cliffs.

Chapter Ten

In the days after her visit to Hayton it did nothing but rain. Louisa was forced to remain indoors, sitting often with her aunt in the parlour while she read or passed the time with light conversation.

Louisa had sensed some tension between Clarissa and herself, ever since the night of the ball. She knew it was her doing, that the way she'd spoken to her aunt about Sir Isaac had made the older woman wary. She regretted that this was the case, but she did not know how to remedy it. To bring up the subject would be uncomfortable, and might lead her aunt to begin the discussion about the master of Hayton Hall anew—which was the last thing she wanted. But to avoid it, as she had done thus far, allowed it to fester between them, making the memory of her cross words no doubt a source of mortification for them both.

Oh, how she wished she hadn't spoken out of turn.

How she wished she'd said nothing about Sir Isaac at all. Especially not a lie—and it was a lie. She knew she'd have enjoyed a second dance with him very much indeed.

Nan was driving her to distraction, too, fussing around

her as she tried to read a book or write a long-overdue letter to her mother, to whom she hadn't written since she'd sent word of her safe arrival several weeks ago. She knew her maid had found the adjustment to a smaller household difficult, and that having to assist with kitchen or cleaning tasks did not suit her as well as keeping solely to the duties of a lady's maid. Nonetheless, she found Nan's frequent intrusions irritating; she didn't need anything brought to her and she didn't desire company. If anything, she wanted to be left alone: to think, to reflect and—dare she admit it?—to daydream a little. It had been a long time since she'd allowed herself a luxury such as that.

On the first fine day in almost a week Louisa ventured outdoors as soon as the calling hours were over. She'd done her best to make it appear like an impromptu walk, deflecting her aunt's suggestion that she send a note to Charlotte by insisting throughout the morning that she planned to stay at home, only to then change her mind at the last possible moment. Such deceit had left her feeling flustered, but she knew she couldn't take Charlotte with her, or indeed anyone else. Nan had made some vague overtures about accompanying her, but had been easily put off when Louisa had let it be known that she planned to walk up to the cliffs and take the sea air.

'I'll come if you wish, miss,' she'd said, gesturing at the sewing in her lap, 'but then this mending will need to wait until later.'

'Oh, no, Nan,' Louisa had replied hastily. 'I don't want to keep you from your work. Besides, I will only be gone a short while.'

A short while—indeed, it would have to be.

As Lowhaven's busy streets increasingly gave way

to countryside, Louisa reflected upon the risk she was taking. Meeting a man, unchaperoned, was not something any young woman should do. She tried not to think about what Aunt Clarissa would say if she knew, how she would lecture her and insist she ought to know better.

She tried not to think about the rumour and gossip she would be subjected to if she was seen. Instead, she tried to calm her nerves, to retain some perspective. After all, she had already met Sir Isaac on the cliffs once, and she had been alone then, too. To a casual observer this might simply appear to be a chance encounter between two acquaintances. Besides, she reminded herself, he might not even come. He might be busy, or he might have reflected upon his own recklessness in suggesting it and thought better of it.

Louisa began the slow ascent along the rough track leading to the cliffs, her boots sliding on the muddy ground which had been saturated by days of rainfall. It wasn't too late for her to turn back, she considered. To return to her aunt's house and forget all about Sir Isaac Liddell and his unusual suggestion. Perhaps that would be wise. And yet, despite her reservations, she kept going, spurred on by an instinct, a sort of curiosity she could not quite name. God knew, wisdom had never been her strong suit…

Isaac arrived on the clifftops a little before four o'clock. For the first time in a while he was alone, which in itself was a luxury he permitted himself to enjoy after all the socialising he'd done recently.

He'd had to put on a convincing show for Samuel in order to escape without arousing his brother's suspicions. Freshly shaven and smartly dressed, he'd joined Samuel for a late luncheon. Halfway through his third piece of cold meat and his second cup of tea, he'd casually announced that he planned to take some air later, now that the weather had improved.

'Then I will gladly accompany you, brother,' Samuel had predictably replied.

Isaac had put on his best and most cheerful smile. 'In fact, if you don't mind, I would prefer to ride alone today. It is nothing untoward, I promise you. I merely feel the need for a little quiet contemplation. I've spent a lot of time in company of late.'

Samuel had seemed unconvinced, but not prepared to challenge his brother further on the matter.

As ever, the early afternoon had brought no callers to the door of Hayton Hall, and after several hours at his desk, attending to estate matters, Isaac had ridden out to that spot on the cliffs where he and Miss Conrad had first met. Now, as he sat on a rock and stared out at the vast blue sea, he contemplated what a fool he was. He had no idea if she would come today or not. She'd said she intended to walk here on the next fine day, but that had doubtless been a flustered response to his impertinence. It was entirely possible that she'd returned to her aunt after meeting him that morning in Hayton and thought better of it. Indeed, he would hardly blame her if she had.

'You should never have asked her, Liddell,' he muttered, giving the ground a swift kick with his left boot.

'Do you often talk to yourself?'

Isaac sprang to his feet, turning around as she approached him. The sight of her took his breath away, from the perfect blonde curls tamed into place by her bonnet to the casual spatter of mud along the bottom of her violet day dress.

He removed his hat, running a swift hand over his black hair. Thank God there was no strong wind to tousle it today. He wished to give her no occasion to remember the wild, dishevelled creature he'd been at their last clifftop meeting.

'Miss Conrad,' he mumbled, greeting her with an awkward bow.

She returned the gesture with a polite nod, before raising her eyebrows expectantly at him. 'Well?' she asked.

He frowned briefly, before her meaning dawned upon him. 'Oh!' he replied, laughing. 'Yes, I'm afraid I am guilty of giving myself a quiet lecture or two when the occasion demands it.'

'And does sitting by oneself on the cliffs require such a thing?' Her question seemed serious, but her eyes, he could see, were smiling.

He felt a flush of colour rise in his cheeks. 'Only if you're the sort of man who recklessly suggests that a woman meet him upon those cliffs alone,' he confessed. 'Forgive me, Miss Conrad. I am very glad you came, but truly I do not know what came over me when we met in Hayton. I know just as well as you do that we should not meet alone.'

She gave another small nod, her expression unreadable. 'I won't tell if you won't,' she replied.

He gave her a small smile. 'There is no one for me to tell—except my brother, perhaps. But I've always found confiding in Samuel to be unwise.'

'Oh?'

Isaac let out a wry chuckle. 'Samuel is younger than me by almost ten years. I find telling him anything usually leads to either teasing or a lecture—although recently it's been more of the latter than anything else. He has become very insistent that I should make more of an effort to go into society. I have not found it easy to be in company since my wife's death.'

Isaac paused, realising he was saying far too much already.

'Forgive me, Miss Conrad,' he continued after a moment. 'I do not know why I am telling you all this. Would you like to walk? Or perhaps to sit awhile on the rocks?'

'We could walk a little,' she replied. 'Although I promised my aunt that I would not be out for too long.' She glanced at his horse, standing obediently at his side. 'Will he be all right to walk with us?'

Isaac had almost forgotten the poor creature was there. 'What? Oh, him! Yes, it was not a long ride from Hayton. He will not be tired yet.'

He gathered the reins tightly in his hand, and with all the courage he could muster he offered Miss Conrad his free arm. His breath caught in his throat as he watched her hesitate, her dark eyes seeming to search his for something—he didn't know what. Then, before he could retract the gesture and apologise once more, she reached out and took it. Her nearness warmed him like the sun could never hope to, and it alarmed him to acknowledge how quickly his thoughts turned to letting the damned horse go and enveloping her in his embrace.

Louisa's heart hammered in her chest as they took a gentle stroll along the coast. She'd barely known what to do or to say since she'd arrived here. The way he looked at her, the way he spoke to her with such openness and familiarity—she could not fathom it.

Why her? What had she ever done apart from be defensive or reserved or muted in his presence? Now, as she walked with her hand clutching his arm, she tried to focus on her surroundings—the squawking of the gulls, the sound of the waves crashing against the rocks far below. Anything but the heat of his arm against hers… anything but the proximity of him.

Those thoughts, she knew, led to other thoughts—brazen, forbidden thoughts. Not the thoughts of a spinster. No, she told herself, this would not do. She was allowing this tide to carry her along, but she had been here before, and she knew what it would cost her. She had to remember the vow she had made to herself. She had to remember what was at stake if she didn't.

'Why—why did you ask me to meet you, Sir Isaac?' she asked, rushing out the words before she could change her mind.

He turned to look at her, studying her face, and she realised he was trying to understand what had prompted her question. She pressed her lips together, trying to swallow down her turmoil. Then he looked away again, staring far into the horizon as he spoke.

'I am drawn to you, Miss Conrad, in a way that I have not been drawn to another human being for a long time. I mentioned my wife before… You must know I lost her, and my son—it is an oft-repeated tale around these parts.'

'Yes,' she interjected. 'My aunt told me not long after that last time we met here on the cliffs. I was sorry to hear of it. Losing those you love brings much suffering.' She felt the truth in those words with a tightening in her chest.

He drew a deep breath. 'Since their deaths I have

struggled. I have kept away from society, tried to protect myself by remaining alone. But that is a fool's errand which brings only misery. Then I met you, and I feel as though I'd like to get to know you.'

He turned his gaze to meet hers once again, and there was no mistaking the warmth in his eyes.

'I know you are not in Lowhaven for long, and I do not ask nor expect you to have the same interest in me. But, nonetheless, if you would consent to spending some time in my company, I believe I would enjoy that.'

'You seek my friendship?' Louisa asked him, desiring clarity.

He nodded. 'If you will give it.'

She smiled then. 'Readily I will give it, sir. You do yourself a disservice if you think I have no interest in you.'

'Even after the last time we met up here?'

She laughed. 'Well, perhaps not after that…but I will admit you redeemed yourself a little when we danced together at the ball.'

'Only a little?' he teased.

'All right, perhaps slightly more than a little,' she replied, still smiling.

He looked at her again, that azure gaze of his growing more serious now. 'You must call me Isaac. If we are to be friends, it is only right.'

She hesitated for a moment, remembering how easily she'd slipped into more familiar terms with Charlotte after only a brief acquaintance. But this felt different— more significant somehow. She wasn't sure she could countenance it—not yet.

'I shall call you Sir Isaac, for that is the name you properly deserve. But I will not object if you'd prefer to call me Louisa, and perhaps, in time, Isaac will do just as well on its own.'

'I will hope for it, Louisa,' he replied, and it didn't escape her notice how broad his smile had grown. 'Even the mere promise of it will do very well for me.'

Louisa drew a deep breath, averting her eyes to concentrate once more upon the seascape. She'd agreed to be his friend, and indeed she sensed that a good friend was something he needed as much as she did. Nevertheless, she knew she had to draw firm lines in their acquaintance—and if that meant maintaining some formality in addressing him, then so be it.

A friendship was all well and good, but any deepening of affection between them could not be permitted. It was clear that Sir Isaac had suffered a great deal, and although he did not know it, so had she. Nothing good could come of becoming too attached, for either of them. Anything beyond friendship was, quite simply, out of the question.

Chapter Eleven

On the day of their next clifftop meeting Isaac found himself gripped by a potent mix of good humour and crippling self-reproach—and he was not sure which feeling disconcerted him the most. He was not renowned for having a cheerful disposition—even before Rosalind's death a solemn countenance had always come easier to him than a smile—and although he'd been a contented spouse, he'd been ill at ease showing it.

He'd often considered it was the force of habit...that his position in life—eldest son, then landowner and baronet—and all the years of bearing so much responsibility had etched a profound seriousness upon his soul. The loss of Rosalind and his child had also meant the loss of his reasons to smile, and so he hadn't.

Not until this summer.

Not until he'd met Louisa.

Acknowledging how much he enjoyed the lady's company, however, came with a considerable amount of guilt. That inner voice which berated him for betraying Rosalind's memory seemed to grow louder, as though it sensed he was contemplating his own readiness to move on. And he was, wasn't he? He'd emerged from the worst of his grief some time ago, and slowly he'd begun to accept just how much he hated being alone.

That acceptance had now bred other feelings—feelings which he had never expected to experience again. The enjoyment of a lovely woman's company. The pleasure of her hand holding his arm. Bit by bit his resolve had weakened, his desire for companionship increasingly defeating his commitment to solitude.

But it was only companionship, he reminded himself. It was only friendship. Surely fostering a friendly acquaintance with a lady during the course of a summer was not such a terrible transgression? In any case, he doubted that Louisa would have any interest in anything more than friendship with an older, morose man such as him. She was young and beautiful, charming and refined. She was hardly likely to consider disagreeable and damaged Sir Isaac Liddell a catch.

Such murky thoughts continued to preoccupy him at breakfast, combining with his growing anticipation of his later clifftop meeting to make him feel quite sick. As he forced down several slices of toast in the company of his brother he made a concerted effort to appear nonchalant about his plans for the day ahead. Fortunately, Samuel made life easy for him in this regard, informing him that he would be detained all day in Lowhaven on matters of business, and that he would not return before dinnertime.

'I am sorry, brother,' Samuel said regretfully. 'It cannot be helped. I hope you will go out riding without me. I can see all the fresh air you've enjoyed recently has done you the world of good.'

Isaac nodded. 'Indeed, I do not mind some time by myself. In fact, I think I might take a long walk today.'

Samuel looked up from his newspaper. 'Oh?' he said. 'Anywhere in particular?'

Isaac shrugged. 'No,' he replied, pushing his empty plate away. 'I am happy to see where the wind carries me.'

Of course the strong sea breeze took him to the coast, and the afternoon sun was shining down from its high position in the sky by the time he reached their meeting place. To his surprise, Louisa was already there, and inwardly he chastised himself for not leaving earlier. Clearly walking to the cliffs had taken him much longer than he'd anticipated.

As he approached, he offered her a warm smile, feeling his mood lift once more as she smiled back at him. He could not help but notice how lovely she looked in a cream and cornflower-blue dress, its vertical stripes seeming to lengthen her petite frame and make her appear taller as she stood to greet him. He'd seen her wear blue more than once now, and thought the colour suited her very well—a thought he would keep to himself, he decided. He'd asked for a friendship, not a courtship, after all.

'I am sorry to have kept you waiting, Louisa,' he said as he reached her, tipping his hat in greeting.

'I have not been here long,' she answered him, glancing back towards the sea. 'Indeed, I have enjoyed watching the waves. It is nice to have a little peace and quiet now and then.' She turned back to him, frowning as she peered over his shoulder. 'You have not brought your horse today?'

'No, I felt like walking to meet you. Besides, he is a

grumpy creature—like his master. It is better not having him here, forced to follow us around.'

Louisa laughed at that. 'I do not think you are so very grumpy,' she countered.

He grinned appreciatively at this compliment of sorts, then offered her his arm, which she accepted without hesitation. Together they began to walk, sauntering slowly along the clifftops, neither of them apparently in any hurry to go anywhere in particular.

He stole a glance at her, spying her contented expression beneath her bonnet. She seemed more relaxed today...more at ease in his company. He wished then that he could be so calm. In truth, the closeness of her, the feeling of her hand resting in the crook of his arm— all of it had ruffled him again, made him think about things which mere friends were not meant to consider.

'So...peace and quiet,' he said, determined on some meaningful conversation. 'You do not have much of that in Lowhaven, I expect?'

She shook her head. 'Such is life in a busy port town, I believe. It is all very new to me. I am far more accustomed to living in the country.'

'And what is the country like in Berkshire?'

'Tranquil.' She smiled fondly. 'And very green. Although there I am without the pleasure of seeing the sea every day.' She gestured towards the vast expanse of water stretching to the horizon. 'I will miss this when I leave Cumberland. The coastal air here has agreed with me very well.'

He nodded, accepting the compliment on behalf of his county. 'Do you enjoy walking at home, too? Or riding, perhaps?'

'Oh, yes—both. Although walking is by far my favourite outdoor pursuit. Indeed, it's a habit I have continued here, much to my aunt's displeasure. She does not think it is right for a young woman to be out so much on her own.'

'Ah, well, of course your aunt's concern is entirely justified,' he replied, giving her a mischievous grin. 'The unchaperoned lady is vulnerable to approaches from all sorts of ruffians and scoundrels.'

She laughed as she looked up at him, giving his arm a squeeze. 'Indeed,' she said. 'As I know only too well.' Her smile faded, and those brown eyes seemed to darken as her face grew serious once more. 'Aunt Clarissa means well, but I do wish she would not make such a fuss. I have been of age for some years now, and I am very accustomed to taking care of myself.'

'You are?' Her declaration surprised him. 'Forgive me, Louisa,' he said, frowning, 'but I assumed you lived with your parents.'

She nodded. 'Yes, I do. Our home is a lovely country estate, and when my parents and brother are in town—which they frequently are—I do very well staying there by myself.'

'You do not go into town with them?'

He watched as she seemed to hesitate, as though his simple question was giving her pause for thought. 'No,' she said after a moment. 'Not usually.'

How odd, he thought. In his experience, unmarried young women were seldom permitted any respite from the watchful gaze of a parent or guardian. Seldom permitted even the semblance of a reprieve from society or from the task of securing a husband.

'And your mother? She is quite content with this arrangement?'

The question slipped out before he could properly consider it, and the moment he uttered the words, he could see that he had overstepped the mark. Immediately Louisa looked away from him, staring straight ahead, her pretty features hardening against what she doubtless perceived to be criticism.

Inwardly, he chastised himself. After avoiding society for so long, what right did he have to question her apparent preference for doing the same?

'Forgive me,' he began. 'I…' His voice faltered, and he found himself at a loss as to how to explain himself.

She glanced at him then. 'There is no need to apologise, Sir Isaac,' she said stiffly. 'My mother is as content as I am. While in residence alone I am properly cared for by my maid, and I send regular reports to my parents, who are always anxious to be reassured of my good health. So, you see, there is nothing for you to concern yourself with on my account.'

Her rebuke, though politely delivered, stung him. What a prying, interfering man he must have seemed to her. How insulting he must have appeared towards her family. He'd been so gripped by his curiosity, by his desire to get to know her, that he'd managed to offend her all over again.

His earlier buoyant mood all but evaporated, and in its place the mist of malaise began to settle once more.

'I see,' he replied, his expression grim. 'I am glad the arrangement suits you. I can only hope that your time in Cumberland will bring you similar joy.'

Louisa could see that she had upset him, but in truth she was at a loss as to how to repair the damage. The fault was undoubtedly hers—there had been no need to mention her self-sufficiency, or her unconventional familial arrangements, and yet for some reason she had. She'd been momentarily unguarded and had said too much about herself. She'd given Sir Isaac cause to wonder about her unusual manner of living. Indeed, was there a gentleman alive who would not have wondered at it?

Her father had only reluctantly accepted her wishes, and that was because he understood the reasons for the choice she'd made. To an outsider it must seem baffling, but she could hardly explain herself. She could hardly admit to her past, which had given her little option but to embrace a solitary existence.

She needed to make amends to her new friend—she knew that. However, she also needed to put a stop to any further discussion about her life in Berkshire. On that subject, she needed to be the closed book she'd promised herself she would be. Her past was hundreds of miles away, and for this summer, at least, that was where she was determined it would remain.

'Tell me about some of your favourite places here,' she said, resolving to change the subject. 'Where do you like to ride, or to walk?'

She was relieved to see his face light up at her question. 'Anywhere quiet. I avoid the town whenever possible—not that there is anything wrong with Lowhaven, of course, but such a busy place inevitably presents the possibility of being seen by an acquaintance and forced by duty to converse.' He paused, glancing at her. 'You must think me very dull, Louisa. Or very disagreeable. Or both.'

She shook her head. 'Not at all. I think you are none of those things. The point in being out riding or walking by oneself is to be alone, not to seek out company. I would avoid the town too, in your position.' She offered him an encouraging smile. 'Please, tell me about a place you like to go.'

'There is a village a little way down the coast called St Bees. Before you reach the village there is a headland which reaches out west. It is a stunning spot, and home to all kinds of sea birds. There is a legend that an Irish princess called St Bega was shipwrecked there in the ninth century, after fleeing from being forced to marry a Viking prince. She became an anchoress, devoting herself to a life of piety and solitude. The village is named after her, and the priory there is dedicated to her.'

'How fascinating,' Louisa replied. 'Does the legend say what became of her?'

'She lived in St Bees for some time, but fearing the pirates who were raiding along the coast she eventually went east, perhaps into Northumberland.' He grinned at her. 'She appears to have caught your imagination, just as she catches mine.'

Louisa felt her cheeks begin to colour, although she wasn't sure why. 'It's quite a story,' she replied, turning to look ahead and steadfastly avoiding his gaze. 'I wonder if it is true.'

'I often ponder the same question,' he replied, not seeming to notice her unfathomable discomfort. 'I must confess, over the past couple of years I have often found myself sitting on that headland, staring out across the sea towards Ireland and reflecting on her perilous escape and her decision, once safe, to remain alone. I've had solitude forced upon me by the unhappiest of circumstances, but she chose it.'

'As you said, it was a matter of religious devotion,'

Louisa countered. 'There are many good reasons why people choose to remain alone.'

She bit her lip, realising that once again she'd said more than she ought to. She felt the weight of his gaze on her as he considered her assertion, but still she avoided looking at him. Indeed, she did not dare, lest he read something in her expression which she did not want him to see.

'I wonder if you speak from experience,' he ventured, apparently not quite daring to ask the question.

Perhaps it was the fine day, or the sea air, or the note of earnest concern in Sir Isaac's voice, but something in that moment caused Louisa's resolve to soften. She looked up at him, her heart lurching at the sincerity of his intense blue gaze, just as it had when she'd first learned of all that he'd lost. When she'd first understood just how much they had in common.

'I lost someone once,' she began, the words falling from her lips before she could truly contemplate them. 'Someone I loved very much. He died in the war.'

She paused, trying to ignore her racing heart, trying to remind herself that she'd said nothing more to Sir Isaac than she'd confided in Charlotte. Yet as she stared up at him, watching the frown gather between his eyes as their shared understanding dawned upon him, she knew that this would be nothing like talking to Charlotte. Nothing at all.

Chapter Twelve

'His name was Richard. He was a captain in the navy.'

Instinctively Louisa drew closer to Isaac, glad of the comforting feeling of his arm holding hers. It had been a long time since she'd talked properly about Richard, and longer still since she'd said his name. She'd begun this story now, for reasons which seemed quite beyond her understanding, and she was committed to telling it. Or at least part of it.

The parts she would tell were painful enough. The parts she would omit were wholly unutterable.

'We met at a ball, at the home of some friends of my family, who live near Reading. Richard was a relation of theirs, and had come to stay with them in the country while recovering from an injury he'd sustained when his ship was badly damaged in a storm. I was young...only nineteen; Richard was a little older at six-and-twenty. Suffice to say we danced and we talked, and were quite taken with one another. Over the following few months I saw a lot of him; our affection grew, and before long we were engaged to marry. By this time Richard's injury had healed and he'd received word that he was to return to sea. He'd applied for a new ship, his old one having been declared unfit for service, and had been appointed to another command. I'm not sure why, but it all seemed to happen very quickly, and we agreed we would marry once he returned.'

Louisa paused, swallowing hard. Even after all this time, telling this story seemed to affect her physically. Her mouth was dry…a dull ache was spreading through her chest.

'However, it was not to be. A couple of months after he took command, Richard's ship was sunk in the English Channel by the French. None of the crew survived.'

Beside her, she heard Isaac draw a deep breath, and she found herself looking out towards the sea, a strange sort of weariness settling over her like mist. She'd parted with as much of the story as she was willing to, and even that had been a trial. She prayed he would accept the sorry tale, just as Charlotte had done. She prayed he would not ask too many questions of her.

'I am very sorry for your loss, Louisa,' he said, his voice grave and sincere. 'And I thank you for telling me. I am sorry if my remarks about your living arrangements in Berkshire caused you any distress. I understand perfectly now why you remain alone.'

She offered him a tight smile. 'It's not a story I tell very often,' she replied. 'At home, it's a story everyone knows, and here… Well, it's been nice that almost no one knows.'

'I can understand that,' Isaac replied. 'After Rosalind and our son died I wearied quickly of all the condolences, all the pity. I just wanted to escape. I couldn't do that, so I retreated instead.'

'It is surprisingly easy to hide on a country estate,' Louisa mused, half to herself.

She felt the pain of guilt grip her as she thought about all the reasons she'd been hiding. About all the things a man like Sir Isaac could never know.

'It seems we have more in common than I'd realised,' he observed. 'I am sorry that you have had your life marred by sadness at such a young age, and before you were even wed. I have always been grateful that at least Rosalind and I did have some years together.'

She nodded. 'Our time together was so very short. Sometimes it feels as though I dreamt him—as though he was never in my life at all.'

'I often think that about my son, since he was here so briefly,' Isaac replied, his voice almost a whisper. He shuddered, as though brushing off unwelcome thoughts. 'It's been two years since they died, you know, and sometimes I wonder if I will ever fully recover from my grief.'

'I don't believe you ever do,' she replied. 'I think you simply learn to live with it…that it becomes a part of who you are.'

'Indeed. As long as you do not let it consume your whole self,' he said pointedly. 'Grief cannot be allowed to govern your life, to dictate to you over every decision you make.'

Louisa bristled, feeling his insinuation sharply. In the wake of losing Richard her grief had been utterly consuming, but even then it had not exercised full control over her choices. She pressed her lips together, thankful that Sir Isaac did not know anything of the other circumstances she'd grappled with during those long, dark months.

Sir Isaac seemed to notice her discomfort, because

after a moment he smiled wryly at her and added, 'I re-alise that I have no business saying that. I've spent much of the last two years allowing my grief to do exactly that. But it a lesson which I think I am beginning to learn.'

Louisa found she could only answer him with a tight smile. The growing wind whipped at her face and she drew closer to him once more, as though the mere feel of him could ground her, could stop her from thinking too much. Her summer in Lowhaven was meant to be a reprieve, and this walk with Sir Isaac was meant to be an enjoyable interlude with a new friend. Thoughts of the past, of her reasons for being here and her choices, had no place here.

Clutching his arm ever tighter, she drew a deep breath, burying those thoughts in the back of her mind as she so often did.

For a brief moment she felt the muscles beneath her fingers tense, before he brought his other hand to rest over hers. It was a tender, reassuring gesture, and one which, despite her instincts, she allowed herself to ap-preciate. He had responded to her sorry tale with kind-ness and sincerity, and had related to her grief with something far deeper than mere sympathy. It was hard to believe that this gentleman, who spoke to her so gently and honestly, was the same sullen and disagree-able man she'd first met.

Sir Isaac was right; they did have much in common. She'd recognised that herself, when she'd first learned of all that he'd lost. But she also knew that their shared knowledge of grief, of pain and of self-imposed solitude was only the half of it. The other half—the unspeakable half—was something Sir Isaac could never know. The other half of her story, she reminded herself, was something which no gentleman in his position could countenance.

Isaac replayed her sorrowful story over and over, picking through its details and feeling his heart lurch at the knowledge of her pain. He understood it now. The serious countenance, the aloofness, the reserve. The stoicism, as Samuel had correctly called it.

At the time, Isaac had objected to his brother's remarks about Louisa's character, and yet he'd been right, hadn't he? She was all of those things, and for good reason. For the same reason, it transpired, he had for being solemn and reclusive. Indeed, they had both locked themselves away, both sought refuge from the prying eyes of the world in secluded country houses. They'd both nursed their grief alone.

He could never have imagined on that first day they'd met, when she'd stumbled into his carriage, that they'd have quite so much in common.

Isaac made himself comfortable in his library, sending for some tea to quench his growing thirst after walking home from the cliffs. As he sat back in his favourite armchair, he found himself wondering how Louisa felt about being alone now…if she was as weary of it as he was. He wondered what had brought her to Lowhaven—if it was more than a simple desire to visit her aunt. After all, since she'd been in town she'd evidently not hidden herself away, attending balls and befriending the likes of the Pearsons. Befriending him.

She hadn't hesitated to accept his offer of friendship, had she?

You do yourself a disservice, she'd said, *if you think I have no interest in you.*

How those words had warmed him since.

'Friendship is one thing, Liddell,' he muttered to himself. 'But anything else is out of the question.'

And it was—it had to be. During these past months he'd come far—much further than he could have imagined possible during those early dark days he'd spent shrouded in his grief. He was loath to admit it, but Samuel's insistence that he re-enter society had been good for him.

If he hadn't been in that carriage returning from Penrith that day he would not have met Louisa. If he hadn't attended the ball in Lowhaven he would not have danced with her. If he hadn't been visiting his tenants he would never have had the chance to boldly suggest that they begin to meet. He would not have begun a friendship with her. But no matter how lovely she was, or how much they had in common, he knew it could never be more than that. He'd learned to live with the past now—it no longer dictated to him. But it was still there, nonetheless.

It still weighed heavily upon his heart.

It still surrounded him in every room, every inch of Hayton Hall.

Louisa had said that Richard's presence in her life had been so fleeting that it felt like a dream. For Isaac, it was the opposite. Rosalind was still everywhere in his home—from the rooms she'd tastefully had modernised, with fresh paint and plasterwork, to the clothes and other personal effects which remained tucked within the ancient cupboards and drawers passed down to him by his ancestors.

He'd clung on to her possessions, unable to look at them, but equally unable to let them go.

Well, he reasoned, perhaps it was time to do either one or the other.

Isaac hauled himself out of his seat and walked over to the large walnut chest sitting solidly in the shadows. He pulled open the middle drawer, noticing immediately the musty smell which rose up, as though stale, years-old air had finally managed to escape the confines of that dark, disused space. It caught him off guard, and he felt the past begin to claw at him.

He paused then, before placing a tender hand upon the pretty blue shawl and lifting it carefully. As though it might break. As though the memories it contained might disintegrate as soon as the cloth met the cool library air. He unfolded it, grateful that after all this time it no longer smelled of her. The whiff of neglect which tainted it now was bad enough, but for it to have held on to even the merest hint of her perfume would have been unbearable.

The last time she'd worn this she'd been heavy with child, sitting in the library and poring over one of her favourite novels by Mrs Radcliffe. *The Italian*, probably, but now he thought about it he realised he couldn't recall.

He clutched the shawl against his chest, feeling the fragility of the soft silk beneath his fingers. He was still fragile, too, he realised. His heart, though mended, was scarred for ever. There was no point allowing his thoughts to linger upon just how much he and Louisa seemed to understand each other, or the way his heart skipped a beat as she took his arm, or the way he would lose himself in her deep brown gaze. He'd found solace in her friendship, but he should not imagine that there could ever be anything more between them than that.

He remained rooted to the spot as the door creaked open and a maid delivered his tea, still holding on to that shawl and, with it, all the reasons he knew he could never allow himself to love again even if he wanted to.

The problem was, he reflected as he poured himself some tea, increasingly he suspected that to love and to be loved was exactly what he wanted.

Chapter Thirteen

Louisa sat beside her aunt in the Pearsons' splendid parlour, trying her best to sit still and look interested in the conversation. Outside the sun shone brightly, and from within this dark room, dominated by a deep blue Chinese wallpaper and an over-indulgence in mahogany furnishings, Louisa felt its pull, as though the fine day itself demanded she get up and leave this place at once.

But of course she could not. She had been informed that morning by her aunt that they would be visiting the Pearsons' home for tea, and it had been made very clear to her that she was expected to attend.

'It will be nice for you to see their home. It's a rather fine house on the edge of town. It is a bit of a walk, but I am sure we can manage it together. Unless you have another commitment?' Aunt Clarissa had asked, her eyebrows raised in surprise at her niece's apparent reluctance.

'No, not at all, Aunt,' Louisa had replied, swiftly recovering herself. 'I had just hoped to walk more of the coast this afternoon.'

'I'm sure if the opportunity presents itself Miss Pearson will walk with you,' her aunt had responded. 'Walking with another young lady is preferable, Louisa. You walk too often by yourself. You must have gone out alone not less than four times this past week!'

Four times, indeed, and each time to meet Isaac at the cliffs. Neither of them had hesitated to take advantage of the dry, sunny days, to fill them with conversation and good company. For the past two days, however, she'd been prevented from seeing him. Yesterday, her aunt had asked her to accompany her into town to visit the linen drapers, and today it was what was turning into a lengthy social call.

She tried not to begrudge it, reminding herself that Aunt Clarissa generally made little imposition upon her time. Nonetheless, she found herself repeatedly gazing out of the window, her mind wandering to the cliffs, to the image of Sir Isaac sitting upon a rock, waiting for her. She hoped he would not wait too long. She wished she'd been able to send word, to let him know she would not come today.

She wished, above all, that she could have gone to see him.

He had been so humorous at their last meeting—so light of spirit. Sharing silly anecdotes with her about his childhood and his family. He'd told her some of his memories of her grandfather, the stern but kind village rector, who had enjoyed the respect and affection of his parishioners. His tales had breathed life into her family history, and for the first time since coming here she'd felt the strength of her connection to Hayton. It had dawned on her that this quiet little corner of Cumberland was a part of her story, too.

How they'd laughed at his recollections of his boyhood scrapes! How they had smiled. She had enjoyed seeing that more relaxed, more cheerful side of Isaac— enjoyed, too, the reprieve from the more difficult subjects they'd previously discussed. To her relief, Isaac had asked her nothing more about Richard, and nor had he spoken of Rosalind. It was as though he'd sensed a need to lift the mood between them. To relish the present, rather than dwell on the past.

Not that she regretted sharing something of her past with Isaac. Indeed, telling him about Richard had brought her a sort of solace she hadn't expected. She supposed that was because she'd shared part of her story with someone who understood loss, who'd known grief. She supposed it was because they were friends.

She did not allow herself to contemplate that Isaac was the only friend she had who could cause her stomach to perform somersaults at the merest touch or the briefest glance. There was, after all, no point in considering that.

'Are you quite well, Miss Conrad?' Mrs Pearson asked, interrupting her thoughts.

'Oh, yes, thank you,' she replied, offering her hostess a polite smile.

Mrs Pearson narrowed her eyes slightly, glancing at the window which had held Louisa's attention before returning her focus to her guest. 'Charlotte tells me she has not heard from you since your visit to Hayton. She wondered if you'd been ill.'

Louisa glanced at Charlotte, noting how she sipped her tea and steadfastly avoided her gaze. 'No, not ill,' she began. 'I…'

'You've been quite preoccupied with writing to your friends and family in Berkshire—haven't you, my dear?'

Aunt Clarissa interjected. 'And the weather has been so dreadful of late I don't think any of us will have ventured much outside of our homes.'

'Quite so,' Mrs Pearson agreed, still looking at Louisa. 'I have felt the damp air in every bone in my body. I believe I must ask my physician to strengthen my tincture. Still, the sun has shone a good deal during the past week. Hopefully it will last, and you two young ladies can take the benefit of it together.'

Charlotte gave an enthusiastic nod. 'We could walk to Hayton again, if you like,' she said, addressing Louisa. 'Last time we did not make it as far as Hayton Hall, and it would be a real pity if you did not see it. I suppose if we are fortunate we may even see Sir Isaac and Mr Liddell out riding again.'

Aunt Clarissa looked up, her teacup poised at her lips. 'Again?'

'Oh, don't you know? Sir Isaac and Mr Liddell accompanied them back through the village,' Mrs Pearson explained. 'Charlotte tells me that she talked at length with Mr Liddell, but could not get a word in edgeways with Sir Isaac as Miss Conrad had him entirely under her spell.'

Aunt Clarissa looked squarely as Louisa, her eyebrows elevated in curiosity and surprise. 'Oh?'

'We really only saw them very briefly, as they were visiting Sir Isaac's tenants,' Louisa explained, as evenly as she could manage.

'We talked for as long as it takes to walk very slowly from one end of the village to the other,' Charlotte added with a giggle. 'I found Mr Liddell very agreeable. He was very charming and witty.'

'Younger sons often are,' Mrs Pearson replied, putting her teacup down. 'When the eldest son has the property and the title, wit and charm are the only currency their brothers have to trade.'

'We should go and see Hayton Hall tomorrow,' Charlotte suggested. 'Let's go while the weather remains fine. What do you say, Louisa?'

Louisa sipped her tea, buying herself a moment's thought. She felt the eyes of the room upon her, all three ladies waiting expectantly for her response. What could she say? She didn't have any plans for tomorrow. Only hopes. Only possibilities. She'd had to let those slip by her today, and she would have to do so again. To do anything other than that would appear odd, at best, and rude at worst. She could not risk causing offence.

'Of course,' she replied finally. 'That would be wonderful.'

She hadn't come. Again. As Isaac rode home, furiously whipping his horse, all the possible reasons for her absence whirred around his frenzied mind. Was she unwell? Had he offended her? Had some other commitments detained her for these past two days?

She had not mentioned anything at their last meeting. Indeed, she had smiled and nodded when he'd asked her if it was likely she'd be walking on the cliffs the next day. Nothing had seemed to be amiss when they'd parted. Their conversation had been agreeable. He'd regaled her with some family tales, which she'd seemed to appreciate, before indulging with her in a lengthy discussion about books they'd enjoyed.

She liked to read; he'd learned that. Travel diaries, especially. She yearned to visit the continent, she'd admitted rather bashfully, as though such a sense of adventure was to be berated rather than commended.

He'd held back from telling her that he'd never left England…that his younger brother was superior to him in first-hand knowledge of other countries and cultures. Instead, he'd told her about his love for *Waverley*, and the other novels by the same anonymous author, how he found himself swept to other times and places whenever he lost himself in their pages.

'I know that they are very famous,' she'd said. 'But I confess I have not read any of them.'

He'd thought about all the hours he'd spent in his library, devouring those stories, trying to distract himself from his grief.

'If you like, I can lend you my copy of *Waverley*,' he'd offered, to which she'd assented.

He still had to consider how he would get the book to her, as its three volumes were too large to fit in his pocket. Just as well, he thought. He'd have felt even more of a fool if he'd brought them with him.

Why hadn't she come?

Isaac whipped his poor horse again, riding hard as Hayton Hall came into view. All other possibilities exhausted, he allowed himself now to contemplate the worst. She was ill, or there had been some sort of accident. God, how he wanted to know! How he wanted to help if he could. But how could he? He could hardly turn up at her aunt's house unannounced.

Yet that was all he wanted to do, and it was all he could think of—going to her, summoning his physician to attend her. Anything. Anything that might help.

He shuddered, remembering how he'd sat beside a bed and watched the life of the woman he adored ebb away. He could still see the sickly pallor of her skin, still feel the cold clamminess of her face. Those memories, he knew, would haunt him for ever.

He could not bear to feel such helpless agony again.

He arrived back at his home, all but flinging the reins of his exhausted animal at his groom. He marched inside, the sound of his footsteps thudding on the wooden floor as he made his way down the corridor towards his library. Once inside, he shut the door firmly behind him, leaning his head against it for a moment, trying to gather his thoughts.

He breathed in deeply, perturbed to realise that today he found no comfort in the familiar smell of the old wooden shelves and leather-bound books. His library had for so long been his sanctuary, his place of retreat. Now he realised he no longer wished to be in hiding. He no longer wanted to be alone.

'What the devil is the matter with you, Liddell?' he muttered to himself.

His foolish desire for companionship had really started to get under his skin, conspiring with the worst of his fears and his memories to drive him quite mad. He was a widower almost in his middle years, not some hot-headed youth, and yet here he was, entertaining impulsive ideas about running to the bedside of a woman with whom he'd promenaded a handful of times.

He had to acknowledge that her friendship had come to mean a lot to him even in such a short space of time, that he enjoyed being with her and talking to her. That her company enlivened him in a way he'd believed he would never experience again. He felt as though she understood him. Yet friendship was all there was between them, he reminded himself. It was all there could ever be. Anything else would be a betrayal of Rosalind and a risk to his fragile heart.

He pulled himself up straight. Louisa was his friend, he told himself. Of course he had to know if she was all right. There was nothing more to it than that.

'Isaac?' Samuel's voice sounded muffled through the thick oak door. 'Is something amiss?'

Isaac sighed. The last thing he needed at this moment was an inquisition from his brother.

'I'm well, thank you,' he called back, stepping away from the door and walking over to his desk.

'May I come in?'

'Of course.'

Samuel entered, a deep frown etched on his face as he glanced around him, apparently—and not too subtly—surveying the room. Looking for clues, Isaac thought wryly.

'You came home in an awful hurry. I thought perhaps something might have happened,' his brother said tentatively.

Isaac picked up a handful of papers from his pile of correspondence. 'I was out riding and recalled I had a pressing matter to attend to,' he replied, waving the papers nonchalantly in his hand.

Samuel narrowed his eyes. 'A pressing matter?' he repeated.

'Yes,' Isaac laughed. 'You do not run the estate, Samuel. You do not see the volume of work I have to contend with, even with my steward's assistance.'

'And is that what you have been doing on so many afternoons recently? Attending to pressing estate business?' Samuel asked, clearly unconvinced.

'No, I have been riding, or walking—as you know.'

Isaac tried to maintain an even tone, but he could feel his patience beginning to wane. He did not have time for this.

'For hours on end?'

'I have been enjoying the scenery Cumberland has to offer, and it is a vast county. So, yes, for hours on end, brother.'

'I see,' Samuel answered, in a way which told Isaac that he didn't see at all. 'Well, if there is anything I can do to assist with this pressing matter, you know I am at your service.'

Isaac gave a tight smile, feigning interest in his paperwork once more. 'Thank you, brother. I will bear that in mind.'

Samuel gave a brief nod and took his leave. The moment the door shut behind him Isaac sat down at his desk and got to work. His explanation to Samuel had not entirely been a lie—he did have a pressing matter to attend to. And while his brother had been interrogating him he'd settled upon the only way he could conceive of to address it.

He wrote furiously, committing his words to paper before he could lose his nerve. Before he could think too much about what he said or how he said it. As soon as he had signed his name he folded the letter and enveloped it within another blank sheet, then rang for his butler.

Moments later, the man arrived.

'Yes, sir?'

'Smithson, I need this delivered to Miss Louisa Conrad in Lowhaven,' Isaac instructed, handing over the letter.

Smithson looked at the paper in his hand, upon which Isaac had hurriedly written Louisa's name and address. 'Right now, sir?'

'Yes. Please see to it that this reaches Miss Conrad

as soon as possible. I am anxious to know that the lady is in good health, Smithson,' Isaac added, 'so any information you manage to discover in this regard would be appreciated.'

The butler nodded. 'Very good, sir,' he replied, turning to leave.

'Oh, and Smithson?'

'Yes, sir?'

'Please ensure that this remains confidential. Particularly, that no word of this letter should reach my brother's ears.'

'Of course, sir.'

Isaac sat back in his chair as Smithson left the room, rubbing his face with his hands. The mix of weariness and agitation he felt following the day's exertions was potent, and he knew his judgement was not as sharp as it ought to have been. Writing to her and having her sought out in this manner was impulsive, and if discovered it would provoke comment and speculation.

But damn it all if he cared about that! All he cared about was knowing—knowing what had happened yesterday, knowing what had happened today, and knowing that she was all right. He would endure any amount of trouble for that.

Chapter Fourteen

Louisa knew her aunt had questions for her; she could almost see the words forming upon her lips the moment they left the Pearsons' home in the late afternoon. Their walk home was a quiet one, with little in the way of conversation to divert Louisa from observing the way Clarissa looked at her, with brief but unsubtle glances, as though she was trying to get the measure of her niece and decide upon the best line of enquiry.

Louisa did her best to ignore it, feigning interest in the town's busy streets as they passed along one and then the next. As they approached Juniper Street she noted, as she always did, how the sounds of the port grew louder. She could hear the clatter and shouts of the dockworkers as they loaded and unloaded cargo at its numerous quays.

She recalled how she'd remarked upon its ceaseless din to Isaac, who'd laughed wryly at the observation. It was one of the busiest ports in England, he had told her, with all manner of goods passing through it, from cocoa and sugar being brought in, to coal and lime being shipped out. She'd quite marvelled at the prospect of it, feeling suddenly worlds away from her home in quiet, rural Berkshire. It had been a liberating thought.

Now she found herself considering how frequently her thoughts turned to Isaac and how, in her mind, she called him only that: Isaac.

'Louisa, is there something between yourself and Sir Isaac Liddell?'

Aunt Clarissa put the question to her almost as soon as the door closed behind them. The young maid, Cass, who'd been busying herself with collecting their shawls, gave them both a quick curtsey, sensing the need to take her leave. The awkward moment offered Louisa a brief opportunity to steel herself. She had not expected her aunt to be quite so direct.

'I barely know the gentleman, Aunt,' she replied, as nonchalantly as she could manage.

Clarissa frowned. 'That is no answer, Louisa. Marriages have been made on the barest of acquaintances, and other associations between men and women on far less than that.'

'Aunt!' Louisa protested, feeling the heat rise in her cheeks.

'Do not give me your blushes, my dear. We are both women of the world. Your mother may have tiptoed around these matters with you, but I will not. What Mrs Pearson said today about you and Sir Isaac—she made it sound unseemly. I cannot bear for you to be subjected to such comments again. Not after all that you have endured.'

Louisa sighed, glancing down the corridor, mindful of who might be listening. 'Perhaps we should talk in the parlour, Aunt,' she suggested.

Clarissa nodded in agreement and they moved into

the little room, with Louisa closing the door behind them. Together they sat down, and Louisa took a moment to collect herself. She did not wish to lie to her aunt, but she couldn't bring herself to be entirely truthful, either. She did not wish to contemplate her aunt's response if she knew about her secret clifftop meetings with Isaac. She did not want to consider the consequences of her reckless actions.

Above all, she did not want to consider whether there was, in fact, something more than friendship forming between herself and Sir Isaac Liddell. Something she knew she could not countenance, no matter how their heartfelt conversations and the tender feeling of her hand holding his arm had made her feel.

'There is nothing unseemly or otherwise between myself and Sir Isaac,' she said in the end. 'I will admit that when I have seen him I have enjoyed his company and conversation. He is very agreeable. But that is all. Charlotte is merely being fanciful if she imagines anything else.'

Clarissa gave a tight smile. '"Fanciful" is certainly a word I would apply to young Miss Pearson,' she replied. 'She ought to mind what she says. It's one thing to speak like that to her mother, but what if she recounts her stories in such a way to others?'

'We cannot control how others behave,' Louisa said simply. 'We can only be responsible for our own actions.'

The truth in this last statement made her stomach churn.

Clarissa exhaled deeply, reaching over and patting her niece on the hand. 'I'm sorry, my dear. I feel as though I have interrogated you. I was just so taken aback by Mrs Pearson's remarks.'

Louisa nodded. 'I will admit what she said managed to set me on edge. I fear I have not endeared myself to her of late. She made her displeasure with me plain enough when she alluded to me being remiss in keeping up my friendship with Charlotte.'

'Yes, I noted that. But you are going out with Miss Pearson tomorrow, which I am sure will placate them both.'

Relieved that their conversation had lightened, Louisa rose from the table. 'I think I will freshen up before dinner, Aunt, and perhaps read for a little while. I do find the bedroom you gave me so very peaceful.'

Clarissa gave her niece an appreciative smile. 'It is nice to hear you remark upon it,' she replied. 'Miss Slater used to say the same thing. Or rather, Mrs Knight, as she is now.'

Louisa nodded. 'Do you ever hear from Mrs Knight?' she asked gently.

'She writes to me occasionally, tells me of life in Carlisle. Her Mr Knight keeps her very busy.'

Clarissa was still smiling, but Louisa could not fail to notice the sadness that had crept into her eyes.

'Her marriage seemed to happen very quickly,' her aunt went on. 'But then at our age there is little time left to lose. I suppose she is a reminder that it is never too late.'

'Very true, Aunt.'

Clarissa got to her feet. 'It is true, Louisa, and certainly true in your case. I know you have determined upon spinsterhood, and I understand your reasons why. Nonetheless, I would caution you to think hard about your decision. Remaining alone is far from your only option. The way the likes of Sir Isaac Liddell regard you should be sufficient to remind you of that.'

'Aunt, you surely know that it is my only option,' Louisa replied. 'No gentleman could risk an association with me if he knew all about me. A gentleman like Sir Isaac would imperil his good name overnight. I could not countenance doing such harm to anyone.'

Clarissa sighed. 'As I've said to you before, my dear, you are too hard on yourself. You know that I have never condemned you for what happened, and neither have your parents. There will undoubtedly be gentlemen who would take the same view as I do. Perhaps Sir Isaac might be one of them,' she added meaningfully.

'Perhaps,' Louisa replied, unconvinced. 'Alas, it is a moot point, since there is nothing between Sir Isaac and me,' she reiterated quickly, trying to ignore how hard her heart was beating.

Clarissa gave her knowing look. 'Perhaps not on your part, but you cannot speak for him. He was obviously captivated by you at the ball, and I don't doubt that in essence what Charlotte told her mother about your encounter with him in Hayton was true. I can well imagine that he did not leave your side.'

'We enjoyed only a brief and very polite conversation,' Louisa countered, feeling her cheeks begin to burn as thoughts of their long walks and intense conversations returned to her once again.

'Oh, my dear! It is not so much what is said, but what is left unsaid, believe me.'

'You sound as though you speak from experience, Aunt.'

'I had a life before spinsterhood.' Clarissa's lined face

crumpled and she sat back down upon her chair. 'I was engaged once, you know. Goodness, we were young… and so much in love. His name was Frederick.'

Louisa took her seat again beside her aunt. 'What happened?'

'Frederick was a curate, but he had not yet managed to secure a living. Of course he needed an income, so that we could marry and begin our lives together. After our betrothal he joined the army as a chaplain and boarded a ship bound for the Caribbean. I heard nothing from him for several months. I remember being so worried… Then one day a letter came—not from him, but from his captain. In it, he told me that there had been some sort of epidemic and poor Frederick had perished, not many weeks after they had arrived.'

Louisa felt her eyes prick with tears and she tried furiously to blink them away. She felt every detail of her aunt's story keenly. Indeed, its resonance with her own could hardly be more acute.

'Oh, Aunt Clarissa…' was all she managed to say.

Clarissa gave her a watery smile. 'It was a long time ago. You see, my dear, we are really quite similar. Like you, I loved and lost, and I chose never to marry after that. It was a choice I was able to make as Frederick had left me a small inheritance in his will. Nothing extravagant, but it has helped to give me my independence.'

'And you have been happy all these years?' It was a searching question, but Louisa couldn't help but ask it.

'I have done well enough by myself,' her aunt replied. 'Although it is far from easy, being a woman in my position. You see for yourself how modestly I live, and keeping myself even in this manner has become more difficult since Mrs Knight's departure and the loss of her... Well, her contribution to the household. I find myself a little more reliant on the help of my family than I'm accustomed to—a fact which makes me uneasy.'

Louisa frowned. 'Your family? Do you mean my mother and father?'

Clarissa nodded, then quickly patted her niece reassuringly on the hand. 'But please do not consider that has anything to do with why you are here this summer. You know I would always gladly have you here with me, whatever the circumstances.'

Louisa gave her a meek smile. 'Do you ever wish you had married?' she asked quietly.

Clarissa sighed. 'In truth, I never met anyone after Frederick who could hold a candle to him, so the decision to remain unmarried was relatively easy in that regard. I can't say what I would have done had I found myself falling in love again,' she added, looking pointedly at her niece.

'I do not think I could bear to fall in love again. Not since losing...' Louisa bit her lip, unable to finish her sentence. Unable to say Richard's name. Unable, perhaps, to face contemplating just how close to falling in love again she might be.

'But one day you might, my dear, and if you do please heed my advice—follow your heart. Life is too short to hold yourself to solemn oaths made in the throes of grief.'

Louisa drew a swift breath, poised to argue. Ready to repeat that in her case it was about more than honouring her fiancé's memory. That it would be futile to fall in love again, for surely she could not marry. No gentleman would want her for a wife if he knew the truth.

Then she looked at her aunt's face, racked with the

pain of baring her soul, and she realised that she had not the heart to say any of it.

'Thank you, Aunt,' she answered instead, with a small and unconvincing smile.

All evening Aunt Clarissa's words preyed on Louisa's mind. After dinner she went straight up to her room, where she tried and failed to concentrate on the book perched on her lap. She'd known nothing of her aunt's story, nothing of the loss she'd experienced—a loss which bore such similarity to her own. In grief they were kindred spirits, a fact which made her aunt's words of caution about choosing to remain alone all the more discomfiting.

Louisa knew that for her marriage remained absolutely out of the question. Yet, despite this, the prospect of spinsterhood seemed more daunting than ever.

'A penny for them,' Nan said that night, apparently tiring of her mistress's prolonged silence as she unpinned her long blonde hair in readiness for bed.

'I learned something about my aunt today,' Louisa replied, giving in to the overwhelming need to confide in someone. Nan, she knew, could always be trusted with her secrets.

'Oh?'

'It turns out we have a lot in common. Like me, she lost the man she was meant to marry. He was an army chaplain, and he died in the Caribbean.'

'Your poor aunt,' Nan remarked. 'I wonder why your mother never told you.'

'I suspect she didn't regard it as her story to tell.'

Nan nodded at that. 'That's true, miss. She is very discreet. I suppose that explains why your aunt has never married…why she stayed up here with your grandparents rather than go off to London like your mother did.'

'Indeed.'

Louisa gazed absently into the mirror in front of her, considering her aunt's insistence that her choice had been straightforward because she had never met anyone else. It occurred to Louisa now that her aunt's decision to remain in rural Cumberland, to embrace quiet village life, had all but ensured that she could not fall in love again. This part of the world hardly teemed with eligible men the way London society did during the season.

Although, Louisa reminded herself, they weren't entirely absent.

She shook her head slightly, trying to brush off all thoughts of a certain gentleman standing before her on the clifftops, his thick black hair tousled by the wind and his deep blue eyes staring intently into hers. She spent too much time thinking about him, and it did her no good. She could not allow herself to form an attachment, to indulge in thoughts about anything more than a summer-long acquaintance. She could not allow her heart to rule over her head. She had done so once, long ago, and she knew what it had cost her. She would bear the scars of her choices for the rest of her days.

'Oh, miss, I almost forgot,' Nan said, reaching into the pocket of her apron. 'A note arrived for you today.'

Louisa turned round. 'A note?'

'Yes.' Nan passed a small folded paper to her. 'It was the strangest thing. The man who delivered it would not say on whose behalf he was calling. He would only say that I was to ensure this note reached you, and he enquired after your health.'

Louisa looked down, running her finger over the

letters of her name. She did not recognise the pristine handwriting, but she knew instinctively who it must be from. She felt her heart begin to beat a little faster, and she hoped that in the candlelight Nan could not see the colour creeping into her cheeks.

'And what did you say?' she asked.

'I told him you were well, but that I would not say more without knowing who was asking.'

Louisa nodded, turning back and placing the note upon her dressing table. 'All right. Thank you, Nan.'

In the mirror she could see her maid frown. 'Aren't you going to read it, miss?'

'I will…in a little while.'

She could see immediately that Nan was not satisfied. She watched as her maid parted her lips, ready to speak, before she pressed them together once again. Clearly, out of respect for her mistress, she had decided that she ought to hold her tongue.

She finished brushing and arranging Louisa's hair quickly and in silence, perhaps not quite trusting herself not to say anything more on the subject.

Louisa thanked her quietly, then picked up the note, clutching it in her palm as she climbed into bed. Once Nan had left, she unfolded it, her heart hammering hard in her chest as she found herself anticipating its possible content.

This was ridiculous, she told herself. It was just a note. And yet as she held the paper in her hands and absorbed the words she felt a strange warmth spread from her stomach all the way down to her toes.

My dearest Louisa,
Please forgive me for writing to you in this way,

but I find I am unable to prevent myself from being an utter fool.

I am sure there was a very good reason why I did not see you today, or yesterday, and of course you owe me no explanation for it. Indeed, you owe me nothing, since you have been so generous with your time already.

However, I cannot seem to rid myself of the feeling that something is amiss, that you are unwell or some other dreadful fate has befallen you.

I hope whoever accepted this note at your aunt's home will have been able to give my butler the assurance of your continued good health, which will help to ease my mind.

But, dearest Louisa, I must tell you that my mind is never so much at ease as it is when I am in your company. I hope we will be able to meet again soon.

Yours,

Isaac

Louisa read the note three or four times before sitting back and holding it against her chest. She closed her eyes for a moment and took a few deep breaths, trying to calm her racing thoughts.

Isaac's concern for her was as clear as it was endearing, although she hated to think that her absence had caused him such distress. But the manner in which he wrote told her more than that. His words hinted at a growing fondness for her, a tenderness which she knew she increasingly felt, too.

She had missed his company today. She knew she would have preferred an afternoon spent in the fresh air talking to Isaac over the confines of a stuffy parlour and polite conversation. Nonetheless, the strength of the feelings his note had provoked surprised her. Alarmed her, even. It was bad enough that she spent far more time thinking about him than she should. That she found her thoughts lingering on the sight of his deep blue eyes or the low sound of his laughter. That meeting him on the clifftops had been the best part of an otherwise pleasant but unremarkable week.

To be so overcome by a simple note was too much. It had been a long time since the words of a gentleman had affected her in such a way. It would not do at all. Not when she still bore the scars of the past. Not when she still bore the unmistakable taint of scandal. Not when there could never be any hope of anything more than friendship between them, no matter what her unruly heart might yearn for.

Louisa climbed out of bed and sat down at the writing desk, determined to respond. Indeed, time was of the essence. She was due to visit Hayton again the following day, with Charlotte, during which she felt certain she could contrive a way to call at Hayton Hall and deliver her reply herself.

She would assure him that all was well, but she could not allow him to form an attachment to her. It was quite obvious that their meetings had already sown the seeds of affection between them. She could not, in all good conscience, allow them to grow.

It would only end in heartbreak for them both.

Chapter Fifteen

After sending Smithson out with his instructions to deliver the note yesterday, Isaac had felt himself begin to sink. For the rest of that day he'd sat in his library, staring blankly at the volumes of books on his shelves, a black mood threatening to envelop him. He'd attempted to remedy it with a large brandy, but had managed no more than a sip before setting the glass aside, realising that he did not really want it.

Gone were the days when he'd wished to drown his feelings in the bottom of the decanter. Gone were the days of surrendering himself so completely to his melancholy. And so, with a resigned sigh and a few 'damnations' muttered under his breath, he'd rung for some tea and forced himself to confront what ailed him.

Louisa. Or, more precisely, Louisa's absence.

His anxiety had gnawed at him as he'd thought about the way he'd reached out to her, his mind reeling with the same handful of questions. Had Smithson been able to find her? Was she well? Had she read his note? And if she had, how had it been received?

This latter question had troubled him greatly. He

knew his words had been unguarded, and that he'd written in earnest about how her friendship had made him feel, what the time he'd spent in her company had meant to him. On reflection, his words had been too plain, perhaps, for either of them to countenance.

God, the wait for news had been unbearable.

Finally, just before dinner, Smithson had returned. By then Samuel had joined Isaac in the library, to peruse the newspapers and enjoy a small glass of port. Isaac had noted how his brother lowered the paper, peering curiously over it as Smithson approached his master. Isaac had got up from his chair then, steering the man towards his desk and away, he hoped, from Samuel's keen ears.

His butler, who was as discreet as he was loyal, had delivered his message in hushed, cryptic tones, but to Isaac his meaning was clear enough.

'I did as you asked, sir, and can confirm that all is well.'

It had taken a good deal of effort for Isaac to suppress his smile. 'Thank you, Smithson,' he'd replied, in the most businesslike voice he could muster. 'That will be all.'

'What was all that about?' Samuel had asked, almost as soon as the butler had left the room.

'Oh, just a household matter,' Isaac had lied. 'Nothing to concern yourself with.'

Knowing that she was in good health had buoyed Isaac's spirits, although he still worried about her reaction to the words his note had contained. He'd expressed himself hastily, and although not a word of it was untrue he feared she might be discouraged by his actions. He'd asked Louisa for her friendship, and yet he feared he was starting to behave as if he wanted far more than that.

Perhaps, he considered, he did want more than that. He knew he shouldn't, that there were scores of reasons why allowing himself to love again was a bad idea— not least the memory of his dead wife and the risk to his barely mended heart. Not least the risk of his love being rejected…a risk which was very real, given that he was neither young nor particularly agreeable.

Even Samuel, who had seemed to perceive the depth of Isaac's interest in Louisa before he did, had urged him to be cautious. And yet in sending that note he had been anything but cautious.

Damn, what had got into him?

Today that heavy feeling had returned, weighing him down in his chair as he sat in the library on a warm, sunny summer's day. He fidgeted uncomfortably, un-buttoning his collar in a vain attempt to combat the growing heat in the usually cool room, before shaking his head disapprovingly at himself.

His appearance today left much to be desired. After several hours of restless contemplation his shirt was badly crumpled, and his cravat hung loosely about his neck. He'd spent much of the morning staring wist-fully out of the window, his mind returning repeatedly to the windswept cliffs. He'd briefly considered riding out there, just in case, but ultimately decided against it. She hadn't come to meet him yesterday for reasons which remained unknown to him, and in his note he had not asked to meet her there today.

He'd decided it was best to be patient…to await her reply. God, how he prayed that she would reply.

A knock at the door interrupted his spiralling thoughts.

'Come in,' he replied, rather impatiently. It was probably Samuel, he reasoned, coming to check on him, to ask why he wasn't going out riding, or to insist that Isaac accompany him to some place or other. Truly, there was never any end to Samuel's machinations.

To his surprise, however, it was Smithson. The man looked flushed and a little out of breath, as though he'd run down to the library in a great hurry.

'Forgive me for disturbing you, sir,' the butler panted. 'But I thought you'd want to know that there was a lady at the door just now. She was here to deliver a note.'

Louisa turned away from the front door of Hayton Hall and hurried back down its wide drive. At the gate stood Charlotte, waiting for her, and even from this distance she could see that she was put out: arms folded, lips pouting.

Louisa let out a sigh. Managing Charlotte had been trickier than she'd expected, and she'd almost tied herself in knots trying to explain to her companion why she needed to call here and deliver a note.

'It's a silly thing, really,' she'd said, as casually as she could manage. 'When we met in Hayton, Sir Isaac and I talked a little of the books we like to read. I told him of my love for travel literature and he said he knew of a book I must read, but he could not remember the title. He wrote to me later, to give me the details. Since we are here today, I thought I might drop off a little note to thank him for his kindness.'

Charlotte's eyes had widened. 'You're exchanging letters with Sir Isaac?'

'No.' Louisa had been emphatic. 'It is one note. To thank him. It is only polite.'

'If my mother found out I was writing to a gentleman she'd say I was being improper, even if it was only to converse about books,' Charlotte had retorted.

'Well, your mother is not my mother, and she doesn't need to know anything of this,' Louisa had replied, a little more sharply than she'd intended. 'If you wouldn't mind waiting for me at the gate? I will only be a moment.'

Charlotte had acquiesced, although Louisa wasn't sure she was convinced by her explanation. She'd felt her heart thudding rapidly in her chest as she'd made her way towards the house, and briefly she'd considered Charlotte's insinuation about the propriety of her behaviour. If Charlotte disapproved of her writing to a gentleman, Louisa did not wish to imagine what she would say if she knew she'd been meeting him, alone and in secret.

She'd pushed the thought from her mind, turning her attention instead to the large, grand house before her. It was very old, certainly—much older than she'd expected. It had many lattice windows, and a roofscape rising at several points, giving it a castle-like quality. She'd wondered about its history, and for a moment had yearned to ask Isaac to tell her about it. Then she'd remembered the note in her hand and what she must do.

It was the right course of action. For both their sakes.

At the front entrance she'd knocked hurriedly, before she could change her mind. When the door had been swiftly answered by a grey-haired butler with a kindly face, she'd pressed her note into his hands and mumbled something barely coherent about being grateful if he would ensure that it reached Sir Isaac.

The man had nodded, his mouth agape, as though caught completely by surprise. He'd recovered himself quickly, and had started to say something about fetching his master, but Louisa had all but fled from the door then. It was one thing to deliver this note—quite another to watch Isaac's face as he read it in front of her.

She was certain she could not bear it.

'All that trouble over a book,' Charlotte huffed now, as Louisa finally reached her at the gate. 'You should have let me accompany you. I might have been able to see Mr Liddell if he's at home.'

'A good book is worth any amount of trouble,' Louisa replied, deciding that humour was the best remedy for her friend's growing bad mood. 'And I did not ask if either Sir Isaac or his brother are at home, as I would not wish to disturb them.'

Charlotte sighed as they linked arms and began to walk. 'I do hope I see Mr Liddell again soon. Perhaps there will be another ball at the Assembly Rooms, and...'

'Miss Conrad! Miss Pearson!'

Both ladies spun round to see Samuel Liddell, running down the path towards them. Louisa watched as Charlotte's pout quickly dissolved into the broadest smile.

'It seems you're going to get your wish, Charlotte,' she observed, feeling her heart sink at the prospect of her swift retreat being thwarted.

'I saw you both from the window,' Mr Liddell puffed when he finally caught up with them. 'Did you call at the house? It looked as though you were coming back down the path.'

'Louisa called,' Charlotte answered, before Louisa could speak. 'She had a note for Sir Isaac—something to do with a book.'

Mr Liddell frowned. 'A book?'

Louisa nodded. 'Yes, a travel book,' she explained, trying her best to sound nonchalant. 'I shall not bore you both with the details.'

Her breath caught in her throat as behind Mr Liddell she saw Isaac emerge from the front door of the house. He marched briskly down the path, his eyes intent upon her even from this distance. As he drew closer she noticed he looked more dishevelled than the last time they'd met. His dark hair was untamed, and he wore neither a coat nor a waistcoat over his white shirt, which looked loose and crumpled next to the smooth lines of his pantaloons and Hessian boots.

She swallowed hard, wondering if he'd already read her note. Surely he was not going to speak to her about it now, in front of his brother and her friend, was he?

'Ah! Here he comes now, Miss Conrad,' Mr Liddell said, after briefly turning to follow her gaze. 'I'm sure he will be at your service regarding this book of yours.'

Louisa inclined her head, hoping she looked more serene than she felt. By the time Isaac reached them her heart was pounding so hard that she believed it would burst out of her chest. She stared up at him, locking eyes with that cool azure gaze of his. He looked strained, she realised. His face was pale and drawn, as though something was weighing heavily upon him.

Her stomach lurched as she considered that she might be the cause of his unrest.

'Miss Conrad brought a note for you, Isaac, concerning a book,' his brother informed him.

Isaac nodded in acknowledgement, although his eyes never once shifted from Louisa. 'Yes, I have received it, thank you.' He gave her a tight smile. 'Perhaps we might all step into my library for a few moments? I believe the book you seek is in there.'

Louisa's eyes widened at the suggestion. 'I'm not sure, sir,' she began, feeling increasingly flustered. 'Miss Pearson and I must—'

'Louisa?' Charlotte interrupted her, frowning. 'I thought Sir Isaac had already given you the details of the book and you'd merely written to express your gratitude?'

'She did,' Isaac replied quickly, not missing a beat. 'But there is another book we discussed too, if I recall. The one by the anonymous author. I had promised to lend it to her.'

'Splendid,' said Mr Liddell, clasping his hands together. 'Might I suggest that since you've come all this way we give you both a tour of Hayton Hall? It would be our pleasure.'

Louisa's heart descended into the pit of her stomach. 'No, really…' she tried again.

'That would be wonderful!' Charlotte spoke over her, all but squealing with delight and taking hold of Mr Liddell's arm as soon as he offered it. 'Come, Louisa, let's make haste.'

Louisa continued to stand there, dumbstruck, a wave of horror washing over her as the futility of any further objection dawned upon her. She'd come here today to draw a firm line under an acquaintance which was in danger of becoming far more than it could or should be. Going into Isaac's home, seeing where he worked and ate and read all those wonderful books they'd discussed, was not at all what she had intended.

Beside her, she felt Isaac draw nearer. He did not offer his arm, but simply walked by her side as they sauntered towards the house. No words passed between them. Nothing about her absence at the cliffs, or his note, or her reply. Just silence. Difficult silence.

Ahead of them she heard Charlotte, already deep in conversation with Mr Liddell. She wished then that she could feel so light-hearted, that this was simply an enjoyable tour of a gentleman's ancestral home. That her friendship with Sir Isaac Liddell had not grown so fraught and so complicated.

But as she drew nearer to his fine country house once more, she realised that nothing between herself and the master of Hayton Hall would ever be straightforward. No amount of wishful thinking could change that.

Chapter Sixteen

As they walked through the front door of Hayton Hall and towards his library Isaac wasn't sure what would drive him to madness first: his head or his heart.

His mind was still reeling at her unexpected presence here, and at the words in that damnable note she'd delivered—the one he'd read frantically before screwing it up and flinging it across the room, only narrowly missing poor Smithson's head.

His thoughts raced at the impulsive way he'd invited her into the library. He had meant to lend *Waverley* to her, that was true, but he could not deny that in that moment outside it had been a ruse to secure a few more moments of her company and an opportunity to speak to her. But how on earth was he going to speak in earnest with his brother and Miss Pearson present?

His heart, meanwhile, lurched from joy to despair, her company both lifting his mood and leaving him anxious that he might, in fact, never see her again. Certainly that was what her note suggested, wasn't it? That there would be no more clifftop walks, no more heartfelt conversations. That she would not, it seemed, permit a friendship between them any more.

In the library she seemed nervous, cutting herself adrift from him and pacing a little as she made a point of admiring the many shelves filled from floor to ceiling with his family's collection. He left his brother to attend to Miss Pearson, who lingered by the door with a bored expression on her face, and fetched the first volume of *Waverley* before taking it over to Louisa.

Her eyes seemed to widen as he approached, and her clear discomfort made his heart lurch. Had he really offended her so terribly by writing to her in the way he had? Was his admission that her company soothed him genuinely so distasteful to her?

'This is *Waverley*,' he said, loud enough for Samuel and Miss Pearson to hear. 'Well, the first volume, at least.'

Isaac held the book out to her, and Louisa's fingers brushed against his as she accepted it. Her unexpected touch jolted him, and his mind immediately returned to the clifftops…to the day she told him that she'd loved and lost, just as he had. To how he'd placed his hand over hers. To how deeply they'd seemed to understand one another. That day they'd drawn closer—a fact which he'd been grappling with ever since. Perhaps she had, too. Perhaps that was why his note had caused her to end their friendship so abruptly.

'Thank you,' she replied, offering him a tight smile but avoiding his gaze as she admired the fine leather cover.

'There are two more volumes,' he explained, 'if you will permit me to fetch them. They are not in their usual place, but I am sure they are here somewhere.'

A loud sigh punctuated their strained conversation. 'Forgive me, Sir Isaac, but I am feeling suddenly rather hot and thirsty after our walk,' Miss Pearson interjected, fanning her face with her hand. 'Could I trouble you for some tea?'

'It is rather too warm here in the library,' Samuel replied, before Isaac could utter a word. 'The small parlour is far more agreeable at this time of the day. Perhaps we might all retire there?'

Miss Pearson's face brightened at the suggestion. 'Oh, yes, let's! But do not trouble Sir Isaac and Louisa, Mr Liddell, if they are busy with their books. They can join us when they have finished fetching the rest of *Walpole*, or whatever it is.'

'*Waverley*,' Isaac muttered, raising his eyebrows at his brother.

Samuel, however, seemed helpless in the face of the young lady's machinations. 'Well…of course, Miss Pearson,' he began, looking uncharacteristically flustered. 'If you will be comfortable, then I'm sure we could…'

'Excellent!' Miss Pearson declared, seeming suddenly less fatigued as she took hold of Samuel's arm. 'I'm sure Sir Isaac and Louisa will do very well without us,' she added, casting the words carelessly over her shoulder as she all but dragged Samuel along with her and breezed out of the room.

The door slammed shut behind them and the library grew suddenly very silent. Isaac looked over at Louisa, offering her a smile and hoping it would convey his apology. He'd already noted her discomfort, and knew that being left alone with him would surely only make it worse.

'I will try to find the other two volumes as quickly as I can. Then we can join the others,' he said, returning his attention to his shelves.

'Thank you,' she said again, before adding, 'This is a lovely library, sir, and a lovely house. When was Hayton Hall built?'

'At the beginning of the seventeenth century, by the first baronet,' he replied, turning back to face her. 'My family has lived here ever since.'

'My goodness,' she replied, looking around once more. 'There is so much history here.'

Her expression of sheer wonder brought a smile to his face. 'I can show you the oldest book in the library, if you like.'

She nodded eagerly and, feeling that the ice between them had finally been breached, Isaac rolled up his sleeves and fetched the ladder, climbing up to retrieve the infamous volume without a moment's hesitation.

All the while he felt her hovering at the bottom of the ladder, her eyes upon him, following his swift movements up, then back down again. The observation intrigued him, and when his feet touched the ground once more he saw that she was blushing. *Blushing!* Whatever had he done to make her blush?

'The first book of *Don Quixote*,' he said, handing it to her. 'An early translation. It's about as old as the house.'

Louisa gasped, clutching it tenderly in her hands. 'I have never read it, have you?'

He shook his head. 'I must admit I have not. A book this old feels almost too precious to be read. You might like the story, though. I believe it's about an idealistic traveller,' he added, with a grin.

What on earth was wrong with him? She'd as much as told him that their friendship was over, and yet here he was, trying to tease her.

She smiled back, although he noticed that it didn't

reach her eyes. 'As much as I'd love to travel, I cannot admit to being idealistic,' she replied.

No, she wasn't—he knew that. Her life, like his, had brought her too much heartache for her to be quixotic.

Around them the library remained quiet. By now his brother and Miss Pearson would be enjoying their tea in the parlour on the other side of the house. For propriety's sake they had only a few more moments together. If he was going to speak honestly to her, then it was now or never.

'Have I offended you, Louisa?' he asked quietly, barely able to bring himself to do so.

She stepped back, just a little. 'No.'

'Your note said that we should not meet any more.'

'It is for the best,' she replied. 'We take a risk each time we meet alone.'

'Then we don't have to meet alone,' he answered. 'We can meet here, with my brother and Miss Pearson and even your aunt in attendance, if you wish. Invite the whole of Hayton, for all I care, if it means still spending time with you.'

She bit her lip, casting her eyes down, and he sensed that he was not winning the argument. 'But your note, Sir Isaac, the way you expressed yourself…'

'I was concerned when you didn't come to meet me. I had to know you were all right. And I felt that I must tell you what our time together has meant to me,' he said flatly. 'Please, Louisa, call me Isaac.'

Louisa looked back at him then. 'I had to go to the linen drapers with my aunt, and then to the Pearsons' house for tea,' she explained. 'That was why I didn't come. I am sorry to have worried you. I would not want you to fret on my account.'

Isaac smiled at her. 'I must admit I could not seem to help it,' he replied.

'Do you not think that is exactly why we must no longer meet?' she asked him.

'Why?' he challenged her. 'We are friends, are we not? Would you really wish for me not to care about you?' He sighed heavily, rubbing his forehead as the meaning of her objection suddenly dawned on him. 'You do not care for me,' he stated. 'I understand. I am too old for you, perhaps? Or too sombre. Indeed, I am well aware of my own shortcomings.'

'No.' He felt her hand upon his arm. 'You are neither of those things, Isaac. It is not that.'

His heart lifted at finally hearing her drop the damnable 'sir' from her address. Their eyes met, and before he could think about what he was doing he leaned towards her, his lips tentatively meeting hers.

He knew he shouldn't kiss her...that he ought to think of Rosalind...that he ought to remember the grief that love and loss had inflicted upon him. But, to his shame, those thoughts had flown from his mind, replaced by other, less familiar and more confusing ideas about the warm proximity of this woman, the orange sweetness of her lips.

His senses heightened as she drew closer, placing a gentle hand on his upper arm as she kissed him back. It was all the encouragement his foolish, impulsive heart needed. He wrapped an arm around her, pulling her close, then unfastened the ribbon of her bonnet and pushed it away. He ran his fingers through the loose curls of her hair, his lips trailing kisses from her mouth to her soft cheeks, her delicate jaw, and down her neck.

The taste of oranges combined with the scent of lavender as his senses were utterly overwhelmed by her. When their lips met again her tongue greeted his, and his mind began to entertain thoughts which he knew would be his undoing. *Their* undoing.

She pressed a hand against his chest, pushing him away. 'No, Isaac, we must stop.'

She was as breathless as he was—breathless and beautiful, her lips and cheeks made pink by his attentions. She stepped back from him, reaching down and picking up the bonnet which moments ago had been discarded on the floor.

He held up his hands, half defensive, half frustrated. 'I'm sorry,' he said. 'I should not have kissed you.'

He watched as she replaced her bonnet, noticed how her fingers shook as she tied the ribbon into an untidy bow. 'No, you should not,' she replied, her voice wavering. 'You must know I cannot—not after Richard…'

'Of course,' he replied grimly, his heart still racing, his mind still reeling from the taste of her lips, the feeling of her pressed against him.

What the hell had he been thinking? Had he gone completely out of his wits?

'Please, forgive me. I shall forget it ever happened, Louisa. You have my word.'

She nodded briskly. 'We should join your brother and Charlotte for tea. They will wonder what has become of us.'

'You go ahead,' he replied, giving her a thin smile. 'I will join you in a moment.'

He watched as she hurried from the room, then slumped down in his favourite armchair with a groan. He needed a few minutes to collect himself—and to chastise himself.

What a fool he was. There would be no more cliff-top walks, no more pleasant conversations now. Kissing her had sealed the fate of their friendship, and it was all his fault.

Worse still, he realised, was that for all he'd promised to forget their kiss, he believed that was the very last thing he was capable of doing.

'You're your own worst enemy, Liddell,' he muttered to himself.

It took Louisa a few minutes to locate Charlotte, following the trail of her giggles as they echoed around the ground floor of the house. In the end she found her in a cosy parlour, sitting far too close to Mr Liddell on a green velvet sofa and enjoying a cup of tea. Neither of them got to their feet when she walked in; they were far too deep in some whispered flirtation.

Even in her turmoil, it occurred to Louisa that they were as brazen as each other. She didn't wish to consider what Charlotte's mother would think of this scene, if she was here to witness it.

'Miss Conrad, do join us for some tea,' Mr Liddell said in the end, gesturing towards one of the seats opposite. 'Is my brother not with you?'

Louisa shook her head as she sat down. 'No... No— he has some business to attend to,' she lied. 'He will be here momentarily.'

Mr Liddell clicked his tongue disapprovingly as he poured her a cup of tea and handed it to her. 'That sounds like my brother—all business and no pleasure.'

That last word made Louisa's heart flutter, and she felt a sudden heat grow in her cheeks. 'I'm sure his tenants appreciate his endeavours,' she replied flatly.

'Are you all right, Louisa?' Charlotte asked. 'You look a little flushed.'

Louisa nodded, then sipped her tea, and was grateful when Charlotte and Mr Liddell's attentions returned to each other. She sat rigid in her seat, listening to the pair of them talk about nothing much, while her mind ran skittishly over everything that had occurred in the library.

Isaac had kissed her, and she had allowed it—more than allowed it, in fact, since she had kissed him in return. Her heart thrummed in her chest as she relived the moment: the soft touch of his lips against hers, the rough hint of stubble brushing her neck, the muscular solidity of his arm beneath her hand. She'd wanted to touch those arms ever since he'd rolled up his sleeves and set about fetching *Don Quixote*. A glimpse of his bare skin, sun-kissed and covered by a layer of fine dark hair, was all it had taken to send her mind to places it ought not to go.

She supposed it was little wonder that she'd surrendered herself so completely to his kiss, when even the mere sight of his flesh seemed to place her on the cusp of ruination.

All the more reason that they must no longer see each other.

At least she'd had the presence of mind to end their embrace. To be firm with him. To tell him that it should not have happened, and to remind him of her grief, of the man she'd loved and lost. That had been as much as she'd been able to say.

There was so much more she could never say to him—so much more he could not know. About her, about her past, about why she was not the sort of woman he should attach himself to. If she allowed a romance to blossom between them, she knew she would not be able to build it on lies. Sooner or later she would have to tell him everything, and she would have to endure the look in his eyes and the inevitable extinguishing of his affection for her. That would be too painful—for him and for her.

He'd already lost his wife and child; he had suffered enough. He needed someone who was worthy of him... someone who did not bear her scars.

It was kinder this way. Kinder to let him go.

And yet she'd made her attraction to him evident, hadn't she? She'd complicated matters with her blushes, and her kisses, and her protest that he was not too old, or too sombre, or indeed in any way disagreeable to her. She hadn't been able to feign dislike or uninterest; she could not have been so cruel. She had pushed him away—but not before indulging herself first. She'd allowed momentary passion to rule her head, to lead to her to go against her better judgement. It seemed she had learned no lessons from the past, after all...

'Are you sure you're all right, Louisa?' Charlotte asked, interrupting her thoughts. 'You look suddenly very pale.'

'I'm fine,' she replied, as smoothly as she could manage. 'However, I do think we ought to begin our walk back to Lowhaven. The afternoon grows late.'

She finished her tea and got to her feet, making her intention to leave clear.

Charlotte rose too, somewhat reluctantly, followed by Mr Liddell, who beamed at them both. Charlotte let out a little laugh at his light-hearted attentions and Louisa bristled, not sure which of them was irritating her more.

'I will have the carriage brought round and my driver will take you back to Lowhaven,' Mr Liddell said. 'Miss Conrad is right—we have detained you here for too long. It is the least we can do.'

'Oh, thank you, Mr Liddell, that is so very kind and thoughtful,' Charlotte gushed.

Louisa watched as her companion took hold of the gentleman's arm, trailing behind them both as they walked out of the warm parlour and back into the cool air of the wide, wood-panelled hall.

'It is a pity we did not have time to show you around Hayton Hall,' Mr Liddell said, glancing at her over his shoulder.

'Another time, I'm sure,' Louisa answered.

'Oh, yes, another time,' Charlotte interjected. 'Perhaps next time Sir Isaac and Louisa won't find themselves detained for quite so long in the library,' she added with a giggle.

Louisa bit her tongue, resolving to say nothing. The enjoyment Charlotte clearly derived from making scandalous remarks was beginning to grate on her nerves. Especially when, in this instance, her insinuations were not so far from the truth.

Finally they reached the front door, and inwardly Louisa breathed a sigh of relief. She had never been so glad to leave a place as she was at that moment.

'Miss Conrad!'

Isaac's deep voice echoed around the hall. Slowly Louisa turned around, felt panic creeping in at the prospect of facing him after all that had happened between them. What they both now had to forget.

Isaac strode up to her, clutching something against his chest. Her mind was so fraught that it took several moments before she realised it was a set of books. He held them up, giving her a broad smile, but she could not fail to see that it did not reach his eyes.

'Waverley,' he said, placing three leather-bound volumes in her hands. 'You almost forgot to take it with you. I hope you enjoy it.'

Louisa smiled back at him, conscious of their audience and the need to express a delight she didn't feel. 'Thank you, Sir Isaac,' she replied. 'I am sure that I will.'

Chapter Seventeen

'Come, my dear, we are going to be late.'

Louisa could hear Aunt Clarissa pacing at the bottom of the stairs as Nan hurried to finish pinning the last curls of her hair into place. She sighed wearily, displeased with the turn her day had taken.

She had been resting quietly in her room, engrossed in the third volume of *Waverley*, when her aunt had knocked on the door and informed her that Mrs Pearson had sent a note requesting the pleasure of their company for tea that afternoon. Louisa, unaccustomed to such last-minute demands on her time, had mildly protested about attending, but her aunt, as usual, had been resolute.

Louisa had known that there was little point in arguing, and Nan had been duly summoned to help her dress for the occasion. Now Louisa emerged from her room in a blue day dress, her hair pulled back into a gentle chignon with a handful of curls framing her face. She just about had time to grab her spencer before Aunt Clarissa hurried her out of the house and across town to the Pearsons' home.

They arrived a few moments after the appointed hour and were shown, somewhat breathlessly, into the parlour.

As Louisa walked through the door she felt suddenly as though she had been thrown into a lion's den. There, sitting on the other side of the small, oval table from Mrs Pearson and Charlotte, were Mr Liddell and Sir Isaac. She felt her breath catch in her throat as Sir Isaac put down his teacup and turned to look at her. Like his brother, he rose to his feet to greet them both, but his face was unsmiling and unreadable.

Beside her, Aunt Clarissa took a step back. 'Forgive me, Mrs Pearson, you have other company. I must have misread the day or perhaps the time on your invitation.'

'Not at all, my dear Miss Howarth,' Mrs Pearson replied with a smile. 'Why...did I not mention in my note that Sir Isaac and Mr Liddell would be joining us? How silly and forgetful of me. Please, do sit down.'

Both ladies did as they were bade, with Clarissa taking the seat nearest to Mrs Pearson, leaving Louisa to sit on the only other available chair, beside Isaac. The prospect of such close proximity to him made her heart beat faster, and she found herself thinking about being with him in the library all over again.

He looked well today, dressed for the occasion in a deep blue tailcoat with contrasting fawn waistcoat and pantaloons, his dark hair tamed into order and his face freshly shaven. Louisa felt his eyes upon her as she eased herself into the seat at his side. She did not look his way, but instead sat back as a maid poured her some tea, trying her best to concentrate on the conversation.

'So Charlotte and I were taken with the notion of a ride in the carriage through Hayton, and who should we see in the village but Mr Liddell? Such a happy co-incidence—and now to have you both here to take tea with us… Such a pleasure,' Mrs Pearson was saying.

Louisa glanced at Charlotte, noting the elated grin on her face, and her eyes darting between her mother and Mr Liddell. A coincidence indeed, thought Louisa.

'It is certainly very good to see you both,' Clarissa agreed. 'Until the ball I had not seen either of you for some time.' She looked apprehensively at Sir Isaac for a moment, then turned her attention back to Mr Liddell. 'I believe you have been travelling in Europe, sir?'

Louisa listened intently as Mr Liddell regaled his audience with tales of his continental travels. Like Mrs Starke, he could no doubt write a book describing his experiences of Paris, Geneva, Rome, Florence and Vienna. He spoke about the places he'd visited so vividly that Louisa could imagine them—although she found herself comparing his accounts with those committed to paper by Mrs Starke, which she had pored over many times.

When he mentioned his visit to Château de Voltaire in Ferney, on the French-Swiss border, she couldn't help but interject.

'Oh, yes, I know of Monsieur Voltaire's house. Mrs Starke wrote of it in her *Letters from Italy*. She says it is unchanged, and that those who have owned it since Voltaire's death have gone to some lengths to preserve it.'

Mr Liddell raised his eyebrows and smiled in delight at their shared enthusiasm for the subject. 'Quite so, Miss Conrad. Although I must tell you that there is one notable thing missing from Monsieur Voltaire's home, and that is his library. It was purchased in its entirety by Catherine, the Empress of Russia, and moved to St Petersburg.'

'Astonishing!' Mrs Pearson exclaimed. 'And you, Sir Isaac, have you travelled, like your brother?'

Isaac gave his hostess a grim smile. 'Unfortunately seeing all that Europe has to offer is not a luxury afforded to a gentleman with an estate to care for— especially when that estate becomes his responsibility at a tender age.'

'Indeed, indeed…' replied Mrs Pearson, apparently somewhat taken aback by Isaac's directness.

'Louisa would like to travel,' Aunt Clarissa said, nodding warmly at her niece. 'I do believe her mother told me that it was one of the reasons she wished to visit me for the summer. Lowhaven isn't quite Lausanne, I grant you, but it has been good for her to see another part of England, I think.'

'I'm not sure I am so keen on the idea of travel,' Charlotte interjected, wrinkling her nose slightly. 'I think I'd much rather remain in a pretty little English village like Hayton and hear all about Europe from Mr Liddell.'

'Of course, my dear,' Mrs Pearson cooed. 'Like Sir Isaac, you know that your responsibilities are here, in Cumberland. Sons and heirs must do their duty, and so must daughters.'

Isaac gave a polite nod. 'Indeed, madam.'

To Louisa's consternation, Charlotte blushed, and she watched as Mrs Pearson eyed her daughter and Isaac keenly. Then she dropped her gaze, occupying herself with drinking her tea and wishing that the ground itself would open up and swallow her whole.

What the devil had he wandered into this afternoon?

Isaac sipped his tea, quietly cursing his brother, who had been responsible for agreeing to this visit in the first place. It was bad enough that since the moment he'd arrived he'd had to endure Mrs Pearson's obvious attempts to place her daughter in front of him, making sure that he knew every detail of her accomplishments. Now the giddy young woman was blushing at nothing, and Louisa had joined them to witness the spectacle.

He wondered if she'd noticed Mrs Pearson's machinations. Certainly, she looked uncomfortable—but then that could be due to his presence more than anything else. For his part, he found it hard to be in the same room as her, drinking tea and knowing what it was like to taste her lips, to feel her pressed against him. He had not expected to see her again so soon; in some ways he had not wished to. Forgetting what had happened between them had been difficult enough, but one glance at her pretty face rendered it impossible.

Isaac fidgeted in his seat. If only he had not come today! He hadn't wished to come, but had felt duty-bound to do so when Samuel had informed him that he'd accepted the invitation on their behalf. He considered himself too honourable a gentleman to deliver such a snub, even to people like the Pearsons, about whom he had to admit to feeling rather wary even before he'd been treated to the mama's scheming.

His brother's growing interest in Miss Pearson had prompted him to make some enquiries about the family, and what he'd discovered was less than encouraging. A trail of bad debt seemed to follow the father, and they lived almost entirely at the whim of his creditors. He'd tried to speak to Samuel about what he'd learned, but he had rebuked him with a speech so well prepared that Isaac suspected his brother of being all too aware of the family's situation.

'If I was to marry Miss Pearson—and I daresay it's too soon to consider that—then the wealth of her family would matter not a jot to me. I have invested my inheritance wisely and I manage my own affairs. When the time comes, I will support my own household. Large dowries and heiresses are no inducement to me.'

Isaac had quickly dropped the subject, in the face of his brother's iron will, and submitted to attending the tea party with resignation. He'd had no idea that Louisa and her aunt would be in attendance also. He still could not decide if that knowledge would have made him more or less likely to attend. All he knew was that between the shock of Louisa's sudden appearance and Mrs Pearson's dreadful efforts to match him with her daughter under his brother's nose, a swift return to the sanctuary of his library felt more tempting than ever.

'Have you managed to read any of *Waverley*, Miss Conrad?' he asked, leaning towards her and speaking quietly in the hope that they might share a conversation.

Fate in the form of Mrs Pearson had forced them together, he reasoned. They might as well make the best of it.

He watched as she hesitated for a moment, as though astonished that he was speaking to her at all. Out of the corner of his eye he could see Miss Pearson observing them, no doubt seeking to include herself in their discussion. He wished then that she would return her attention to his brother, who was engaged in a lively exchange with Mrs Pearson and Miss Howarth.

'Yes,' Louisa replied, 'in fact, I am reading the third volume.' She gave him a reticent smile. 'I must thank you for lending it to me. I have very much enjoyed it.'

'Well, I am glad to hear that. Though I cannot believe

you are almost at the end already. You must have spent a good deal of time reading these past days.'

'I confess that at times I have been unable to tear myself away from the story. The way the author describes the Scottish Highlands is so precise and so vivid that I find myself wishing I could visit.'

Isaac found himself nodding vociferously in agreement. 'I will admit that I entertained the same notion.' He glanced at Miss Pearson, who had mercifully lost interest in their literary discussion and had now been engaged by Samuel on another topic. 'As I think I told you once, I very much lost myself in the pages of that book.'

He watched as Louisa's face coloured slightly at this reference to one of their clifftop conversations.

'I can understand that now that I have read it,' she replied.

She pressed her lips together and he found his eyes lingering on them, his mind wandering to that kiss in his library once again.

'Pray tell, what are the two of you whispering about over there?' Mrs Pearson asked loudly, giving them both a stern look.

'We are just discussing a novel which Sir Isaac has given me to read,' Louisa replied, before Isaac could answer. 'It is called *Waverley*, Mrs Pearson. Perhaps you know of it?'

'No, I don't believe I do.' Mrs Pearson shrank back into her seat. Clearly a conversation about a book was not what she had been expecting to uncover.

'Ah, yes, one of my brother's favourites,' Samuel interjected. 'Its author chooses anonymity, but his identity is a secret not very well kept. I have heard it said

on more than one occasion that the poet Walter Scott
is the author of *Waverley*.'

Isaac bristled as he observed Louisa's eyes widen in
wonder. Trust Samuel to manage to impress with such
an assertion, he thought.

To his surprise, Louisa turned to him for confirmation. 'Did you know this, Sir Isaac?'

He shrugged. 'It is mere London tittle-tattle. I would
not give it any credence unless the poet acknowledges
it to be the truth.'

His answer earned him a nod of agreement from her.
'Indeed,' she replied, 'I would not credit even half of
what is said in society.'

He could not mistake the note of displeasure in her
voice. He glanced at her, frowning. The impassive expression on her face revealed nothing, but he couldn't
help but feel that she was talking about far more than
the secret identity of a writer.

'Since we are all gathered here today,' Mrs Pearson
interjected, clapping her hands together, 'I would like
to extend an invitation to you all. Mr Pearson and I have
recently considered how very nice it would be to spend
a little of the summer away from Lowhaven. Shortly we
intend to travel to our country home, Langdale Hall, and
we would be honoured if you would join us there for a
few days—perhaps on the Friday after next, if that is
suitable?'

Isaac blinked, thoroughly taken aback by the invitation. It was bad enough that Samuel had dragged him
here today, but now he faced the prospect of a prolonged
social engagement—one which would take him away
from his own estate. One which would involve spending several days in Louisa's company.

He stole a glance at her, observing how she stared at Mrs Pearson in apparent astonishment. Clearly she had not expected this either.

'Mrs Pearson, my brother and I would be delighted to accept your invitation—wouldn't we, Isaac?' Samuel said, in his usual flawless way.

'Wonderful,' Mrs Pearson declared, clasping her hands together. 'We will hold a dinner in honour of your visit—won't we, Charlotte?' she added, her keen gaze shifting to her daughter. 'We can invite our neighbours the Suttons and the Coles to join us.'

Miss Pearson gave a vigorous nod, clearly enthused by her mother's obvious machinations. 'With dancing, Mama,' she added. 'Surely we will have dancing?'

'Indeed,' Mrs Pearson replied, clapping her hands together once more. 'Then it is settled.' She turned to her other guests, who still sat, apparently dumbstruck. 'My dear Miss Howarth, Miss Conrad... I hope you will both attend as well?'

Isaac noticed how Louisa's gaze shifted towards her aunt, in the clear expectation that she would answer for them both. The older woman, meanwhile, seemed to take a moment to find her tongue.

'Oh, well...yes, Mrs P-Pearson,' she stammered. 'Indeed we would love to come. But I'm afraid that, as you know, we've... Well, we've no means by which to get ourselves to Langdale Hall.'

The way Clarissa Howarth's face reddened at that final admission made Isaac's heart lurch in sympathy for her, and he felt the heat of indignation rise in his chest at the difficult position Mrs Pearson had put her in. He hoped it was mere thoughtlessness, but he suspected it was not.

'We could take a stagecoach, Aunt,' Louisa interjected, trying to be helpful. 'That will at least get us to the nearest town.'

The thought of Louisa setting foot inside another damnable coach after what had happened to her earlier that summer set Isaac's teeth on edge.

'No,' he said, the word sounding more forceful than he'd intended. He paused momentarily, composing himself. 'It would be our pleasure to escort you. You shall travel with us in our carriage.'

Louisa looked at him then, her dark gaze guarded and unreadable, as somewhere in the background her aunt uttered hurried words of gratitude. In truth, Isaac wanted none of this: no tea parties, no visits to the Pearsons' country home, no long journeys with Louisa sitting in his carriage. But he was a gentleman. He had no choice but to accept invitations and offer his assistance to a fair maiden and her aunt when they needed it.

A fair maiden, he thought to himself. It had been some time since he'd called her that. Much had happened since then—much which could not be undone. Much which, if he was honest with himself, he did not wish to undo.

Isaac glanced at Louisa again as all around them excited chatter about the visit to Langdale Hall grew.

Several days away from Hayton Hall. Several days of seeing Louisa's face each morning. Several days of eating and sleeping under the same roof as her.

Could he bear it? He wasn't sure. One thing he did know, though, was that it would make forgetting that kiss all but impossible...

Chapter Eighteen

The journey to Langdale Hall took Louisa into the depths of Cumberland's hilly, rugged countryside and away from the sea for the first time in weeks.

For the first couple of hours, as the horses pulled them along at a gentle pace, Louisa gazed out of the window, half listening to her aunt and Mr Liddell make polite conversation, but mostly preoccupied by the increasingly dramatic scenery as it unfolded before her eyes. It was either that, she realised, or risk meeting the eye of the man sitting opposite. A man who sat as quietly as she did, but whose presence nonetheless seemed to fill the entire carriage as they rattled along the uneven country roads.

He had surpassed himself today. The deep blue of his frock coat contrasted sharply with a high white cravat and buff waistcoat, and his attire was completed with a smart pair of fitted grey pantaloons. The only aspect of him which was not agreeable was the expression he wore on his face. His brows were knitted together in a near-permanent frown, his lips pressed together in forbearance. It reminded her of that day, weeks ago, when he and his brother had come to her rescue in the aftermath of the stagecoach accident.

Despite herself, Louisa smiled at the memory. Back then she'd thought him so rude and disagreeable. Now she felt she understood him better. She understood his tendencies to solitude, his aversion to polite society. Indeed, in many ways she shared his feelings.

To her, the invitation to Langdale Hall had been as vexing as it had been unexpected. There was little doubt in her mind that Mrs Pearson had orchestrated this sojourn to further Charlotte's marriage prospects, and increasingly she suspected that Mrs Pearson wished to match Isaac with her daughter.

Charlotte might have spent much of the summer encouraging the attentions of Mr Samuel Liddell but, as Aunt Clarissa had once observed, the Pearsons' circumstances meant that Charlotte needed to marry as well as possible. For her mother, a younger son simply would not do.

The thought of spending several days witnessing Mrs Pearson manoeuvring to secure a baronet for her daughter during endless dinners and dances filled Louisa with dread. The idea of Isaac being betrothed to Charlotte made her stomach churn, as did the prospect of spending so much time in his company after that day in his library. After that kiss.

In truth, she was still reeling from it—from its tenderness, from her unguarded response to it. From the way she'd kissed him back. It brought colour to her cheeks each time she thought about it—which she was alarmed to concede was often. Seeing him every day at Langdale Hall would do nothing to help her forget about it.

The carriage jolted on the road, causing Louisa to start. She caught Isaac's eye, saw the sombre way he regarded her, his gaze holding hers for just a moment too long. It occurred to her then that perhaps the prospect of her presence at Langdale Hall was what vexed him, too.

Around noon they stopped at an inn for luncheon, and to change the horses. Louisa followed her aunt out of the carriage, determined to stay close beside her guardian as they went in search of a parlour and some refreshment. Yet Clarissa, it seemed, had other ideas, and before Louisa could intervene Isaac's brother had joined her aunt and they were striding together across the courtyard, leaving Louisa and Isaac behind.

Louisa couldn't help but wonder if that had been deliberate.

'I'm not sure who is livelier—your aunt or my brother,' Isaac said, moving to stand beside her. 'They barely stopped talking enough to draw breath all the way here.'

Louisa looked up at him, forcing a smile in an effort to seem cheerful and serene. She needed to be at her best, she reminded herself, even if she did not feel it. It was a simple matter of duty.

Isaac moved closer, offering his arm, and she felt herself hesitate—not because she did not want to hold on to him, but because she was frightened of what she would feel if she did.

Something in her demeanour must have betrayed her reluctance, because after a moment Isaac's expression darkened and he withdrew. 'Do you not wish to speak to me, Louisa?' he asked. 'Are we to travel in silence all the way to Langdale?'

His directness perturbed her, and she found herself looking away. 'I doubt that very much since, as you say, my aunt and Mr Liddell are both apt to converse. Besides,' she added, 'I have been enjoying the scenery. I seem to recall you did much the same thing yourself, the first time we travelled in a carriage together.'

Isaac grimaced at the recollection. 'Oh, please don't remind me. I must have seemed like the most disagreeable man on earth that day.'

Louisa nodded, sensing the ice between them breaking. 'You did, but it is all right. I know you much better now.'

Isaac grinned at her, apparently warming to her gentle teasing. 'Should I dare to imagine that I have gone up in Miss Louisa Conrad's estimation?'

She returned his smile. 'Well, you do have excellent taste in books,' she retorted playfully. 'What I mean to say is, I can imagine that a muddy, dishevelled woman and her maid clambering into your carriage was probably the very last thing you needed that day.'

'I was actually most concerned that you were injured,' he replied, his expression growing serious once more. 'Every time we hit a bump in the road you clutched at your side.'

She raised her eyebrows at that. Now she understood why he'd been so insistent about sending his physician to attend her. It seemed that Isaac had not been quite as uninterested as he'd appeared, after all.

'I am sorry if I am not an agreeable travelling companion today,' she said softly, slowly walking in the direction in which her aunt and Mr Liddell had headed. 'I am sorry if my aunt and me are an imposition.'

'I have hardly been talkative and full of cheer, have I?' he answered. 'But you must know that you could never be an imposition, Louisa. Contrary to what my sombre countenance might suggest, it is my pleasure to escort you and your aunt to Langdale Hall.'

'Thank you,' Louisa replied, inclining her head politely. 'And you must know that I understand if our visit to Langdale Hall is the reason you are not feeling so cheerful.'

She drew a sharp breath, poised to change the subject. Their brief conversation had been quite candid enough; she was not keen to know where else it might lead.

'Now, let us go and find my aunt and your brother and something to eat. I am very hungry.'

As his carriage made its way along the drive leading to Langdale Hall, Isaac almost found himself breathing a sigh of relief. The journey had been long enough, taking much of the day and leading them into the very heart of Cumberland with its enticing landscape of lakes and mountains.

Usually the sight of such wilderness would be sufficient to preoccupy him for the hours it took to pass along the web of winding, uneven roads, and he would be content to sit there, watching it unfold and admiring its beauty. Instead, he'd begun the journey in a terrible 'black mood', as Samuel would call it, and had barely noticed the scenery outside.

He was still annoyed with his brother for accepting this invitation and for leaving him no choice but to come. The idea of spending several days with the unsubtle Mrs Pearson and her giddy daughter was bad enough—and that was before he even considered how he felt about Louisa's presence there.

How *did* he feel, exactly? He wasn't sure. The sight

of her sitting across from him in his carriage, silent and steadfastly avoiding his gaze, had provoked him, although he was at a loss to explain why. After all, given the way he'd apparently lost his mind in his library that day, and given the way he'd kissed her, the lady could hardly be blamed for wishing to keep her distance from him. Yet despite knowing this he'd found himself craving a look, a glance, even the smallest interaction.

When they'd stopped for lunch and had that brief conversation he'd felt his bad mood begin to lift. He'd even managed to smile. He'd suggested to her that he was glad to escort her to Langdale Hall—a sentiment which he'd been unaware of until he'd put it into words.

It was all very disconcerting and confusing. Ever since that kiss, it was as though all his thoughts and feelings had been thrown up into the air. They were still falling like autumn leaves, and he was still gathering them up and trying to make sense of them. Trying to understand how he could both long for companionship and yet still feel compelled to remain alone. Trying to understand how to reconcile his grief and his loyalty to Rosalind's memory with his growing attraction to Louisa.

That was what it was, he realised—it was attraction. It was more than mere interest…more than friendship. Those things, he knew, did not lead a man such as him to kiss a woman, or to light up in her company the way that he did.

Louisa understood him—that much was clear. She'd observed his foul mood today and known the reason for it—and, what was more, she'd felt moved to tell him that she knew.

I understand, she'd said, *if our visit to Langdale Hall is the reason you are not feeling so cheerful.*

When he'd resumed his seat opposite her, after luncheon, he'd begun to wonder whether the prospect of their stay at Langdale discomfited her too. Feeling suddenly anxious to put her at ease, as well as craving more of her conversation, he'd decided to engage her on a topic he knew she would relish, given her love of the subject matter.

'Did you finish reading *Waverley*?' he'd asked.

'Oh, yes,' she'd enthused, a smile spreading across her lovely face. 'I did, and it was wonderful. I could hardly bear to tear myself away from it! I have brought the books with me. They are packed away in my portmanteau, and I will return them to you later.'

The visible joy those books had given her had stirred something deep within himself, and it had taken all the strength he'd been able to muster for him to acknowledge her intention with a serene nod.

Finally the carriage drew to a halt outside the entrance to Langdale Hall. It was an attractive house—too petite to be called a mansion, but nonetheless impressive, with its red brickwork and elegant embellishments around the windows and doorways.

He wondered how the Pearsons managed to maintain a home such as this, given what he knew about their financial circumstances. Then he reminded himself that it was really none of his business. It was his brother who was nursing a great interest in Charlotte Pearson, not him.

Isaac stepped out of the carriage, swiftly turning and offering his hand to Louisa, who he was heartened to see accepted it without any hesitation. He'd been perturbed when she hadn't taken his arm at the inn, as though she was signalling to him that things between them had changed, that they could never return to the easy familiarity they'd enjoyed before that kiss. That had saddened him—although, to his consternation, he'd realised that it did not lead him to regret embracing her that day in his library.

The Pearsons had come outside to greet them, and a whirlwind of pleasantries were exchanged as all four weary travellers disembarked.

Mr Pearson was briskly introduced to Isaac and Samuel. Isaac was amused to note that the portly, red-haired man looked unenthused, wearing the sort of expression a gentleman wore when he desired nothing more than a newspaper, a stiff brandy and some peace and quiet. Confirmation, if it was needed, that this sojourn had not been his idea.

'I do hope Langdale Hall will feel like a home away from home to you, Miss Conrad.'

Mrs Pearson's shrill voice pierced Isaac's thoughts as she addressed Louisa.

'From what your aunt tells me, you live on a large and very grand estate. Is that where you spend much of your time?'

He watched Louisa hesitate, pressing her lips together momentarily before answering. 'Yes, indeed, I prefer to be in the country,' she replied. 'And, as you say, my home is very lovely. I prefer to spend my time there.'

Mrs Pearson raised her eyebrows. 'But you must spend at least some time in town, surely?'

'I seldom go to town, madam,' Louisa answered her quietly.

'But if an unmarried woman does not go to town, how does she expect to find a husband?' Mrs Pearson continued. 'You must give your mother cause to fret.'

Isaac saw a discomfited look flicker across Louisa's face at such an interrogation, and he felt the temperature of his blood begin to rise in indignance. Clearly Mrs Pearson knew nothing of Louisa's bereavement, or if she did she was being unforgivably callous. He wondered why the older lady felt the need to raise the matter at all. What did she hope to gain, other than to make her guest feel uncomfortable?

'I daresay all ladies are entitled to keep their own counsel on such matters, Mrs Pearson,' he said, giving the woman a stern look.

'Indeed, sir, indeed...' Mrs Pearson stuttered, apparently thoroughly taken aback by his intervention. 'I was merely reflecting upon the concern of all mothers, which is to see their daughters married.'

'Hmm...' he responded, unable to quite trust himself to say anything further on the subject.

Certainly, marriage was foremost in Mrs Pearson's mind. He believed that this was why they'd been invited to Langdale Hall, and he suspected, too, that he was the gentleman Mrs Pearson intended to secure for her daughter, not his brother. Well, Mrs Pearson would have to be gravely disappointed in that regard. Frankly, there was more chance of Louisa kissing him again than there was of him marrying Charlotte Pearson.

Where the hell had that thought come from?

The grateful look Louisa gave him was unmistakable. Emboldened by it, he walked over to her, offering his arm once again. She took it, and as they walked together through the front door of Langdale Hall, he brought his other hand to rest ever so briefly over hers. It was a caring gesture, acknowledging her discomfort at Mrs Pearson's line of questioning. But more than that he hoped to convey how defensive he'd felt of her, and how much solidarity he felt with her.

Earlier today she'd let him know that she understood him. Now, more than ever, he wanted her to know that such understanding was mutual. They were, without doubt, kindred spirits—in grief, and in solitude. In the losses they'd borne, and in the terrible circumstances they'd both had to face.

Still, as he walked by her side he suspected that such an affinity could not begin to explain the way he'd felt when his lips had met hers...or, for that matter, what had possessed him to kiss her at all.

Chapter Nineteen

Dinner that evening was a trying affair, and to her own surprise Louisa began to look forward to the arrival of the other guests the day after next. At least the presence of some less familiar faces might bring fresh possibilities for mealtime conversation.

Tonight, she was seated at the end of the table, next to Mr Pearson, who had little enough to say to her beyond trivialities about the fine weather and the quality of the soup. Unsurprisingly, that well of superficial talk quickly ran dry, and before long Mr Pearson turned to Isaac, and the two men became engrossed in a discussion about business and investments.

Several times Isaac caught her eye, his expression unreadable, as Mr Pearson wittered on about the price of this or that commodity. If he was bored, he did not show it. Truly, he was every inch a gentleman.

Faced with subjects upon which she could hardly hope to converse, Louisa found herself observing the interactions taking place elsewhere. Directly across from her Charlotte looked flushed, the flirtation between her and Mr Liddell so relentless that Louisa felt almost

176 Spinster with a Scandalous Past

embarrassed to witness their whispers and smiles. Not that they seemed to notice; they were so preoccupied with each other that they barely looked in her direction.

Still, she thought, at least her peripheral position spared her from participating in Mrs Pearson's topic of choice. Even from here she could hear her engaging Aunt Clarissa at length on the favoured subject of her poor health.

Fortunately, after dinner the evening and the opportunities for good conversation seemed to improve. The ladies retired to the drawing room, where they played several hands of whist, while the gentlemen remained in the dining room, no doubt nursing glasses of port.

For whist, Louisa partnered with Charlotte, who thankfully seemed more composed now she was separated from Mr Liddell, although she was as hopeless at the game as Louisa was. Nonetheless, the card game served to occupy her mind, and for the first time in a while Louisa found herself beginning to relax. Perhaps, she reasoned, this visit to Langdale Hall would not be so bad as she'd feared.

The journey earlier today had served to alleviate much of her discomfort about her forced proximity to Isaac. In fact, at the inn and during the final few miles of the carriage ride, she'd found herself remembering just how much she enjoyed his company and his conversation. Just how open and kind he could be.

Furthermore, she had not been able to help the feeling of admiration which had washed over her when he'd stepped in to defend her against Mrs Pearson's onslaught of questions about marriage. He'd done so with such ease and such tact, but he had known what it had meant to her—the way he'd touched her hand afterwards had told her he had. She could only hope that his intervention had been sufficient to ensure that Mrs Pearson would have no more difficult questions for her, although she suspected that was wishful thinking.

'Oh! We lost again!' Charlotte cried out, startling Louisa from her thoughts.

Louisa smiled bashfully. 'I did say I am no good at this game—whereas I happen to know my aunt is particularly skilled at it. Truly, we did not stand a chance, Charlotte.'

Aunt Clarissa clutched her hand to her chest in faux outrage. 'Me? Whatever do you mean, my dear?'

'I mean my mother told me you and she were an unbeatable partnership as young ladies, Aunt,' she replied with a grin.

'It is all about memory,' Mrs Pearson interjected. 'If you are the sort of person who never forgets a detail, then you can be very successful at whist.'

'Which explains why I am hopeless at it,' Charlotte retorted with a giggle. 'I forget everything.'

'Just as long as you remember to do your duty, Charlotte,' her mother replied, giving her a pointed look. 'We can forgive a lack of skill at cards.'

The sharpness of Mrs Pearson's words cut through the jovial atmosphere like a knife, and Louisa was relieved that at that moment the gentlemen walked in to join them. Instinctively she sought out Isaac among them, catching his eye and offering him a small smile in greeting as he approached their table. He smiled back, then quickly adjusted his cravat and smoothed a hand over his dark hair, which was threatening unruliness again.

She thought of the first time she'd seen him on the

cliffs, his clothing and hair thoroughly windswept. She reflected that, as handsome as he looked in evening attire, dishevelment came very easily to him, and she was alarmed to find herself pondering which version of him she preferred. Clearly she'd had too much wine at dinner.

'Shall we retire to the comfortable chairs?' Mrs Pearson suggested, rising from her seat before anyone could answer. 'I will ring for some tea.'

Louisa did as their hostess bade, sitting down beside her aunt on a well-cushioned sofa. It struck her that the drawing room, like the rest of Langdale Hall, was immaculately furnished and decorated. Nothing about the Pearsons' country home suggested that their circumstances were as dire as Aunt Clarissa believed them to be. In which case, Louisa thought, they had to be living far beyond their means…

'So, who won at whist, Miss Conrad?' Isaac asked her as he took a seat on the sofa opposite.

'My aunt and Mrs Pearson—resoundingly,' she replied, inclining her head towards Aunt Clarissa, who was by now engaged in conversation with Mr Pearson. 'I seldom play the game, so there was little hope for Charlotte and me, I'm afraid.'

Isaac nodded. 'I daresay you prefer to spend the evening reading.'

She let out a small laugh. 'You know me well, sir.'

'Indeed, Miss Conrad,' he replied, lowering his voice. 'I believe I do.'

Although the expression on his face was earnest, Louisa found herself colouring at all the possibilities that remark could contain. Of all that it might suggest. He did, after all, know her mind well. But he also knew the taste of her lips…the feel of her body pressed against his. She knew instinctively that he had not been referring to that, and yet somehow, for some reason, that was where her thoughts had taken her.

'That reminds me—I still have your books in my portmanteau,' she said, grasping at any subject to draw her errant mind back from places it ought not to wander. 'I will fetch them for you shortly.'

He smiled. 'There is no hurry. I know they are safe in your keeping, since you treasure the story as much as I do.'

Louisa inclined her head politely before lowering her gaze, realising to her great mortification that she was still blushing. Truly, what had come over her this evening?

'Miss Conrad,' Mrs Pearson called, interrupting her thoughts. 'I had meant to tell you earlier that it seems we have a mutual friend in Berkshire.'

Louisa looked up at her hostess. 'Oh?'

'Yes—one of the Gossamers. Their estate is not far from Reading. I do believe that you know them?'

Louisa's stomach churned at the mention of that familiar name. 'Indeed, we are acquainted.'

'Mrs Gossamer is an old friend from my youth—our family estates were next to each other in Northumberland. We still write to each other frequently. In fact, I mentioned you to her in my most recent letter…' Mrs Pearson paused, giving Louisa a pointed look. 'I received her reply just a few days ago. She sends you her warmest regards.'

Louisa's heart pounded so hard that she could hear its rhythm in her ears. She'd been blushing before, but now her face burned fiercely, and she was sure she must appear crimson to everyone, even in the dim candle-light. A feeling of utter dread washed over her. Terror at the possible nature of the enquiries Mrs Pearson had made about her, and fear at what might have been contained within the reply.

She glanced at Isaac and saw that he was watching her intently, a small frown betraying his concern. She was sure that he'd read her reaction, that he'd seen her horror. He must be wondering what on earth had provoked it.

She gave Mrs Pearson a polite smile, trying her best to recover. 'Thank you,' she replied, relieved that she sounded more serene than she felt. 'Please convey my best wishes to Mrs Gossamer in return.'

Isaac stood on the terrace and drew in a lungful of the cool night air. He stared out absently, barely noticing the moonlit gardens which sprawled before him. It had been a long day and he was exhausted, his limbs heavy and his senses dulled by tiredness and, he conceded, rather liberal quantities of port. Yet the night was young, by polite society's standards, and as a gentleman he could not retire just yet.

A few moments in the fresh air ought to be sufficient to restore him before he returned to join the party. Although the thought of yet more company and conversation made him inwardly groan. He'd had quite enough of Mr Pearson's talk of wild money-making schemes over dinner—and after dinner, for that matter. It was little wonder he'd indulged in more port than was sensible; it had been all he could do to get through it.

He'd have much preferred to talk to Louisa. He'd sought opportunities to engage her at dinner, but Mr

Pearson's monopoly on his attention had made that all but impossible. That had irked him; he'd felt as though she'd been quite neglected. With a prickle of irritation towards their hostess, he'd had to observe that Louisa's peripheral position at the table was largely responsible for that.

After dinner the ladies had departed for the drawing room, and he'd found himself oddly impatient to join them. When finally he had, he'd been pleased to see that Louisa appeared to be enjoying herself, finding an endearing amount of amusement in being thoroughly beaten at whist. Grace in defeat, he'd thought with a smile. Her face had fallen, though, when Mrs Pearson had mentioned their mutual acquaintance.

That had been odd... It was a fairly innocuous topic, and yet Louisa had reacted like someone awaiting a dreaded punchline at their expense, her eyes widening and her cheeks glowing scarlet. Now that he thought about it, that entire brief interaction had been inexplicably strange...

'Ah! There he is, Miss Conrad.'

Hearing Louisa's name caused Isaac to start. He spun around to see his brother standing in the doorway, grinning, his eyes sparkling after an evening of merriment. Next to him stood Louisa, clutching something in her hands. She looked tired, mustering only a small smile as her eyes met his. He suspected that, like him, she'd had quite enough of being in company today.

'I was just taking the air,' Isaac explained, giving them both a polite nod.

'He's hiding, he means,' Samuel quipped, and let out a hearty chuckle.

Isaac flinched, acknowledging that there was some

truth in his brother's remark. It was all right for Samuel. Social situations always seemed to bring out the best in him, and tonight he was undoubtedly in high spirits. Isaac had not failed to notice that Miss Pearson had been very receptive to Samuel's wit and charm over dinner—a fact which had no doubt contributed to his brother's exuberant mood. Indeed, their flirtation had been so overt that everyone must have noted it... including Mrs Pearson.

Perhaps that would put an end to any ideas the young lady's mother might have about matching her daughter with the older brother.

Isaac could only hope.

'Miss Conrad was looking for you, brother,' Samuel continued. 'She has brought you your books.'

Louisa took a step towards him, holding out the three pristine volumes he'd lent to her that day she'd visited Hayton Hall. That day he'd kissed her.

He forced a smile as he moved to accept the books, pushing that particular memory from his mind.

'I am about to retire for the night, but I wanted to make sure you had these back in your possession first,' she explained.

He nodded. 'Thank you, Lou— Miss Conrad,' he replied, inwardly chastising himself for his accidental familiarity when his brother still stood nearby.

Without doubt Samuel had noticed Isaac's slip, flashing him a mischievous look before clearing his throat. 'Well, I am in very great need of some more tea before I retire. Please excuse me—and goodnight, Miss Conrad,' he added, before bowing and swiftly taking his leave.

'You are retiring?' Isaac asked, turning back to Louisa as Samuel disappeared from view. 'Is everything all right? Are you unwell?'

'I have a slight headache,' she replied, 'but it is nothing to worry about. I am sure I will feel restored in the morning.'

He nodded. 'I daresay sleep will help; you must be fatigued after the journey. Please, let me know if there is anything I can do to assist you.'

'Thank you, Isaac, you are always very kind.'

He watched as she hesitated briefly, before continuing.

'I wanted to thank you for intervening earlier today… when Mrs Pearson asked me about marriage.'

Isaac bristled at the recollection. 'I still cannot understand what possessed her to speak to you in such a way. Does she know about your bereavement?'

'I suspect she does,' Louisa replied quietly. 'Charlotte knows a little of the story. I would be surprised if she had not repeated it to her mother.'

Isaac grimaced. 'Then that is even worse.'

Louisa shrugged. 'I suppose not everyone views these matters in the same way. There is still an expectation in our society that gentlemen and women will go on to marry or remarry after such losses.'

'But not you—or me,' he mused, with a conviction he was discomfited to observe he did not feel quite so strongly as he once had.

'Indeed. Anyway,' she said with a slight shiver, 'it is best forgotten.'

She rubbed her arms, clearly beginning to feel the chill of the night air through the thin muslin of her cream evening dress. Without thinking, Isaac put down the books he was holding and removed his tailcoat, draping it over her shoulders before either of them had time to contemplate the intimacy of the gesture, or how the distance had suddenly closed between them. How, momentarily, his hands had come to rest on her shoulders.

Isaac stepped back, clearing his throat. 'You looked cold,' he explained, as though words were needed.

'Thank you.'

He watched as she ran a careful hand over the sturdy blue fabric.

'If ladies could wear these in the evenings, instead of flimsy gowns, we'd certainly be much warmer.'

'You could try doing that,' he suggested, 'although I daresay you really would provoke comment from Mrs Pearson then.'

She let out a soft laugh, her dark eyes alight with amusement. The sound of it, and the sight of her, did strange things to his heart.

Before he could really understand what he was doing, he stepped towards her again. 'We have never spoken about that day in my library,' he said quietly. 'When I kissed you.'

She looked up at him, her expression unreadable. If she was taken aback by his remark she did not show it.

'You promised you would forget about it,' she said. 'We both should.'

'I did promise to forget,' he replied. 'But I must confess that has proved to be difficult. You know how much I have come to value your company and your friendship, Louisa,' he continued, rubbing his forehead with his hand. 'But I find myself wondering if, perhaps, something more than friendship has started to grow between us.'

Louisa shook her head, just slightly. 'Isaac…' she began.

Behind them, the sound of doors opening and the din of voices intruded.

Louisa glanced nervously over her shoulder. 'We must not discuss this now,' she said, hastily removing his coat from her shoulders and handing it back to him. 'I should go. My aunt will expect that I have retired by now.'

She hurried away, leaving him staring after her, clutching his coat in his hand. What the devil had got into him? He had not meant to say those things—he had not meant to express feelings he was still grappling with himself. Yet in those snatched few moments alone with her he'd done exactly that. He could try to blame fatigue, or port, but he knew it was neither. He knew it was the truth.

Since that kiss he'd felt something shift between them, and within himself. Something he felt less and less able to resist.

As the lively chatter of the rest of the party drew nearer Isaac suppressed the urge to groan. What in damnation was he going to do?

Chapter Twenty

Isaac sat alone in the breakfast room, clutching a cup of tea in his hands. In front of him his plate sat barely touched as he stared out of the window, his thoughts far from the business of eating.

He'd risen late that morning, after a fitful night's sleep, and had come downstairs to discover that his hosts and the other guests had already breakfasted and gone out to enjoy the morning sunshine in the gardens. Quietly, he had been relieved; he was tired, and out of sorts, and some peace to collect his scattered thoughts was exactly what he needed.

Isaac breathed in deeply and picked up a slice of toast, resolving to eat. The way his conversation with Louisa had ended last night had sent his mind into a maelstrom. He still could not fathom what had possessed him to speak the way he had.

After retiring last night, he'd turned the words over and over in his mind, and somewhere during the small hours he'd confronted his own raw honesty about his deepening affection for a woman who'd wandered quite unexpectedly into his life. He'd never thought he'd feel this way again. His heart had been so broken by grief that he'd genuinely believed himself incapable of such feelings.

Now he realised how wrong he'd been. He had not been incapable, merely unwilling. He'd erected defences around his heart…he'd shrouded himself in solitude. He'd allowed that inner voice to rule him, telling him that to remain alone was to honour his wife's memory, that love was a risk too great and that allowing himself happiness was a betrayal. Over the course of a single summer, though, those defences were being eroded, and if last night was any indication there were not many left to fall.

But how did Louisa feel? That question had plagued him for the remainder of the night.

In the library she'd returned his kiss with an ardour she'd been unable to disguise, yet ultimately she'd ended the kiss, reminding him immediately of the impediment to her heart, of her loyalty to the memory of her dead captain. Last night she'd done little more than remind him of his promise to forget the kiss, said that they should both forget it. Did that mean that, like him, she was unable to quash the memory of it?

How he wished they had not been interrupted—that they had been able to talk for a little longer. How he wished to know what else she might have said, if given the chance.

'Good morning, sleepyhead.' Samuel's cheery voice intruded as he walked in, a merry spring notable in his step.

'Good morning, Samuel,' Isaac muttered, pushing away his plate.

'I regret to inform you that while you were slumbering you missed a truly lovely promenade in Mr and

Mrs Pearson's gardens.' Samuel's grin faded as he sat down opposite his brother. 'Isaac, what's amiss? You look wretched.'

'Nothing. I didn't sleep well that's all,' Isaac replied, getting to his feet and avoiding Samuel's scrutinising gaze. 'I suppose I ought to give my apologies for my tardiness. Is everyone still outside?'

Samuel nodded. 'They are. Come, they'll be pleased to see you. Perhaps you might even manage to rouse a smile from Miss Conrad. She looks about as happy as you this morning.'

Isaac ignored his brother's jibe, following him wordlessly into the fine formal gardens which sprawled at the rear of Langdale Hall. He wondered if Louisa was as tired as he was…if she had also had a restless night. His heart sank into the pit of his stomach as he contemplated that his words might have upset her, and that she might not share similar feelings to his at all.

'Oh, Sir Isaac, a very good morning to you!'

Isaac squinted in the bright light as Mrs Pearson made a beeline for him, her daughter following dutifully at her side. The fabric of their immaculate day dresses swished as they approached, parasols in hand to shade them from the glare of the near-midday sun. He had to admit that Miss Pearson looked very becoming in the soft blue she wore, with loose curls of her red hair framing her youthful face. She gave him a pretty smile, which seemed to illuminate the smattering of freckles on her nose. For all that he had never warmed to her giddy demeanour, he had to admit that it was not difficult to see why his brother was so utterly smitten with her.

He inclined his head politely at the two women. 'Mrs

Pearson, Miss Pearson… I do apologise for my lateness this morning.'

'Oh, do not fret, Sir Isaac,' protested Mrs Pearson. 'I trust you slept well?'

He nodded, offering a smile which he hoped would mask his lie. 'I hope you are well this morning, madam?'

'Oh, yes, very well—very well indeed,' gushed Mrs Pearson. 'I feel considerably restored today. Like you, I rose late. My delicate health requires that I sleep a good deal.'

Isaac looked about him. 'And Mr Pearson is also well?' he asked, noticing that the man was not present.

'Indeed, he has gone wandering in the woods,' Mrs Pearson informed him, waving a dismissive hand in the direction of the trees clustered beyond the gardens. Her eyes shifted briefly to her daughter. 'Charlotte wondered if she might give you a tour of the gardens—perhaps show you some of our prized plants.'

Isaac hesitated, glancing at Samuel. He saw a look of confusion flit across his brother's face before he quickly composed himself once more.

Beyond Samuel, and a short distance away, he spotted Louisa walking alongside her aunt. The two women were sauntering at a snail's pace along the path which led to a walled garden. Their backs were turned to him, but he could see from the gentle shake of her aunt's head and the movement of her hands that they were deep in conversation.

He suppressed a sigh, resigning himself to an invitation which politeness dictated he must accept. He thought about Louisa's observation last night, that society was quite content to see widowed gentlemen like him lining up next to eligible bachelors on the marriage mart. Quite frankly, the thought of spending the rest of his days being sought after by ambitious mamas like Mrs Pearson made his toes curl.

Swallowing his misgivings, he offered Miss Pearson his arm. 'I would like that very much,' he replied, forcing another smile.

The sweet fragrances of the flowerbeds combined with the woody scent of conifer hedges to give Louisa a welcome sense of peace. She'd forgotten how much gardens and greenery could soothe her...how she felt better able to cope with her cares and worries after spending time among plants and trees.

At home they had beautiful gardens, carefully planned and every bit as splendid as those at Langdale Hall. Over the past years she'd walked in them daily, in all seasons and weathers, sometimes with others but often alone. Those daily walks had steadied her, had been her anchor when she'd felt the tides of madness and despair trying to sweep her away.

She realised now that her coastal walks in Lowhaven had been a continuation of that habit, although when it came to the walks she'd taken with Isaac, she suspected they had been less about grounding herself and more about wishing to cast her cares away on a sea breeze. About longing to somehow wipe the slate clean and start anew. About enjoying the solace that friendship could bring.

Only somewhere along the line something more complicated than friendship had begun to flourish, hadn't it?

This morning she was neither losing her mind nor at her wits' end, but she was tired and still reeling from the whirlwind of yesterday. The journey to Langdale, the hours spent so close to Isaac, the way his company and conversation had been her favourite things of the day… The way Mrs Pearson had mentioned her friend in Reading, and how that fleeting piece of conversation had opened old wounds. How she'd worn her pain and her panic on her face.

And then the manner in which Isaac had spoken to her last night—his admission that he still thought of that kiss, that he was thinking about more than friendship. She'd been so lost for words that she'd been almost relieved when they were interrupted by the rest of the party. She was all too aware that, despite herself, her feelings for Isaac had grown too, that she regarded him with an affection and an admiration which went far beyond a friendly acquaintance.

She could not deny that she was attracted to him—that he was capable of provoking desires within her that until this summer she'd believed she'd long since suppressed. However, she also knew that this—whatever it was—could go no further. There could be no future for them; her past had seen to that.

She had to talk to him. She had to find the right words to explain herself. She could not reveal any more about her past—telling him about losing Richard had been as far as she'd been prepared to go. But she could assure him of her friendship. She could appeal to their shared knowledge of grief and loss and ask him to understand that, for her, marriage to any man was out of the question. She could make him see that although she cared for him she could not risk falling for him. Because she could only ever be a spinster, not a wife.

'Are you even listening to a word I say?'

Clarissa had turned to face her niece, raising an inquisitive eyebrow at her. Louisa averted her gaze, staring instead at the handful of sparrows pecking at the ground, hunting for their breakfast. Or was it luncheon? Truly, she'd lost all sense of the time.

After a moment the birds flew away; she listened to the gentle flutter of their wings, wishing she could join them. Right now she wanted to be hundreds of miles from here. She wanted to be in the Neapolitan countryside, or on the shores of Lake Geneva, or indeed anywhere but Cumberland or Berkshire.

Cumberland, she realised, had become as suffocating as her home. She'd absorbed too much of it, let it soak through her skin, allowed it to become familiar with her. She thought again about the pointed way that Mrs Pearson had told her they had a mutual acquaintance in Berkshire. The blessed anonymity she'd enjoyed was ebbing away, and the past had got her firmly in its clutches once more.

'Louisa?' her aunt prompted her. 'What is the matter? Are you unwell?'

Louisa shook her head, taking hold of her aunt's arm once more and leading her through the entrance to a pleasing walled garden bursting with floral displays.

'Last night, after dinner, did you hear Mrs Pearson ask me about the Mrs Gossamer?' she asked quietly, hoping the old stone walls surrounding them did not have ears.

'Yes, your mutual acquaintance—I do recall Mrs Pearson mentioning her. Sometimes it's a small world, is it not?' Clarissa's smile dissolved into a frown as she regarded Louisa once more. 'Why do you ask?'

'Mrs Pearson said she'd mentioned me in a letter to

Mrs Gossamer, and that Mrs Gossamer had replied, acknowledging our acquaintance. The Gossamers are related to...' she paused, struggling to form the words '...to Richard, the man I was to wed. He was their nephew. What if—what if Mrs Gossamer spoke of us in her letter?'

The furrow on Aunt Clarissa's brow deepened. 'I don't quite see the problem. Why would it matter if Mrs Pearson knew about your betrothal?'

Louisa huffed out a breath. 'It wouldn't. In fact, I daresay she's already been informed about it by Charlotte, who I rather foolishly confided in a little while ago. But what if Mrs Gossamer has said more than that?' She shot her aunt a meaningful look. 'They are Richard's relations, after all. We met at a ball they hosted, and he was staying with them at the time. They know far more than most about everything that happened between us.'

She watched as Clarissa chewed her lip thoughtfully. 'Perhaps... But, as his relatives, they will surely wish to guard his memory. Try not to fret, my dear. I doubt Mrs Gossamer has said anything in that letter beyond stating that she knows you.'

'I hope you are right.' Louisa sighed again. 'I wouldn't like to think that I've brought trouble to your door...that my reputation might tarnish yours.'

'I'm an old spinster and the daughter of a long-dead clergyman. No one cares a jot about me—which is exactly how I like it.' Clarissa gave her a knowing look. 'What you're really worried about is Sir Isaac knowing your story. That's what is troubling you.'

Louisa raised her eyebrows at her aunt's perceptiveness. 'Perhaps.'

Aunt Clarissa chuckled. 'There's no "perhaps" about it, my dear. I've observed the two of you often enough by now to see the affinity between you for myself.'

'Isaac knows some of my story,' Louisa admitted. 'He knows I was engaged, and he knows about Richard's death.'

'Ah, so the two of you have discussed more than your favourite books, then?' her aunt teased. She held up a defensive hand. 'Fear not. I don't intend to interrogate you again about the exact nature of your acquaintance with the master of Hayton Hall. You made yourself very clear the last time. I do still wonder about his feelings towards you, however. Certainly he seems to enjoy your company more than that of anyone else here.'

Louisa felt herself begin to crumple. 'He has admitted to me that he feels there could be more than friendship between us,' she blurted, feeling the sudden urge to confide in someone she knew she could trust.

Aunt Clarissa's expression grew serious. 'I see. And what did you say?'

'I did not say anything. I did not get an opportunity as our conversation was interrupted.'

Clarissa frowned. 'Well, you must say something, Louisa. What if he offers marriage?'

'You know I could not marry him, Aunt.'

'Then you must find a gentle way to tell him so—a way of explaining yourself which you can both live with. Do you think you can do that?'

Louisa swallowed hard. 'I hope so,' she replied.

'You don't sound sure.'

'I…'

Louisa's words caught in her throat as over Clarissa's shoulder she spied Isaac, walking up the path with Charlotte on his arm. She felt a strange twinge in the pit of her stomach as she observed the smiles on their faces, and in particular Charlotte's unmistakable giggles and admiring glances as he pointed—presumably to different items of horticultural interest around the vast gardens.

The most powerful heat coursed through her—flames of indignation at the sight of Charlotte walking at his side, clutching his arm and gazing admiringly into his eyes. The strength of the feelings the scene provoked in her were alarming, and not at all reasonable. She could never be anything more than his friend. She could never be his wife. She could not begrudge him if ultimately he sought happiness with another.

Clarissa glanced over her shoulder, following her niece's startled gaze. 'Ah, yes,' she said, taking her by the arm and turning her away as they began to walk once more. 'I hope you are certain of your decision, Louisa, because it seems to me that there might soon be someone else vying for Sir Isaac's affections. And I have the distinct feeling that a certain young woman's flirtatiousness paired with her mother's ambitions will be quite a formidable force.'

'Then let us hope that the end of the summer arrives soon,' Louisa replied, blinking away the sting from the tears which had begun to gather in her eyes. 'Because at least then I will not be here to see it.'

Chapter Twenty-One

Louisa struggled to eat much at luncheon, her stomach turning somersaults each time she caught Isaac's eye. She forced herself to make polite conversation with the rest of the party, even struggling through a lengthy discussion with Mr Pearson, who seemed keen to tell her all about the undulating fortunes of Lowhaven's port.

She listened as he wittered on, doing her best to look interested, although she'd learned much of what he told her already, from Isaac. She pretended to be thoroughly absorbed in the subject of imports and exports, ignoring the painful hammering of her heart in her chest each time her mind wandered to the conversation she knew that she and Isaac needed to have.

It was for the best, she told herself. She would find a way to be clear with him and then, in a day or two she would return to Lowhaven. Shortly thereafter she would travel home. Isaac would become a distant memory, and in time he would forget about her, too.

'So, you see, Glasgow is the place for tobacco now. It has completely taken that trade over from Lowhaven in every respect,' Mr Pearson continued.

'John, you must be thoroughly boring Miss Conrad with all that talk of trade.'

For once, Louisa was grateful for Mrs Pearson's interjection. She watched as her husband's already rosy cheeks deepened their colour, his head wobbling indignantly on his shoulders.

'I'm not sure what you mean,' he objected. 'These are matters which ought to greatly occupy us all. There can be few in this part of Cumberland who are not heavily invested in the fortunes of the port, and...'

'I wonder...' Isaac began, raising his voice above the ensuing argument.

His interjection caused the assembled party to fall silent, and he smiled appreciatively at them before beginning again.

'I wonder if anyone might wish to walk with me this afternoon? I find the country air is very agreeable on such a fine day.'

Louisa felt her breath hitch as those deep blue eyes of his rested on her, making it clear to whom his invitation was primarily directed. She felt her cheeks colour to match Mr Pearson's, then looked away.

'Charlotte will join you,' Mrs Pearson replied, patting her daughter on the hand.

Charlotte nodded her agreement, although Louisa could not help but note her uncharacteristic lack of enthusiasm for the suggestion. It was not at all like Charlotte Pearson to be so quiet.

Isaac smiled at Mrs Pearson, although Louisa noted that the warmth of it did not reach his eyes. 'Delightful, Mrs Pearson. In that case, I am sure my brother would be happy to accompany us also.'

'Indeed I would,' replied Mr Liddell, inclining his head politely at both ladies.

Charlotte uttered some polite words of acquiescence, fixing a less than convincing smile upon her face. Her mother, meanwhile, appeared thoroughly chastened; her lips pursed, her already pale face turning chalk-white.

Little wonder, really, thought Louisa. No one in the room could have failed to notice how adeptly Isaac had side-stepped her blatant attempt at matchmaking.

'In that case Louisa must go, too,' Clarissa interjected, regarding her niece. 'As a companion for Miss Pearson.'

'Of course,' Louisa replied quietly, accepting her duty to Charlotte as she knew she must.

She bristled as she caught Mrs Pearson glaring at her, clearly still displeased at her machinations being thwarted and apparently now regarding Louisa as an obstacle. That was hardly fair, Louisa thought. Her presence was required for propriety's sake, after all. She could hardly refuse, even if she wanted to.

Did she want to?

She was not sure.

For all that she knew she needed to speak to Isaac, she doubted she would get an opportunity with his brother and Charlotte both present. Perhaps, she reasoned, the walk would be good for her, nonetheless. A little fresh air always helped to restore her and to clarify her thoughts, and Louisa felt keenly the need to do both after last night.

'Excellent,' Clarissa replied, a little too enthusiastically, and Louisa suspected that offering her niece as a companion had been motivated by more than propriety. Indeed, it seemed that Mrs Pearson was not the only woman at the table who was intent upon meddling...

'That's settled then,' Isaac said, clasping his hands together and giving such a genuine smile that Louisa could not help but find it endearing.

Immediately she chastised herself for the thought. She needed to be a good deal more resistant to his charms than that if she was going to speak frankly with him. From now on, she reminded herself, it was her head which had to rule her, not her heart.

Isaac was delighted to discover that Miss Pearson was completely out of sorts. The party of four set out at a steady enough pace, but it was not long before the young woman fell behind, complaining that she had a sore ankle and that she was unable to keep up. Samuel, ever dutiful and attentive, stayed with her.

Isaac had to suppress a chuckle at hearing his genuine concern for her welfare, his pondering aloud if they ought to in fact turn back. Truly, his brother was smitten.

Louisa, on the other hand, seemed determined to march ahead. Together they walked along, side by side, the distance between them and the other two growing by the moment. For some time neither of them spoke, both apparently enjoying the pretty sprawl of the surrounding countryside as they made their way up a gentle incline and into the shadow of the mountains and hills beyond.

Isaac allowed himself to steal the occasional glance in her direction, watching as the wind whipped at her skirts and loosened her blonde curls from under her bonnet. As usual she was immaculately dressed, wearing the same patterned pink day dress she'd worn this morning and at luncheon, and protecting herself from any chill wind with a rose-pink spencer. He tried not to notice how the increasingly rocky, uneven path forced her to lift her skirt away from the ground, revealing a hint of the bare skin above her ankle boots.

With some difficulty he averted his eyes, focussing instead upon the horizon, although his mind remained on improper thoughts of what he had seen—and what he had not.

'I do not think Charlotte finds walking quite so agreeable today,' Louisa said, finally breaking the silence.

'Indeed. Although I believe the fresh air agrees with you very well,' he observed. 'You seem very content.'

She inclined her head politely. 'I'm not sure if I could ever be anything but content in surroundings such as these.' She paused, glancing briefly behind her. 'It seems our companions have turned back. Should we join them, do you think?'

Isaac shook his head, not turning around. 'My brother is more than equal to the task of assisting Miss Pearson.'

'It was clear that Mrs Pearson wished for you to accompany Charlotte. She seemed quite put out when you insisted that Mr Liddell would join you.'

'I was hardly going to promenade with Miss Pearson alone, whatever her mother may or may not wish,' Isaac countered with an amused laugh. 'Besides, it is my brother's duty to assist Miss Pearson, since it is he who wishes to court her.'

'I think Mrs Pearson wishes it to be you who is courting her daughter.'

Her directness took him aback. He looked at her, observing the obstinate way she set her jaw, half intent upon the path in front of her, half intent upon—what? Provoking him?

He thought again about their conversation last night...

the way he'd spoken of his feelings. The way that she'd remained silent about hers. Was she trying to tell him something about them now?

'Do you think that I should?' he asked, choosing to answer fire with more fire.

'I think that would hurt your brother, given his obvious attachment to her,' she replied.

'And what about how *you* feel, Louisa?'

Again, she clenched her jaw. She did not look at him. 'We are friends, are we not? I wish for you to be happy, Isaac. Just perhaps… Well, perhaps not with Charlotte Pearson.'

He raised his eyebrows in amusement at her assertion. 'Do you not regard Miss Pearson as being a suitable match for me?'

She glanced at him, a smile pulling at the corners of her mouth. 'With all due respect to Charlotte, I think her excitable nature would drive you to distraction.'

He gave a brisk nod. 'Very perceptive. Fear not, Louisa, my interest does not lie with Miss Pearson, but elsewhere. Indeed, I think I said as much to you last night.'

Isaac watched as she drew a deep breath, realising that his heart was thudding in anticipation of what she might say. He did not wish to vex her, but he had to speak with her honestly, had to understand how she felt. To understand if she might feel the same way as he did. And it had to be now—just the two of them, alone in the countryside, with Miss Pearson and his brother well and truly out of sight. It was possible that they might not get the opportunity to speak like this again.

'I do care for you, Isaac,' she said at length. 'But I cannot be anything more to you than a friend. I decided long ago that I would remain unwed. Surely you must understand why, given all that you have also lost?'

'I do understand,' he agreed, his heart at once sinking at the plain tone of her refusal whilst also being buoyed by her admission that she cared for him. 'I have spent much of the past two years convincing myself that I should remain alone, that love is something to be altogether avoided—feared, even. But nursing such convictions, I have discovered, brings much unhappiness.' He gave her a hopeful glance. 'If we both care for each other, then perhaps that is something we ought to embrace.'

She gave a slight shake of her head. 'It is not possible, Isaac. I came to Cumberland to visit my aunt for the summer, and I will be going home to Berkshire soon. We will be hundreds of miles apart. Indeed, we are unlikely to ever see each other again.'

'You do not have to go,' he ventured, his throat suddenly dry at the prospect of her departure. 'That day on the cliffs when you told me about Richard, you said how much you liked it that hardly anyone here knows your story. Perhaps that anonymity has afforded you the fresh start you needed. Perhaps the distance between you and Berkshire has liberated you. Perhaps it has helped you to move on.'

'But the past is always there, Isaac,' she replied. 'You know that as well as I do. Surely that was why you were content with my friendship? Because, like me, you could not truly countenance anything else?'

'Even asking for your friendship was a considerable step forward for me,' he admitted. 'After Rosalind died, for the longest time it was as though I had died, too. I wallowed in my library. I drank too much and ate too little. And I saw no one but my servants. But over time I began to remember that I am in fact alive, and moreover I began to want to live. This summer, for the first time in two years, I have lived a full and happy life. I have been dancing, I have visited my tenants, I have enjoyed tea and conversation in parlours and I have walked arm in arm on the clifftops with a captivating woman.'

He smiled bashfully at his own frankness.

'The past is always there,' he said. 'But so is the future. It seems to me that what has grown between us this summer represents another chance of happiness, if only we will take it.'

They halted as a stream crossed their path, its fast waters flowing noisily over the stones it had carried down from the nearby peaks. Isaac glanced up, noticing how heavy grey clouds had started to gather on the hilltops, and he wondered how much time they had left. He leapt over the stream before turning back and extending his hand towards Louisa, indicating that he would help her. He bristled to see her hesitate, glancing down first at the stream and then at her skirts, as if to assess the situation for herself.

After a moment, and apparently accepting that she had no viable alternative, she hitched up her skirt slightly with one hand and grasped his hand with the other, before leaping towards him. She reached the other side, narrowly missing the water's edge and losing her footing, causing her to stumble.

Instinctively Isaac caught her, and found duty dissolving quickly into pleasure as he grew conscious of his own hands upon her slim waist. Despite his better judgement he did not release her once he felt her feet become steady on the ground. Instead, he allowed his arms to encircle her, pulling her closer to him. To his surprise she did not resist. At first her hands pressed against his chest, before moving up on to his shoulders. Her dark eyes gazed into his, the tips of their noses touched, their lips were barely an inch apart...

'Isaac...' she began.

He pressed his mouth against hers, stemming the flow of her words. The kiss was as fierce as it was urgent, and the strength of his ardour surprised even himself. Even more disarming was the way Louisa responded in kind, looping her arms around his neck, her body clinging tightly to his.

Even through his frock coat he was aware of every detail of her petite, alluring form, from the legs he'd glimpsed earlier brushing his to the soft curve of her breasts pressed against his chest. His heart pounded as desirous thoughts ran unbidden through his mind, warming the blood in every part of him.

Around them the wind continued its frenzied dance, and behind them the stream continued its ceaseless babbling. Time marched on even as he willed it to stop, willed it to suspend them both in this perfect, delicious union. Alas, he knew it would not. He knew that words must be spoken...that questions must be answered.

'Please stay in Cumberland, if only for a while longer,' he breathed. 'Being with you this summer has made me see my life clearly—made me see that I've allowed my grief to cast its shadow over everything for too long. Being with you has made me confront what it is that I truly want, and it is not to be miserable and alone. I want laughter and conversation, companionship and affection. I do not want to forget the past. I want to live with it rather than allowing it to rule me. My brother once said to me that Rosalind would have wanted me to be happy. At the time he made me angry, but he was right—she would. And I believe Richard would have wanted only happiness for you, too.'

'It is not as simple as that...'

She pulled away from him, stepping back towards the water as though she might turn and flee at any moment. The look of horror on her face in response to his honesty made his heart lurch.

'I do not understand,' he began, shaking his head. 'You have said that you care for me. I did not realise that the admission of my feelings would be quite so unwelcome.'

'I do not mean to offend you...' She paused, her lip trembling as tears welled in her eyes. 'I do care for you, Isaac. Please believe that.'

He stepped towards her again. 'Then do not deny yourself happiness, Louisa. You deserve so much more than to do that.'

'I do not deserve anything,' she replied, tears running unabated down her cheeks. 'I care for you, but this...this affection between us—it must cease. I cannot allow myself to love you, Isaac, and for your own sake you cannot love me. I am not the sort of woman you should have in your life.'

He frowned. 'I do not understand. What does that mean? Are you trying to tell me that your objection to me is about more than your lost sea captain?'

She shook her head. 'I am sorry, Isaac. I cannot explain...'

'The devil you can't!' he replied, his frustration growing. 'Surely you must know by now that you can trust me, Louisa,' he continued, doing his best to soften his tone. 'If there is more to your story than I know, then please tell me. Tell me whatever it is, so that I can assure you that it makes no difference to how I feel.'

Those brown eyes stared into his, and he watched as she bit her trembling lip, trying to regain some modicum of control. 'I am sorry, Isaac, but I will never be able to bring myself to say those words to you.'

'I see,' he said, his voice grave. 'Then you are a coward, Louisa. Plain and simple.'

Overhead the sky had darkened further, and the thick clouds seemed to beckon the low but persistent rumbles which could be heard in the distance. Isaac let out a sigh of resignation, his mood blackening like the weather as he realised there was nothing more he could say to her. He cared for her, and she cared for him, and yet it seemed he was doomed to lose her without even understanding why.

'Come,' he said grimly. 'Let's make haste and return to Langdale. There is a storm brewing.'

Chapter Twenty-Two

Just as Isaac had predicted, a storm did indeed arrive, bringing heavy rain which battered Langdale Hall's windows, and thunderclaps loud enough to set everyone's nerves on edge during dinner. Not that the inclement weather was the only reason that tension hung in the air—as Louisa knew only too well.

Dinner was a torturous affair. The sight of Isaac seated across the table from her, immaculately dressed in his deep blue tailcoat, made Louisa's breath catch in her throat and her heart race.

She was far beyond the point of being able to deny her feelings for him, even to herself. She cared deeply for him and was hopelessly attracted to him. Her eyes sought him every time she entered a room. She craved his attention, his conversation. His embrace. Worse still, she now knew the depth of the regard he had for her. She'd heard it in his every word today, felt it in that kiss. And yet those feelings were all for nought. There could not be any future in what they felt for each other.

As she sat at that table, sipping her wine and wishing she could muster an appetite for the food in front of her, it occurred to Louisa how different this was from her attachment to Richard. Back then she'd been so youthful, so simplistic about love. She'd also been naïve, trusting in that affection as it carried her along, never thinking it would bring her such heartache. Now she knew better. Indeed, it was that awareness, that experience, which made her involvement with Isaac so complicated.

Standing by that stream, with the sky looming thunderously above them, she had so desperately wished she could tell him everything—that she could trust her feelings just as she had all those years ago. Knowing she could not…knowing how the truth would only serve to condemn her in his eyes and confirm that they were lost to each other…was as painful as refusing his affection had been.

There had been no good choices today—but then, Louisa reflected, that had been the case for her for a very long time.

After dinner, Louisa retired to the drawing room, occupying a window seat away from her aunt and the Pearson ladies and nursing a cup of tea. She watched absently as bolts of lightning lit up the black night sky, making a pretence of being fascinated by the spectacle so that she might remain undisturbed. She was not in the mood for light conversation tonight.

The gentlemen hadn't joined them yet, clearly preferring to remain around the table with their glasses of port—a fact which Charlotte had remarked upon several times in as many minutes, her head bobbing up and down to look at the door.

She'd seemed uncharacteristically on edge ever since returning from her walk, and Louisa had caught enough of the whispers exchanged between her and her mother to surmise that the outing had not proceeded according to either of their plans. If she'd been in a better state of mind Louisa might have tried to speak to Charlotte herself, to discover what was amiss. As it was, she found herself still consumed by the events of her own afternoon, replaying them over and over, tormenting herself with every last detail.

The way Isaac had spoken of his feelings for her. The way he'd kissed her. The way he'd insisted that whatever had happened in her past did not matter.

That final declaration had torn the ground from beneath her feet. How could he say that when he did not know the nature of what he so readily dismissed?

A gentleman like Sir Isaac Liddell could not love a woman like her; it was out of the question. Even if he could care for her in spite of her past, his association with her would taint him and his good name. The whiff of scandal would plague them for ever. It would destroy her. It would destroy them both.

No, she reminded herself. Of course she could not tell him. She could not risk ruining herself further, or seeing the light go out in his eyes when he regarded her. It was better this way, even if it meant Isaac thinking that she was a coward. Better that than him thinking she was a scandalous woman.

'Are you all right, my dear?'

The kindly face of Aunt Clarissa looking down at her startled Louisa from her thoughts. She nodded, forcing a smile for good measure as her aunt sat down beside her.

'Mrs Pearson and Miss Pearson are going to retire for the evening,' she said, as both ladies departed from the room with the briefest and, it seemed to Louisa, the most curt of farewells.

'Charlotte has not seemed happy this evening,' Louisa observed, once the door had closed behind them.

'Nor have you,' Clarissa countered.

Louisa inclined her head, deciding not to deny it. 'I daresay Charlotte's reasons are different from my own.'

'Or perhaps not, since I suspect both of you have reasons that are rooted in your feelings for a certain pair of brothers.' She patted her niece on the hand. 'Come, we are alone, and I think the gentlemen are unlikely to join us now. Tell me what happened.'

'I spoke to Sir Isaac earlier today. I made it clear that we could not be more than friends.'

Clarissa's eyes widened. 'Oh, I see. And what did he say?'

'He left me in no doubt about the depth of his feelings for me.' Louisa felt her lip begin to tremble, her fraught feelings bubbling to the surface once more. She tried to quash them, but to no avail. 'He spoke so honestly, Aunt, and I am afraid I said more than I wished to when I refused him.'

'Did you tell him about your…about all that happened?' Clarissa asked, lowering her voice to a whisper as she chose her words carefully.

Louisa shook her head. 'I could not bring myself to. He knows there is more to my past than losing Richard, but that is all. He told me that whatever happened doesn't matter to him, but surely that cannot be true?'

Clarissa frowned. 'Sir Isaac is no starry-eyed youth, Louisa. He is a respectable gentleman. If he has given his word to you, then what reason do you have to disbelieve him?'

'His respectability and status are the very reasons

why I would be entirely unsuitable for him, Aunt—you must see that.'

'Oh, my dear, perhaps it would have been better if you'd just told him and let him judge the situation for himself,' Clarissa replied.

'Please do not be angry with me, Aunt,' Louisa replied, sobbing. 'I could not do it. I could not bring myself to tell him. What possible good could come from him knowing? All it would do is serve to ruin me all over again—this time in his eyes.'

Clarissa placed a comforting hand on Louisa's shoulder. 'You have a lot of regard for the opinion of a gentleman you once claimed barely to know,' she observed, giving her niece a knowing look. 'I'm not angry with you, my dear. I am saddened, though. Your summer in Lowhaven has not turned out as I'd hoped. I wanted you to leave here with a lighter spirit and a spring in your step, not weighed down by more difficulties.'

'Oh, but I have enjoyed my time here with you,' Louisa said, sniffing as she finally brought her tears under control.

'Yes, but it has not been the respite that I wished for. I wanted Lowhaven to be an escape for you…to be somewhere you could feel free from the past, even if only for a month or two. And, rather selfishly, I had hoped you'd grow to love it so much that you might wish to stay.' Clarissa paused, a watery smile spreading across her thin face. 'Your company has brought me great comfort these past weeks. It is not an easy thing, to be on your own. That is something you will learn, Louisa,' she added pointedly.

'I admit I have much to learn when it comes to being independent. But if I have learned anything in Lowhaven it's that I cannot run from the past, no matter how much I might wish to, or how hard I might try. I will live with its consequences for the rest of my life. And the only way I can do that is on my own.'

'And in doing so you are prepared to deny yourself love?'

Louisa wiped her eyes with a firm and steady hand. She had shed enough tears today. 'Fate has denied me love, Aunt,' she replied. 'God has denied me love. Napoleon himself denied me love when he took Richard from me. I lost all hope of love a long time ago.'

'I'm the wrong brother, Isaac. That's the problem. I'm the wrong brother...'

Isaac sat at the dining table with Samuel, the pair of them finishing off what had once been a healthy decanter of brandy. Mr Pearson had departed a few moments earlier, summoned to bed by his wife, and, rescued from the need to sustain an interminable conversation about investments, or gambling, or some other gentlemanly pursuit, the brothers had seized the chance to speak frankly for the first time in days.

Samuel had started first, his tongue loosened by drink and his heart apparently sore after today's ill-fated promenade with Miss Pearson.

'She has as good as told me that I must end my pursuit of her,' Samuel said miserably. 'She's made it clear that her father will not permit any such courtship, and has declared she is not ready to marry. She said that her mother plans to take her to London soon, so that she might experience "proper society", and that it will be a long time before she will return.'

'This is the mother's doing,' Isaac replied, before

gulping down another generous measure of the strong drink. 'A typical ambitious mama, if ever I've seen one.'

'Indeed... Why have the younger brother when you could have the baronet?' Samuel replied, and the bitterness was unmistakable in his voice.

Isaac raised his eyebrows at that. 'Mrs Pearson's efforts to foist her daughter on me have not gone unnoticed, brother, but I can assure you I am completely indifferent to that young woman. Let them try their luck in London, for they shall have none here. I am bone-weary of the female heart,' he added sourly.

'Oh? Pray tell, brother, which female heart has so grievously wounded you? Dare I suppose that it is the heart of a certain Miss Conrad to which you are referring?'

Isaac groaned, rubbing his temples with his fingers. 'I have told Miss Conrad that I care for her,' he admitted.

Samuel sat bolt upright. 'Good heavens, why on earth did you do that?' A mischievous grin spread across his face. 'I knew there was something between the two of you—although I did not imagine for one moment that you'd reached the stage of professing your undying love.'

'I most certainly did not do that—and besides, there isn't anything between us,' Isaac replied, shaking his head. 'She told me that anything more than friendship is impossible.'

Samuel's face fell. 'Really? Why?'

Isaac hesitated. As miserable as Louisa had made him, he could not stop himself from feeling protective towards her. 'It transpires that a number of years ago she had a fiancé—a naval captain who was killed fighting

Napoleon. It seems that her grief still troubles her,' he explained, settling on telling half the story.

The half he knew, he reminded himself, since the rest remained mere conjecture. Mere imagination, since she had given nothing away.

Samuel frowned. 'But you are a widower, and you are clearly prepared to remarry.'

'Perhaps there is more to the story than Lou—than Miss Conrad is willing to say,' Isaac replied, feigning a nonchalant shrug. 'Or perhaps she really is quite content to be alone, whereas I am not. I quite despise it, if the truth be told.'

'Then let that be the lesson here, brother,' Samuel said, refilling both their glasses. 'If meeting Miss Conrad has made you realise that you want a wife, then a wife is what you must find.'

He paused, holding his glass up in front of him as though considering its contents.

'I have seen a change in you this summer, Isaac. And if some of that is because of Miss Conrad then, frankly, we ought to thank her. You must keep moving forward now. If you do not want to be alone, then do not remain alone. If Miss Conrad will not have you, then you must find a woman who will.'

He took an enormous gulp of brandy, almost draining the glass in one swift movement.

'But not Miss Pearson, because I would never forgive you.'

Isaac laughed. Despite the trials of the day, the brandy-fuelled conversation with his brother had somewhat lightened his spirit.

'You've clearly drunk too much of this, Samuel,' he said, waving his glass, 'if it is giving you wild ideas about Miss Pearson and me.' He drew a deep breath, not quite able to believe what he was about to say. 'You are right, though, about me finding a wife. I think it is time I made a concerted effort to remarry—for companionship, yes, but also to fulfil my duty to this family. I am not getting any younger, and we Liddells need sons and daughters if we are to survive.'

Samuel rested his chin on his hands, giving Isaac a considered look. 'And what about love?' he asked.

Love. Indeed, Isaac thought, what about it? Love had been the sight of Rosalind, dressed in white, walking down the aisle towards him. It had been the smile on her face as she'd patted her swollen belly. It had been the cold clamminess of her hands as she'd gripped the bedsheets and clung to the hope of living.

This summer he'd come to hope for love once more—only to have those hopes dashed in the midst of the Cumberland countryside by a woman who'd wept as she'd rejected him. A woman who cared for him but could not bring herself to tell him the truth about her past.

All love seemed to have done, Isaac thought, was break his heart.

He gulped down the last of his brandy. 'Perhaps, brother, I've had quite enough of love,' he replied.

Chapter Twenty-Three

Louisa sat beside her aunt in the drawing room, running her finger absentmindedly over the rim of her wine glass and paying little attention to the surrounding conversation. The party had assembled for dinner, dressed in their finest clothes as they awaited the arrival of the handful of further guests who would be attending for the evening. Two had just joined them—a Mr and Mrs Sutton of Ashwell Park—and a further three were apparently expected at any moment.

Louisa suppressed a shiver, feeling cold in the pale blue muslin gown Nan had packed for her. She leaned towards the fire, grateful for its heat. She'd declined to have much involvement in the selection of her dresses— a decision she now regretted. Sometimes, she reflected, she could be her own worst enemy.

The day had passed quickly, with most of the household preoccupied with preparations for the evening's festivities. Keen to keep out of the way, Louisa had embraced the excuse to keep to her room as much as possible, busying herself with her books until the appointed hour, at which time a maid had arrived to help her dress for dinner.

She had not spoken to Isaac since they'd returned from their walk yesterday, their interactions having been restricted to polite nods of acknowledgement at mealtimes. She had noticed his sombre countenance whenever their eyes met over the dining table, and she didn't doubt that she looked just as unhappy. Being in the same room with him had become such torture that she longed to return to Lowhaven. Except, she reminded herself, it was Isaac's carriage which would take her back tomorrow.

The very thought of spending so many hours sitting close to him, after all that had passed between them, made her chest tighten and her stomach churn. She had no idea how she was going to bear it.

'Miss Howarth, Miss Conrad...may I present Mr and Mrs Edmund Cole and their daughter, Miss Carolyn Cole?' Mr Pearson said, interrupting her thoughts.

Louisa got to her feet, inclining her head politely at the final guests to arrive. Mr and Mrs Cole acknowledged her stiffly, before turning back to be introduced to Isaac, who had now joined the party in the drawing room. Their daughter, however, gave her a warm and hopeful smile. She seemed young, perhaps even younger than Charlotte, her green eyes filled with the anxious wonder of a woman not long out in society.

Louisa smiled in return, musing on the composition of the assembled party. The small size of it struck her, as did the obvious omission of eligible young gentlemen. It was a clear indication that Mrs Pearson's schemes had indeed been focussed upon securing one of the Liddell brothers for her daughter, and Louisa had well-founded suspicions as to which one she preferred.

Her smile dissolved as she spotted Charlotte sitting

quietly beside her mother, looking unmistakably glum. She wondered again what might have happened to provoke such a change in her, and felt a stab of guilt that she had not tried to find out.

'Are you quite well, Miss Conrad?' Miss Cole asked her. 'You look a little uncomfortable.'

'Oh, yes I am well...just a little cold in this dress,' Louisa replied as smoothly as she could manage. 'It seems I am not yet acclimatised to summer in Cumberland. I am visiting from Berkshire, you see.'

The young woman's eyes widened. 'Indeed! I daresay it is warmer in the south, though I have never been. I should be so happy to go—especially to London. I suppose you will have been to London many times?'

Louisa laughed, finding it hard not to be encouraged by Miss Cole's enthusiasm. It was hard to remember how exciting a prospect London had seemed to her at one time. 'Yes, although these days I prefer life in the country. It is possible to tire of town, after a while.'

'Oh, I don't believe that! Cumberland is so dull that I hardly think I could be anything but merry in London,' Miss Cole gushed.

Louisa smiled, and without even thinking found herself gazing over the young woman's shoulder towards Isaac. She drank in the details of him, from his immaculate deep blue tailcoat and crisp white cravat to the curl of his dark hair, which had been tamed into order.

As though sensing her looking, he turned his head, and for a moment their eyes met. She watched as feigned indifference melted into curiosity, and felt a familiar heat rise in her belly as the hue of those blue eyes deepened with desire. She looked away, unable to bear the intensity in them a moment longer. Unable to bear the longing his stare had conveyed. Unable to bear knowing just how much he cared for her when his affection was futile.

'I find that Cumberland could be described in many ways,' she replied, recovering herself, 'but in my experience "dull" is most certainly not one of them.'

Dinner was announced, and the party made their way into the dining room to find their seats. Louisa found herself hoping that she might be seated near to Miss Cole. The young woman had a pleasant and easy manner about her, and the sort of light conversation she would doubtless offer would make this difficult final evening at Langdale Hall more bearable.

Alas she was not, and furthermore Louisa's bad luck was Charlotte's good fortune, since the young ladies had been placed opposite each other at one end of the table. Suppressing a sigh, she continued to peruse the name plates, hoping that at the very least she'd been placed near to her aunt. Heaven forbid that she should have to endure another meal beside Mr Pearson...

'You are at the other end, Miss Conrad, beside my brother,' Mr Liddell called over to her, with an unmistakably mischievous smile.

Louisa nodded, trying to conceal her alarm at the placement. She watched as Samuel Liddell rested a hand upon his own seat, beside Charlotte, arching her eyebrows as Charlotte immediately turned away from him with a look of haughty indifference. It was quite a change from the ceaseless flirtation of recent days, and Louisa could not mistake the look of hurt as it flickered across Mr Liddell's face.

Something indeed was terribly amiss.

'Forgive me, Miss Conrad, I do believe my brother

has swapped the name plates.' Isaac spoke discreetly, his low voice behind her making her stomach flip. 'I am sure we can change it if you like.'

'It is fine,' Louisa replied, in an equally hushed tone. 'I daresay your brother has his reasons for the change, although I fear his suit does not fare well.'

'Indeed,' replied Isaac, his eyes momentarily shifting towards Mr Liddell. 'It seems that neither of us has had much recent success when it comes to matters of the heart.'

Louisa stared at him open-mouthed, unsure how to retort. It seemed that tonight she did not have the monopoly on forthright remarks.

She watched, dumbstruck, as Isaac turned his attention to Mrs Pearson, giving her the most magnanimous smile.

'I must compliment you on your table settings, madam,' he said.

Mrs Pearson beamed at him, although her smile quickly faded as she observed Louisa taking her seat at Isaac's side. A seat Louisa had not even wanted. And now, thanks to Mr Liddell's meddling, she had provoked Mrs Pearson's ire once more.

Louisa sipped her wine, trying to ignore how her senses were heightened with awareness at Isaac sitting so close to her. Trying not to remember the warm feeling of him as he'd wrapped her in his arms and kissed her beside that stream. Trying not to think about just how much she wished she could reach out now, touch his hand and tell him that she would be his.

Truly, she thought miserably, tomorrow could not come soon enough.

* * *

The sight of her in that sky-blue dress was positively arresting. From the moment he had spotted her coming down the stairs he had been unable to tear his eyes away from her. All the resolutions he'd made during his conversation with Samuel the previous night had immediately fled from his mind, his thoughts fixed instead upon the glow of her fair skin, bared by a plunging neckline and short sleeves, and the neat curve of her waist as the floaty fabric skimmed over it.

Unable to entirely trust himself, he'd not followed her into the drawing room, but lingered instead in the hall, feigning interest in the portraits on the wall. Now she sat beside him at dinner, her familiar lavender scent wafting beguilingly towards him, haunting his senses, provoking his memories. How foolish he'd been to think that he could simply set aside his feelings for her and seek someone else. How awful he'd been to consider a union without love.

If he could not have Louisa he would have no one else.

'The game is very good, is it not, Sir Isaac?' Louisa asked, nodding approvingly at her fork.

He agreed, then continued with his own meal. Conversation between them was stilted, at best, and he wondered if she too was trying to maintain her composure in the presence of so many listening ears. Certainly, Louisa's aunt seemed to be paying close attention whenever they spoke to each other. He wondered how much her guardian knew about their involvement this summer.

'I daresay that here in Cumberland we have the finest fare—wouldn't you agree, Miss Conrad?' Mrs Pearson asked, having clearly caught Louisa's remark.

'I would certainly agree, Mrs Pearson,' Louisa replied. 'There are many things I will miss about Cumberland when I return to Berkshire.'

'Chief among them are my cook's cakes, I should think,' her aunt interjected, provoking a few murmurs of amusement around the table.

'I imagine you will miss the beautiful scenery as well, Miss Conrad,' Mrs Pearson continued. 'Indeed, you must have spent a long while enjoying it yesterday, since I hear that neither you nor Sir Isaac returned to Langdale for some time after Mr Liddell escorted Charlotte home with her injured ankle.'

The woman paused, staring at Louisa, her expression impassive as she let the damning insinuation her words contained sink in around the table.

'Charlotte feared you had both become lost, after you continued walking. She said you were completely out of sight,' she added, apparently for good measure.

Isaac felt the heat of indignation rise in his chest. He could not believe what he had just heard—could not believe that Mrs Pearson had the audacity to sit at the dining table and make such thinly veiled scandalous accusations for all her guests to hear.

It was bad enough to hear such suggestions being made about *him*, to have *his* honour called into question, but as a gentleman he knew he would survive it. For a lady like Louisa reputation was everything—once ruined, it could never be recovered. Such was the cruelty and such was the difference in standards applied to men and women by so-called polite society.

Isaac glanced at Louisa, saw how her cheeks had reddened and her eyes had widened in horror. It was true that they had been alone together yesterday. They had talked of their feelings. They had embraced. But Mrs Pearson could not and would not know anything of that. He would make sure of it.

'I'm afraid you are mistaken, madam,' he replied, meeting her eye with a cool and steady gaze. 'Miss Conrad and I turned back immediately. However, Miss Conrad had twisted her ankle on the rocky path, and had to rest, which meant we returned to Langdale a few moments after my brother and Miss Pearson did.'

He watched as the older woman's nostrils flared. 'That is not what I was given to understand...' she began.

'Perhaps Miss Pearson's recollection is not complete, given she was in such discomfort. But I can assure you we never lost sight of either Miss Pearson or my brother.' Isaac turned to Samuel, who was regarding him carefully, his fork poised in his hand. 'Indeed, did I not wave to you several times, brother, to assure you we were just a little way behind?'

'Yes,' Samuel replied seamlessly. 'That is correct.'

Isaac gave Mrs Pearson a satisfied smile. 'I hope this eases your mind, madam. I'm sure that, as her guardian, Miss Howarth appreciates your concern for her niece.' He glanced at Louisa's aunt, who looked thoroughly dismayed at what was unfolding before her. 'It is regrettable that sometimes accidents happen...especially in the countryside. However, I can assure you both that Miss Conrad was appropriately attended throughout the entire short promenade. You have my word as a gentleman.'

Briefly he regarded Louisa. She acknowledged his explanation, inclining her head gracefully, and he felt another wave of protectiveness grip him as he noted the look of sheer relief in her eyes. How he wished he could reach out and place his hand over hers, reassure her that all was well, that he would always be there for her. That he would not allow the likes of Mrs Pearson and her spiteful tongue to harm her. That he wanted to care for her always, if only she would let him.

Around the table his final remarks were being met with murmurs of agreement about how dangerous the paths could be, and how regrettably commonplace such injuries were. Mrs Pearson, however, looked rather as if she had just swallowed a lemon. He watched as the woman exchanged a glance with her daughter. Whatever the look communicated, it seemed sufficient to wipe the small smile from the younger lady's face.

He suppressed a wave of irritation at their behaviour. How glad he would be to be away from these Pearsons and their scheming ways.

Hopefully Samuel's heartache concerning the daughter would be short-lived.

Hopefully, his own would be, too, although somehow he doubted it.

After their meal was finished, the party retired swiftly to the drawing room for drinks and dancing. It seemed that during dinner Louisa's aunt had been persuaded to do the honours on the pianoforte, and despite her mild protestations of being out of practice, before long she was delighting them all with a merry tune from her repertoire.

Isaac watched with some amusement as Samuel keenly assembled the dancers, persuading first the Suttons and then the Coles to participate in a dance. To his surprise, his brother then approached Miss Cole and requested a dance, and he watched as she accepted his hand with a shy smile. On the other side of the room the Pearsons had gathered, watching the festivities unfold, clutching glasses of wine as red as their faces.

It would have been an uncomfortable scene if it had not been so thoroughly deserved.

'Won't you dance, brother?' Samuel asked him.

'I hardly think Miss Pearson looks in the mood to take a turn,' he replied, making the observation quietly enough so as not to be overheard.

'What about Miss Conrad?' Samuel persisted.

'I believe she is turning the pages for her aunt,' he replied, inclining his head to where Louisa stood by the piano.

'I daresay someone else could do that,' Samuel said, raising his voice. 'What do you say, Miss Howarth? Could you spare your niece so that she may dance with my brother?'

'Gladly, sir,' Louisa's aunt replied. 'It is surely the duty of all young people to be dancing on such an occasion, is it not?'

Isaac did not miss the wily look the woman gave her niece, and nor did he miss the look of consternation Louisa gave her aunt in return. He strode towards her, holding out his hand and giving her the broadest smile.

Perhaps it was the wine, or perhaps it was the breathtaking sight of Louisa in that pale blue dress, but something emboldened him—made him determined to charm her once more. It was as though this summer, each clifftop walk, each conversation, each kiss, had led them to this dance. To spending a few final, fleeting moments in each other's arms, quietly acknowledging all that had passed between them and all that could never be.

'Pray tell us, brother, what dance would you have us perform?' Isaac asked, as Louisa accepted his hand.

Her touch seemed to set his fingers alight, and he found himself swallowing hard, grappling with the sudden tide of emotion which threatened to overwhelm him.

Samuel grinned at him, clearly enjoying himself. 'I had thought a country dance, but in truth I am now minded towards a waltz.'

Miss Cole's eyes widened, and Samuel smiled at her with what could only be described as rakish charm. For a moment Isaac almost pitied her. She was young, and only just entering society, and he hoped that his brother was not simply suggesting the performance of such an intimate dance in order to make Miss Pearson jealous.

Although if that was his intention it seemed to be working. Miss Pearson still hovered on the periphery of the room, looking completely put out, whilst her mother's pinched face had turned white with anger. Still, he thought, conscious again of Louisa's hand resting in his, he could not concern himself with his brother's romantic entanglements—not when he had such an insurmountable one of his own. How his heart would survive waltzing with her, he did not know.

Miss Howarth began to play, and the couples took their positions in the centre of the room. He smiled warmly at Louisa, trying his best to compose himself, to calm his racing heart. Louisa, however, looked worried, casting her eyes down and chewing intently upon her bottom lip.

Isaac felt his resolve begin to waver. 'What is the matter, Louisa?' he whispered.

'I don't believe I know the steps,' she admitted with a heavy sigh. 'It has been a long time since...'

Her voice faltered, but he knew her meaning well enough.

Isaac smiled again, taking his position at her side and holding her hands in his. The last time he had danced a waltz it had been with Rosalind. How many lifetimes ago that felt now.

'Please do not worry,' he said. 'Just follow my lead and all will be well.'

Tentatively he led her through the first few marching steps before turning to face her, their eyes meeting as he took one of her hands in his, above her head, and placed his other hand upon her waist. The feeling of her form curving below his fingers took his mind back to their country walk, and his blood heated with thoughts of the embrace they'd shared the previous day.

Louisa's hand came to rest on his shoulder, and if he'd been warm before, now his flesh was searing at the temptation offered by her touch. She looked up, those brown eyes bewitching him, daring him to hold her gaze, to be this close and yet not kiss her.

They turned and turned again, melded together, fixed on each other, not caring if the room around them was empty or full, not concerned about whether everyone or no one was watching. It had been a long time since Isaac had felt so light, so uncontrolled.

'Thank you for what you said earlier,' Louisa said quietly. 'To Mrs Pearson...about our walk. What she was suggesting...it was...'

'Let us not speak of her now,' Isaac murmured.

He felt her draw closer to him. 'I just want you to know what it meant to me. You defended my honour.'

'You must know by now that I would do anything for you, Louisa,' he replied. 'You can trust me.'

She nodded, her expression heavy with thoughts he could not read. 'I know.'

'You are the most beautiful lady in this room,' he whispered. 'I wish you knew how happy being with you makes me feel.'

Her dark eyes widened a little more, and her lips parted as she searched his face in earnest. 'I think about you all the time...' she breathed. 'I confess, I do not know what to do...'

The music stopped, ending the dance, breaking the spell. Louisa stepped back, taking her hand from his and smoothing it over her skirts as she cast her eyes about—first at the other dancers, then towards her aunt. He saw at once the rapidity of her breath, the flush of colour in her cheeks. She had felt it, too. Undeniably, she had felt it.

'Louisa, I...' he began, reaching towards her.

He had to say something, and yet at that very moment words seemed to fail him.

She took another step back, wrapping her arms around herself. 'Forgive me, Sir Isaac,' she said. 'I am a little cold. I need to fetch my shawl.'

Isaac blinked at her, as though startled, his arm still suspended awkwardly in the air. She had cut him adrift once more, and there was nothing he could do but watch as she turned away from him and hurried out of the drawing room.

Chapter Twenty-Four

The rules of etiquette forced Isaac to remain with the other guests, to keep a smile fixed upon his face and pretend that nothing was amiss.

The dancing continued, and mathematics conspired with politeness to ensure that he participated. With more ladies than gentlemen present, he could hardly decline—much as he wished to. Much as he wanted to run from that room and seek out Louisa. Much as he wanted to kiss her fiercely upon the lips and ask her all over again to stay in Cumberland, to stay with him.

At length he took two turns with Miss Pearson, after the sullen young woman's mother all but shoved her daughter towards him in the aftermath of Louisa's sudden departure. Fortunately that single waltz seemed to have sated Samuel's appetite for the borderline scandalous, and the party occupied themselves with a cotillion, followed by a lively country dance.

Still Louisa did not return, and Isaac found his gaze repeatedly drifting towards the door, wondering how it could take so long to retrieve a simple shawl.

'I am sure Louisa is quite well, Sir Isaac,' Miss Pearson insisted in the end, clearly trying to recapture his attention. 'She has always struck me as very…robust.'

Isaac forced a smile, not wishing to indulge her on this subject. 'An astute observation, Miss Pearson,' he replied, immediately regretting the note of sarcasm which had crept into his voice.

Thankfully, Miss Pearson did not seem to notice. 'Still,' she continued, 'if she does not return then you will have to dance with me for a third time! But I should not wish to hear us *talked* about,' she said, with laughably feigned concern. 'I should not wish anyone to think that we have formed an *attachment*.'

Isaac suppressed the urge to roll his eyes. The young woman was as ridiculous as her mother. What his brother saw in her, he could not fathom.

'Miss Pearson,' he replied, giving her a steely look, 'I do not think that anyone could look at the two of us and believe we are attached.'

Her nostrils flared, and to his eternal shame he felt no small measure of satisfaction at having provoked her.

'I daresay it is impossible to tell who has become attached to whom from mere observation,' she said smoothly. 'My mama says people will always surprise you—that those you dismiss are often the ones who remain constant, whilst those you pursue are most likely to trifle with your heart.'

He scoffed at that. 'You mean just as you did with my brother's?'

Miss Pearson's face flushed scarlet. 'I do not know what you mean, sir.'

Mercifully, at that moment Louisa's aunt stopped playing, signalling the end of the dance. Conscious of the sudden quiet in the room, Isaac checked himself, painting an insincere grin on his face as he bowed politely at his dancing partner, who gave him a furious curtsey in return.

'I am sure you do not, Miss Pearson,' he replied. 'Now, please, excuse me.'

With a reassuring nod in Samuel's direction, Isaac walked out of the drawing room as casually and confidently as he could manage. Once out in the hall he paused, taking a lungful of cool air. It was chilly tonight, he realised, and those light, fashionable gowns women wore were no match for the northern climate, even in summer. Little wonder Louisa had felt the need of her shawl.

But that did not explain why she had stayed away for so long. The reason for that, he expected, lay in what had passed between them during that waltz. It had enraptured him, and he was still in thrall to his feelings. Goodness knew what effect that dance must have had on a woman determined to deny herself love if she'd felt even half of what he had.

He made it across the hall and up the first half-dozen steps of the staircase before his thoughts forced him to pause again. What was his intention now, exactly? He could hardly burst into her bedroom, even to ask her if she was all right.

He took a deep breath, felt his heart rattling inside his ribcage. As improper as it was, he would knock on her bedroom door and ask to speak to her. He would not go in; he could say what he wished to say in the doorway. But he had to say it. This was likely the last chance he would get.

When he reached her door he knocked tentatively, his sense of honour rendering him uncertain about his chosen course. He was Sir Isaac Liddell, a baronet and a gentleman—not the sort of rapscallion who went about summoning women from their bedchambers. His means might be questionable, but his intentions were noble, he reminded himself. Noble and tender.

'Louisa?' he said softly. 'Louisa, it's Isaac. Are you all right?'

His words were met with silence. He stood still for a moment, his ear hovering close to the door, listening for any sound coming from within. But there was nothing—no answer, no footsteps...nothing.

'Louisa?' He tried again. 'I only wish to make sure you are well. I...' He faltered, trying to decide what to do. 'I will go,' he continued after a moment, 'but I will ask Mrs Pearson to send a maid to attend you.'

With a sigh he walked away, his footsteps heavy on the floor as he headed back along the corridor and down the stairs. He felt his mood shift from concern towards frustration. If she was not in her room, then where the devil was she? And if she *was* in her room, why had she ignored him? Why would she not simply speak to him? Tonight they'd found themselves in each other's arms once again, forced to confront all that had blossomed between them this summer, and she'd chosen to run from it.

She'd run from him.

Outside the drawing room he paused, feeling suddenly unable to face the party, to disguise his misery with a smile and bury his lovelorn heart beneath layers of obligatory merrymaking. Instead he turned away, making his way down towards the Pearsons' library. He would re-join the party in a little while, but right now he needed a few moments of sanctuary in the sort of place where he could always find solace.

He wandered in and shut the door, glad to be greeted by the same scent of leather-bound books that gave him such comfort at home.

Except that wasn't all that was there to greet him.

She was sitting in a wingback chair, a shawl wrapped around her shoulders, her legs curled up beneath her. She looked up at him, her dark eyes wide, surprised and unsmiling. As though he was intruding. As though he was the last person she'd expected to see.

That makes two of us, he thought to himself.

He had not expected this at all.

'Louisa,' he said, finally finding his voice. 'What are you doing in here?'

'I could ask you the same question.'

Louisa stared at him in something of a daze. She hadn't answered his question because she did not have an answer. She still wasn't sure what had possessed her to wander in here after fetching her shawl. Despair, perhaps. Desperation. The realisation that she could not return to the party and face everyone as if nothing had happened.

As if she hadn't just danced a waltz with a man whose gaze, whose touch, whose mere presence made the earth shift beneath her feet.

'I needed a few moments of peace,' he replied, both his expression and his tone remaining sombre. 'Do you mind if I join you?'

'It's not my library, Isaac,' she replied. 'Strictly speaking, we ought to ask Mr Pearson's permission to be in here.'

Strictly speaking, she thought, they ought not to be in here together and unchaperoned at all. She did not wish to imagine what Mrs Pearson would make of it if she caught them.

She watched as Isaac removed his tailcoat and sat down opposite her with a sigh. For several moments she continued to stare at him, drinking in the sheer deliciousness of those dark features against the sharp white linen he wore. His hair, threatening disobedience as always, had begun to curl on top, and she found herself dwelling on what it would feel like to run her fingers through it.

'I don't think I could live without the peace and quiet of a library to retreat to,' he said softly, casting his eye over the Pearsons' immaculate room.

'I could not live without books,' Louisa replied. 'Without being able to escape into the worlds they contain.'

He nodded. 'Hiding away in libraries and stories is a reliable way to avoid life's difficulties,' he said, looking at her pointedly.

He knew—of course he knew. He always did. He knew her. He understood her. He deserved to know everything, whatever the consequences.

'Isaac, I...'

She got to her feet, and so did he. They moved towards each other, drawing close. Through his shirt and waistcoat she could see the rapid rise and fall of his chest and instinctively she reached out, laying a hand over his heart, feeling its furious rhythm playing against her skin. She dropped her gaze, staring at the broad, solid frame hidden so tantalisingly beneath the fine fabric of his attire. He hooked a finger under her chin, lifting her eyes to meet his. Blue—so blue. Just like the ocean.

'Isaac…' she began again, searching his gaze, struggling to find the right words.

'Stay…' he breathed. 'Do not leave Cumberland. Stay here with me.'

Even as she began to shake her head she found herself pulling him towards her, running her hands over his shoulders and around to the back of his neck, her fingers finding those curls of dark hair. She pressed her mouth against his, revelling in the firm, muscular warmth of him, feeling the heat of passion rise in her as he wrapped both his arms around her waist and pulled her closer to him.

She knew she should not kiss him—that what she was about to tell him would likely break their bond for ever. That he would never look at her in the same way again. Perhaps that was why she kissed him—to feel his closeness, to feel his affection one final time before the truth parted them for good.

'Isaac.' She tried yet again. 'I have to tell you what happened—with Richard. I have to tell you everything…'

He shook his head. 'I do not need to know,' he replied, caressing her cheek. 'It is in the past. It can make no difference to this—to us.'

'You do not know that,' she replied, stepping back from him. 'When Richard and I were together, before he returned to sea, we…' She faltered again, the words sticking in her throat. Words she could hardly bear to speak. Words she'd have to live with from the moment they fell from her lips to the end of her days.

'I am sorry that I called you a coward yesterday,'

Isaac said quietly. 'I should not have said that. And I should not have asked you to tell me everything. I understand how much pain it causes you to speak of this; I can see it. Please, do not tell me.'

He placed a tender kiss on her forehead, and despite herself, despite all her better judgement and reason, Louisa pulled herself close to him once more.

He brushed the curls back from her face as his lips found hers, softly and gently, and the earlier passion she'd felt dissolved into an overwhelming need for comfort and solace. For reassurance. For a kiss to say everything that she had not been able to put into words. For it to tell him her secrets so that she might never have to speak them…

'Well, I daresay *this* will cause a scandal.'

A shrill voice intruded, causing them both to fly apart.

Louisa felt her cheeks begin to burn, the intimacy of a moment suddenly overcome by the sting of shame. She heard Isaac cough, saw him press his fist to his mouth, as though he too was struggling to compose himself. Her eyes flew towards the door, although she already knew from the voice she'd heard who had entered and caught them together.

Her heart sank as she met that familiar cold gaze and observed the self-satisfied curl of those thin lips. There was no doubt in her mind that this discovery would be her downfall.

'I am quite shocked,' Mrs Pearson continued, in a voice which did not sound very shocked at all. 'Although, given what I know about Miss Conrad, I cannot say I am altogether surprised that she has seduced you, Sir Isaac.'

Isaac took several steps towards her. 'She has not…
What on earth can you mean, madam?'

Louisa bowed her head, feeling her heart and her
stomach descend into her feet.

Mrs Pearson knew. She knew it all.

Mrs Pearson, meanwhile, was smiling. Louisa could
not see it, but she could hear it, along with the note of
something like triumph that was ringing in her voice.

'Oh, Sir Isaac, she hasn't told you, has she?' she
continued, her tone honeyed even as her words bit like
vipers. 'Then it is fortunate that I arrived when I did.
I think there is something about Miss Conrad that you
should know.'

Chapter Twenty-Five

Isaac glared at the spiteful older woman, challenging her to do her worst. He watched as she dallied towards them both, running a carefree hand over the back of a nearby armchair, her expression haughty and disapproving. Beside him, he sensed Louisa's frozen form. He glanced at her, beholding her ashen face and staring brown eyes. It was as if all of her was suspended in dread. Mrs Pearson, meanwhile, seemed to be relishing the moment, a smile twitching at the corners of her mouth as she turned to look at him once more.

'Well?' he demanded. 'You should know, Mrs Pearson, that I care little for idle gossip.'

'Oh, this is not gossip, Sir Isaac,' she replied, her tone irritatingly silken. 'You see, I have learned the truth about Miss Conrad from a very good authority on the matter.' She looked at Louisa, clicking her tongue disapprovingly. 'And to think, when she first arrived in Lowhaven I thought she would be an improving influence upon my dear Charlotte...'

He saw how Louisa visibly shuddered, and instinctively he reached for her hand. His heart sank as she drew herself away from him, retrieving her shawl, which had earlier fallen from her shoulders, and replacing it around her even tighter than before.

'I presume Mrs Gossamer did not spare any detail in her letter?' Louisa spoke quietly, her voice suddenly hoarse.

Mrs Pearson chuckled at that, which only served to rankle Isaac further. He frowned, his thoughts racing as he tried to make sense of what was unfolding.

He recalled Mrs Pearson's talk of an acquaintance she shared with Louisa, to whom she wrote. Her name was Gossamer, wasn't it? He thought about that dinner, and how perturbed Louisa had seemed when Mrs Pearson had raised the subject. At the time he found it strange. Now he was beginning to realise there had been an undertone to her words, a threat contained within them which he had not understood.

'Who is this Mrs Gossamer and why should I give a single damn what she says?' he asked, anger flashing through him now. Anger at Mrs Pearson—at her intrusion, her taunts.

At length, it was Louisa who answered him. 'Mrs Gossamer is…was Richard's aunt,' she whispered, venturing to look at him. 'You might recall that when I talked of him I told you that we'd met while he was staying with his relatives? Their family name is Gossamer.'

He nodded, holding her gaze, pained to observe how broken she looked. She had said that. He searched her dark eyes, as though he might be able to find answers in their depths. Mrs Pearson knew Richard's aunt—why was that significant? What on earth could the correspondence of two women contain that would leave Louisa looking so defeated?

Mrs Pearson, meanwhile, was not to be discouraged. 'Ah, but it seems to me, Miss Conrad, that you have not told Sir Isaac all that you ought to have told him about your dalliance with that young captain.'

'It was no dalliance, Mrs Pearson,' Louisa bit back. 'Had life dealt us a kinder hand he would still be here and we would be wed.'

'Life is cruel, to be sure,' Mrs Pearson answered her, just as sharply. 'Although a young woman can do much to protect herself against its evils if she is of good moral character. If she is not prone to wanton behaviour.'

Incensed, Isaac stepped forward. 'Mrs Pearson, I hope you are not suggesting…'

'Indeed, I am, Sir Isaac,' the woman spat. 'Imagine my horror to learn from a dear old friend that her poor dead nephew's memory has been sullied by his association with this strumpet! To this day, she remains so appalled by what was said that she could barely bring herself to write the details to me. Were it not for the duty she felt, to warn me against any association with such company, I doubt she would ever have mentioned any of it. To lose such a dearly beloved young man to war is bad enough, but then to hear society whispering about him leaving a woman behind, unwed and with child, is simply unthinkable.'

'A woman?' Isaac repeated. 'You cannot mean…?'

He turned to Louisa, searching her expression for something—he did not know what. A denial, perhaps? An explanation? Had he any right to ask for either? The colour had returned to her face now, and a hot fury was gathering in her cheeks to match the indignant look with which her eyes beheld Mrs Pearson.

The older woman, meanwhile, continued her dramatic remonstrations.

'Have you no shame, Miss Conrad?' she asked, her arms wildly outstretched. 'Have you no sympathy for the pain already borne by his grieving family?'

'I understand their pain well enough, Mrs Pearson,' she replied, her voice low but steady. 'Their loss was also mine. As for shame—I cannot own the portion you would give me, since I am not guilty of all that you have accused me of.'

'So, you were *not* with child?' Mrs Pearson rounded on her. 'You did *not* accuse that young man of going to war and leaving you in such a condition?'

For the longest moment Louisa just stood there, not answering, not even looking at her accuser but staring beyond her, her brown eyes eerily vacant and unmoved.

Isaac watched her intently, awaiting and dreading her answer in turn. So much made sense now—so much of what she had said to him over these past weeks and so much of what she'd left unspoken. Yet at the same time there was much still to be untangled—a good deal of rumour and insinuation which needed to be separated from the truth. Louisa's truth. The only truth, frankly, that he cared to hear.

'Louisa…' he prompted her gently.

Her eyes snapped back to Mrs Pearson then, but where that affronted expression had previously been, Isaac now saw only sadness.

'I was with child,' she replied, her voice trembling as her tears began to fall. 'Richard's child. The child did not live.'

Instinctively Isaac moved towards her, overwhelmed by the desire to comfort her, to wrap her in his arms and to never let her go. To make her understand just how profoundly he understood her sense of loss. To tell her just how little the opinions of society and its preoccupation with so-called scandal mattered to him.

But Louisa simply shook her head and stepped away. 'Now you see why I can never marry,' she sobbed, rushing past Mrs Pearson towards the door. 'Please forgive me. I should not be here.'

Then she left the library, leaving unanswered questions hanging in the air and, he realised, her dancing shoes abandoned on the rug.

She never allowed herself to think of the child. For these past years she'd made Richard the sole focus of her grief—a grief she'd worn like a shroud, owning it as a justification for her melancholy, her insistence upon solitude and her complete withdrawal from society.

She'd loved and lost, it was true, but she had not permitted herself to count those losses or to acknowledge the depth of them.

As she ran up the stairs and into her bedchamber it struck her that tonight was the first time she'd spoken of the child since he'd slipped from her body, limp and small, his tiny lungs not yet ready for breath.

Her child.

Her son.

Pressing herself against the door, she wept as she thought of the words that had been placed alongside him. Dalliance...wanton behaviour...strumpet. Shame. She had felt shame—shame for being swept away by passion, for her secret being discovered despite her efforts to conceal it. For all the things Berkshire society had said about her—some true, but most not. For not having the good sense to marry the man she had loved before taking him to her bed.

But she had not felt ashamed of the child. As she'd brought him into the world and watched him pass straight on to the next she'd felt overwhelming guilt and the deepest sorrow, but never shame. Perhaps that was why she could never bring herself to think of him. Because confronting that pain was hard enough without being reminded of what she was expected to feel but could not.

Feeling suddenly weak, she let her weight drop to the ground, slumping down on the cold, hard wooden floor. Isaac had known how she felt; she had seen it in his face—seen his own pain breaking through as he'd placed it next to hers. They'd long since realised that they shared an understanding; now they both knew just how deep it ran.

Except Isaac's was an acceptable sort of loss. Hers was not.

Not that any of it mattered now, of course. Isaac knew the truth about her, and whatever his feelings were for her he knew, just as she did, that any association between them was at an end. Cumberland, it seemed, had not been far enough away for her to outrun the past. It had got her in its grip once again. She could feel its pull, dragging her back to Berkshire, to loneliness and isolation, to daily reminders of all that had been and all that was gone.

It was time to go home.

Taking a deep, shuddery breath, Louisa forced herself off the floor and hauled herself to her feet. She glanced down at her flimsy gown in irritation, suppressing the memories it provoked—memories of tonight, of dancing, of Isaac holding her in his arms as they twirled.

Such dresses were no good to her now. She would have to change into some warmer clothes and put on some boots, since she realised now that she had nothing on her feet. Furiously, she pulled off her evening clothes and dressed herself in the plainest day dress she could find, along with the largest bonnet, the thickest shawl and the single pair of boots she'd brought.

Thank goodness Nan had had the good sense to include some items suitable for long country walks in her portmanteau. Her heart lurched as she thought of her loyal maid back in Lowhaven, blissfully unaware of her mistress's imminent departure as she retired for the night. How worried she would be when she learned of it. How worried Aunt Clarissa would be, too.

She hurried over to the little desk in the corner of the room, scribbling a brief note to her aunt. She would leave it on the hall table, just before she departed.

Louisa adjusted her bonnet and wiped her watering eyes, steeling herself. She retrieved her reticule, tucking the note she'd written into it and hoping that the money she'd brought with her to Langdale would be sufficient for her journey home. Not that there would be any coaches going south at this time of the night; she would have to wait until morning for that.

In the meantime she would have to find somewhere to hide—somewhere that no one would find her. Somewhere that Isaac would not find her. Quietly, she slipped out of the bedchamber, every step accompanied by a silent prayer that the solid floors of Langdale Hall would not betray her as she made her bid to find sanctuary and thereafter to get away unseen.

* * *

Isaac didn't know how long he'd been staring at those dancing slippers. Long after Mrs Pearson had departed, with a brisk nod and a muttered goodnight, he found himself still fixated upon them, as though a simple pair of shoes might hold the answer to what on earth had happened that evening.

Merely an hour or two ago he'd held that beautiful, beloved woman in his arms, losing himself in her gaze as they waltzed together. In the library he'd asked her to stay, he'd embraced her and told her that the past did not matter. But then Mrs Pearson had intruded, and she'd brought it all crashing down with her stories and her gossip.

How that dreadful woman had crowed over Louisa… how determined she had been to bring her low. Well, he told himself now, he was just as determined that she would not succeed. He cared nothing for scandals, for reputations. The only part of that sorry tale to affect him had been learning about all that Louisa had lost. He did not wish to condemn her, only to console her.

Only to love her.

That thought made his breath catch in his throat, but it was true. What he felt for her had ventured far beyond the friendship they'd begun earlier that summer. He loved her. He understood that now.

He picked the slippers up, holding them tightly in his hands as he hurried out of the library and up the stairs towards the bedrooms. He would go to Louisa and he would declare himself to her.

It had been a little while since she had left the library. He could only hope that sufficient time had passed for her to calm herself, that they might talk candidly now that they'd been freed from Mrs Pearson's poisonous presence.

He needed her to know that what he'd said was true—there was nothing in her past that could change his feelings towards her. If anything, knowing about her past had only served to deepen his affections. She had borne terrible losses and had been greeted not with the sympathy she deserved but with callousness and censure from those in society.

He understood now that she'd been all but forced into a life of solitude, robbed of the right to properly grieve as a widow and a bereft mother otherwise might. Her past was not a scandal; it was a tragedy.

'Louisa?' he said, knocking loudly on the door. 'Louisa, please—I need to speak to you.'

He waited for several moments but received no reply. Tentatively he placed his hand on the doorknob, in a quandary about what to do next. He ached to be with her, to speak to her, but bursting into her bedchamber was hardly the right or proper thing to do.

He listened at the door, trying to detect the smallest movement, the subtlest sound. He felt sure she must be in there. After all that had unfolded in the library, he could not imagine she had returned to the party. Perhaps, he reasoned, she'd been so exhausted and overwrought that she'd simply fallen asleep. Or perhaps she just could not bring herself to face him right now.

Either way, he decided he ought not to intrude. He let go of the doorknob, resolving to leave her in peace. He would speak to her in the morning. He would hope that in the light of a new day she would be able to see that all would be well. That his intentions and his affections remained steady and unchanged.

'Goodnight, Louisa,' he said softly. 'I will see you tomorrow. I want you to know that this changes nothing when it comes to how I feel about you.'

Isaac withdrew and walked towards his own bedchamber, his head swimming with the evening's events and his heart still yearning for her to change her mind and open her door to him. To see her face, to feel her embrace. To hear, at the very least, a 'goodnight' in reply.

Chapter Twenty-Six

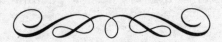

Louisa slumped down against the wall of an old stone hut, listening to the wood pigeons as they cooed on the roof. She groaned, clutching her ankle as it throbbed painfully in her boot and chastising herself for not being more careful. She'd been sore enough already as it was, her legs aching after hours on her feet, and her back and neck stiff from spending the night in the cramped linen cupboard she'd found at Langdale Hall.

Not that she'd slept, she reminded herself. Indeed, each time she'd closed her eyes she'd revisited that scene in the Pearsons' library, from the condemnation in Mrs Pearson's words as she'd revealed Louisa's scandalous past to the sympathy and sadness Louisa had seen in Isaac's eyes.

In the early morning she'd crept out of the cupboard and then out of the house, leaving the note addressed to Aunt Clarissa on the hall table, before making her way to the stables. There she'd asked a bleary-eyed young groom for directions to the nearest coaching inn from which she might begin her long journey south. A look of confusion had flashed momentarily across his face, but he had imparted the necessary instructions, which had seemed straightforward enough.

In practice, however, she'd quickly lost her way, the seemingly endless woodland and lack of discernible landmarks leaving her disorientated. The burning heat of panic had begun to rise in her chest, clouding her thoughts, and moments ago she'd stumbled over a tree root, painfully twisting her ankle and falling to the ground with a thud.

Now she was filthy, and she was injured. She needed rest, but there was no time for that. She knew she had to carry on. It was either that, she realised, or return to Langdale Hall.

Going back, she knew, was not an option.

Wearily she hauled herself upright, gritting her teeth as she forced the injured leg to bear her weight. Tears pricked in the corners of her eyes as the overwhelming desire to escape which had driven her all morning began to give way to the harsh reality of the situation she faced. She had no idea where she was, or how far it was to the nearest inn, or indeed if she was heading in the right direction at all. She had some money, but no food or drink to sustain her. She had to find her way, and soon, otherwise she really would be in peril.

'Stop it,' she muttered to herself. 'Fretting will do no good at all.'

She swiped a hand across her watering eyes and forced her mind to focus. She had to get out of the woodland and on to a road—preferably one with inns and coaches, with other travellers and people who could tell her where she was. There was nothing else she could do; there were no other options. She had to keep going.

With renewed determination she began to limp along,

biting her lip at the pain which pulsed through her ankle. At least the day was fine and bright, with the sun streaming through the gaps in the trees. She inhaled deeply, filling her lungs with the crisp air as she forced herself to keep moving forward. Around her the pigeons sang their farewell, and although she was tired and sore she gave them a watery smile.

She would find the road, she told herself. She had to. Her life, as bleak and lonely as it was condemned to be, likely depended upon it.

'I've asked the groom to ready the horses. She cannot have got very far.'

Samuel's insistent words cut across the silent room. Isaac dragged his hands down his face, the shock of her sudden disappearance giving way to his sheer horror at the thought of her out in the countryside alone.

A myriad of thoughts raced through his mind. If only he had gone to her last night... If only he'd decided to walk into her bedchamber and offered his reassurance and his heart... If only he had not waited until morning to speak to her... If only he had not risen later than usual, after a fitful night's sleep...

Then he might have discovered her disappearance sooner. If only he'd been more impulsive and less gentlemanly, he might have been able to prevent her from fleeing at all.

'The young groom said that Miss Conrad approached him early this morning and asked where she could find the nearest coaching inn,' Samuel continued. 'However, she did not give him any indication as to where she might wish to travel from there.'

'And this groom did not think it odd? A lady like Miss

Conrad leaving Langdale alone shortly after dawn?'
Isaac snapped.

'He's a boy, Isaac,' Samuel replied. 'He was hardly
going to be disobliging.'

'You're right…forgive me,' Isaac said, rubbing his
forehead.

In truth, he did not know what to do with himself.
He could do nothing until he knew Louisa was safe and
well. Until he had her back here, with him.

'At least we know which coaching inn she is heading for,' Samuel continued. 'We also know that she is
on foot. On horseback, we should be able to catch up
with her.'

'Unless she reaches the inn before that and catches
a coach,' Isaac replied. 'If that is the case we will have
no idea where she is going.'

'I think I know.'

Louisa's aunt walked into the parlour, her lined face
drawn, her eyes red and swollen with tears. She had
been the one to discover Louisa's disappearance, having gone into Louisa's bedchamber after knocking and
receiving no reply. She had not stopped weeping since.

Miss Howarth held up a letter. 'One of the servants
just found this in the hall. It is from Louisa, and addressed to me. She thanks me for welcoming her into my
home, but says that she must return to Berkshire now,
and that…' The older woman paused, pressing her handkerchief against her mouth as she fought to suppress her
sobs. 'She says that now everything about her is known,
regrettably her time in Cumberland is at an end.'

'Please try not to fret, Miss Howarth,' Samuel said,
doing his utmost to comfort her. 'We will find her safe
and well, I'm sure of it.'

'She seemed troubled last night,' Louisa's aunt continued between sobs. 'I should have gone after her when she left the dancing. I should have spoken to her last night instead of waiting until this morning. I should have known, after all she's endured these past years...' She looked up at Isaac. 'This is my fault, sir. I suggested that it might be better if you knew all about her. I never imagined—' Her voice broke, her words faltering once again.

Isaac regarded her grimly. Such a remark, so laden with meaning, left him in little doubt that Miss Howarth knew the whole story of her niece's past. He drew a deep breath, knowing he had to say something. That he had to try to explain.

'Samuel, perhaps you could check on the horses,' he suggested, knowing that speaking with Miss Howarth about something so delicate could only conceivably be undertaken in private.

His brother gave him a look of surprise, but quickly caught on. 'Ah—yes, of course,' he acquiesced.

Isaac gave his brother a grateful nod as he left and closed the door behind him, before he turned back to Miss Howarth, who dabbed her eyes with her handkerchief.

'I know how profoundly your niece has suffered, Miss Howarth,' he began, speaking quietly. 'I know all of it. But I can assure you...'

'So that is why she has run away, then,' she sobbed, interrupting him. 'Oh, my poor Louisa! She never speaks of the baby, you know. Never. Telling you would have taken a deal of strength, and clearly she cannot bear it. Oh, my dear girl...'

Isaac's heart lurched at her assumption that Louisa

had confided in him. How he wished that she had. How he wished that he'd let her. How he wished that he'd heard the story in her own words, rather than from Mrs Pearson's venomous tongue.

He decided that he wouldn't tell Miss Howarth about Mrs Pearson's involvement in its revelation—at least not yet. Knowing about that right now would only cause her more grief.

'What a frightful journey for her to attempt…on the stagecoach alone!' Miss Howarth continued. 'Think of it—a young woman, unchaperoned, wandering about the inns…'

Isaac could not decipher the rest, since Miss Howarth had buried her face in her handkerchief, her words muffled then eventually overtaken entirely by a set of deep, racking sobs.

'I promise you, Miss Howarth, I will do all that I can to find your niece.' He spoke gently, in an effort to calm her. 'Please do not blame yourself. You must know that I care for her a great deal, and what I know now does not alter that. I will ride all the way to Berkshire for her, if necessary.'

The older woman nodded, composing herself as she attempted a watery smile. 'I believe you will, sir.'

A knock at the door startled them both, and before Isaac could answer it Samuel burst in. 'Sorry to disturb you, but I thought you'd want to know that the horses are ready.'

Isaac gave his brother a brisk nod, walking closer to where he stood in the doorway. 'We should leave immediately and go directly to the inn,' he said.

'Assuming she has found her way to the inn,' Samuel added. 'She cannot know this country well, given that she has been here for such a short time. She might just as easily be lost.'

'And if that is the case I will search every inch of Cumberland,' Isaac replied, rubbing his face with his hands.

He needed to wash, having had time only to change for riding. Alas, that was something else which would have to wait.

'I have to try everything, Samuel. I will not rest until I find her.'

His brother rested a sympathetic hand on his shoulder. 'I know,' he said.

Isaac sighed, glancing over his shoulder at Louisa's aunt. 'Before we leave, perhaps you could ask someone to come and sit with Miss Howarth.'

He sighed heavily, considering the options. The Coles and Suttons lived nearby and had left late last night in their carriages, before Louisa had disappeared. The Pearsons, meanwhile, had apparently not risen yet. Not that Isaac wanted to see any of them right now.

'Fetch a maid, perhaps,' he suggested, 'and ask her to bring some tea.'

Samuel nodded. 'I'm surprised Mrs Pearson has not been down to console Miss Howarth,' he mused. 'Where *are* the Pearsons, anyway? I have not seen any of them since last night.'

Isaac suppressed a growl at the mention of that family. He could not wait to be many miles from them—but he had to find Louisa first.

'Making themselves scarce, I hope,' Isaac replied. 'Mrs Pearson in particular.'

'Oh?' Samuel stared expectantly at his brother, frowning.

Isaac's gaze shifted briefly to Miss Howarth, who had begun to weep all over again. 'I will explain all while we ride,' he replied, his tone hushed. 'But believe me when I say that I wish never to lay my eyes upon that woman again.'

'I'm not sure which part of this I find most shocking,' Samuel remarked as they rode on to the turnpike road, having been apprised of all that had been revealed last night. 'That the sensible and serious Miss Conrad has a scandalous past, or that Mrs Pearson has the capacity for such ill behaviour. And to think I'd been considering pressing my suit with her daughter just days ago.'

'Indeed,' Isaac grunted, cantering alongside him. 'I'd say you had a lucky escape, brother.'

'I could say the same for you, Isaac, if all that Mrs Pearson has said is true. Miss Conrad has done you a good turn by refusing your affections.'

Isaac looked at his brother sharply. 'My feelings are unchanged, Samuel, and I intend to tell her so once we find her,' he said. 'Indeed, I wish to marry her if she will have me.'

Samuel looked aghast. 'But there will surely be a scandal. It does not sound as though Mrs Pearson can be relied upon to keep her own counsel on the subject. The news of Miss Conrad's disgrace will be the talk of Lowhaven soon enough.'

'What disgrace, Samuel? I should think it a terrible misfortune, not a disgrace, to lose the one you love to war.'

'But she was with child and unwed. You are no fool, Isaac. You understand how society views these things.'

'I knew Rosalind before we were wed,' Isaac said,

shooting him a meaningful look. 'If Rosalind had ended up with child, and I had died before the wedding could take place, she would have been left in the same situation. It is rank hypocrisy from so many among our society to condemn others for falling foul of risks that they themselves have often taken. And I would wager that you, brother, are no innocent, but are as yet unwed. Which means that...'

'Yes, all right, your point has been well made,' Samuel interrupted, screwing up his face in discomfort. Then he shook his head, smiling at Isaac in disbelief. 'You really have fallen for Miss Conrad, haven't you?'

Isaac looked straight ahead, not meeting his eye. 'I believe that I love her, Samuel. And I believe that she loves me, too.'

'Then you have my blessing. Not that you need it, of course.'

Isaac glanced at him then, offering a small smile. 'Thank you. I might not need it, but I do value it, brother.'

'Now, let's find this woman you wish to wed,' Samuel declared. 'We are not so far from the inn now, and look—there is a mail coach stopped ahead. We will ask the driver and guard if they've seen a woman walking along here.'

Before Isaac could say anything Samuel galloped ahead. Inwardly Isaac groaned. Its requirement for speed and efficiency meant that the postal service never took kindly to any imposition on its time. And if they were stopped here, and not at an inn, that meant they were already delayed. He was not keen to provoke an irritable guard, armed with pistols and a blunderbuss.

By the time he caught up with Samuel he saw that

his brother was already in conversation with the driver, an older man with a keen stare and a roughly shaven face. The red-coated guard, meanwhile, watched warily from his perch at the back.

'Thank you for your offer of assistance, sir,' the driver was saying. 'But we are about to be on our way. We hit some tree branches on the road a little further back; they got caught in the wheels and one of the horses seemed spooked. You can't be too careful.'

'Quite right,' Samuel agreed enthusiastically, effortlessly deploying that easy manner of his. 'Before you go, I wonder if you might have seen a young woman walking along this road? She has a very handsome face, brown eyes and fair hair. She might have seemed a little…distressed.'

The driver raised an eyebrow. 'I see, sir. Well, I daresay the course of true love never did run smooth for any of us.'

'It is not like that,' Isaac interjected, feeling suddenly defensive, although he wasn't sure why. 'The woman has had some bad news regarding a relative who lives some distance away,' he explained, the lie falling easily from his tongue. 'We fear she may try to catch a coach going south, and are gravely concerned about her making such a journey alone.'

'I see, sir,' the driver said again, although he looked far from convinced. 'Well, I'm afraid we haven't seen such a woman on the road.'

He inclined his head politely and began to ready his reins.

'There was that young lady at the last inn, John,' the guard reminded the driver. 'She looked much like the woman the gentleman has described.'

The driver nodded. 'Oh, aye—in a bit of a state, she was. Her dress looked all muddy and she was walking with a limp. She approached me just as we were leaving; she must have seen we'd nought but the mail on board and thought she'd try her luck. This last leg of our route can be quiet, as a lot of passengers leave us at Penrith. Anyway, she seemed tearful when I told her we were bound for Lowhaven.'

Isaac and Samuel exchanged a look, half hopeful, half fretful. If this woman was indeed Louisa, then she had already reached the inn. It also sounded as though she was injured.

Isaac felt his stomach lurch, a potent mix of anxiety and desperation gnawing at him. The need to find her was more pressing than ever.

'Thank you both,' Samuel said with an obliging nod. 'I think we will ride to the inn and make some enquiries.'

The driver began to ready his horses once more. 'You'd best make haste if you wish to find her there, sir. Many coaches pass through in the morning. She's bound to find a seat on one of them.'

Isaac did not need urging twice. With a brisk word of thanks he was off at a gallop, his brother speeding to catch him. Coaches be damned, he thought to himself. Let them all be filled. Let her be still stranded at the inn.

Quietly he appealed to his maker, casting out something like a prayer as his horse's hooves frantically churned dust on the road beneath. He hadn't prayed in a long time, but he would do so now. He prayed for Louisa, and for her safe return to Langdale Hall.

For her safe return to him.

Chapter Twenty-Seven

Louisa sat alone in the lowly kitchen, picking at an unappetising meal of stale bread and cheese, accompanied by a sour-tasting watery beer. Moments ago the room had been a flurry of activity, with half a dozen travellers hurriedly helping themselves to the refreshments on offer while their stagecoaches changed horses outside.

All scruffily dressed and smelling ripe, they'd eyed her suspiciously as they'd shovelled bread and beer into their mouths before departing to take their seats once more—no doubt the cheapest ones, outside and atop the coach, exposed to all the elements.

Seats Louisa would have never contemplated occupying, until today.

Now she would take any seat, any means, to get where she wanted to go.

Upon arriving at the inn she'd received a hostile reception; travellers on foot, it seemed, were not particularly welcome. The portly, rosy-cheeked landlord had glared at her before pointing her wordlessly in the direction of a woman whom Louisa presumed to be his wife, a short and no less rotund individual, whose manner had been equally inhospitable. She'd pursed her lips as she'd looked Louisa up and down, no doubt noting the filthy fabric of her skirt.

Louisa had tried to enquire about coaches travelling south, but the woman had brushed her questions away with a brisk shake of her mob-capped head.

'You'll need to get to Penrith for that,' she'd said, her voice thick with the local accent. 'Penrith coaches do come through here, but you'll be lucky to get a seat on one.'

The woman had been right about that. After an hour or more of trying, Louisa had not managed to find a seat on any of the coaches travelling in the right direction. In the end, feeling faint with hunger and exhaustion, she had tearfully admitted defeat and approached the woman again, this time to ask if there was any possibility of a drink and a warm meal.

'There's the parlour,' she'd said, raising her eyebrows as she regarded her dirty clothing once again. 'Or there's bread and beer in the small kitchen, which you might prefer.'

Not wishing to make a spectacle of herself in the parlour, and conscious that she needed to keep most of her money for coach fares, Louisa had settled upon the cheaper option. The woman had directed her to this cramped, untidy room at the rear of the inn, and it was here that Louisa had sat ever since, forcing herself to eat the unappealing fare and trying to gather her strength for the long walk ahead. If she could not get a coach to Penrith, then she would have to get there on foot.

She shuddered, pulling her shawl tighter around her shoulders as she considered what lay ahead of her. Getting herself this far had been a trial. Her ankle had worsened, growing more painful and swollen with each mile, and conspiring with her growing fatigue to hinder her progress as she limped along. She wasn't sure how she was going to face more hours on her feet, enduring pain and lacking both sleep and proper sustenance. She did not even know if she would reach her destination before dark, or where she would rest if she did not.

'What is the alternative, Louisa?' she muttered to herself, shredding the dried bread with her fingers. 'You can hardly go back—not now.'

A tear slipped down her cheek as for a moment—the briefest moment—she allowed herself to despair. Last night, her life had seemed to unravel at such an overwhelming pace that she'd felt she had no other option but to flee. Yet her flight had not lightened her load; instead, it had only added further difficulties, which seemed to multiply and mount up by the hour. Running away, it turned out, had been no answer. It was self-destruction, plain and simple.

She wiped her eyes as a young maid flew in through the door, her small hands laden with dirty bowls which she dumped unceremoniously on the table in front of her. Servants had been to-ing and fro-ing like this ever since she'd been there, using this small area to abandon the used crockery that they had presumably collected from the parlour.

This maid, however, did not leave immediately; she lingered, her pretty emerald eyes regarding Louisa curiously for a moment. Normally Louisa would have found this impertinent, but she had no energy for such feelings today. Instead, she offered the maid a small smile, then filled the silence with another sip of the flavourless beer.

'Is your name Louisa?' the maid asked after a moment.

'Y-yes,' Louisa stammered, taken aback at being so bluntly addressed. 'Why?'

'There's a fine-looking gentleman in the parlour asking about a young woman called Louisa something-or-other. The description he gave sounded like it might be you.'

Louisa felt her heart descend to the pit of her stomach. It was Isaac—it had to be. She ought to have realised he would come looking for her. Ought to have considered that, whatever he thought of her now, her sudden disappearance would grieve him.

'Oh,' she replied. 'And what did you say?'

'Nothing,' the maid scoffed. 'He didn't ask me—he asked Mrs Sym. She's keeping tight-lipped, of course. Doesn't like to get involved with runaways. We get a lot of that here, what with being close to the border. Mind you, if he offers her a few coins that'll likely loosen her tongue,' she added. 'Anyway, miss, you might want to slip out of here now—if you don't wish to see him, that is.'

Louisa nodded her thanks, but didn't move from the hard wooden stool upon which she was perched. She sipped her beer again, her heart still racing but her mind strangely blank. She was tired, and she was injured, and at that moment she realised that she had neither the will nor the energy to carry on.

The young maid regarded her carefully, her freckled face screwed up in confusion. 'Or perhaps you do wish to see him, after all?' she asked.

Louisa felt the heat of tears prickling in her eyes as she considered the question. 'Yes,' she whispered finally. 'But I cannot. It is better this way.'

The maid's brow furrowed deeper. 'With all due respect, miss, I don't see how moping in here is better than going out there to talk to him. If it makes any difference, the gentleman looks as miserable as you. Worried, too. I'll bet he's travelled miles, trying to find you. If I had a gentleman like that looking for me, I wouldn't be staying put in Mrs Sym's kitchen for a moment longer, that's for certain.'

Her spirited tone made Louisa smile. 'So, if you were me you'd go and see him?' she ventured to ask.

The maid grinned. 'I'd do more than see him. I would marry him and go to live in whatever grand house he's come from. Then I wouldn't have to work all hours in this place and give most of my pay over to my father just so he can spend it on ale. That's what I would do.'

Louisa sighed. 'I ought to have spoken to him last night, instead of running away from him. I was just so overwhelmed, and I got it into my mind that it would be best if I left.' She tugged at her skirt. 'Now look at me—all I've managed to do so far is injure myself, be a nuisance to every coach driver I've encountered today, and no doubt upset everyone who has ever loved me.'

'The gentleman must care very much about you,' said the maid thoughtfully. 'Whatever has happened, is it really so terrible that you must run away?'

Louisa grimaced, thoughts of last night's revelations flooding unbidden into her mind. 'Yes, it was terrible,' she replied, slowly getting up from her seat. 'However, I don't think I am running any more.'

'Are you going to see him, then?' the maid asked, raising an eyebrow. 'If you are, you'd best hurry.'

Louisa nodded, suppressing a groan at the pain that shot through her ankle as she began to walk. 'Thank you,' she said. 'If it wasn't for you I'd have never known that he was here.'

The maid shrugged. 'I just thought you had a right to know. That way, you could decide what you wanted to do about it.'

'I'm still not sure I have decided,' Louisa replied. 'I just know that I need to talk to him.'

'Then you *have* decided, in a way,' the maid answered her. 'Now, go on, miss—go and find him. But take care with that leg; you've turned very pale all of a sudden.'

Louisa smiled at her, her head feeling suddenly light as pain, nerves and anticipation potently mingled. Mustering the very last vestiges of her strength, she limped out of the room, trying to ignore the way the ground swayed beneath her feet and the world swam before her eyes.

Isaac made his way back across the courtyard to where Samuel was patiently waiting with the horses. Frustrated, he kicked at the dusty ground, cursing aloud and causing a couple of young grooms lingering nearby to cast him wary looks. The innkeeper's wife had been rude and evasive, and had all but refused to answer his questions.

'It's a busy place,' she'd kept telling him. There was no way to account for who passed through or when they might have been there.

Her unwillingness to look him in the eye had told him that she was lying, but there was precious little he could do in the face of such obfuscation.

'Did you not offer her a few coins for her trouble?' Samuel asked, when Isaac informed him that he'd failed to discover anything. 'Everything has a price in these establishments—even information. She might have been a bit more forthcoming with a shilling or two in her pocket.'

'No. I hadn't thought of that,' Isaac replied, putting his head in his hands. 'Perhaps I should have sent you in there instead, brother, for it seems I am truly hopeless. Louisa could be anywhere by now. What am I going to say to her aunt? To her family?'

To his surprise, a slow smile spread across Samuel's face as he looked over Isaac's shoulder. 'You can tell them that you've found her. Look.'

Isaac spun round, his heart leaping into his throat as he laid his eyes upon the slight young woman limping towards him. For a moment he did not believe it could be the same lady he'd waltzed with just a day earlier, such was the extent of her transformation. Her bonnet looked to be damaged, and some of her fair curls had escaped from it and come to rest on her shoulders, which were adorned with a filthy shawl. Her dress was in an equally ill condition, and as she drew closer he saw that her pale face seemed almost grey, with pronounced dark circles beneath her brown eyes. She looked up at him, attempting a smile, but managing only a grimace.

'Good God, Louisa,' he said, darting towards her. 'What has happened to you?'

Without thinking he wrapped a supportive arm around her. She looked fragile enough that one gust of wind might blow her away.

'Please don't fret. I am quite well,' she said, but her voice contained an odd, strained note which told him that she was anything but fine. 'When I heard you were here I realised I must see you. I needed to tell you I am sorry…'

Isaac gathered her into his arms. 'No, *I* am sorry. Sorry for what happened last night. Sorry for everything that has happened to you. Sorry that you felt you had no choice but to leave Langdale. To leave me.'

Her lip trembled. 'I should not have run away. I should have spoken to you and…' She paused, a pained look flickering across her face as she leaned against him, grabbing hold of his coat and clinging on for dear life. 'I am sorry. My ankle…it's…'

She did not have to say another word. Without a moment's hesitation Isaac lifted her up, taking her into his arms and striding towards the inn. He carried her through the door and into the parlour, where a dozen or so gawping genteel faces awaited, with their wine glasses and their steaming bowls of soup.

He cared nothing for their whispers, nor their judgement. Propriety be damned, he thought. Society be damned. Society had brought Louisa nothing but condemnation and misery. It had left her feeling as though she deserved no happiness…as though she had no good choices left to make. If this was what society and its rules would do to a woman, then he wanted no part in it.

'Your best room, man—now!' Isaac bellowed to the ruby-faced innkeeper. 'With fresh sheets and a fire lit. And send for a physician immediately. Tell him that Sir Isaac Liddell of Hayton Hall requires his assistance. This lady is injured.'

'You're making a scene,' Louisa said quietly. 'You'll be the talk of Cumberland.'

He gave her a tender smile. 'Then so be it. Let them gossip. I care nothing for it as long as you are by my side.'

She searched his gaze, her brown eyes seeming to

darken further. 'You cannot mean that. Not now. Not after learning the truth about me.'

'I mean it more than ever,' he replied, as the inn-keeper beckoned them into a large and comfortable room. 'Indeed, Louisa Conrad,' he added, smiling at her once more, 'I mean to marry you, if you will have me.'

Chapter Twenty-Eight

He wanted to marry her.

As the young maid she'd met in the kitchen had fussed around her, and a physician had arrived to tend to her, Louisa had turned Isaac's words over and over in her mind. He cared nothing for gossip. He wanted her by his side.

He wanted to marry her.

She'd been unable to answer him at the time, such had been her shock at his declaration, and as propriety had required him to leave the room once the maid had come to help her remove her filthy dress and get into bed, he'd not had the opportunity to say anything further. Now, as the physician finished bandaging her ankle, she found herself wondering where he was. Wondering when she would be able to speak to him again and say all the things she knew needed to be said.

'It will heal,' the physician said brusquely, inclining his head towards her foot. 'With a few days of rest and a good deal of care there should be no lasting damage.'

Louisa offered him a meek smile and a nod of thanks before the maid escorted him to the door. The room she'd been given was comfortable and warm, with a low fire burning in the grate and the curtains drawn against the world outside. She sank back against the crisp bedlinen, trying to rest as she'd been instructed, but finding she could not relax.

Her mind raced, her thoughts scattering like leaves in the wind. He knew every detail of her scandalous past, and yet he wished to marry her. She'd run away from him like a reckless coward, and yet he wished to marry her. How was this possible?

A knock at the door startled her, and the maid flashed her a knowing smile. 'That'll be your gentleman, I expect.'

'He's not my gentleman,' Louisa said, sitting herself upright.

'He most certainly is,' the maid insisted. 'I'll let him in, shall I?'

Louisa nodded her agreement.

Inexplicably, she held her breath as the door creaked open and she caught sight of those familiar blue eyes, that dark, dishevelled hair with a will of its own. He was, without doubt, the most handsome man she knew. He was kind, and loving, and decent. And he wanted to marry her.

'Come in, sir,' the maid said. She gave Louisa another knowing look. 'I do believe Mrs Sym is looking for me, so I shall leave you both in peace.'

Hurriedly the maid departed, pulling the door shut behind her. For several moments neither of them spoke. Isaac busied himself by fetching a chair from the corner of the room and bringing it to her bedside. Louisa, meanwhile, found herself watching him, her eyes lazily wandering over his tall frame, over his broad shoulders.

He had removed his coat and wore only a shirt which had been rendered off-white, no doubt by his exertions. The sting of guilt rose in her stomach then, as she was reminded of all the grief her actions would have caused him.

'I have sent Samuel back to Langdale,' Isaac said, sitting down next to her. 'He will return in my carriage with your aunt and your portmanteau. The physician has advised that you would be best to rest here for a day or two, so you will need some provisions for that.'

Louisa nodded, lowering her gaze and feeling suddenly very conscious that she wore only her chemise beneath the bedsheets. 'Thank you, Isaac,' she replied. 'For everything. You must think me very foolish and reckless.'

'I do not think you are either of those things,' he countered. 'The way Mrs Pearson behaved towards you was unconscionable. It is little wonder that you felt you had to leave.'

She bit her lip, still not looking at him. 'I do not just mean that. What I did in the past…'

Isaac shifted in his seat, clearing his throat. 'What happened to you in the past is not your fault, Louisa. You were dealt a cruel hand, but neither you nor your fiancé did anything different from what scores of men and women have done since the beginning of time.'

She smiled. 'You sound like my aunt.'

'Well, your aunt is right.' He paused, as though searching for the right words. 'I just— I wish I had allowed you to tell me what happened. I wish I had not had to hear it from that dreadful Mrs Pearson.'

She felt her smile fade as her thoughts were overtaken by recollections of that scene.

'I think the satisfied look on her face will haunt me. Her version of events…the insinuations she made…' Louisa bit her lip, shaking her head in disbelief. 'I am not a strumpet. And I never accused Richard of anything. And I never—I never lay with anyone but him. By the time I discovered I was with child he was at sea. I told no one—not even my mother. Instead I waited, hoping beyond hope that he would return soon, that we could marry quickly and no one would be any the wiser. Then the news of his death reached me. It all… it all unravelled after that. I told my parents—I had to. But I told no one else. To this day I do not know how the rumours began—the careless talk of a maid, perhaps, or the prying eyes of a visitor who spotted my swollen belly. Being with child and unwed was scandalous enough, but some of the things which were said were appalling—that I had taken many lovers, that I was no better than a harlot. I've often wondered if it was Richard's family who said those things—to discredit me and to protect his memory, I suppose. It seems that the vitriol spouted by Mrs Pearson is some confirmation of that.'

Louisa sniffed, wiping crossly at the tears which had begun to form in the corners of her eyes. Isaac, meanwhile, got up, and to her surprise he perched on the bed next to her, taking her hand in his.

'You said yesterday that you lost the child,' he said. 'My son did not live for many hours after his birth… nor did Rosalind. She succumbed to fever a day later.' He paused, a pained expression briefly flashing across his face. 'I understand all too well the grief you feel. But I'm not sure I can put into words my anger at the way Mrs Pearson tried to shame you, or my sorrow for your loss. I am so sorry, Louisa.'

She gave him a watery smile. 'Thank you. You are the first person to say that to me. Even my parents, as kind as they were in the circumstances, never could bring themselves to say they were sorry.' She felt her face crumple as more tears began to fall. 'I wish I had confided in you, Isaac. I wish I'd trusted that you would understand.'

He squeezed her hand. 'Perhaps you would do me the honour of putting your trust in me now,' he said quietly, searching her gaze. 'Will you marry me, Louisa?'

She hesitated. Ever since he'd first uttered his intention as he'd carried her into this room, she'd been grappling with her answer. With what her heart desired and what her head still told her she could not have.

'You are a gentleman of impeccable repute, Isaac,' she said. 'Please consider what connecting yourself to me would mean for your name, for your family.'

'Reputations be damned,' he replied. 'I will not live my life for society's approval. I will be forty years of age soon, and I have endured quite enough pain in my life. I love you, Louisa. I wish to be happy, and I wish to make you happy. More than anything. Please, trust me. Trust that this is all that matters to me—not society, nor scandal. Just you. Just us.'

She nodded. 'I do trust you,' she replied, feeling the depth of truth in those words.

She could trust him—he had more than proved that to her. Over these past days he'd defended her, protected her, cared for her and sought to rescue her, even after learning her terrible truth. Now, when he said her past was no impediment to his heart, she trusted him. She believed him.

'Then the only question that remains is, what do you want, Louisa?'

His eyes continued to search hers and she knew he was glimpsing her answer, even if she had not yet put it into words.

She had spent so long fixed upon the past that she had never allowed herself to consider the future. Never permitted herself to contemplate being happy. Never dared to imagine loving and being loved in return. Yet the desire for those things had always been there, she realised now, lying dormant beneath layers of grief, sorrow and shame. This summer Isaac had awoken that desire—perhaps in the candlelight of the Assembly Rooms or on the breezy clifftops, or perhaps in his old library, when she'd first enjoyed his warm embrace.

She could not truly say. What she did know, however, was that this was a desire she must finally admit to.

She swallowed hard, holding his gaze. 'I want you,' she said. 'I will marry you, Isaac.'

By the time Louisa's aunt arrived with Samuel, Isaac felt as though he was ready to burst with joy. He wanted to rush downstairs and announce his news to his brother in the middle of the inn. He wanted to tell all of Cumberland that Louisa Conrad had accepted him. As it was, he tried his best to maintain his composure, reminding himself that there was a proper way to handle these matters. And as Louisa's guardian, Miss Howarth needed to be informed first.

After showing her to Louisa's room he tried to excuse himself, believing it was best to give the two ladies some time alone to reconcile, and for Louisa to deliver her news in her own way. However, Louisa would not permit it, insisting that he should remain. She seemed anxious about seeing her aunt again, and he suspected she was worried that the older woman would be angry with her for leaving the way she had. As it was, she need not have feared. More than anything, Miss Howarth seemed relieved to find her niece safe and well, except for an injured ankle.

Now that they were all happily far away from Langdale Hall, Isaac took the opportunity to inform Miss Howarth about Mrs Pearson's regrettable involvement in the revelation of Louisa's past. It was a task he did not relish, but he knew he had to do his duty.

Miss Howarth's mouth fell open in horror as the full extent of the woman's unpleasantness became apparent to her, and she turned back to her niece, regarding her tearfully.

'Oh, my dear, I am so sorry,' she said, shaking her head. 'I must admit that I was perturbed when I heard the suggestions Mrs Pearson made at dinner, about you and Sir Isaac promenading alone, but now I am truly horrified. I cannot believe she did that to you. It is no wonder that you ran away from Langdale.'

'Even so, I am sorry I caused you such distress, Aunt,' Louisa replied. 'I hope you can forgive me.'

'There is nothing to forgive,' Miss Howarth insisted. 'On the contrary, it is me who should be asking you for forgiveness. I regret the day that I ever introduced you to Mary and Charlotte Pearson. Please know that I will never welcome either of them into my home again. Our acquaintance is at an end.'

With that, Miss Howarth seemed to consider the matter of her callous former acquaintance closed, and their conversation turned to the future—specifically, the next few days.

In his elated state, Isaac had given little thought to

the practicalities of what lay beyond today, and he found himself rather taken aback to witness Louisa's aunt take charge of the situation. Neither he nor Louisa seemed to be able to get a word in edgeways as the older woman launched into listing all that needed to happen, and all that needed to be done.

'And Mr Liddell has been very attentive, and has secured me a very nice room here,' she continued, singing the praises of Isaac's younger brother. 'So I will stay while you convalesce, as is right and proper. Oh, and I will need to write to your mother. I know she is expecting you back in Berkshire by summer's end, but I will write to explain that there may be a delay on account of your injured ankle.'

'Aunt…' Louisa began, clearly trying her best to interject.

'Oh, but how shall we travel back to Lowhaven once you are well enough?' Miss Howarth began to fret. 'Sir Isaac and Mr Liddell will surely have departed by then.'

Louisa tried again. 'I doubt Sir Isaac will have gone, Aunt, since…'

'Oh! Well, then, sir, would you be so kind enough to take us back to Lowhaven in a day or two?'

Isaac glanced at Louisa, an amused smile twitching at the corners of his mouth to mirror the one she already wore. 'It would be my pleasure, Miss Howarth,' he said, beginning to chuckle.

Louisa's aunt furrowed her brow, regarding them both seriously as Louisa began to laugh, too. 'Pray tell, what is so funny?'

'I have been trying to tell you, Aunt,' Louisa replied, obviously composing herself. 'Sir Isaac has asked me to marry him, and I have accepted.'

The older woman clasped her hands together in delight. 'Oh! How wonderful!' she exclaimed. 'Why on earth did you not say anything before? I feel rather foolish now, talking of writing to your mother about your return to Berkshire. I shall have to write and tell her there is to be a wedding. Oh—and in your grandfather's old church, too. She will be delighted.'

He watched as Louisa sat bolt upright. 'The church in Hayton?' she repeated.

Miss Howarth nodded. 'Well, of course—the master of Hayton Hall can hardly get wed anywhere else, can he? I'm sure the whole village will turn out for it—and probably a good number of families from Lowhaven, too.'

Isaac saw Louisa's smile fade. She closed her eyes, a small frown gathering between them, as though she was trying to steady herself. His heart lurched as he realised something troubled her. Something that he sensed she was not prepared to reveal in front of her aunt.

'Miss Howarth, perhaps you would be so kind as to give me a moment or two alone with your niece?' he asked.

Perhaps noticing the sudden tension in the room, Louisa's aunt assented and swiftly departed, closing the door behind her.

Isaac sat down at Louisa's side, his heart thudding in his chest, his emotions swelling up into a lump in his throat. Dread. Anticipation. Agony. Hope.

'Is something the matter, Louisa?' he said softly. 'Do you not wish to marry me, after all?'

'Of course I wish to marry you,' she replied without a moment's hesitation. 'It is not that. It is…it is the thought of the banns, of church. Of the whole village watching us wed. Of what they will say.'

'You know I care nothing for any of that.'

'It is easy to say that you do not care when you have never been marred in scandal,' she countered. 'Besides, you are a gentleman, and a baronet—you will always command respect, even if tainted by your association with me. I, on the other hand, will always be considered a disgrace. I am not sure I can face the scrutiny... if I can manage to stand up in church in front of society and endure their whispers while making my vows.'

An idea dawned on him then, and he could not repress his smile. 'Then don't,' he said. 'Let's not marry in front of them at all. We don't have to marry in Hayton, and we don't have to wait until the banns are read. Indeed, I do not care for any of it as long as we are wed.'

She frowned. 'What do you mean?'

He took hold of her hands, clasping them in his. 'I mean, let's go to Scotland. Let's elope, Louisa, to Gretna Green. We can travel as soon as you are strong enough.'

Her eyes widened at the suggestion. 'An elopement? That will cause another scandal!'

He drew her fingers to his lips and kissed them. 'It might, but it will be our scandal. Together.'

She smiled. 'Sir Isaac Liddell, I do believe that you've lost your mind.'

'Oh, I have,' he answered her, laughing. 'Earlier this summer a beautiful woman climbed into my carriage after a stagecoach accident, and days later my horse almost collided with her on the clifftops near Lowhaven. My life has not been quite the same since.'

'Nor has mine,' she replied, stroking his rough, unshaven cheek. 'I'm not sure what I expected from my summer in Lowhaven, but I certainly did not expect this.'

'Well, you did once tell me that you wished to travel,' he said. 'And, since we both adored *Waverley*, Scotland seems as good a place as any to start.'

'To start?'

'Indeed,' Isaac answered with another smile. 'I think you and I have had our fill of hiding away. There's a world out there, and I'd like us to see it together.'

The look of utter joy on her face was a sight to behold. Isaac leaned over once more, enveloping her in his embrace and saying a quiet prayer that he would always manage to make her as happy as this.

Chapter Twenty-Nine

They were married not before an altar but an anvil, in a short ceremony conducted by the village blacksmith. Louisa did not take her eyes off Isaac throughout, and the words of the would-be priest washed over her as she assuredly made her vows.

The past few days had been strange and exciting, taking them across wild open countryside and into a succession of comfortable but often raucous inns as they made their way north.

Isaac had insisted that they take their time, travelling only as far as the horses could manage each day. She was still recovering, he'd pointed out, so a more leisurely pace would be better for her health. Louisa, in turn, had expressed her desire to be wed as soon as possible.

'I may have to reconsider my opinion that you are neither foolish nor reckless,' Isaac had teased.

She'd laughed and conceded the point, agreeing to be sensible just this once.

Their church on that fine summer's day was the blacksmith's shop, a humble building with whitewashed walls and a ceiling supported by exposed wooden beams. Their congregation comprised two witnesses tempted out of the nearby inn with a few coins for their trouble. For wedding clothes they'd made do with their country attire, although Louisa did not believe Isaac had ever looked a finer gentleman than he did now, in his dark frock coat, fawn pantaloons and black Hessian boots.

It was all very irregular, and far from sensible, and yet Louisa could not have been happier. Standing there in that little room, observed by no one who knew them as she committed herself to the man she loved, she realised that for the first time in a long time she felt truly free.

Isaac took hold of her hands as the blacksmith brought his hammer down on his anvil, sealing their union with the tools of his trade. Then he pulled her close, confirming it himself with a lingering kiss on her lips. She kissed him back ardently. Their first kiss as husband and wife.

'A very handsome couple,' one of the witnesses remarked. 'I wonder why they had to run away to get wed.'

'Let them wonder,' Isaac whispered in Louisa's ear. 'Although they are right,' he added, kissing her on the cheek. 'The bride in particular is a great beauty.'

Louisa blushed, glancing down at her plain cream day dress, conscious of the curls she'd struggled to tease into order that morning bouncing around her face. For all her delight at the way in which she'd been wed, she had missed the help of her maid.

Aunt Clarissa had assured her that Nan would remain at her home in Lowhaven until she could be reunited with Louisa when the new mistress of Hayton Hall returned. The thought of it caused Louisa to pause. That was what she was now: the new mistress of Hayton Hall. Isaac's wife. It was hard to believe the changes to her life which had been wrought by one summer sojourn to visit her aunt.

Aunt Clarissa, for her part, had been somewhat taken aback by their decision to elope. Ultimately, though, she had been supportive, understanding their reasons for doing so, albeit with some reservations about exactly what Louisa's parents would make of it.

Sharing her aunt's concern, Louisa had written to her mother directly before they departed for Gretna, explaining her decision and expressing her hope that her parents would be happy for her.

'We will invite them to visit once we return to Hayton,' Isaac had said when she'd broached the subject of how her parents might greet her news. 'I have no doubt that will allay any concerns they may have.'

'Are you telling me that the brooding Isaac Liddell plans to charm my parents?' Louisa had teased him.

'No, I thought I'd let Samuel do that,' he'd replied, grinning. 'For my part, I intend to impress them with my large estate and title.'

Smiling now at the memory, Louisa leaned against Isaac, steadying herself. Her ankle was slowly healing, but it still ached after any length of time spent on her feet.

'This has been quite an adventure, hasn't it?' she remarked, gazing up at him. 'Once we return to Hayton, I think it will feel like a dream.'

Isaac grinned at her. 'Alas, I have no plans for us to return to Hayton just yet.'

'You don't? But what about the estate?'

'I have written to Samuel, and I'm sure he will manage my affairs for a little while longer,' he said, wrapping his arm around her waist as together they walked outside to where their carriage was waiting.

'Poor Mr Liddell... I fear he has been rather put upon of late,' she remarked, referring to all the to-ing and fro-ing the poor man had done across Cumberland, seeing Aunt Clarissa home safely and bringing the eloping couple provisions before returning to Hayton himself.

Isaac chuckled. 'He has enjoyed it. As a very beautiful and perceptive lady once told me, my brother likes to arrange things. And, please, call him Samuel. You're my wife now; hearing you call my brother "Mr Liddell" sets my teeth on edge.'

'In that case, shall I expect to hear you calling my aunt "Clarissa" when we next visit her for tea?' Louisa asked, unable to suppress her smirk.

'Oh, heavens, no! She will be Miss Howarth until the end of my days.'

They paused next to the carriage, and he pulled her closer to him.

'Anyway,' he continued, his thumb caressing her cheek, 'do you not wish to know where we are going, if not back to Hayton?'

She gazed up at him. 'Indeed. Enlighten me.'

'It occurred to me on our journey to Gretna that I'd like to see something of Scotland with my wife. How does Edinburgh sound?'

'Edinburgh sounds wonderful,' she gushed, resting her head against his chest. 'I love you, Sir Isaac.'

Isaac placed a tender kiss on top of her head as the driver opened the carriage door, signalling the start of their next journey together. Beyond the charming little border village were more miles of roads, more open country, and eventually a city beckoned.

'I love you too, Lady Liddell,' he replied.

* * * * *

RESCUING THE
RUNAWAY HEIRESS

For David

Chapter One

September 1818

A loud cry pierced the cool, still air of the early autumn evening, causing Samuel to startle. He had been enjoying his usual slow promenade around Hayton Hall's fine gardens, appreciating the quiet calm, observing the changing light and admiring the late blooming plants as one season ebbed into the next. Or at least, so he told himself. He found that he told stories to himself frequently these days, as though such works of fiction, if repeated often enough, could eventually embody the truth. He'd tell himself that he was simply a country gentleman, relishing some moments of peaceful solitude before retiring for the night. That he took just as much pleasure in doing his duty as he always had. That he was his own man, in charge of his own destiny. That he did not mind being alone. That he did not spend most evenings walking in that garden, listening to his doubts as they whispered to him, about just how bleak his prospects now seemed.

Samuel looked around him, shaking his head at himself in an uncomfortable acknowledgement of the darker turn his thoughts had taken before that brief, shrill noise had intruded. The gardens of Hayton Hall fell back into silence once more, readying themselves for the impending dark as, above them, the sky's pink hues deepened. His gaze shifted towards the wood beyond, its trees still thick with summer's lush green foliage, the leaves only now hinting at beginning to turn. He stood still for several moments, listening for anything which might betray the origin of such a sound. All he could detect, however, were the occasional caws of the crows as they came home to roost for the night.

'You see, Samuel,' he muttered to himself, 'you've naught but the birds for company.'

Naught but birds, and his servants, of course. Or, rather, his older brother's servants, since it was Sir Isaac Liddell who was the master here. Samuel was merely the caretaker, appointed to look after the family estate while his brother travelled with his new bride.

As Samuel turned his back to the woods and continued his gentle promenade, he found himself counting the weeks since Isaac and Louisa's departure, and considering how much, and how little, had changed since. At first, he'd embraced the responsibility his brother had bestowed on him with his usual cheerful enthusiasm, but although he believed he'd discharged his duties competently, he'd quickly wearied of just how solitary and tedious running a country estate could be. It pained him to admit it, but he resented how it tied him, quite literally, to its acres. He'd never have thought it possible, but he was tired of the sight of his ancestral home. Tired, too, of his own company.

Yet solitude, he'd discovered, was infinitely preferable to being the subject of ceaseless gossip. As happy as he was for his older brother, he could not fail to acknowledge that Isaac had left quite a scandal in his wake, and the news of his elopement with a woman who'd borne a naval captain's child out of wedlock had quickly spread. For the first time in his life, Samuel had become disenchanted with Cumberland society, as he found himself either invited to dinner parties to answer questions about the scandal, or not invited at all. In the end, declining such invitations had been a blessed relief, but it had made his world grow smaller still. It was hard to believe that last year he'd been on the Continent, enjoying picnics on the shores of the Swiss lakes and attending lavish dinner parties in cities like Geneva, Milan and Venice. It was hard to believe that he'd been surrounded by so much culture and good company, and yet now...

A crow cawed again, taunting him.

Resigned to his lonely routine, he sauntered back towards Hayton Hall, to the servants waiting to greet him, to offer their deferential smiles whilst always keeping their distance. They played their roles as well as he knew he had to play his. He'd seen that clearly, the first and only time he'd ventured to suggest that Smithson, his brother's butler, join him for an evening brandy. The ageing man's jaw had just about hit the floor, and Samuel had reddened at his transgression, unable to decide what was worse—the awkward excuses the butler offered as a refusal or the look of pity in his eyes.

Since then, he'd not strayed from his side of the line which divided servants and masters, even though he was not master of anyone—not truly. It was just a part he had to play for a little while longer, until the real master of Hayton Hall returned. Then he would revert to his real role, that of the younger brother, free to do as he pleased, to spend his time and inheritance as he wished. Of the unattached gentleman, untroubled by land or titles.

Or, more realistically, of being the less attractive prospect, the wrong brother. Or at least that was what his rejection by a certain young lady that summer had taught him. As he drew nearer to Hayton Hall he shuddered—at the cooling air, perhaps, or at the memory of her bright red hair, the smattering of freckles across her nose, her broad smile. Remembering her biting words to him that afternoon as they'd walked together and he'd dared to suggest he was fond of her, that he would like, with her father's permission, to begin a courtship.

'Why would you think to even ask such a thing? When I am my father's only daughter, and you are a younger son. When you have no property, no title...'

Samuel grimaced, his mind suddenly filled with the images of her usually pretty face contorted into a look which was part-offence and part-mockery as she quashed his hopes and stamped upon his heart. He held no affection for her now; he'd seen her true fickle nature too clearly for that. But her rejection of him had been thoroughly humiliating and whilst the hurt he'd felt no longer burned his insides, it still stubbornly smouldered somewhere within him, its embers always ready to be rekindled in his quiet, contemplative moments. And, as God only knew, he'd had too many of those during the preceding weeks.

'Pull yourself together, man,' he muttered under his breath, reminding himself that in the coming days his solitude would be over. His friend Charles Gordon had mercifully responded to Samuel's plea that he should visit, gladly accepting and venturing to suggest that he bring his sister with him too. He had much to look forward to, Samuel reminded himself. He'd met Charles during his Continental travels, taking an instant liking to the man's convivial demeanour and outrageous sense of fun. Seeing his friend again would lift his spirits, and he was intrigued about making the acquaintance of Henrietta Gordon, especially since, until Charles had mentioned her in his letter, Samuel had not known about the existence of a sister at all.

Another loud yell breached the silence. It was deeper this time, longer and angrier, almost a roar. Samuel spun around, his eyes darting warily back towards the wood. Up in the trees the crows began to squawk frantically, and it occurred to him then that it could be a fox. He decided he would mention the noise to his brother's steward; the estate's tenants would need to be put on their guard, especially those who raised sheep.

Then, before he could think any more about it, a final cry rang out. This one, however, put paid to any theories he'd entertained about foxes, instead betraying its origins as being unmistakably human. This one, he realised as he ran instinctively towards the trees, was not a scream or a roar, but a plea.

'Help!'

As she lay on the ground, pain pulsing through her as she watched a murder of crows circling overhead, all Hope Sloane could think was how much easier her bid to escape would have been if only she'd had a breeches role. Men's clothing was without doubt far more suitable attire for dashing across the countryside than a flimsy gown of muslin and lace. However, if there was one thing that life had taught Hope, it was that you played the hand you were dealt, and you seized your opportunities when they came. And so she had, running for her life across fields and through woodland, hoping she could get far enough away before falling under the cloak of inevitable darkness.

Unfortunately, the only thing she'd fallen upon was the uneven, branch-strewn ground. She hadn't gone down quietly either, letting out an almighty scream at the pain as it seared through her. Truly, she could not have announced her whereabouts more clearly if she'd tried. She could only hope that her disappearance had not yet been discovered, that there might still be sufficient distance between herself and those who sought to capture her.

Namely her father and the man to whom she'd been promised as though she was nothing more than contraband to be smuggled and traded.

Hope shivered, the short sleeves and thin fabric of her gown doing nothing to ward off the early autumn chill. They'd made her put on this gown, her father and the man. They'd insisted that she should look nice and tidy her hair and make an effort. She was going to celebrate with them, they'd told her, for in a matter of days she would be wed. The following day she would depart for Scotland, where she would smile and make her vows before God, or risk her father's wrath. Then she would go to live with this man, the one her father called George, although she had not cared to even know his name. She would spend the rest of her days on his farm near the Solway Firth, only leaving the place to run whisky over the border and into England by wearing a belly canteen which made her look as though she was heavy with child.

'Except when you're actually having a bairn, of course,' the brute George had said as he leered at her, placing an unwelcome arm around her waist and pulling her roughly towards him.

Both men had laughed and raised their mugs in a toast while Hope had bitten her tongue, resolving to say nothing and to bide her time. Foolishly, after making her change her clothes, they'd left her unbound, instead ordering her to wait on them hand and foot. Recognising the opportunity for what it was, Hope had turned on the charm, forcing a smile on to her face for George's benefit while she'd plied both men with more and more drink. There was no stronger liquor in Cumberland than that which came from her father's stills. All she'd had to do was wait until they passed from stupor into slumber. The moment they did, she'd hurried to escape.

Hope shivered again, wincing as she pulled futilely at the muslin sleeves as though they could somehow be stretched to cover her bare arms. Forcing her to wear that gown had been a form of mockery, she knew that. It was the gown she'd been wearing when they'd grabbed her that night at the theatre, not long after the play was over. It was her Lady Teazle gown, a beautifully embellished but ultimately thin piece of frippery befitting the flirtatious and spendthrift gentleman's wife she'd played in Sheridan's *The School for Scandal*. It was a relic from a life she might never know again, thanks to her own naïve foolishness.

Why had she not tried to excuse herself, when she learned her theatre company were to tour in Cumberland in addition to their usual destinations in Westmorland? Why had she not feigned illness, or injury? She was an actress, after all.

Why had she ever thought that several years of absence and a stage name would be enough to protect her from recognition? Why had she fooled herself into thinking she could slip in and out of Lowhaven, undetected by her father's many spies? Why, on that day five years ago when she'd crept out of her family's damp cottage for the final time, had she believed that running away to Yorkshire would ever be far enough?

Hope's teeth began to chatter. And why, she asked herself for the umpteenth time, had she not taken a breeches role? She was going to freeze to death in that ridiculous gown! A potent mix of anger and anxiety coursed through her veins as she forced herself to sit, desperation and determination gripping her as she realised she must drag herself, somehow, towards shelter.

Using all the strength she could muster, she tried to pull herself to her feet, only to fall down once more as a dizzying pain in her head overwhelmed her, and her right leg refused to bear her weight. Furious now, she pounded her fists into the ground, letting out a loud, guttural cry—at the pain, made worse by the sudden movement, and at her predicament. At the unfairness of it all.

She'd run away once before; back then, she'd had more time to think and to plan, to pack clothing and gather coins to aid her escape. She'd got on one coach, then another; she'd put many miles between herself and Cumberland and carved out a life she could call her own. A life which was not beholden to the whims of cruel men, or to the tides of fortune which dictated whether she escaped the grasp of constables and excisemen, or found herself in gaol, facing the noose. A life in which she'd played many different parts, and lived many colourful lives. A life she could enjoy once again, if only she could get herself out of this terrible mess.

Above her the crows still circled, their squalls growing louder and more urgent as though they too understood the severity of her situation. Hope cast her eyes around, trying to get some sense of where she was. Trying to ignore the way pain spread from her head to her neck as well as searing up her leg. Through the trees, she caught glimpses of stonework in the near distance, and her heart began to race at the prospect of having stumbled upon a house, upon the possibility of rescue and shelter.

Play the hand you've been dealt, Hope, she thought to herself as a fresh wave of dizziness threatened to consume her. *Play the hand, even if it means placing yourself at the mercy of fortune's tides once more.*

At the top of her lungs and with the last vestiges of her strength, Hope mustered one final cry.

'Help!'

By the time Samuel found her, the crows had fallen silent, and so had she. Above him, the sky was ink-blue and the sun was long gone, leaving the woodland to languish in the gloomy shadows of its many trees. He bent down at her side, his instincts racing ahead of his thoughts as he tried to assess the situation. The woman before him lay very still, her eyes shut, her arms perishingly cold to the touch. Little wonder really, he thought, since the evening gown she wore was completely unsuitable attire for wandering about the countryside at dusk. She needed warmth, and the attention of a physician. Whoever she was, and whatever had happened to her, it was clear that something was gravely wrong.

Carefully, he lifted her off the ground, simultaneously concerned and reassured by the brief groan which escaped her lips in response to the movement. At least she still lived, although how badly injured she was, he could not tell. Holding her in his arms, he walked back towards Hayton Hall, calling out for his servants once he reached the formal gardens he'd been sauntering around just a little while ago. The noise he made seemed to rouse her slightly, and she began to murmur again—pained moans littered with sobs, and in amongst all that, a few words. Words which seemed to distress her greatly.

'No…not going with him…' she whimpered.

'Hush,' he replied softly, anxious to reassure her. 'You're safe now.'

The woman's eyes rolled and closed once more and, to his horror, he sensed her grow limp in his arms. With increasing urgency, Samuel hurried towards the door of Hayton Hall, from which several servants were rushing towards him, their brows furrowed as they responded to his calls.

'Prepare a bedchamber!' Samuel barked his orders, playing their master once more. 'Fetch some water and light a fire! This lady needs our help.'

Chapter Two

Hope's eyes fluttered open, the brightness of the midday sun immediately overwhelming her blurry vision. She blinked several times, trying to see better, trying to understand where she was. The bed she lay in was large and soft, her head resting upon a pile of pillows as she remained tucked beneath crisp white sheets. She shifted her gaze, wincing at the discomfort that this slightest movement of her head caused as she observed the light streaming through lattice windows, illuminating a room dominated by dark furniture, wooden panelling and heavy tapestries. An old and very fine room, to be sure, but where? And how had she ended up here?

She licked her dry lips, conscious suddenly of feeling desperately thirsty as she tried to remember what had happened. She'd been in some woodland, running as fast as she could. She'd slipped and she'd fallen—she'd felt pain everywhere. She'd cried out, and then...

A voice—deep and reassuring. A tide rolling in, lifting her off the bracken-strewn ground and carrying her away, its undulating waves rocking her, conspiring with sleep to distance her from her pain. Except it hadn't been the sea at all, had it? It had been a man, the one the voice had belonged to, taking her into his arms, offering gentle words to calm her as he carried her away from the woods. She'd been found, but by whom? Where on earth was she? And, more to the point, was she safe?

Or had she been found by yet another of her father's many acquaintances? Had he been alerted to her whereabouts? Was he on his way to take her again, right now?

Hope's heart began to race, and in a sudden panic she tried to pull herself upright. Pain shot through her back and her neck, causing her to cry out. Her head throbbed; she touched the back of it gingerly, wincing as her fingers grazed over a swollen lump. What had she done to herself? Just how badly injured was she? The heat of coming tears burned her eyes and she blinked furiously, forbidding them to fall. Crying would do no good; it never had.

Crying hadn't helped on the day that she'd found her mother's lifeless body strewn across her bed, having finally succumbed to laudanum's charms. Nor had it helped her stop herself from being drawn into her father's underworld of illicit stills and free trading, a world in which she'd never been able to decide whose wrath she feared more, that of her kin or that of the law. Her tears and her pleas had not prevented her father from trying to force her into a marriage, either five years ago or yesterday. The man was immune to tears, and so should she be. The only thing which had helped, then and now, was running away.

She had to run. But first she had to get out of this bed.

Pushing the bedsheets away, she forced herself upright, gritting her teeth as a fresh, sharp agony stabbed at her lower back. Glancing down at herself, Hope was surprised to see that the pretty, thin gown she'd been wearing last night had gone, along with her stays, leaving her wearing only her white linen shift. She felt her cheeks redden at the realisation—who on earth had done that? Not the man who'd carried her, surely? No matter, she decided. She would run across the countryside wearing her undergarments and no shoes, if she had to.

Persevering despite the pounding which grew in her head, Hope shuffled to the edge of the bed and let her toes touch the floor. Her right ankle began to throb and she looked down to see that someone had covered it with a bandage. The rug below her feet felt soft and reassuring as she pressed against it. However, her injured ankle protested, a sudden pain shooting through it and causing both her legs to buckle. Before she could stop herself, she was falling down, landing on the floor with a hard and graceless thud.

'Ow!' she cried out and this time, despite herself, the tears did fall.

Clearly the commotion she'd caused had been heard. Beyond the bedchamber, someone else in the house stirred, and all Hope could do was sit helplessly on the floor, tears flooding down her cheeks as footsteps approached. Quick, frantic footsteps, growing louder by the second. Then, after a moment, the door creaked open and a face peered around it. A man's face, etched with concern, his brow furrowing as he spied her on the floor.

'What the devil are you doing down there?'

He was impeccably dressed; that was the first thing she noticed. As he strode towards her, she drew her first, hurried conclusions about him, taking in his tidy, sand-coloured hair, his high collar and cravat, his immaculate blue coat. A gentleman, certainly, although that was no surprise to her really, considering the fine surroundings she'd awoken in. She stared up at him, meeting his grey-blue eyes for the first time and finding, to her great relief, kindness there. Whatever he saw in her gaze was presumably less reassuring; she watched in confusion as he hesitated, averting his eyes and half turning back towards the door.

'Sir?' Hope croaked, her mouth desert dry.

'Forgive me,' the man said, still looking away. 'I should not have burst in like that. I shall fetch a maid to attend to you.'

A maid to attend to her. Yes—he was definitely a gentleman. Hope glanced down, her confusion clearing like mist as she caught sight of the linen shift she wore once more. Ah, of course. Now she understood his hesitation.

'Thank you, sir. Also, if it is not too much trouble, I would be obliged to you for some water,' she added politely, instinctively slipping into the voice she'd used on stage just days ago—soft and refined, clear and articulate. She didn't know why. Perhaps because she feared that even a word spoken in her own voice, laced as it was with the Cumberland accent, would tell him exactly who she was? Or perhaps because sitting here, in this grand room, speaking to the well-dressed gentleman who'd saved her life, she felt that she ought to smooth over her coarse ways?

She watched as the man glanced at the water jug sitting atop the table. He sighed heavily before turning back around and stepping towards her once more.

'This is ridiculous,' he muttered as he bent down, gently lifting her off the floor and placing her back upon the bed. Despite the discomfort that the movement caused, the brief feeling of his arms around her was warm and strangely reassuring, bringing back those vague, confused memories of the previous night. She did not even need to ask if he'd been her rescuer; instinctively, she knew that he had.

'What is ridiculous, sir?' she asked him.

The man walked around the bed and poured some water into a cup. 'Fetching a maid to help you when I can just as easily do it myself,' he replied, handing the cup to her. 'Anyway,' he continued, 'you did not answer me. What were you doing on the floor?'

'I was trying to get up,' Hope replied between thirsty sips. 'I am grateful to you, sir, but I am sure I have been a burden for long enough. If you could see to it that my dress and shoes are returned to me, I promise I will leave within the hour.'

'The devil you will,' the man replied, frowning at her once more. 'I'm afraid you're not fit to go anywhere right now. Your right ankle is badly injured, and you've suffered a nasty blow to the head. I don't know what happened to you in the woods, but my physician says you're purple and blue with bruises.'

'Your physician?' Hope repeated, her heart pounding once more. She pulled the bedsheets tighter around herself, as though they could protect her. As though anything could protect her.

'Yes, my physician. He attended to you last night. He assures me that your ankle is not broken, and that all your wounds will heal. But he says you must rest.'

Hope, however, was not listening. 'Did you say anything to him about me? Did you tell him where you found me?' she asked, her questions rapid as she began to panic. Did her father know any physicians? Was it possible that this physician knew who she was? Might he betray her whereabouts?

'I told him that I discovered you lying injured in the woods,' the man replied. 'That was all I could say, since I do not know anything about you.' He paused, holding her gaze with his own for a long moment. 'I dare say that's something we ought to rectify. Perhaps you'd like to begin by telling me your name and whether there is someone I should inform of your whereabouts.'

Hope's heart raced even faster, the pain in her head reaching a crescendo as she felt the room begin to spin. 'Someone you should inform?' she repeated.

'Of course,' the man said. 'Surely a lady such as yourself has loved ones who are desperately worried about you? They'd be welcome to stay here too, of course, while you convalesce. Indeed, that would be best, for propriety's sake. I will have to ask them to arrange for some of your clothes to be brought to you. That gown you were wearing last night is unfortunately beyond repair.' He gave her an affable smile, but she could not mistake the curiosity lingering in his eyes. 'I do wonder what you were doing, wandering in the woods by yourself in such a fine evening gown.'

Hope drew a deep breath, trying to calm herself, trying to read between the lines. She thought about the way he behaved towards her—calling her a lady, talking about her fine gown, panicking at the impropriety of being in the same room as her while she wore only a shift. Did he think she was like him? Had he mistaken her for a gentleman's daughter? For the offspring of some grand duke, or of a wealthy merchant?

Hope sipped her water again, buying herself some time as she considered her options. Telling this man the truth about herself was out of the question; the nature of her father's business, such as it was, meant that he was known across Cumberland society. It was well known that Jeremiah Sloane supplied his contraband to many of the fine houses, and many of the magistrates, thus ensuring they happily continued to turn a blind eye to his activities. For all she knew, this was one such house, and one such gentleman. And yet she knew she had to tell this man something. If she had to remain here for the moment, she needed him to understand her requirement for secrecy; she needed him to help her hide. Surely, she reasoned, she could come up with a story which explained why, one which met with the assumptions he seemed to have made about her. Surely she could create a suitably genteel and imperilled character for herself. She was an actress, after all. This would simply be another role for her to play.

She cleared her throat. 'Please understand, sir, that no one can know I am here. Promise me that you will not whisper my whereabouts to a single soul. It is bad enough that your physician and your servants already know...'

Her plea seemed to grab the man's attention and he drew closer, his sympathy evident in his expression. 'Of course, I promise I will say nothing. And please, do not worry— my servants' discretion can be trusted, and my physician is a good man. Besides, no one even knows your name— including me.'

Hope gave an obliging nod. It was the sort of nod she'd cultivated on stage when playing high society types—subtle and reserved. 'My name is Hope...' She paused, searching for a family name. 'Hope Swynford.' Inwardly she groaned; that name was uncomfortably similar to her stage name, Hope Swyndale. She might be a decent actress, but it was already becoming apparent that she was a hopeless playwright.

'Ah! Like the third wife of John of Gaunt,' the man said, a grin spreading across his face. It was a handsome face; she noticed that now, her attention drawn to his blue-grey eyes, sparkling with interest, to his straight nose, his fair complexion, his full lips...

'Oh, John of Gaunt—yes, indeed,' she replied, forcing herself to concentrate on their conversation. She knew that name from a play by Shakespeare, but could not recall which one. Nor could she recall a wife, much less three of them. What on earth had got into her?

The man extended a hand towards her, and she accepted it gingerly. His fingers were gentle and warm, just as his arms had been both times she'd found herself within them. 'Delighted to make your acquaintance, Miss Swynford,' he said. 'My name is Samuel Liddell.'

She offered him a polite smile. 'It is a pleasure to meet you, sir, and thank you once again for coming to my aid. I believe you saved my life.'

'I was glad to be of assistance to you.' He let go of her hand, his expression growing serious once more. 'Perhaps, Miss Swynford, you might tell me what happened to you last night, and why you do not wish for your whereabouts to be known. I would like to help you, if I can.'

The look in his eyes was so genuine that for a brief moment Hope considered telling him the truth. Perhaps this Samuel Liddell really was a good man, perhaps he knew nothing of her father. Perhaps he would be willing to help Hope Sloane just as much as he wished to help Hope Swynford. Yet, as much as she wanted to be honest, she knew that it was not worth the risk. If life had taught her anything, it was that the only person she could really trust was herself.

Hope drew a deep breath, committing herself finally to her deceit. 'I am running away from my uncle, sir,' she began, improvising, the story and her lines unfinished even as she uttered them. 'I am running away from a marriage he wishes to force upon me. From a marriage I do not want.'

Chapter Three

If Samuel's prayers for company had been answered, he could not decide if it was God or the Devil who'd granted his wish. As he made himself comfortable in a small armchair which he'd pulled nearer to her bedside and began to listen to Miss Swynford's sorry tale, he realised that last night in the woods he'd found trouble. Quite literally, it seemed, since by all accounts this uncle Miss Swynford described was a deeply unpleasant character. Hellbent on carving up her inheritance between himself and an acquaintance, he'd concocted a plan to kidnap her and take her to Scotland, where he would force her to marry the co-conspirator, thus transferring her wealth to her new husband, who would then give the uncle his share. It seemed they'd travelled first to Lowhaven, to meet this awful acquaintance off a boat from the Isle of Man, before continuing northwards for the wedding. With her parents both deceased, the poor lady had been powerless in the face of his machinations, until some commotion at an inn had afforded her an opportunity to run away and board a mail coach.

'The coach was bound for Lowhaven, where we had just come from—not that I cared where it was going,' she continued, grimacing as she shifted in the bed. 'I just knew that it was fast, and it would get me away from them both.'

'Did your uncle or this other man see you board the mail coach? Did they try to pursue you?' he asked, trying to ascertain whether she remained in immediate danger.

She bit her lip. 'Unfortunately, I think they did. Two men were fighting in the courtyard, and one landed a blow on my uncle. This distracted them long enough for me to get away from them, but not without them seeing how I'd made my escape.'

She shifted again, clearly uncomfortable. Without thinking, Samuel leapt to his feet, plumping and adjusting the pillows behind her back. This prompted her to let out a nervous laugh, and he realised then just how close he was to her. Just how cream-coloured her bare arms were in that white shift. Just how deep the brown colour of her hair was, how it spilled over her shoulders in thick, wild tendrils.

Truly, he thought, he had found trouble, and not only because of the tale she was telling. He'd realised he'd found it the moment he'd walked into this bedchamber and observed those emerald eyes staring up at him. Something had stirred within his sore, lonely heart then. Something unwise. Something which he could only blame on the long weeks he'd spent in solitude. Something he felt certain this poor lady could do without, given her recent ordeal. He could do without it too, he reminded himself, given his own recent failed romantic endeavours.

'So what did you do, once you got back to Lowhaven?' Samuel asked, retreating to his armchair and forcing himself to focus on their conversation.

'I did not make it as far as that. I'd scrambled atop the coach as it was about to depart, and handed over the only two shillings I had. It turns out that two shillings doesn't get you very far. I've been trying to make my way on foot across the countryside ever since.'

'And where were you hoping to go?'

'London.'

'You were going to walk to London?' Samuel asked, incredulous.

Miss Swynford gave him a sad smile. 'In the circumstances, I had little choice. Anyway, I got thoroughly lost and utterly exhausted, before falling and hurting myself in the woods near to wherever this is. The rest you know.'

'Hayton,' Samuel informed her. 'You're in Hayton, and this house is Hayton Hall. So then, why London?' he continued. 'Is that where you're from?'

She seemed to hesitate. 'No, not really,' she replied evasively. 'But I have a good friend there. A married friend. I was going to go to her and her husband for help, and for protection.'

Samuel nodded, sensing for the first time that there was something she wasn't telling him, but deciding not to press her further. She barely knew him, after all, and could hardly be expected to trust him with every detail of her life, especially in the circumstances. Indeed, given all that she'd endured, she'd be entirely justified in never trusting anyone again.

Samuel rose from his seat, offering her a polite bow. 'You have my promise, Miss Swynford, that you will be well protected here. Once your injuries have healed and you are well enough to travel, I will accompany you and see to it that you reach your friend in London safely.'

He watched as those bright green eyes widened at him, unsure if it was mere surprise or sheer horror he saw in her gaze. 'You do not have to do that, sir,' she protested. 'Please, do not inconvenience yourself on my account.'

'It is no inconvenience. I have thought often about how some time away from Cumberland and a little society would do me the world of good,' Samuel replied, giving her a broad smile. How true that statement was, after so many long, lonely weeks. 'We will travel together, in my carriage. If anyone asks, I will say that you are my sister.'

Miss Swynford pressed her lips together, appearing to accept his plan even if her serious expression told him that she remained unhappy about it. Again, he reminded himself, she was hardly likely to jump for joy at the prospect of travelling with a man she'd only just met. A man who, for all she knew, could prove to be just as much of a rogue as those she'd recently fled from. A man who she had no reason to put any faith in. He made a silent promise then that he would work hard to earn her trust. That by the time they set off in his carriage she would have no reason to harbour any more reservations about Samuel Liddell.

'Do you have a sister, sir?' Her question, softly spoken though it was, pierced the silence which had hung between them.

He shook his head. 'No. We'll have to invent one, I'm afraid.'

She chewed her bottom lip, considering his answer. He found himself staring at her, drawn to the pretty features of her heart-shaped face—her slim pink lips, her small button-like nose and those big emerald eyes which had so taken him aback when he'd first walked into the room. She was, without doubt, uncommonly beautiful. And he was, without doubt, uncommonly ridiculous for entertaining such thoughts about a lady whose only concern was evading her fortune-seeking uncle and finding sanctuary in London.

'What about a brother?' She continued her line of questioning, thankfully oblivious to the inappropriate turn his thoughts had taken. 'Or a wife?'

He chuckled wryly at that. 'I am as yet unwed,' he replied, trying to sound nonchalant. 'I do have a brother, but he is not here at present,' he added vaguely, finding that for some reason he did not wish to talk about Isaac.

'So you live here alone?' She stared at him, incredulous. 'All by yourself?'

'Not entirely alone,' he countered, feeling suddenly defensive. 'My brother will return and…well, there are servants here, of course. Indeed,' he continued, moving away from her bedside and towards the door, 'I think it is past time that I arranged for a maid to attend to you.'

He placed his hand on the door knob, ready to leave, his inner voice giving him a stern talking-to. Why had he not just explained the situation? Why had he not simply told her that his solitary life was only temporary while he cared for his ancestral home and estate in his brother's absence? That the real master of Hayton Hall would return soon and resume his duties, liberating his inconsequential younger sibling to do as he pleased once more.

'Yes, thank you, and please forgive me, sir,' she called after him. 'I did not mean to offend you. I was merely curious.' She glanced around the bedchamber. 'This is a lovely room. I'm sure the rest of Hayton Hall is very fine. Hopefully, when my ankle is strong enough, you will be able to show me.'

He smiled proudly. 'It is indeed a fine country house. A little old-fashioned, perhaps, for modern tastes, but I believe it will stand the test of time. It was built around two hundred years ago, by the first baronet.'

He realised as soon as he said that word that he'd given her the wrong impression. That she'd made an assumption about him, an assumption which he ought to immediately correct. Along with the other assumption he'd undoubtedly led her to—that Hayton Hall belonged to him, that he was the master of a grand house and a vast estate.

And yet, as he looked up and met her lovely green gaze, he found himself unable to say the right words. To tell her that it was Isaac who was the baronet, and Isaac to whom the estate belonged.

'I promise you will be safe here, Miss Swynford,' he said instead, opening the door. 'Safe and well cared for. I'll ask for a tray to be sent up from the kitchen too. You must be famished.'

What in God's name had got into him?

Samuel paced up and down in the library, this same question circling around in his mind. He'd always regarded himself as a very straightforward, decent sort of fellow. He'd travelled all over Europe and mingled with all sorts of people, from country squires to wealthy merchants, to the sons and daughters of earls and dukes, and he'd never once felt any temptation to present himself as anything other than what he was. He was Samuel Liddell, a Cumberland gentleman, a younger son, a man sufficient in both means and good sense to enjoy a very comfortable life. A man who was glad not to have the responsibilities which came with an estate and a title. And yet there he'd stood in that bedchamber, allowing that lady to believe that everything here was his. That he was the master of Hayton Hall, and that he was the baronet. It was unfathomable.

Samuel slumped down into an armchair, sighing heavily and tugging uncomfortably at his collar. Outside, the day had grown dull and blustery, the loss of the earlier sunlight combining with the wind to usher in an autumnal chill. By contrast, however, the library felt stifling, the warm air heavy with the scent of leather-bound books and old wooden shelves. Samuel had no idea why he'd fled in here; this room was Isaac's domain, with everything about it pronouncing the real baronet's taste and temperament— from the dark green leather of its chairs to the decanter of brandy with a single glass and a newspaper placed neatly by its side. It was a quiet, brooding space, and one which had never suited the irrepressible cheer and sociability of the younger brother. Until recently, anyway. Bound by duty to the estate and disinclined towards society, thanks to the whiff of scandal Isaac had left in his wake, it was clear to Samuel that he'd been emulating many of his brother's habits during these past weeks. That glass and that newspaper, after all, were for him.

'None of which makes it all right to let Miss Swynford believe you're the baronet, you foolish man,' he muttered to himself. 'The question is, what are you going to do about it now?'

He had to tell her the truth, of course, before matters went any further. After all, he had not lied to her, exactly. But he had unwittingly misled her, and upon realising he had done so, he had failed to clarify who he in fact was. It was this clarification that he had to now offer, as soon as possible. It would be embarrassing, but by dealing with this swiftly, a simple apology for not explaining the situa-

tion to her immediately would suffice. He would not need
to offer any further explanation about his reasons for ini-
tially misleading her.

What were his reasons, exactly? Why had he not been
able to bring himself to utter a handful of simple words,
explaining that neither Hayton Hall nor the baronetcy were
his? Had these past weeks of effective isolation sent him
quite mad? Was he so in want of company that one short
conversation with an emerald-eyed young lady was enough
to make him lose all reason? It would seem so.

Samuel put his head in his hands, letting out a heavy
sigh. Allowing himself to attribute his behaviour to lone-
liness, no matter how convenient an explanation it was,
would not do. There was little point in lying to himself,
in failing to acknowledge that the thought of contradict-
ing the lovely Miss Swynford's assumption about him had
brought back those painful feelings of the summer. How
it had reminded him that he was not quite good enough,
that he'd been assessed on society's marriage mart and had
been found lacking.

How it had reminded him of the way a certain flame-
haired beauty had looked down her nose at him as he confessed his growing affection for her for the first time. The
way her words had cut him down and put him firmly in
his place—a place which was far below every titled man
in England.

*'Mama says I must have a London season, for that is
where the very best gentlemen are found. I dread to think
what she would say if she knew what you have asked of
me today...'*

Samuel shook his head, trying to push the humiliating,
hurtful memory from his mind. The fact that he still rumi-

nated upon it was bad enough, but allowing it to cloud his judgement when it came to being honest about himself was ridiculous. Quite apart from anything else, he'd no intentions towards Miss Swynford, or indeed towards any lady. This summer he'd thrown himself wholeheartedly into the turbulent waters of courtship and where had that left him? Washed up, rejected and deserted—quite literally. It was not an experience he was in any hurry to repeat.

He groaned, dragging his hands down his face. He had to put the recent past firmly behind him. And he had to be honest with Miss Swynford—as soon as possible.

His resolve suitably strengthened, Samuel rang for the butler. A moment later the older man arrived, one wiry grey eyebrow raised as he waited expectantly for his orders.

'Smithson, Miss Swynford will remain with us while she recovers from her injuries. Please see to it that she is kept comfortable and please ensure that no one outside of this house learns that she is here. It seems that the poor lady has fled from the clutches of a nefarious uncle who was seeking to force her into a marriage.'

'Poor Miss Swynford,' the butler remarked. 'Of course, sir, I will make sure the staff treat the lady's presence here with the utmost secrecy.'

Samuel inclined his head gratefully. 'As soon as she is well enough, Miss Swynford plans to travel to London,' he continued. 'I have promised to escort her; my absence won't be prolonged, and I'm sure that between you and the steward, the estate will be well cared for,' he added, offering the man an appeasing smile.

'Indeed, sir. Unless Sir Isaac has returned by then, of course.'

The mention of his brother caused Samuel to wince. 'Ah—

yes,' he began. 'You see, Smithson, Miss Swynford seems to have formed the opinion that I am the master here…that, um, well, I am Sir Samuel, I suppose.'

That wiry eyebrow shot up again. 'Miss Swynford has formed this opinion?' the butler repeated. 'Can such things be considered opinions, sir?'

'Perhaps it is more of an impression then,' Samuel replied, grimacing.

Smithson nodded slowly. 'I see. And to be clear, sir, this impression was formed by the lady herself, rather than given to her by someone else?'

Samuel groaned. 'The lady formed the impression and someone else—namely me—failed to clarify matters.' He gave the butler an earnest look. 'I do intend to give that clarification when the appropriate moment arises. However, the lady is vulnerable and her health is clearly delicate, so it is important that the clarification comes from me, rather than a servant, wouldn't you agree?'

He watched as his brother's loyal servant pressed his lips together, his brow furrowing deeply for a moment as he considered his words. 'Just to be clear, sir—you want the household to pretend that you are the baronet?'

Samuel felt his face grow warm. 'I'm not asking anyone to lie, Smithson. I'm simply asking them not to say anything until I can…'

'Until you can clarify matters?'

Samuel nodded. 'Exactly.'

Smithson gave Samuel another tight-lipped look. 'I will ensure everyone in this household does as you wish,' he replied after a long moment. 'I would only caution you, sir, that often what begins as a small deception tends to have a way of getting out of hand. It would be best to be honest, sooner rather than later.'

'I fully intend to be, Smithson.'

The butler nodded, apparently satisfied. 'I dare say you'll need to have clarified matters before your friends arrive, in any case.'

Samuel frowned. 'My friends?'

'The ones due to visit from Lancashire, sir,' Smithson reminded him. 'Mr Gordon and his sister. Are they not arriving next week?'

At this Samuel groaned, dragging his hands down his face once more. In the midst of everything that had happened since last night, he'd quite forgotten about Charles and Miss Gordon's visit. They couldn't possibly come now, not while there was a lady hiding in his home. A lady whom he'd sworn to protect. A lady whose whereabouts he'd promised to keep secret.

'I'll write to Charles and ask him to postpone. I'll tell him I'm unwell,' Samuel replied. 'I cannot possibly entertain guests while Miss Swynford is convalescing in secret. I gave her my word that no one else would know she was here.'

Smithson nodded politely. 'Very good, sir,' he replied. 'Hopefully, the letter will reach Mr Gordon in time.'

Indeed, thought Samuel, it had better. As much as he'd been looking forward to seeing Charles, and meeting his sister, keeping Miss Swynford safe and hidden, and keeping his promise to her, was more important. He might not be a baronet or a landowner, but he was still a gentleman. A foolish, heartsore gentleman, but a man of honour nonetheless.

Chapter Four

The next few days passed in a blur of sleep and soup—the latter served eagerly by a maid named Maddie, who'd been charged with Hope's care. For the first time in her life, Hope discovered what it was like to be waited upon hand and foot, to recuperate in a house which was warm and comfortable, and where no one wanted for anything. As a child, the spectre of illness had frequently cast its shadow over their humble farmer's cottage, taking all of her siblings before they were old enough to help in the fields. Even the merest hint of sickness or injury had spelled danger in a home which was always damp and where there was never quite enough to eat.

If she was being generous to him, she could understand why, in the face of such hardship, her father had turned to more illicit ways of earning a living. What she could not understand, however, was how he'd allowed it to corrupt him so utterly. How he'd allowed it to drag her mother down, her spirit so broken by his cruelty that she'd sought solace in her deadly tinctures.

How he'd been able to face remaining in that cramped cottage near Lillybeck once everyone else had gone. Hope shuddered, her thoughts briefly returning to the night she'd been dragged back there, how it had struck her that nothing about the cottage or him had changed during her five-year absence. The place was still bitterly cold, and so was he—icy and filled with contempt for the daughter who'd disobeyed him and dared to have a life of her own.

Shuffling beneath her sheets, she brushed the memory aside. She could not dwell upon Hope Sloane's difficulties, not when she was meant to be Hope Swynford. After all, the runaway heiress she'd invented had enough problems of her own.

'Can I fetch you anything, miss?' Maddie asked, noticing Hope's discomfort. She was an attentive woman, perhaps ten years Hope's senior, her dark eyes framed by thick brown brows which were drawn together with concern for her charge. Hope tried not to dwell on what Maddie would think if she knew who the woman she waited upon really was.

Hope shook her head, offering Maddie a reassuring smile. 'No, thank you,' she replied. 'Honestly, you have cared for me far better than I have ever cared for myself.'

That much was true. In many ways, life in the theatre had been just as unforgiving as the precarious existence of a farmer turned free trader's daughter. The hours spent rehearsing and performing were long and relentless, while life off-stage presented endless dangers for her to avoid, from gin and opium to men who regarded actresses as little more than harlots. There had been no respite, and little opportunity to either eat or sleep well.

Maddie beamed at her. 'Oh, thank you, miss,' she replied, the colour rising in her cheeks at the compliment. 'I must say, you are looking much better already.'

Hope was inclined to disagree with that. With Maddie's

help she'd managed to wash earlier, and had caught sight of herself and her wounds in the mirror. She was indeed purple and blue, just as the physician had said. Thankfully, her face was unscathed, but her pallor was horribly grey, and her lower back bore a particularly nasty, swollen bruise. In short, she looked anything but better. She had to admit that she was beginning to feel better, though; the pain in her head had largely abated, and while her ankle remained swollen, it was not as sore as it had been. After washing, Maddie had given her a clean shift to wear, which had helped to lift her spirits further.

'It's one of mine,' the woman had remarked. 'It's a bit big for you, miss, since you are so slender, but it'll do until we can sort out some proper clothes of your own.'

Hope had nodded, wondering what Maddie had meant by that. Lending her a shift to wear in bed was one thing, but poor Maddie couldn't be expected to give items of clothing to her indefinitely. In the end, however, she'd decided not to question her further. Since becoming Hope Swynford and pouring out her deceitful tale, Hope had decided that remaining silent and compliant was the best approach. Saying too much, and asking too many questions, risked those around her growing suspicious. Lies had a way of tying you in knots if you weren't careful, and Hope had already told enough of them in the cause of concealing her true identity.

An identity which, thus far, she had successfully hidden. It seemed to be a stroke of incredible luck that she'd not encountered any familiar faces at Hayton Hall. There did not appear to be anyone here who knew who she really was. Perhaps the master of this fine house was completely unacquainted with her father and his unscrupulous dealings. She had no way of knowing; despite being situated mere miles from Lillybeck, she knew nothing of Hayton or its foremost family.

Before running away and joining the theatre, her world had been small, revolving around that damp cottage, household chores and keeping watch over her father's stills, tucked away in nearby caves. A world which only expanded when she was required to accompany her father into Lowhaven, or forced to assist with one of his night-time runs to the coast to shift contraband under the cover of darkness. Hardly a reprieve. Still, she thought, perhaps Hayton was far enough away to offer her sanctuary. Perhaps she had been very unlucky, after all, to have been recognised in Lowhaven.

Hope remained relieved and somewhat surprised too that her hurriedly invented tale had been accepted so readily by Sir Samuel, as she assumed she ought to call him now. When he'd questioned her, she knew she'd been vague and foolish with her answers. Goodness knew why she'd said she was going to London, of all places! Her careless words had not gone unpunished, with Sir Samuel's insistence upon escorting her on her journey south, meaning that she would now have to go there and work out how to survive in a city about which she knew nothing and where she was acquainted with no one. A city which was many miles south of Richmond, of her theatre company. Of her real life.

Her lies, indeed, would tie her in knots. She would have to be careful not to become trapped in a tangled mess of her own making.

A knock at the door broke the silence which had descended in the bedchamber. Maddie gave Hope a knowing look. 'The master again, no doubt.'

Hope smiled, smoothing the bedsheets down in front of

her. It was true that Sir Samuel was a frequent visitor, coming in periodically to see how she fared, or to ask whether she needed anything—which, of course, thanks to Maddie, she never did. Sometimes he'd simply sit by her side for a few moments, talking about nothing much beyond the weather or where he'd been on the estate that day, before apologising for tiring her and taking his leave. She supposed he wished to reassure himself that she was recovering well, that he saw this as his duty, since she was in his home and therefore in his care. Yet she also sensed there was more to his visits, that he did in fact desire her company. She recalled the remark she'd made during their first conversation, about him being at Hayton Hall all by himself, and how that had seemed to offend him. She wondered if, despite his protestations to the contrary, Sir Samuel was in fact lonely.

'Come in!' Hope called.

She raised a brief smile as Sir Samuel entered, although her expression quickly dissolved into one of consternation when she saw the pile of clothing he carried in his arms. She watched as he placed them down gently on the end of the bed, then stood with his hands on his hips, surveying them with a pleased look on his face. He had the most genuine, open smile, one which made gentle creases gather around his grey-blue eyes. The sort of smile which could illuminate a room. The sort of smile which, she reminded herself, she had no business paying quite so much attention to.

'These are for you,' he began. 'I thought you would need something more suitable to wear, once you're well enough to come downstairs.'

Hope glanced down at the clothes, a feeling of panic rising in her chest as she noted the fine lace and muslin on display. 'That is kind of you, sir,' she replied. 'But really, you should not have gone to so much trouble on my account. I cannot repay you at present…'

'Repay me?' Sir Samuel raised his eyebrows in surprise. 'Oh! Heavens, no! I did not purchase these, Miss Swynford. No, in fact, we…er…that is to say, they were already in the house. They belong to my cousin, you see. She stayed here a few years ago, with my aunt as well, of course, until she married. For whatever reason, she neglected to take these items with her, in her trousseau.' He gave a nonchalant shrug. 'So now they are yours—for the time being, at least. I do hope they fit as my…er…cousin is perhaps a bit taller than you, if I recall.'

His awkward acknowledgement of her small stature made Hope laugh. 'I find that most ladies are taller than me, sir,' she replied.

He grinned, apparently too much of a gentleman to comment further. 'Indeed, well, I'm sure Madeleine is more than capable of making any alterations that might be required,' he replied, nodding briefly towards the maid, who gave him a distinctly displeased look. Perhaps, Hope reasoned, she wasn't quite so adept with a needle and thread as her employer believed.

Sir Samuel, meanwhile, had paced over to the window, surveying the view outside with his hands clasped behind his back. Hope found her eyes roaming approvingly over his trim physique, his broad shoulders and slender waist on perfect display in a deep green tailcoat, whilst his fitted fawn pantaloons showed off the strong legs of a man who spent much of his life on horseback. Every impeccably tailored inch of the man announced his wealth and his power, his status as a gentleman, a landowner and a member of Cumberland's elite. A status which was far beyond her own.

Hope swallowed hard, barely daring to contemplate what this man would say if he knew that he'd come to the assistance not of a genteel heiress, but an actress and the daughter of an outlaw.

'Do you think you might feel strong enough to come downstairs today?' Sir Samuel asked, turning back to face her. 'I thought I might show you a little of the rest of the house.'

His question surprised her. 'Perhaps for a little while, although I cannot walk very well, sir.'

He narrowed his eyes, looking thoughtful. 'I may have something which will assist you in that regard, although I will need to go and look for it.' His eyes shifted briefly to Maddie, who hovered beside the pile of clothes. 'Madeleine will help you find something suitable amongst all that, and can let me know once you are ready so I can escort you downstairs. If you are sure you are well enough, that is.'

Hope nodded. 'I am sure, sir.'

Sir Samuel gave her another of his broad smiles, then with a brief bow he took his leave.

Hope watched as Maddie held up each gown one by one, apparently assessing their size and suitability with a keen eye and careful hands. There were more dresses in that pile than Hope had ever owned in her entire life. Most of what she'd worn over the past few years had been costumes; her clothing had belonged to the characters she'd played, not to her. But then, she supposed, so did that pile of dresses. They'd been given to Hope Swynford out of kindness, and to allow her to present herself in a way which befitted her position in society. Gowns like those were not meant for the likes of Hope Sloane.

'It was very kind of your master to fetch those himself,'

Hope remarked, feeling discomfited by the stony silence which had settled in the room. 'I would have thought he'd be too busy.'

'Yes, well, he's very…organised,' Maddie replied. 'Likes to take charge of matters.'

'I suppose that is a good trait to have in a gentleman with an estate to run,' Hope pondered.

Maddie appeared to flinch before answering. 'Suppose so.'

'You don't agree?' Hope asked, her curiosity defeating her resolution not to ask too many questions. 'I did notice that you looked a little displeased with him. Is he not a good master to work for?'

The maid eyed her carefully. 'He's fine, miss, honestly. Except when he calls me Madeleine. I have said that he can call me Maddie, like everyone else does. That's just his way, I suppose—very proper. Very exact. Not a hair out of place, so to speak. He's not at all like…' Maddie paused, pressing her lips together as she made a show of examining a pretty blue dress.

'Not like whom?' Hope prompted. It was clear the maid had said more than she ought to.

Maddie ran a gentle hand down the fabric, brushing away imaginary creases. 'His brother,' she said flatly, avoiding Hope's gaze.

'What about his brother?'

It was clear, however, that the maid was not going to elaborate further. 'I think this one will do very well,' she continued, holding up the dress. 'And I don't think it requires altering, which is a relief.'

Hope nodded, giving the maid a wry smile. The woman really did not like sewing, that much was obvious, but to describe it as a relief seemed a little dramatic. Hope shuffled forward, wincing as she pulled herself out from beneath the bedsheets. Sir Samuel's invitation to come downstairs had intrigued her, and she was keen to see something beyond these same four walls. Nonetheless, she would have to take care not to exert herself too much.

'Let's try it then,' she said to Maddie. 'But without my stays. I'm not sure my bruises could withstand them.'

With a brisk nod, Maddie set about assisting her, and no more talk passed between them—not about brothers, or dress alterations, or anything else. It seemed the maid had decided to hold her tongue, and despite her vow to remain quiet and indifferent, Hope could not help but wonder what it was that the woman was unwilling, or unable, to say.

Chapter Five

Samuel waited at the top of Hayton Hall's stone staircase, clutching his father's old walking cane in his hand. He'd asked Smithson to retrieve it for him, and requested that some tea be brought shortly to the small parlour, as Miss Swynford would be coming downstairs for a little while today. Smithson had given a brief nod of assent, but Samuel had not been able to overlook how the man had pressed his lips together, as though to prevent himself from saying what was on his mind. Not that he needed to: over the past few days, Hayton's butler had left Samuel in no doubt about just how much he disapproved of the situation unfolding in the house.

'The servants are very unhappy about keeping up the pretence that you are the baronet, sir,' Smithson had told him in no uncertain terms. 'Especially Maddie. The poor maid is terrified that she's going to slip up and accidentally say the wrong thing to Miss Swynford.'

'Madeleine's only job is to ensure Miss Swynford is kept comfortable and that all her needs are met while she recovers, Smithson. She hardly needs to discuss my family's history with her and, in any case, I doubt the lady would be interested,' Samuel had replied, conscious of how hollow his protestations sounded. He was, without doubt, making life difficult for his servants. 'I fully intend to explain everything to Miss Swynford,' he'd added. 'When the opportunity arises.'

Smithson had been unmoved, reminding his master of the perils of deception, that even the most banal lies had a habit of getting out of hand. Now, as he waited to escort Miss Swynford downstairs, Samuel found himself reflecting upon just how true this was. Not only had he compelled his servants to join him in deceiving Miss Swynford, but today he'd told her an outright lie, this time about the clothing he'd brought to her. In truth, there had been no cousin who had left her gowns behind; those items he'd gathered up and taken into Miss Swynford's bedchamber had belonged to his brother's beloved and sadly deceased first wife, Rosalind. Since her death two years earlier, they'd remained tucked away in Hayton Hall's old drawers and clothes presses, and Isaac had thus far neglected to do anything with them.

Samuel had agonised over giving Miss Swynford some of Rosalind's old clothes, but ultimately he'd concluded it was the most sensible solution. After all, the lady needed something suitable to wear, and given that she was in hiding from her wicked uncle, he could hardly take her to a dressmaker in Lowhaven. Telling her that the gowns had belonged to the deceased Lady Liddell had, of course, been out of the question—he might be a fool and a scoundrel for allowing Miss Swynford to believe he was the master of Hayton Hall, but pretending that his brother's loss had been his own was a step too far, and so he'd concocted the tale about his imaginary cousin instead. He'd barely been able to meet Madeleine's horrified gaze as he'd laid out the fine garments once worn by her mistress and dared to suggest they might need to be altered. He did not even wish to consider what Isaac would say if he knew. He'd damn him to hell, at the very least.

Feeling increasingly agitated, Samuel began to pace back and forth down the hallway. He'd insisted to Smithson, and to himself, that he'd be honest with Miss Swynford as soon as possible, and yet so far he'd failed utterly to find the right moment. Every time he'd knocked on the door to her bedchamber, and every time he'd sat beside her bed and made polite conversation, he'd resolved to tell her the truth. Then he'd looked at her smiling, welcoming face, at those green eyes regarding him in earnest, and the words had died in his throat. He'd procrastinated, telling himself that she was still weak from her injuries, that the awkward truth ought to wait until she was feeling stronger.

However, if he was honest with himself, he knew it was more than that. There was something about Miss Hope Swynford which had captivated him. Perhaps it was the soft, articulate sound of her voice, or the feeling of her petite form as he'd carried her in his arms, or the way she managed to make a maid's old shift look becoming, but something about her made him want to impress her. He knew that the moment he corrected her assumptions about him, the moment he confessed to being little more than Hayton's caretaker, he would be put back firmly in his unimpressive place.

'I do not mean to be unkind, Mr Liddell. You are very witty, and very charming. Perhaps if you had been born into your brother's position, things might have been different...'

Samuel shuddered as a certain red-headed young lady's words haunted him once more. Like it or not, memories of how it had felt to be rejected not for who he was but for what he was not had thus far rendered him hopelessly silent. That bitter experience had taught him that as soon as Miss Swynford knew the truth she would likely be very disappointed indeed.

Not that he was planning to court her! Of course not. His only role was to protect her, to ensure she recovered from her injuries before seeing her safely to London.

The sound of Madeleine calling to him from down the hallway startled Samuel from his thoughts, and he walked back towards Miss Swynford's bedchamber, twirling the walking cane in his hand with renewed determination. If Miss Swynford was indeed well enough to join him downstairs, then he would delay his embarrassing confession no longer. He would apologise for not clarifying sooner and he would renew his commitment to protect her. He would seek to put the lady at her ease, to make the best out of the situation in which they'd found themselves. To hopefully find enjoyment in each other's company during the short time that circumstances had conspired to bring them together.

When he reached her doorway, however, he felt himself freeze, the cane growing suddenly still in his hand as his gaze came to rest on his houseguest. Gone was the maid's hand-me-down shift, replaced by an elegant cream gown and matching shawl. Her dark hair, meanwhile, no longer hung loose about her shoulders but had been pinned up, except for one or two curls which framed her heart-shaped face. Standing there in the doorway, she looked every inch the refined, genteel young lady he knew her to be. She greeted him with a cautious smile and he found himself swallowing hard before he could return it. She was, without doubt, a thoroughly striking beauty.

Miss Swynford shuffled forward, leaning heavily against Madeleine, and a wave of protectiveness washed over him as he was reminded of what had happened to her. Of why she was here, and what he had pledged to protect her from.

'I want you to have this,' he said, holding out the walking cane. 'It belonged to my father. I thought it might help while your ankle heals.'

She gave him a grateful nod. 'Thank you, sir,' she said, accepting the cane and limping towards him, her steps tentative and unsteady after so many days of being confined to her bed.

Samuel offered her his arm, walking slowly at her side as they made their way towards the stairs. Her hand, like the rest of her petite form, was small and delicate, and he tried not to dwell on how pleasant it felt resting in the crook of his elbow.

'You must tell me if you feel at all fatigued, Miss Swynford,' Samuel insisted. 'I will return you immediately to Madeleine's care. I just thought that you may enjoy some respite from staring at the same four walls.'

'Thank you.' She inclined her head again. 'I will be sure to tell you, sir. I believe the walking cane will make moving around easier. It is fortunate that you still had it.'

He chuckled at that, gesturing around him with his free hand. 'Old family houses like this tend to collect people and their things, storing them within its walls like memories. At least instead of collecting dust, that old cane has come in useful. Alas, I am sure I do not need to tell you that, Miss Swynford,' he added. 'I'm sure you've enough dusty ancestry of your own somewhere.'

He watched as she nodded, her expression suddenly guarded and unreadable. 'Oh, indeed,' was all she said in reply.

Miss Swynford managed the short walk along the hallway well enough, but when they reached the stairs he saw her hesitate, glancing down with trepidation before turning to look at him. 'I'm not sure I can…' she began, shaking her head with regret. 'My ankle is not strong. I am worried I may fall, sir.'

'Of course,' Samuel began. 'Forgive me, it was silly of me to bring you out of your bedchamber so soon. I will return you to Madeleine.'

'No, sir, I am sorry,' she said. 'I admit, I was rather looking forward to seeing some of the house.'

The look of genuine disappointment in those large green eyes did strange things to his insides, and before he could give it due consideration, an idea had come into his mind.

'Then, if you will permit me…' he began, giving her a bashful smile as he scooped her up into his arms. 'I carried you up these stairs days ago. I believe I can carry you back down again.'

The sound of her laughter echoed around him. 'I have only a vague recollection of that, but I do distinctly remember you lifting me back on to my bed after I was unwise enough to try to get out of it and leave Hayton in naught but my bedclothes.'

That memory alone would have been enough to bring the colour to his cheeks, but coupled with the feeling of her wrapping her arms around his neck and clinging to him as he carried her, he was certain he must be glowing scarlet. Samuel tried to focus on taking one step at a time, to pay no heed to the way her alluring form had settled so perfectly into his arms. It was ridiculous to entertain such thoughts, he reminded himself. The lady was only in his home because of the unhappiest of circumstances; his duty was to protect her, not to admire her. Not to allow his recent lone-liness to put ideas in his head which he had no business entertaining. Ideas which he most definitely did not want to have, after his recent brush with rejection.

'So where are we going, sir?' she asked softly, thankfully oblivious to the inappropriate turn his thoughts had taken.

'To my favourite room in the house—the small parlour,' he replied. 'For tea and cake—in my opinion, two of the very best things in life.'

Tea, cake, and confessions, he reminded himself silently.

'That sounds lovely,' she replied. 'I feel very safe here, with you. I do find myself wondering whether, should my uncle learn that I was here, the risk of offending an impor-tant local gentleman such as yourself might dissuade him from seeking me out.' She paused for a moment, her eyes wide as they searched his. 'After all, a gentleman in your position must be closely acquainted with those charged with upholding the law. That ought to make him think twice about doing anything…untoward,' she added quietly.

Her words were tentative, laced with fear, and Samuel felt his blood heat as the need to protect her gripped him. 'I can assure you that the Liddells have always been known to do what is right, Miss Swynford, and have always main-tained a good relationship with the local magistrate. Please do not worry,' he added as he reached the bottom of the staircase and released her from his arms. 'You are indeed safe in this house.'

She smiled at him, those emerald eyes brightening with relief. 'I do believe that I was fortunate indeed to stumble into the home of a baronet.'

Samuel forced a smile in return, his heart lurching and descending rapidly into the pit of his stomach. The hopeful look in Miss Swynford's eyes, and all that it implied, was unmistakable. She believed that his position as the master of Hayton Hall, as a landowner and a baronet, meant that he could protect her better, that he had a standing in society which no wicked uncle could overcome. That his title and his estate could shield her. And in many ways she was right—except neither of those things were truly his!

But how could he tell her that now? How could he tell her that she did not enjoy the protection of a titled gentleman but a mere younger son, playing the master in his brother's absence? How could he, in all good conscience, dash her hopes of receiving the very best protection? How could he knowingly allow her to feel anything less than completely safe with him?

He knew the answer to all of that—he simply couldn't. As they made their way slowly towards the parlour, he almost groaned aloud. Lord help him, but he was going to have to be the baronet for a while longer yet.

Hope sipped her tea tentatively and took a moment to observe the neat little parlour into which Sir Samuel had brought her. She could immediately see why he liked this room, with its compact size and good number of windows making it both warm and bright. Her gaze fell briefly upon the fireplace around which the sofa and chairs were arranged, and she found herself imagining how cosy it must feel to sit in front of the fire on a cold winter's day.

She doubted she'd ever experienced such comfort in all of her life; even with the hearth lit, her childhood home had always felt so cold and damp, whilst the wages of an actress had only ever afforded her the most meagre accommodation, invariably shared with other women who made their living on the stage. She pushed the thought from her mind, reminding herself who she was now. Or at least, who she was pretending to be. Hope Sloane might sit in awe of a simple parlour, but Hope Swynford never would.

'Do you have everything you need, Miss Swynford?' Sir Samuel asked.

The master of Hayton Hall had sat down opposite her, leaning forward slightly as though anxious to ensure she was well before he would relax. Upon bringing her into the room he'd placed her gently upon the sofa, then set about fetching cushions for her back and a footstool upon which to rest her injured ankle. Truly, his attentiveness was rather endearing, and she found herself struck by how pleasant it was to be treated thus by a gentleman. She found herself thinking too about those few moments she'd spent in his arms as he'd carried her down the stairs. How she'd found the courage to broach the subject of his acquaintance with local men of the law, looking for even the merest hint of crookedness or, God forbid, of dealings with her father. How Sir Samuel had not hesitated to tell her what she'd already begun to suspect—that the Liddell baronets were decent, upstanding men.

How reassured she had felt, in that moment. How relieved to be in his home, to enjoy his protection. And how safe she had genuinely felt as she'd wrapped her arms around him and clung to him for dear life.

It was a disconcerting idea, and one which she pushed swiftly from her mind. No doubt she was simply in awe of this gentleman, of his grand home and his impeccable kindness to her. The gentlemen she'd encountered in theatres were usually very different—at best, drunk and unintelligible by the final act, and at worst, downright lewd and trying to procure the sorts of services she absolutely did not offer. She felt herself begin to blush at the thought of it. She was quite sure Hope Swynford would never have to put up with such humiliation.

'Miss Swynford?' he prompted her, and Hope realised she had not answered.

'Yes, thank you, sir,' she replied, offering a smile which she hoped would be reassuring. She glanced out of the window, spying the view to the front of the house. Neat gardens, stone walls and fields as far as the eye could see. From this aspect, Hayton Hall felt remote. But was it remote enough to keep her hidden? She had to hope so.

'So what is Hayton like?' she asked him. If they were going to drink tea and converse, she reasoned that she might as well learn a little more about exactly where she was.

'It's a small village, just a short walk away,' Sir Samuel replied. 'It has an old church, and a single inn. It is a quiet place. Not a great deal happens in these far-flung corners of England, Miss Swynford,' he added with a grin.

'It sounds lovely,' she remarked, thinking how like Lillybeck it sounded. Thinking too how small places so often appeared sleepy and innocent on the surface. Peel back the layers, though, and there was always some darkness to be found.

'And what about…wherever it is that you are from?' Sir Samuel asked.

Hope hesitated. She had not yet managed to invent a satisfactory explanation of where exactly she'd come from. In truth, her knowledge of England was piecemeal, confined largely to Lillybeck, Lowhaven, and the handful of northern towns she'd visited whilst travelling with her theatre company. She could not risk claiming to be from any of them; if Sir Samuel happened to know any of the prominent families from those areas, her story would quickly come unstuck. The south, meanwhile, was unknown to her; she could not convincingly claim to be from any part of it. Perhaps, she reasoned, it was best if she did not explain at all.

'If you will forgive me, Sir Samuel, I would prefer not to speak of home,' she said quietly, her heart beginning to thud in her chest. She avoided his gaze, hoping he would not press her further. Hoping he would not somehow sense the truth among the lies, that the last thing she ever wanted to tell him about was Hope Sloane's life in Lillybeck with a free-trading father and an opium-eating mother.

He held up his hands. 'Of course, of course. It was thoughtless of me to ask, after all you've endured of late,' he replied. 'Although if you'd said you were from Lancaster, I'd have definitely grown suspicious about your connections.'

Hope frowned, her stomach lurching as a wave of anxiety gripped her. 'What do you mean, sir?'

Sir Samuel grinned at her. 'I was referring to Katherine Swynford,' he replied. 'I am sorry, it was a terrible joke. An inaccurate one too, since the lady was likely from Hainault.'

Hope shook her head, still not understanding. 'Forgive me, I…'

'John of Gaunt's third wife,' he reminded her. 'I was referring to a remark I made when you first told me your name. You share the same name as the third wife of John of Gaunt, who was the Duke of Lancaster. As I said, a terrible joke.'

'Oh, yes,' she replied, recollecting now. Recollecting too the play from which she knew the name. 'John of Gaunt, from the play by Shakespeare *The Life and Death of King Richard the Second*,' she added, allowing herself a brief indulgence in her memories. Her company had performed that play during her first year in Richmond. She'd had only a small part as one of the Queen's ladies, but it had not mattered. Newly liberated from her father's clutches, everything about her life then had seemed so fresh and new. So full of possibility.

Sir Samuel nodded enthusiastically. 'Indeed, from Shakespeare and from history, of course. John was a younger son of Edward III. The story goes that John fell in love with Katherine, but he was already wed and so took her as his mistress. Together they had several children, and after the death of his second wife, he married her.' He regarded her carefully. 'Forgive me, I am perhaps telling you something you already know.'

Hope pressed her lips together, unsure if this was something which a genteel lady like Hope Swynford ought to know. Hope Sloane did not, but then what Hope Sloane knew had been learned from books and plays, from observation and conversation. It was knowledge grasped during a colourful and chaotic life, not the result of orderly tutoring or instruction.

'It is quite the love story, is it not?' she observed after a moment, choosing words which would neither suggest knowledge nor convey ignorance.

Sir Samuel chuckled. 'I suppose it is. Alas, neither of them lived many years after their marriage. And, of course, their offspring's descendants, the Beauforts, went on to be thoroughly embroiled in the quarrel between the roses, as Mr Hume called it.'

'Of course,' Hope replied, feeling thoroughly lost now. 'A love story with unintended consequences, then,' she added thoughtfully.

'Ah—yes, very good,' Sir Samuel agreed. He paused, finishing his tea. When he met her gaze again, she saw his blue-grey eyes seemed to have darkened. 'I don't know about you, Miss Swynford, but it seems to me that there are always consequences when it comes to matters of the heart.'

His words, though smoothly delivered, seemed raw, and Hope found herself wondering at the cause of such an observation. During the short time she'd known him, Sir Samuel had seemed to her to be a kind and gentle sort of man. The sort of man who would be generous with his affections, and perhaps the sort of man whose own feelings were easily wounded.

By contrast, she had always guarded her emotions closely; grim experience had taught her that she had to be the master of them, that feeling anything too deeply was unwise in a life dominated for so long by crime and cruelty. And as for love—that was something others traded, whether it was her father making her his part of a bargain with a fellow outlaw or the actresses she'd known, selling their affections for little more than trinkets and the whispers of gentlemen who made empty promises of a better life. No, she thought, love had played no role in her life thus far.

'Alas, sir,' she answered at length, 'I must confess I have little enough experience of these matters, beyond facing the prospect of a forced marriage, but that had nothing to do with love.'

As the words fell from her lips, Hope was pained to acknowledge that this was the most honest sentiment she'd expressed to Sir Samuel since they'd met. Pained too to note the look of earnest sympathy he gave her as she reminded him of her misfortune. An unexpected, unfathomable feeling rose within her, one which made her yearn to tell him more about herself. To tell him truths she'd never uttered to another person. Perhaps even to tell him the truth.

Hope swallowed down the rest of her tea, as though the hot liquid might bring her back to her senses. As benevolent as her rescuer appeared to be, he could not know the truth about her. No one here could. Her entire future likely depended upon it.

Chapter Six

After that first afternoon they spent together in the parlour, something of a routine was quickly established at Hayton Hall. Sir Samuel would spend the morning attending to his duties on the estate, leaving Hope to rest in her bedchamber. Around noon, Maddie would serve her luncheon in her room and then help her to dress before Sir Samuel arrived to collect her and carry her down to the parlour for tea.

If Hope was honest with herself, she'd already begun to look forward to their meetings, perhaps more than she should. After all, every conversation they had carried a risk—a risk that she might accidentally reveal some detail about her real self, or a risk that she might say something to provoke Sir Samuel's suspicions about the authenticity of the story she had told him.

Despite these risks, Hope did her best to immerse herself in the role she had created, allowing herself to enjoy the fine dresses she wore, the comfortable sofa she sat upon and the quality tea she sipped while getting to know her host better. Sir Samuel seemed to understand that she did not wish to talk much about herself. Since she'd politely refused to answer his enquiry about where she was from, he had not asked her anything specific about her life at all.

Instead, he engaged her on less contentious topics, every-thing from the minutiae of the day to discussions about fa-vourite pursuits. Hope learned that he'd travelled widely, that his knowledge of the Continent, of its different countries and cultures, was second to none. She found his descrip-tions of all that he'd seen fascinating; from lakes flanked by towering mountains in Switzerland to crowds of boats on the Venetian lagoon, it was as though he was revealing new worlds to her through words alone.

'You are fortunate to have seen so much of the world,' she'd mused one afternoon as he concluded one of his tales. 'Especially with an estate to manage.'

'Well, of course, all of this took place before I had such responsibilities,' he'd replied, giving her an odd, strained look.

Realising he must have been referring to the time when his father still lived, she'd glanced at the walking cane she'd placed beside her, suddenly struck by all that had passed from father to eldest son. 'It must be a strange thing to in-herit all of this,' she'd remarked, waving a hand delicately about her. 'For all the security it surely brings, it must also place limitations upon a gentleman. You cannot freely do as you please when you have duties to your family, your land and your tenants.'

Sir Samuel had given her a tight smile. 'I hardly think any gentleman born into comfort and wealth has any right to complain about his lot, however much he might wish to.'

His reticence had made Hope grin. 'Surely everyone has the right to complain sometimes,' she'd replied. 'It strikes me, sir, that running an estate well is very hard work.'

'Indeed it is,' he'd agreed, 'and not only for gentlemen, as you may discover, should you one day marry and find yourself the mistress of some grand house with many acres attached to it.'

Her smile had faded quickly at that. 'That seems un-likely,' she'd replied, grappling for the right answer, the one which Hope Swynford would surely give. 'My uncle all but dragged me to the border to wed a stranger,' she'd reminded him. 'He might not have succeeded, but I hardly think that detail will matter. I am doubtless ruined in the eyes of so-ciety.'

She'd half expected Sir Samuel to argue, but instead he had agreed. 'Polite society is apt to condemn, and apt to make ill-founded judgements upon others,' he'd remarked with such resignation that Hope could not help but wonder if his words had been provoked by more than her retort.

'Oh, I almost forgot,' he'd said, swiftly changing the subject as he lifted a pile of books off the nearby table. 'All that talk about John of Gaunt and Katherine Swynford the other day prompted me to remember these books. Mr Hume's *A History of England*. I thought they might help you to pass the time while you convalesce. That is, if you have not already read them.'

Hope had shaken her head, accepting the six volumes as Sir Samuel handed them to her. 'No, I confess I have not read them,' she'd replied as casually as she could manage. Again, she'd no idea if a woman like Hope Swynford would be expected to have read such books or not.

To her relief, Sir Samuel had seemed not at all perturbed by her admission, which was just as well because Hope had felt unsettled enough for the two of them. As much as she enjoyed Sir Samuel's company and conversation, it was mo-ments like that which reminded her of all she was pretend-ing to be, and all that she was really not. Sir Samuel was a learned gentleman, well-tutored and well-travelled. By contrast, Hope was fortunate that she could read at all; as a girl, she'd been taught her letters by her mother, but they had not owned books like the ones Sir Samuel had given to her. As a woman, she read broadsides and chapbooks, and perhaps the occasional well-thumbed novel which had been passed between the actresses.

Life had taught Hope most of the lessons she knew, and latterly, the theatre had been her schoolroom. Indeed, the theatre was the one area in which she could perhaps match Sir Samuel's knowledge, albeit whilst implying that she'd become acquainted with Shakespeare's plays from a seat in a box at Covent Garden or Drury Lane, and not because she'd spoken his words on stage at Richmond's Theatre Royal.

Unfortunately, it seemed to Hope that fate had more discomfiting moments in store for her. Today, as they rose to leave the parlour, Sir Samuel suggested that they dine together in the evening for the first time. Hope was reluctant; until now she'd eaten her evening meal in her bedchamber, under Maddie's watchful eye but with no expectation of displaying the proper manners or refinement. She knew enough about the habits of the wealthy to know that dining formally with Sir Samuel would be an entirely different matter, and one which she was not confident she would manage. Indeed, the thought of sitting at his fine table, completely lost in the face of all those dishes and all that cutlery, made her feel quite sick.

'I'm afraid my appetite is not as it should be,' she explained, trying her best to thwart him as gently as she could. 'I do not think I could manage it.'

'I do not propose we get through a pile of game and a

mountain of jelly by ourselves,' he replied. 'Indeed, most evenings I sit down to a bowl of soup followed by a small plate of fish and vegetables.'

That admission caught her by surprise. 'That is what I am served most nights, in my room.'

'That's right, because that is what my cook has made for us both,' Sir Samuel answered with an amused smile. 'You look startled, Miss Swynford.'

She shook her head. 'I do not know why, I just had not imagined you were eating the same meal as me.'

He began to laugh. 'Oh, heavens! Now I'm concerned you must have imagined me dining downstairs upon fifteen courses while Madeleine served you meagre soup and fish. I'm a country gentleman, Miss Swynford, not the Prince Regent.'

Hope felt her cheeks begin to flush. 'I can assure you, sir, I did not think that. It is just that I have found my meals very restorative and I assumed they had been served to me for that reason.'

Sir Samuel nodded. 'Yes, and what is good for you is also good for me. I prefer simple, hearty fare. I am not a great enthusiast for rich sauces or heavy puddings.'

'Except cake,' she countered. 'One of the two best things in life, if I recall.'

He grinned at her. 'That's right. Now then, on the promise of a small, simple meal, will you dine with me this evening, Miss Swynford?'

Hope felt her hesitation melt in the face of his convivial persuasion. That was something else she'd observed about Sir Samuel—what he had in learning was easily matched in charm and good humour. She found herself reflecting momentarily upon his qualities, his affability and aptitude for conversation, and contrasted that with what she knew of his life at Hayton Hall, alone and unwed. She wondered why that was, wondered too if it had anything to do with the remark he'd made just days ago about matters of the heart and their consequences. Then she pushed the thought aside, deciding it was none of her business.

Instead, she returned his smile, knowing that whatever misgivings she still had, there was only one answer to his invitation that she could possibly give. 'That sounds lovely, Sir Samuel.'

Samuel took a mouthful of his evening meal, believing it to be the best mackerel he'd ever tasted. Weeks of dining alone had led him to become largely disinterested in what was on his plate, the business of eating having become a mere necessity rather than a pleasure. This evening he was reminded just how much he enjoyed dining in company. He'd been delighted when Miss Swynford had agreed to join him, although acknowledging this delight had made him feel instantly guilty as he was forced to remember that he was enjoying her company under false pretences. That he was allowing this lovely young lady to believe she was dining with Hayton's baronet. Swiftly he had buried the thought, reminding himself of the reason for his ongoing deception. It made Miss Swynford feel safe and protected. That alone made the lie a worthy one, didn't it?

He'd wrestled with that question, and his conscience, ever since that moment at the bottom of the staircase when he'd made the decision to hold his tongue. He'd wrestled too with the uncomfortable knowledge that as honourable as his intentions were in keeping the truth from her, maintaining the deception had also saved him from seeing her evident disappointment when she learned who he truly was. He had to admit to himself that whilst his desire to make her feel secure with him was paramount, he was still allowing his wounded pride to rule his head, at least in part.

Across the table, Miss Swynford caught his eye and he offered her a smile. Like him, she'd dressed for dinner, the cream day dress she'd worn earlier now replaced by a very becoming periwinkle blue gown. Several times his gaze had been drawn to how the colour contrasted so sharply with her dark hair, how the silk fabric flattered her slender form, before he reminded himself that he had no business admiring her. Especially not when it was another of Rosalind's dresses that she wore.

Miss Swynford returned his smile shyly, before taking a tentative sip of the fine claret he'd had Smithson fetch from Hayton's cellars. She seemed on edge tonight, surveying the food and drink before her with wide eyes, consuming them slowly and deliberately, as though she was unsure of herself. As though she was unsure of him.

Samuel felt his smile fade, gripped now by the worrying thought that he might be responsible for her apparent discomfort, that perhaps dining together like this had been a step too far. However compelling the reasons were for her to remain in his home at present, she was nonetheless an unchaperoned, unmarried woman, convalescing in close confinement with an unmarried man. Perhaps she'd been able to countenance tea and cake in the afternoon light of a parlour, but the presence of claret and candles as day faded to night felt too intimate. He had not considered it like that before but, now that he did, he could see how dining like this could be construed in that way. How it might give rise to concerns about his intentions, and just how dishonourable he might in fact be. He reminded himself again of all that she'd endured of late. Certainly, her wicked uncle and his equally dreadful conspirator had given her no reason to trust a gentleman.

'I hope you will forgive me for asking you to join me this evening, Miss Swynford,' Samuel began, possessed now by the urge to say something, to explain himself.

She looked up from her plate, fork poised. 'Forgive you?'

'Indeed, it was very selfish of me. I occupied you for much of the afternoon in the parlour, and ought to have left you to rest this evening.'

She wrinkled her brow at him. 'Do I look tired, sir?'

'Well, no, of course not...'

She gave him another of those small smiles. 'Then all is well. I will be sure to say, if I wish to retire.'

'Yes, of course, very good.' He paused, momentarily unsure how much more he wished to say, before swallowing his pride and adding, 'I would just like to assure you that I have only the most honourable and gentlemanly intentions in inviting you to dine with me. I merely felt it would be nice for us both to have some company during dinner, that is all.'

Miss Swynford sipped her wine again, lingering somewhat over it, and he could tell that she was considering his words. Inexplicably, his stomach started to churn, and he began to regret eating that mackerel quite so enthusiastically. He would have to ask Smithson to have the cook prepare for him some of that sweet ginger drink she always swore aided digestion.

'I am relieved to hear it, Sir Samuel,' she replied at length. 'I cannot tell you all the wild thoughts I had been entertaining since we sat down to our soup.'

Samuel felt his heart skip a beat. 'Really?'

The horror on his face must have been comical, because Miss Swynford began to laugh. 'No, of course not,' she said between chuckles, clearly trying to retain a modicum of self-control. 'I cannot think why you would even feel the need to clarify your intentions, sir. I know we have only known one another for a matter of days, but you have given me no reason to think of you as anything other than the very best of gentlemen.'

He raised a smile at her compliment, even as it made him feel utterly wretched. Would she still think that if she knew he was not really Hayton's baronet? 'I only wished to put you at your ease,' he said after a moment. 'I am sorry to observe it, but you looked uncomfortable from almost the moment you sat down to dine.'

In the dim light offered by the candles and the coming dusk outside, Samuel was sure he saw her expression darken. 'I am not used to dining in this manner,' she replied quietly, 'with such fine food and drink, such civilised company.'

He frowned. 'What do you mean?' he asked, a furious heat growing in his chest as his mind raced to contemplate all that her words might imply. 'What happened to you, Miss Swynford? In what manner was this uncle of yours keeping you?'

She shook her head gently, declining to answer. When she looked up, her expression had brightened once more. She reached for her glass again. 'The wine really is very good, sir,' she remarked, taking a sip and, he suspected, collecting herself. Something was amiss, but he was damned if he could fathom what it was.

He nodded, lifting his glass in agreement. 'A Bordeaux wine, and one of my particular favourites, although I only indulge when in company. Drinking such fine wine alone always seems rather a waste,' he added.

'I must confess to wondering why you are alone here, Sir Samuel,' Miss Swynford replied, meeting his eye. 'Forgive me, but you must surely be one of Cumberland's most eligible gentlemen.'

Her directness took him aback. 'I'm not sure about that...' he began, before realising that he had no idea what to say. How could he possibly explain himself? He did not want to let yet more falsehoods fall from his tongue, to portray himself as some sort of humourless baronet, so committed to managing his estate that he had not yet troubled himself to find a wife. Yet he could not bring himself to tell her the truth either, that he was a lesser prospect, a younger brother, a recent reject on Cumberland's marriage mart because he had not quite passed muster. That final fact, in particular, was too humiliating an admission to contemplate.

It was clear from the expression on her face that Miss Swynford had seen his discomfort. 'I am sorry,' she said softly, before he could settle upon an explanation. 'It is none of my business. In any case, I dare say it will not be long before I hear of your marriage to some well-connected society beauty with a large fortune.'

Samuel gave a wry chuckle. 'She sounds...intimidating.' His smile faded. 'To be frank, I think I'd prefer genuine companionship, Miss Swynford. Wealth and connections might matter a great deal to some people, but not to me. If I marry, I would rather it was for love than status.'

Miss Swynford's eyes seemed to search his, as though she was surprised by this admission, as though she was trying to determine if he was in earnest. Truly, she must have only ever been acquainted with the most dreadful gentlemen if she could be so astonished by his heartfelt confession. Then again, hearing those words fall from his own lips had come as something of a surprise to him too. He'd heard the sharp edge in his own voice as he'd spoken about other people's considerations, and the frankness when he'd confessed his own.

He had not meant to be quite so blunt, to speak of marriage and love—two things he'd sworn off for now, and for very good reasons. Truly, what had come over him lately? Clearly, those smouldering embers of the hurt and humiliation he'd experienced had been given cause to reignite. Or perhaps, he considered, they'd never quite ceased to burn in the first place.

Samuel shook his head at himself. 'Forgive me…'

The sound of the door opening caused them both to startle and Samuel turned to see Smithson burst into the dining room, somewhat breathless, his cheeks flushed.

'Sir, I am sorry to disturb you at dinner,' the butler began. 'But I need to speak with you urgently.'

Samuel pushed back his chair impatiently, nodding an apology to Miss Swynford before turning to regard the older man. 'What on earth is amiss?' he asked as he strode towards him. 'Has there been some accident? Is it one of the servants?'

'No, sir.' Smithson spoke in a hushed tone, giving Miss Swynford a worried glance. 'No accident. But I must tell you that there is a carriage coming up the drive. A carriage I do not recognise. Someone is coming to call at Hayton Hall, sir. Tonight.'

Chapter Seven

Samuel hurried towards Hayton Hall's grand entrance, his heart hammering in his chest. Usually, he left the business of answering the call of visitors to the butler, but he'd instructed Smithson to escort Miss Swynford and find somewhere for her to hide. Besides, he reasoned, he was damned if he was going to put any of his servants in harm's way. In his brother's absence, he was the master of the house; dealing with unwelcome visitors was ultimately his responsibility. If, indeed, that was who awaited him in the carriage outside. It was possible that both he and the butler were jumping to the wrong conclusion, that this unexpected evening call had nothing to do with Miss Swynford's presence here, that her whereabouts had not somehow been discovered by those who sought her. That it was not the uncle coming to claim his niece, or the would-be groom coming to claim his unwilling bride.

But if it was not them, then who else could it be?

At the door, Samuel paused, pressing his eyes shut momentarily as he collected himself. As he prepared himself for the worst. Since Isaac's elopement and Samuel's retreat from society, Hayton Hall had received no visitors for weeks and, in any case, there was not a single person of his acquaintance who would consider calling uninvited at this late hour. Suppressing a groan, Samuel turned the door-knob and opened the door with trepidation. The chances of whoever waited outside being here to pay him a friendly call seemed vanishingly small.

Outside, the light was fading fast, and Samuel found himself peering at the carriage which had drawn to a halt before Hayton Hall's front steps. A driver had dismounted, opening the door for the person or people sitting within, and Samuel felt his breath catch in his throat as he watched a man step out. An imposing man, very tall and thickset, wearing a greatcoat and a conical hat.

A man, he realised immediately, who he did in fact know. A man whom he'd invited to visit before circumstances in the form of Miss Swynford had prevailed upon him. A man to whom he'd written and asked not to come at present, but who had apparently come nonetheless. Samuel felt his mouth fall open, his stomach lurching as his relief at see-ing a familiar face came into conflict with his awareness of the other difficulties this unexpected arrival presented.

'Charles?' Samuel called out, hurrying down the steps to greet him.

'Hello, Sammy,' Charles replied with a hearty chuckle. 'I am sorry we are so late. The roads rather wreaked havoc with this dear old thing. Father let us take the family coach—I suppose it is well suited to long journeys but I do so pre-fer the landau.'

'Oh, I see, yes, very good,' Samuel stuttered, still col-lecting himself.

Charles reached back into the carriage and Samuel watched as a gloved hand accepted his. A young lady stepped out, immaculately dressed in a deep blue bonnet and matching pelisse. Samuel watched as she brushed a swift hand down her long coat, keeping her eyes fixed on the ground as she stood dutifully beside Charles and awaited the necessary introduction.

'Sammy, this is my sister, Miss Henrietta Gordon. Sister, this is Mr Samuel Liddell.'

Finally regaining his composure, Samuel inclined his head politely at Miss Gordon, who mirrored his gesture but did not lift her eyes to meet his. She was uncommonly tall, much like her brother, but, unlike him, she was extremely slender, a fact which leant her stature a willowy, almost fragile air. Samuel found himself rather unwittingly contrasting her with the diminutive Miss Hope Swynford, a thought which prompted him to remember that poor Miss Swynford was still hiding somewhere in the house, fearing her imminent discovery. A thought which also reminded him that he was now going to have to find a way to explain that young lady's presence in his home to his unexpected guests.

A young lady who still believed he was the master of Hayton Hall. At that moment, Samuel could have groaned aloud. What on earth was he going to do?

Charles regarded Samuel with a half-amused, half-puzzled expression on his face. 'You look rather astonished to see us. Had you forgotten our little visit this week?'

Samuel shook his head. 'Of course not. Only…only I had written to you, to ask if we could perhaps postpone for a few weeks. I presume you did not receive my letter.'

At this, Charles laughed, patting Samuel playfully on the back. 'Doubtless your letter arrived at Shawdale, but Henrietta and I have not been there for almost three weeks, have we, sister?'

Miss Gordon shook her head, still not meeting Samuel's eye. 'We have been in Buxton, taking the waters.'

'Why did you wish to postpone?' Charles asked, glancing up at Hayton Hall. 'Is something amiss? Are you unwell? You do not look unwell.'

'I am fine,' Samuel replied, bristling as he recalled that it was illness which he'd used as an excuse to postpone in his letter. 'It is just that…well, I have a guest already. She arrived rather unexpectedly several days ago and…'

'She?' Charles interrupted him. Samuel watched as his friend's gaze shifted briefly to his sister. 'Is this conversation suitable for a lady's ears, Sammy?'

'Of course it is—it is nothing untoward. The lady was injured…she needed somewhere to stay, to recover, and… listen, I will explain everything when there is more time. Poor Miss Swynford is inside; I need to go and tell her that all is well, that she can come out of hiding.'

Charles frowned. 'And who exactly is Miss Swynford? Why is she hiding? What the devil is going on?'

'I will explain everything in good time,' Samuel said again, wringing his hands in front of him.

He was anxious to return to Miss Swynford now, but that was not the only reason he felt so on edge. Determining what to tell Charles about how Miss Swynford had come to be in his home was difficult enough, but the thought of owning his deception of her caused panic to rise in his chest. Smithson's words of caution rang in his ears. Lies did indeed have a way of getting out of hand. Certainly, this one was entirely out of his hands now; Samuel had no choice but to place it into the keeping of his friend, and hope that he would understand or, at the very least, that he would keep the knowledge of it to himself. In that regard, he was cautiously optimistic—for all that Charles was loud and enjoyed a good piece of gossip, Samuel knew that he could be relied upon when it mattered most.

Besides, what choice did he have? The alternative was to risk Charles bursting into his home and unwittingly revealing Samuel's deceit to Miss Swynford. The notion of her learning the truth from someone else was unthinkable. No—it had to come from him. If he could ever find the right moment, the right words to explain…

The right words to reassure her that she would always be safe with him, whether he had a title or not.

Samuel stood in front of his guests, his back momentarily turned to Hayton Hall. 'I need to ask for your co-operation in one matter, though,' he began, lowering his voice.

The furrow in Charles's brow deepened. 'Sammy?' he prompted.

'If Miss Swynford refers to me as Sir Samuel, please do not contradict her,' Samuel blurted, detesting the words as they fell from his lips.

A mischievous smile spread across Charles Gordon's face and he glanced up at the grand house once more. 'The lady thinks all this is yours, does she, Sammy?' he asked. 'Good grief. Just what sort of trouble have you gone and got yourself into?'

Hope shuffled on her chair, grimacing at her ankle as it throbbed in protest at the evening's exertions. The imminent arrival of that carriage had thrown Hayton Hall into a panic, and Smithson had worked quickly to find her a suitable hiding place. She'd followed him down into the servants' quarters at a pace which had been far from comfortable, leaning heavily on the walking cane as the butler swiftly placed a chair inside a pantry and instructed her to wait inside. There she'd sat ever since, feeling sore and restless in equal measure as her mind reeled with a myriad of discomforting thoughts.

Guilt possessed her first of all—guilt at acknowledging that, unlike Sir Samuel and his butler, she did not fear that those arriving in that carriage were looking for her. Guilt at realising how her deception had made her host fearful of an uncle and a co-conspirator who did not exist, whilst keeping him in the dark about the menacing spectre of men who definitely did.

If her father or indeed the man she'd been meant to marry were seeking to find her, they would not come in a carriage. They would not call at the front door and announce themselves. Men who lived as they did, who were involved in the sorts of things they were involved in, were never so conspicuous. Men like them worked under the cover of moonless stormy skies or in the deep black of Cumberland's caves; they drew their power from the places where shadows and chaos reigned. If they ever came for her then, without doubt, they would have her in their possession before Sir Samuel even knew anything about it.

Hope suppressed a groan, dragging her hands down her face in despair as the evening's events forced her to consider just what a tangled web she'd woven with her deceit. Moments before that carriage's arrival she'd been sitting at that fine dining table, sipping wine, allowing its potency to blur the lines between the real and the imagined, between who she really was and who she was pretending to be. She'd let her mask slip too many times; she'd allowed the veil of ladylike refinement she'd worked hard to draw across herself grow too thin. Hope reddened to recall her response to Sir Samuel's efforts to reassure her about his good intentions, how she'd teased him quite wickedly about wild thoughts, and, worse still, how she'd met his observation of her discomfort with something alarmingly approaching the truth. Why had she not simply said she was tired, or out of sorts? Whatever had possessed her to all but admit that she'd never dined like that before? Why did she seem so intent upon allowing glimpses of Hope Sloane to be seen?

Because she did not like lying to him, that was why. Because since the moment she'd arrived at Hayton Hall he'd been unfailingly kind and candid, and the knowledge that she'd repaid him with nothing but deceit gnawed at her. Worse still, the guilt she felt seemed only to grow with every passing day and every conversation. With every new thing she learned about him. With every growing doubt that the master here would be the sort of man to have any acquaintance with her father or his business dealings. She had not known what to do with herself tonight when he'd spoken so honestly about his desire for genuine companionship over more worldly considerations.

'If I marry, I would rather it was for love than status…'

Hope straightened herself and forced her mind to cease lingering upon those words. Indeed, she'd had no right to draw them from him in the first place, to ask him such searching questions about his life. She definitely had no right to be impressed by them, no matter how heartfelt or genuine they had seemed. Not when she was deceiving him. Not when those words had been intended for Hope Swynford, and not for the ears of Hope Sloane.

The door to the pantry swung open, causing Hope to startle. Her alarm, however, quickly dissolved into relief when she saw that it was Sir Samuel who had come, presumably to collect her and take her back upstairs. Drawing a deep breath, she reached for the walking cane and got to her feet, resolving to set aside all that she'd spent these past interminable minutes mulling over. There was little point in dwelling upon her guilt or fretting over what she'd said or done. There was nothing she could do about that—there were only the consequences of choices she had already made. Those choices, she reminded herself, had left her with a role to play.

'Is all well?' she asked him. 'Was it my…my uncle? Did you send him away?'

Sir Samuel sighed. 'Not quite.'

Hope watched with growing confusion as he glanced over his shoulder before stepping into the pantry to join her and closing the door behind him. She became aware, quite suddenly, of the confined space around them, of the shelves crowded with jams and grains. Of his close proximity to her, of the soft rhythm of his breathing, of the lemon scent of his cologne.

'The good news, it was not your uncle,' he began. 'The bad news, a friend of mine has arrived, along with his sister. Their visit was arranged prior to your arrival here, after which I wrote to Charles and asked to postpone. It seems he did not receive my letter.' Sir Samuel shook his head. 'Suffice to say, I cannot simply send them away now.'

'No, of course not,' Hope replied quietly. 'I am only sorry that you felt you had to cancel their visit on my account. If I had known how my presence here would inconvenience you…'

Sir Samuel reached out, placing his hand on her arm. 'You have not inconvenienced me,' he insisted, his grey-blue gaze holding hers. 'Please, do not think that.'

Hope nodded her assent, conscious of the warm reassurance of his fingers against her bare skin. 'Then what are we to do?' she asked. 'I suppose I could pretend to be a servant here.'

'No.' He retracted his hand, leaving her feeling oddly bereft. 'Regrettably, we cannot do that, Miss Swynford.'

She frowned. 'Why not?'

'Because I am an utter blockhead,' he replied with a heavy sigh. 'Charles turning up like that had me in such a panic and I…well, I may have told him that I already have a guest staying with me.'

Hope felt her heart begin to race. 'I see. Does he know anything else about who your guest is?'

'Only your name, and that you arrived unexpectedly and are staying here while you recover from some injuries.'

Her eyes widened at him. 'You promised you would not tell a single soul about me…' she began. 'You may as well put up posters in the nearby village telling everyone my whereabouts and have done with it, sir.'

Sir Samuel met her eye, and she watched as he pressed his lips together as though he was trying to collect himself. It was an odd change on a face which was usually either serene or cheerful, and it irked her to observe that he wore a grave expression just as well as he wore a happy one.

'You must know that I would never deliberately put you in harm's way, Miss Swynford,' he said. 'My words to Charles were careless but he is a good man and, besides, he does not know the whole story. I am sure we can come up with something. Indeed, we must tell him something…'

Hope shook her head, feeling the heat of tears prick in the corners of her eyes. Not more stories. Not more lies piled upon lies. She could not countenance it. She huffed a breath then moved to step past Sir Samuel, suddenly possessed of an urge to leave that cramped little room, to retire to her bedchamber and put some distance between herself and this man. To envelop herself in dark silence and try to reconcile the conflict currently raging in her weary mind between her angry disappointment at Sir Samuel's momentary indiscretion and the guilt-ridden knowledge that he'd done little more than repeat a small portion of her tall tale. And she would have done all of that, had it not been for the walking cane she leaned on. Instead, the perfidious thing seemed to catch against the uneven stone floor. She jolted, losing her footing as her weakened ankle failed to bear her weight, and fell forward.

Straight into Sir Samuel's arms.

He caught her—of course he did—raising her slowly back to her feet, his gaze intent upon her own. She felt her breath hitch, felt her hands pressed against his chest, apparently powerless to move. Felt the furious beat of his heart through his white shirt, felt his hands remain gently upon her waist just a moment longer than was necessary. Felt the closeness, the sheer heat of him. She'd never stood like that with a man before. It was strange, intoxicating, and not at all unpleasant.

Then Sir Samuel cleared his throat and took a step back. 'Forgive me.'

'No...yes, of course,' Hope said, giving him a tight smile and doing her best to compose herself. She moved to step past him again, this time successfully. 'Excuse me. I think I shall retire for the night.'

'Indeed, you must be exhausted,' he replied with a brittle nod. 'I will need to go and attend to my guests. We can save formal introductions for tomorrow but, in the meantime, what would you like me to tell them about you? I'm afraid Charles is surely going to ask.'

Hope pushed the pantry door open, letting out a resigned sigh. 'Tell him the rest of the story,' she said, her head still spinning with the odd intensity of what had momentarily passed between them. 'I dare say that there's little else to be done about it now.'

Chapter Eight

'Well, Sammy, that's a fine mess you've made for yourself.'

Charles Gordon sat back in his chair and sipped his brandy as Samuel nodded glumly, finding it hard to disagree with his friend's assessment. Miss Swynford had retired some time ago, without so much as casting another word or glance in his direction, leaving him to entertain his new guests. After a hasty supper of whatever the cook could cobble together at such short notice, they had retired to Hayton Hall's largest and finest room to converse. Predictably, Charles had pursued the matter of Miss Swynford, and Samuel had rather uncomfortably answered his questions, acutely aware of just how much having her story told would displease his other guest. Although, of course, there was little for him to tell, since he knew only the barest details; she'd refused to tell him where she came from, and he knew neither the uncle nor the other man's names. Clearly, the lack of meat on the bones of the story dissatisfied Charles, and before long he'd returned to marvelling at his friend's pretence of being Hayton Hall's baronet.

'I simply cannot fathom it—Samuel Liddell, lying to a lady,' Charles continued, shaking his head slowly. 'I would never have thought you capable of it.'

'Unlike you, brother,' Miss Gordon interjected. 'As I witnessed for myself in Buxton.'

Samuel raised an eyebrow in surprise. Charles's sister had had little to say for herself during supper, and since sitting down in the drawing room she'd apparently preferred to sip her tea and stare rather vacantly at the fire which roared in the grate. The nights were growing colder, and in the larger, infrequently inhabited rooms of Hayton Hall the chill was particularly notable. He watched as Miss Gordon adjusted her shawl across her thin frame, tearing her eyes finally from the fireplace to meet the discomfited gaze of her sibling.

'Please, do tell, Miss Gordon,' Samuel prompted her, relieved at the opportunity to turn the conversation away from his own shortcomings.

Miss Gordon raised a tight smile. 'We attended several balls at the Assembly Rooms during our stay. I cannot say if it was the strength of the punch or the sheer quantity of eligible young ladies which made my brother dizzy, but something possessed him to tell some really rather tall tales about himself. By the end of our stay, several had been led to believe that Charles had been closely acquainted with the late Duke of Devonshire himself.'

'It is not so unbelievable, is it?' Charles replied, an unbecoming shade of scarlet creeping up from beneath his cravat. 'The duke has only been deceased for a handful of years and, as everyone knows, he took a keen interest in Buxton and its improvement. It is entirely possible that I might have known him or…or met him, at the very least.'

Samuel chuckled, shaking his head at his friend. 'I thought you would have learned your lesson during our travels, Charles. As I recall, you came unstuck on more than one occasion when a young lady discovered you were not the son of an earl or a duke as you had claimed to be.'

Miss Gordon's eyes widened and she leaned forward before saying, 'Did he, indeed?'

Samuel nodded. 'They were all most disappointed to learn that Viscount Faux-Title here had no aristocratic connections at all.'

Charles let out a heavy sigh. 'Alas, where some men shall inherit castles, I shall inherit calico printworks.'

Samuel let out another amused chuckle. 'To listen to you, anyone would think you were not from one of the wealthiest families in Lancashire. Perhaps if you spent more time telling young ladies about that and not pretending to be someone you are not, you would have more success.'

He watched as both his guests stared at him, mouths identically agape as the irony of what he had just said sunk in. He suppressed a groan as wearily he rubbed his brow, his mind wandering to the lady sleeping upstairs, the one who did not have the faintest idea who he really was. The one whose company he had been enjoying once again just hours ago, as they'd dined together, as they'd talked. The one who'd fallen into his arms in the pantry, and whom he'd relished catching more than he cared to admit.

Samuel gulped down the last of his brandy, flexing his free hand against the arm of the chair, still feeling the ghost of her waist against his fingers. After the abject misery of confessing his deceit to Charles, he'd gone down to the pantry, resolved to tell Miss Swynford the truth there and then. However, his resolve had wavered in the face of how panicked she'd been at the thought of his guests knowing even the barest facts about her, and how rightly upset she'd been with him over his poor judgement and loose tongue. He was reminded at once that she already had enough to worry about, that she was in very real danger. A danger which she believed that he, and the title and status she believed him to have, could shield her from. His duty, first and foremost, was to protect her, not to burden her with any further worries.

A duty which certainly did not involve letting his thoughts linger on the feeling of holding her in his arms, he reminded himself. No matter how pleasant such thoughts were.

'I realise I have no business lecturing you, Charles,' he said after a long moment. 'Please, forgive me.'

Charles shrugged. 'There's nothing to forgive, Sammy. I can be a complete cork-brain and I know it. But you, my dear fellow, are not. What I do not understand is why you told Miss Swynford that you were a baronet in the first place.'

Samuel hesitated. 'I did not tell her exactly…she assumed, and, to my great shame, I did not correct her. I've been torturing myself with exactly why that was ever since—foolish pride, I suppose. I've been either a younger son or my brother's heir all of my life and, God willing, now that he's wed again, I will not be his heir for much longer. When Miss Swynford presumed I was more than that, I suppose I just got a little carried away.' He paused, deciding that was all he was prepared to say. Charles was his friend but, even so, he was not about to confess to him just how much of a wounding his pride had suffered of late. Or indeed how much of a role his humiliating rejection in the summer might have played in his willingness to be the baronet.

Charles grinned. 'So it is not because you want to court her, then?'

'Hardly.' Samuel bristled at the suggestion, alarmed to

note the image of her looking up at him, her hands pressed against his chest, returning to him once more.

'In that case, why don't you simply tell her the truth?'

'I was on the cusp of doing so,' he replied miserably, 'but then Miss Swynford told me how safe she feels here, how protected. It's clear she attributes this protection in no small part to my title and standing in Cumberland—or at least the title and standing she believes me to have. How could I undermine that when she is in my home, alone and vulnerable? How could I knowingly allow her to feel unsafe? And what if I confessed all and she felt so unsafe that she left Hayton Hall before she had properly recovered and ended up back in harm's way with her uncle?'

'The Sammy doth protest too much, methinks,' Charles replied, chuckling.

'Shakespeare—yes, very good,' Samuel grumbled. He slumped back in his chair. 'Perhaps I should just tell Miss Swynford the truth, whatever the consequences.'

'No, I think you're right.' Miss Gordon spoke up, nursing her tea thoughtfully. 'Miss Swynford is here in your care, and as you've no intentions towards her beyond offering her comfort and shelter while she convalesces, then I'd leave the situation as it is rather than risk her fleeing and coming to harm.'

Samuel inclined his head at Miss Gordon's interjection. She was an odd lady, carrying herself with such an air of disengagement, of disinterest, and yet it was clear she was listening to everything that was said, weighing it up and drawing conclusions. There was a cold clarity, a steeliness about her which her loud, affable brother had never possessed. How different two siblings could be, but then,

Samuel already knew that. He'd grown up with a far more sombre, far more reserved older brother, after all.

Samuel found himself wondering about Miss Swynford's family then, about who had been there for her before her uncle had her in his clutches. Her parents were dead, he knew that, but had there ever been any brothers, any sisters? He reflected on that strange remark she'd made at dinner, about how unused she was to enjoying good food and drink, and civilised company. How long had it been since anyone had truly cared for her? A heavy feeling settled in his stomach as he found himself contemplating the possibility that no one had, that apart from her wicked uncle she was all alone.

'Well, if Henrietta agrees, then who am I to argue?' Charles said, placing his glass upon the table and rising from his seat. 'I will go along with it, Sammy.' He grinned. 'Or, should I say, Sir Faux-Title?'

Hope sat up in bed, the first volume of Mr Hume's *History of England* perched upon her lap. She'd awoken some time ago but, oddly, Maddie had not yet come to attend to her, and Hope suspected this had much to do with the arrival of the other guests. Proper guests, she thought, feeling her heart sink. The sort who were accustomed to maids and butlers, to grand houses, large dining rooms and lavish meals.

An uncomfortable feeling settled over her then, as she recognised that the familiar routine she'd hitherto enjoyed at Hayton had come to an end. There would be no more mornings spent with Maddie fussing over her; the maid simply would not have the time for that. There would be no more parlour meetings with Sir Samuel either, no more af-

ternoons of cake and conversation. That particular thought
bothered her most and she fidgeted, trying to cast it from
her mind.

'You're just out of sorts, Hope, that's what's the matter
with you,' she muttered. 'You just don't want to go and meet
these new guests.'

That was true, certainly. Playing the role of Hope Swynford was challenging enough in front of Sir Samuel and a
handful of servants; adding two further scrutinising pairs
of eyes to the audience of people she had to convince was
the very last thing she wanted. She looked down at her book
again, forcing herself to concentrate on its lofty prose about a
queen called Boadicea and her battles with the Romans, and
trying not to think about last night. The way she'd allowed
candlelight and fine wine to loosen her tongue at dinner.
The way she'd reacted when she'd learned that Sir Samuel
had told his visitors about her presence there. The way she'd
fallen into Sir Samuel's arms in the pantry.

Hope felt the colour rise in her cheeks as she recalled
how her senses had seemed to heighten, at once acutely
aware of the muscular solidity of his chest beneath her
hands, of the warmth of his arms as they circled her waist,
of how his blue-grey eyes had searched hers, as though trying to discern the answer to a question which had not been
put into words, as though...

As though he might kiss her.

Hope sat bolt upright in bed, pushing the book to one
side in growing irritation at herself. What a fanciful notion to entertain! Of course a gentleman like Sir Samuel
had not been about to kiss her, and nor had she wanted him
to. Nor could she want him to—not when she was a guest
in his home, enjoying his faultlessly kind and considerate

hospitality under false pretences. Her ankle throbbed, giving her a timely reminder of the consequence of her clumsiness, and of the reason she was here at all. Hayton Hall was a place of refuge and its master had been a Good Samaritan to her, but there was nothing more to it than that. Indeed, she reminded herself, if he knew who she really was, and if he knew just how fundamentally she'd lied to him, he might not be so hospitable.

A knock at the door startled Hope from her thoughts. 'Come in,' she called, smoothing the sheets down in front of her and placing the book back in her lap. It was almost certainly Maddie, come at last to ask her what she would like for breakfast, and to help her dress. The poor maid must have been run ragged by the other female guest in the house if she had been detained until now.

'I am in no hurry, Maddie, so please…'

Hope's words died in her throat as Sir Samuel walked in and closed the door behind him. Immediately, thoughts of their close encounter in the pantry ran unbidden through her mind and she felt the heat rise inexplicably in her cheeks.

Stop it, Hope, she told herself. *Stop thinking about it. You're being ridiculous.*

She watched as Sir Samuel took a couple of steps into the room, then seemed to freeze. He stared at her, his eyes wide, his lips parted in surprise.

'Oh, you're not…' he began, waving a flustered hand in her direction. 'Erm, where is Madeleine?'

'Waiting upon your friend's sister, I expect,' Hope replied.

Sir Samuel gave a slow nod. 'I see. Perhaps I should go, then. We can speak once Maddie has been to help you dress.'

Hope frowned. 'Why? You sat by my bedside and talked

to me when I was most unwell.' She pulled irritably at her shift. 'This is nothing you have not seen before.'

Sir Samuel coughed. 'No, indeed, but…there are others in the house now. Others who may think thoughts which ought not to be thought if they…' He faltered, the expression on his face one of excruciating embarrassment.

'If they observe you slipping into my bedchamber in the morning before I am dressed. Or, I suppose, if they observe you coming in here at all,' Hope said, perhaps more bluntly than she should. After all, she doubted Hope Swynford would speak so plainly about such matters. In Hope Sloane's world, however, gentlemen being caught alone with actresses was of very little consequence. Certainly not something that anyone would bother to tiptoe around.

'Indeed,' Sir Samuel replied. 'I should not be here.'

Hope inclined her head in polite acknowledgement, before making a point of turning her attention back to the book on her lap. She could not explain why, but all that talk about the need to behave properly in front of the other guests troubled her. Almost as much as the realisation that Sir Samuel had probably sat them down last night and told them all about the poor runaway heiress sleeping upstairs. The thought of them all chewing over her concocted tale made her feel quite sick.

'Miss Swynford?'

Hope looked up from the pages, surprised to see he had not yet moved. 'Yes?'

'I came only to ask if you wish to come downstairs today. I realise that yesterday must have been quite a trial for you, so if you do not feel well enough then I understand.' He took a step closer, peering at her book. 'Is that Mr Hume's book you are reading?'

She nodded. 'It is. I have just reached the part where the Romans are leaving Britain. I have not managed to read very much of it yet.'

He smiled meekly. 'Of course, and gentlemen bursting into your bedchamber will hardly be helping.'

'Not gentlemen,' she replied. 'Only you.'

Sir Samuel laughed. 'I'm not sure whether I should feel complimented or affronted by that remark.'

'I'll leave that up to you to decide, Sir Samuel,' Hope quipped, trying and failing to suppress a smirk.

To her surprise, however, Sir Samuel's smile faded. 'Call me Samuel,' he said, his voice low and sincere.

Across the room, their eyes met and Hope found her thoughts straying to that odd moment they'd shared in the pantry once again. 'As you wish,' she answered him, trying her best to sound nonchalant. 'And I suppose you should call me Hope, rather than Miss Swynford.'

He inclined his head politely. 'I would like that very much, Hope.'

The way he said her name made the most disconcerting heat grow deep within her stomach. Hope looked down at her book once more. He needed to leave now, and not only because they risked the scandalous remarks of the other guests with each passing moment.

To her relief, Sir Samuel—or, rather, just Samuel now—moved back towards the door. 'I'll ask Madeleine to attend to you,' he said. 'You have waited long enough.'

'It is fine,' Hope replied, waving her hand. 'I am not in a hurry and, besides, it must be a lot of additional work, having all these people in the house who are not usually here.'

Samuel raised his eyebrows as though this was the first time that the extra burden having guests placed upon his servants had crossed his mind. 'Yes, you're right about that,' he conceded after a moment. 'You're right too to be cross with me for telling them about your presence here. I should have spoken to you first, to agree the best approach.'

'What's done is done,' she replied with a small shrug. 'I suppose they know all about me now, do they?'

'I have explained how you came to be here,' Samuel replied. 'I have also stressed how important it is that your presence at Hayton Hall remains a closely guarded secret.'

'Thank you. What did you say their names are? And where are they from? I'm afraid I cannot recall.'

'Charles and Henrietta Gordon, from Lancashire,' Samuel replied. 'I believe their home is called Shawdale, on the edge of a town called Blackburn, where their father does very well in trade.'

'Trade?' That all too familiar word made Hope look up in consternation. 'What sort of trade?'

'Calico printing, I believe.'

Inwardly, Hope breathed a sigh of relief. A proper sort of trade, and perfectly legal—of course it was. She was too quick to think the worst, to jump to the wrong conclusion when, realistically, she probably had nothing to fear. She'd never known her father to have dealings with anyone in Lancashire, much less those involved in calico printing. It did not seem likely that Mr Gordon or his sister would know who she really was.

Samuel's expression darkened. 'Why? Is that a problem?'

'No, of…of course not,' she stammered. 'Why would it be a problem?'

'Because, to some, the idea of associating with anyone who comes to wealth and prominence through means other than inheriting land and a title is offensive,' he said pointedly.

'Oh,' Hope replied, feeling as though Hope Swynford would probably have known that. 'Well, I assure you that I only asked out of curiosity.'

Samuel inclined his head, apparently appeased. 'So, you will come down to meet them today?' he asked hopefully.

Given the offence her questions had almost caused, Hope knew she had little choice. She knew too that meeting them was inevitable; she could hardly avoid them for the duration of their stay. The Gordons' visit was not ideal, but they were here now and that was that. This was the hand she'd been dealt, and she'd simply have to play it, and her role, very well indeed.

'Of course,' she replied, painting on a smile.

Chapter Nine

Samuel sat back in his favourite chair, trying his best to relax. He'd arranged to have tea with all of his guests in the small parlour, and hoped that the cosy familiarity of the room would put Hope at ease when meeting Charles and Miss Gordon. She'd seemed anxious when he'd met her in the hallway to escort her down, and for the first time since arriving at Hayton she'd refused to let him assist her on the stairs.

'I dread to think what your guests would say if they saw you carrying me,' she'd pointed out in a hushed tone. 'Besides, I am feeling much stronger. I managed to go upstairs by myself last night, and I am sure I can manage to walk down them today if I use the walking cane.'

Samuel had acquiesced, but nonetheless he'd remained close by her side as she'd made her way, somewhat unsteadily, down each step. Several times he'd observed her grimace in discomfort, and he suspected her ankle was not as healed as she'd suggested. But she was right; he could no longer be permitted to lift her into his arms, not when there were others in the house. An unexpected wave of regret had gripped Samuel then. Regret that his visitors had turned up as planned, that his letter had not reached them. Regret that his time alone with his unexpected guest had passed. Immediately he'd chastised himself for it. Hope was living in his home under his protection, not so that he might, quite literally, sweep her off her feet. That was something he had absolutely no intention of doing, especially not when he was being so untruthful.

The introductions over, their group had settled into some pleasant, if a little stilted, conversation. To Samuel's surprise and relief, Charles appeared to have decided to be on his best behaviour, engaging Hope in only the gentlest of enquiries about her convalescence and whether she was enjoying her time at Hayton Hall, notwithstanding the circumstances.

'This is the first time I have visited Sammy's home,' he said, looking all about him. 'And I must say that I have never laid my eyes upon a finer country house than this.'

'It is very lovely,' Hope agreed demurely.

Samuel, however, rolled his eyes. 'I am sure I recall you saying the same about almost every house we visited on the Continent,' he replied. 'And I am equally certain that Shawdale can compete with them all.'

Charles made a face. 'Shawdale is very grand, but it is not a country house. It is on the edge of a town and is barely ten years old. It does not have the depth that Hayton has, or indeed that any old family seat has when it has stood long enough to store the centuries within its walls.'

'You must forgive Mr Gordon,' Samuel said, turning to Hope. 'He has an unhealthy preoccupation with having an ancient noble lineage and a castle to keep it all in. You'll have to marry a duke's daughter, Charles,' he added, addressing his friend once more. 'Then you can ask your father-in-law if you can borrow one of his.'

Samuel was amused to see Hope splutter on her tea at that. She seemed to have relaxed a little now, and her laughter had made the colour rise in her cheeks, giving her a healthier glow. He found his gaze lingering upon her as he considered how well she looked in her cream day dress, her dark curls framing her face, her emerald eyes sparkling with merriment. Perhaps, he considered, their little group of four would not be such a bad thing, after all.

'He mocks me, Miss Swynford, but I am going to build my own castle,' Charles continued.

Hope's eyebrows shot up. 'Oh, like the Prince Regent? He builds castles for himself, does he not?'

Charles shook his head. 'The Prince Regent builds mansions and palaces. I shall build a castle which William the Conqueror himself would be proud to live in.'

Samuel chuckled in disbelief. 'You're going to build yourself a Norman castle?'

'Another of my brother's wild schemes,' Miss Gordon interjected drily. Until now she'd sat quietly, so much so that Samuel had quite forgotten she was there. 'When he inherits our father's fortune, he plans to knock down Shawdale and erect his monstrosity in its place.'

Samuel regarded his friend, aghast. 'And what does your father say about that?'

'He does not know.' Charles shrugged. 'Nor shall he.'

'You speak of legacies, Charles, yet you'd readily demolish what your father has built?' Samuel shook his head, unable to fathom it. 'And what about your mother? Or your sister?' he added, inclining his head towards Miss Gordon.

'Oh, I care not,' Miss Gordon said. 'When our father is gone, Charles can do as he likes, and so shall I.' She gave a self-satisfied smile then turned to Hope. 'I presume you had parents at one time, Miss Swynford?' she asked.

Samuel watched as Hope met his eye cautiously before answering, 'Yes, of course.'

'And have you committed yourself entirely to guarding their legacy?'

Hope sipped her tea, and Samuel saw that she was considering her answer. In truth, he was intrigued as to what it might be. In their time together, she'd said so little about herself, about her history. He knew nothing about where she'd come from, in terms of either location or heritage. He wondered now if Miss Gordon's rather abrupt questioning might yield more information than he'd thus far managed to gather.

At length, Hope shook her head. 'I confess I'm not sure I've ever thought much about it.'

'Well, what did they bequeath to you?' Miss Gordon put up her hand. 'And, before you think me impudent, I am not speaking of money. What I mean to say is, do you have happy memories of them to treasure, or would you too be happy to tear down the ancestral home?'

'Sister…'

Charles spoke gently, but the warning contained within his voice was all too clear. Samuel found himself wondering what on earth was going on, how a convivial conversation about Norman castles could have taken such a dark turn. Still, though, he was curious as to how Hope would answer. If she would answer.

He watched as Hope looked up, meeting Miss Gordon's gaze squarely. 'I dare say that, like many people, I can confess to cherishing some memories, while wishing to cast away others like stones.'

'And the ancestral home?' Miss Gordon pressed.

Hope gave a grim smile. 'It can remain standing, but I shall never set foot in it again.'

'I am sorry to hear that,' Samuel interjected quietly, glancing around him. 'I feel fortunate that I can look upon my family's home with such fondness.'

'Ah, and that is why Hayton is such a haven,' Miss Gordon answered, her tone lighter now. 'The perfect place to convalesce, I am sure. Well, except for Buxton. Its waters always do me the world of good, don't they, Charles?'

Charles might have answered but, in truth, Samuel was no longer listening. Instead, he found himself mulling over what Hope had said, trying to discern its meaning. He'd wished to know more about her, but what Miss Gordon's enquiries had revealed had only provoked more questions in his mind. What were the memories she wished to cast away? Why would she never return to her ancestral home? Did any of this have anything to do with the uncle from whom she was currently hiding?

Miss Gordon had spoken of guarding legacies. Well, Samuel thought, Hope was guarding something about her past, he felt sure of it. Something, he suspected, that was painful. Something she'd much rather forget.

Hope wasn't sure if she felt better or worse after her first meeting with the Gordons. Mr Gordon had seemed pleasant and good-natured enough, and she'd enjoyed the affectionate teasing which was clearly central to his and Samuel's friendship. Miss Gordon, however, was a different matter entirely. Frankly, the lady unnerved her, bestowing those dark eyes upon her as though she was peering into her soul, and asking questions in a way which seemed to suck the life out of the room.

Her behaviour had already caused consternation among the servants too. When Maddie had finally arrived in Hope's bedchamber that morning, she'd been flustered, explaining that it had taken several of the female servants to rouse Miss Gordon, such was the depth of her slumber.

'When, finally, she awoke, I thought she was unwell,' Maddie went on. 'She seemed weak and listless, and her eyes kept rolling back as though she was struggling to remain awake. I was ready to send for the physician, but she insisted nothing was amiss and ordered me to help her dress. Rather curtly, I might add.'

Hope had thought little of it at the time, reasoning that Miss Gordon was likely exhausted after her long journey to Hayton. Now, having met her, and having noted the sharp edge to her questions and the brittle way she spoke of family and legacies, Hope realised she would need to be on her guard. There'd been some pain and turmoil in that near-black stare, she felt sure of it. There'd been a story, barely concealed and threatening to spill forth, driving a tendency to want to unravel the stories of others. Hope knew her sort; the theatre had been packed with just such haunted individuals, taking to the stage to escape themselves. Hope wondered now what Miss Gordon's escape was, and whether it had anything to do with her difficulty in waking that morning. That was something she'd witnessed before too.

After tea, they took a walk in the beautiful gardens which sprawled to the rear of Hayton Hall. To begin with, Hope had hesitated about joining the group on their afternoon promenade. The walls of Hayton Hall, she realised, had become a fortress for her. Inside, she felt hidden away, protected from those who might be roaming the countryside, looking for her. The garden, by contrast, felt dangerous and exposed. Instinctively, Samuel had seemed to understand this.

'I can ask Madeleine to fetch your book and some more tea to the parlour, if you'd prefer to stay here,' he'd suggested. 'Although the gardens are very secluded, and we will not venture far from the house.'

Hope had felt the eyes of the other two guests upon her as she'd considered her options. Her gaze had wandered towards the window where, outside, a bright autumn day awaited. She did so long to feel the warmth of the sun on her face again. Surely, she reasoned, the risk of briefly venturing into private gardens, tucked between a large house and sprawling woodland, was not so great.

'I will come,' she'd said in the end. 'The fresh air will do me good. Although I'm afraid that my ankle means that my pace will be painfully slow.'

'There is nothing painful about a gentle promenade,' Samuel had replied, offering her a reassuring smile. 'I find it allows plenty of time for quiet reflection or, if in company, some delightful conversation.'

Equipped with the walking cane and a wide-brimmed bonnet sufficient to shield her face, Hope limped along the orderly paths which wove their way through beds thick with plants and bushes. She clutched Samuel's arm tightly, partly for support and partly, she realised, for reassurance. He had not left her side since they'd walked out of Hayton's rear door, nor had he spoken much, apparently preferring companionable silence to conversation.

Hope told herself that she ought to be relieved; she was still reeling from Miss Gordon's questions in the parlour.

Though her answers had been suitably vague, they had also contained much truth about herself—her real self. In light of that, the chance to keep her own counsel for once should have been welcome, yet instead Hope found herself wishing that Samuel would engage her on some topic, however ordinary. Wishing too to rekindle something of those short few days they'd spent together, prior to the Gordons' arrival.

'Is everything all right?' she ventured to ask in the end, finding herself unable to tolerate the silence any longer.

He gave her a bemused look. 'Of course, why would it not be?'

'You seem unusually quiet, that is all. I thought perhaps something was amiss.'

'I was just thinking about the last time I walked in these gardens.' He smiled at her. 'About hearing a scream coming from the woods. About finding you.'

She nodded. 'I am glad you did. Who knows what would have become of me?'

'I am glad that I did too.' He regarded her thoughtfully. 'You have made a remarkable recovery in…how long has it been? A little over a week?'

Hope drew a deep breath. 'It's odd—it feels as though I have been at Hayton Hall much longer than that. I agree, though, I am feeling much better. I have you to thank for that, sir.'

'Just Samuel,' he reminded her.

'I have you to thank, Just Samuel,' she retorted with a grin.

He chuckled at that. 'I dare say it's actually Madeleine you should thank. She has cared for you, after all.'

Hope inclined her head in agreement. 'It's Maddie,' she corrected him. 'She prefers to be called Maddie.'

He glanced at her again, a frown gathering between his eyes. 'Er...yes, you're right, I do recall her once suggesting that I call her Maddie.'

'Then why do you insist upon calling her Madeleine?'

'I do not know... I suppose because that is her proper name.'

'Well, it vexes her, Samuel. For whatever reason, she does not care for her proper name. Just as you do not care for being called Sammy by your friend,' she observed.

He gave her a quizzical look. 'How do you know that?'

'Because you flinch every time Mr Gordon says it,' she replied. 'However, Mr Gordon is your friend and your equal; if you really wanted to, you could insist that he call you Samuel. But Maddie is your servant—she can hardly challenge you over what you call her.'

Samuel cleared his throat, his countenance shifting into something less jovial, less comfortable. Hope saw that her words had struck a chord. 'Yes, quite,' he replied. 'I did not realise that it bothered her. But you are right, of course.'

She raised her eyebrows at him. 'Yes, I am right. Perhaps I shall begin to call you Sammy too. Perhaps I will do so until you start calling her Maddie.'

'All right, all right,' he said, a smile breaking on his face as he glanced at her. 'You are very direct—do you know that? Very plain-speaking.'

Hope felt her heart begin to thrum faster at his observation, conscious that she'd allowed her true self to be glimpsed once again. 'Miss Gordon seems to speak her mind too,' she retorted, nodding her head towards the siblings, who were now some distance away.

'Miss Gordon speaks in riddles,' Samuel replied, shaking his head. 'Quite what her conversation in the parlour was about, I cannot fathom. She even had Charles looking uncomfortable, and nothing usually ruffles his feathers.'

'I dare say all is not well at Shawdale,' Hope observed. 'Perhaps that is what lies beneath their stay in Buxton, and their visit to you.'

'I think you may be right about that.' Samuel regarded her carefully, his grey-blue eyes holding her own. 'It occurs to me now that when we were on the Continent, Charles never seemed inclined to return home, and he never said much about his family. Indeed, until he wrote to me to accept my invitation to visit, I did not even know he had a sister.'

'That is odd,' Hope mused. 'Although I suppose people have their reasons for not wishing to discuss their families.'

'Like you, you mean.'

Hope realised they'd stopped walking, standing instead in the middle of the path. When had that happened? She felt suddenly and acutely aware of her arm still resting in his, of his proximity, of his eyes fixed on hers. Of the weight of meaning in his observation. Of all that separated them, of the chasm wrought by his wealth and status. Of everything he did not know about her, and everything he could never know.

'Yes, like me,' she said quietly, looking away.

If she had expected an inquisition, it did not come. Instead, Samuel reached over, placing his free hand over hers, which remained in the crook of his elbow.

'Whenever you wish to talk about it, I am ready to listen,' he said.

The gesture was so tender that she could not bring herself to meet his eye. Instead, she simply nodded, not quite trusting herself to answer. Not quite trusting herself not to blurt out her story, and lay the unpalatable facts of her life at his feet.

Chapter Ten

'I am heartily sick of this interminable rain.'

Samuel looked up from his newspaper, suppressing his irritation at Charles's complaints, which were as endless as the biblical torrents falling outside. In the days since the Gordons' arrival the weather had indeed taken a turn for the worse, a fact which Charles seemed to have taken as a personal insult. Samuel had lost count of the number of times Charles had wandered over to the window, only to sigh heavily at the sight which greeted him. He knew from past experience that his friend was like a caged bear when confined to the house; a particularly wet few weeks spent in a villa by Lake Geneva had taught him that. Charles was a man who needed to feel the sun on his face and sense the world at his feet. It was a wonder, Samuel reflected now, that he'd ever returned to the damp confines of north-west England at all.

'There is nothing to be done about the weather, Charles,' Samuel said, chuckling. 'You'd be best to find yourself an occupation—the rest of us have. The ladies both look very content to sit with their books.'

He noticed Hope raise a brief smile at his remark, before returning her attention to the page in front of her once more. They'd retired to the library a little over an hour ago, after Miss Gordon had declared rather brusquely that she had nothing to divert her and Samuel had felt obliged to offer the opportunity to find some reading material. Hope had almost immediately taken the seat nearest to the fire, which burned brightly in the grate and kept the autumnal chill at bay.

His heart had warmed to observe that she'd brought one of Mr Hume's volumes with her and although there was plenty within his newspaper to occupy him he'd found his gaze wandering towards her more than once. He'd watched with some amusement as her upright, ladylike posture had dissolved into something more relaxed, sitting back, her chin resting on her hand, the book balancing on the arm of the chair. Once or twice he'd even seen her move to tuck her feet up beneath her, before remembering either the constraints imposed by her healing ankle or the requirement for decorum—he wasn't sure which. Whatever the reason, he found watching her forget then remember herself rather endearing. The distraction of a good book, it seemed, could make Hope Swynford almost drop her guard. In the end, he forced himself to avert his gaze. His eyes, and his thoughts, lingered upon her far more than they should.

'What do you do for enjoyment in this wet little corner of Cumberland, then?' Charles continued, still complaining. 'Are there no assembly rooms, no theatres?'

Samuel noticed Hope's eyes flick up briefly at Charles's question. 'We have both in Lowhaven,' he answered.

'And where the devil is Lowhaven?' Charles asked.

'A few miles away, on the coast,' Samuel replied. 'It is a busy port town, and has everything we need.'

'Then let us take the carriage there,' Charles suggested.

'We can enjoy a drive around the town. It will pass the time and we may discover what is on at the assembly rooms or the theatre.'

Hope's eyes flicked up again, for longer this time. Samuel met her gaze, saw what looked like panic rising within it.

'You forget that Miss Swynford cannot leave Hayton Hall,' Samuel reminded his friend. 'She is still convalescing and, besides, we cannot run the risk of encountering her uncle.'

'Oh, of course. Well…perhaps Miss Swynford could remain within the carriage?' Charles asked. 'Surely the chances of her being spied through a carriage window are vanishingly small and, anyway, I dare say this uncle has given up searching for her by now. It's been, what, more than a week since she fled from his clutches?'

'Nearly two weeks,' Samuel replied. 'Nonetheless, Charles, we cannot be certain, and I will not take any risks when it comes to Miss Swynford's safety. Take the carriage into Lowhaven if you wish but, regrettably, we cannot join you.'

'Neither of you have bothered to ask Miss Swynford what she wishes.'

Miss Gordon's interjection startled both men. Samuel turned to regard her, observing that she had made her remark without so much as troubling herself to tear her eyes from the pages of her book. She'd selected Walpole's *The Castle of Otranto* from the library's shelves, and clearly the dark and supernatural novel held her interest. How unsurprising, Samuel thought wryly.

'Miss Gordon is right,' Samuel said, returning his mind to the matter at hand. 'Forgive me, Miss Swynford,' he continued, addressing Hope now. 'I dare say you've had quite enough of gentlemen making decisions for you of late—decisions which they've absolutely no right to make. What do you want to do?'

Given the earlier look of panic he believed he'd glimpsed, he expected Hope to decline outright. Instead, however, she appeared to be giving the outing some consideration, chewing her bottom lip thoughtfully as she apparently weighed up her options.

'You have not asked Miss Gordon what she'd like to do either,' Hope replied after a moment, glancing at the other woman.

'Oh, I care not,' Miss Gordon replied airily. 'I find that it is best to remain indifferent, Miss Swynford, when your desires will not be taken into account in any case.'

Samuel saw Charles flinch at his sister's cutting remark. 'Then it is up to you, Miss Swynford,' he said, smoothing over whatever was amiss between the Gordon siblings. Frankly, he could not care less about that right now. 'If you would prefer to remain here, then I will stay with you.'

He watched as she looked towards the window, the rain still running like tears down its old panes. She bit that lovely pink lip once again, and he found himself wondering what she was thinking, if she was as taken with the idea of remaining at Hayton as he suddenly was. If it had occurred to her, as it now had to him, that they could sit together in the parlour and enjoy tea and cake, just as they had before the Gordons had arrived. That they could talk—really talk. That she might bring herself to confide in him, that she might answer some of the questions which had been whirling around his mind about her family, about where her home was and why she would not, or could not, return to it. About exactly what had happened to her to leave her at the mercy of such a wicked relative, and why it appeared she had no one except an unnamed friend in London to turn to.

Not that he had any right to expect such confidences, he reminded himself. Not when he was still deceiving her about who he really was.

At length, when Hope delivered her answer it came as quite a surprise. 'I will come,' she said plainly. 'But I will remain out of sight within the carriage, as Mr Gordon suggests.'

Charles clapped his hands with delight as Samuel mustered an obliging nod in Hope's direction. She met his eye but her expression gave nothing away. Nothing about what had informed her choice to venture out when she'd thus far been so cautious. Nothing about whether cake and conversation with him had even occurred to her and, if it had, why she had rejected it in favour of a rainy carriage ride with the restless Charles and his prickly sister.

'As you wish, Miss Swynford,' Samuel replied, forcing a smile.

Hope shrank back into her seat, her heart beating hard in her chest as the carriage rattled along Lowhaven's bustling streets. She kept her head bowed, allowing the wide-brimmed bonnet she wore to keep her fully in shadow. She'd barely dared to look out of the window, convinced that the moment she did she'd be immediately recognised by some keen-eyed, wicked associate of her father and dragged back to Lillybeck. That had happened to her once before, after all.

She suppressed a shudder at the memory of being hauled away from the back door of the theatre, a coarse hand clapped over her mouth, stifling her screams. Of how pow-

erless she'd felt as they'd dragged her along a lonely alley-
way before binding her hands and feet and bundling her
into a cart.

These past weeks at Hayton, she'd found sanctuary, and
not only from the very real dangers she faced. She'd found
sanctuary from her thoughts too, and from her memories.
By inhabiting the role of Hope Swynford, she'd put some
distance between herself and Hope Sloane's troubles. Now,
in the midst of this busy port town, it all returned to her,
running unabated through her mind. The confusion. The
fear. The desperation.

In her lap, she squeezed her gloved hands together. Why
had she come here? Why had she not simply said she'd prefer to remain at Hayton Hall?

Because Samuel would have remained with her, that
was why. They would have been left alone, and that was
something Hope feared she could no longer countenance.
Ever since that tender moment they'd shared in the garden,
Hope had come to believe that she could no longer trust herself around him. The way she'd reacted when he'd touched
her hand and spoken to her so earnestly…the temptation
she'd felt to surrender to the truth, to admit everything—
it would not do.

It was bad enough that she was clearly in awe of his good
looks, his fine house and his gentlemanly manners. It was
bad enough that she'd allowed her thoughts to linger too
often on how it'd felt to be in his arms as he carried her
down the stairs or broke her fall in the pantry. It was bad
enough that she'd entertained ludicrous ideas about him
kissing her. Now, was she seriously contemplating placing
her trust in him and telling him the truth? What good did
she think could possibly come of that?

No good—that was what.

Sir Samuel Liddell was hardly likely to greet the news that she'd lied to him, that she was no heiress or gentlewoman but an actress and the offspring of an outlaw, with anything other than horror and disdain. For all that he'd shown himself to be kind and decent, such qualities had limits, and a gentleman in his position could surely not countenance allowing a woman like her to remain under his roof. She was the lowest of the low—a common criminal's daughter who'd only managed to escape her father's grasp by taking a profession which, in the eyes of many, made her little better than a harlot. And she had lied about it—she'd dined at Samuel's table, slept in his guest bedchamber and socialised with his friends under false pretences. That, she realised now, was perhaps the most unforgivable part of all.

She had to hold her tongue, she reminded herself, and if that meant avoiding being alone with Samuel and using the Gordons as a shield, then so be it. As soon as they left, she would make plans to leave too. She would allow Samuel to escort her to London as agreed and she would begin her life anew from there, even if that meant making her home in the Rookeries and acting on the makeshift stages of the city's many penny gaffs. This time, she vowed, she would put as many miles between herself and her father as possible. She tried not to consider that the same distance would then exist between herself and Samuel. There was, after all, no point in dwelling upon that.

Hope was so lost in her thoughts that it took her several moments to realise that the carriage had drawn to a halt. She looked up to see Mr Gordon hurry out of the door, before reaching back in to assist his sister as she too disembarked.

'We shan't be long, Sammy,' Mr Gordon called, his tone so cheerful that Hope was sure he'd almost sung the words.

Behind them the carriage door clicked shut, concealing Hope from the outside world once more, and leaving her with the master of Hayton Hall once again. So much for avoiding being alone in his company, she thought wryly. Clearly, fate had other ideas. Across from her, Samuel attempted what looked like a reassuring smile, but it quickly dissolved into an exasperated sigh.

'Goodness knows if either of them will find anything at the assembly rooms or the theatre which will please them,' he said, shaking his head. 'I fear Buxton has spoiled them both. Lowhaven's meagre entertainments and lack of pump rooms can hardly be expected to compete. Do you know, Hope, that we have only seawater here? Appalling.'

Hope smiled at his witty remark. 'I dare say Buxton's plays differ little from Lowhaven's. They're all put on by touring provincial theatre companies, after all.'

'Very true,' Samuel replied, raising his eyebrows at her observation. 'You are quite the theatre enthusiast, I think.'

Hope shrugged, trying to ignore the way her stomach lurched. Once again, she'd forgotten herself. Forgotten who she was meant to be. 'I do enjoy a play from time to time,' she replied, doing her best to sound nonchalant. 'Although, of course, I will not be able to join you and the Gordons at the Lowhaven theatre, should they find a play they wish to see one evening.'

She watched as Samuel knitted his brow. 'No, of course, but as you cannot go, I shall not join them either.'

'But you must,' she protested. 'They are your guests…'

'They know the situation,' he insisted. 'They will understand. I promised that you would remain under my care until I escort you to London. I would be remiss in my duty to you if I left you alone and went to Lowhaven for the evening.'

'I would not be alone. I would have Maddie, Smithson and all the other servants there with me...'

'And what if that blackguard of an uncle were to come for you under the cover of darkness?' He held her gaze, his blue-grey eyes seeming to darken. 'What would my poor old butler or my maid be able to do about it then? I can see that you are fearful of your uncle, Hope. You have looked terrified all the way here, even though Charles is correct—there is little chance of him spying you in a carriage with us, if he even remains in Cumberland at all.'

'Trust me,' she replied, lowering her gaze. 'He will still be close by. He will not give in until he has found me.'

Samuel frowned. 'If that is the case, what difference will going to London make? Does he know you have a friend in the city and, if he does, isn't it possible he will find you there? Can this woman and her husband protect you, or are you simply going to be running for ever?'

'I do not know.'

Beneath her lashes, Hope felt a tear slip out. That was the truth, of sorts: Hope Sloane had as little a notion of what the future held for her as Hope Swynford apparently did. Beyond that, Hope was at a loss for what to say. Her story was quickly coming apart under Samuel's growing scrutiny; the tangled web of deceit she'd hurriedly woven together was disintegrating, and she could not even bring herself to attempt to repair it, to tell yet more lies.

'Forgive me, I have upset you.' Samuel leaned forward, placing his hand over hers, which remained folded in her lap. 'Tell me how to help you, Hope. Tell me what more I can do.'

'You have done enough already, Samuel,' she replied, attempting a watery smile.

'Clearly that is not the case, if I am to deliver you to London so that you may spend the rest of your life living in fear. And what sort of a life will you have there? Can you support yourself? Can you access your inheritance?'

'Please, do not concern yourself...'

'But I am concerned,' he insisted. 'I am very concerned about exactly what this nasty and ruthless individual has done to you. I am very concerned that you do not appear to have any family except him, that there is no one to care about your welfare...'

'You are right—I have no one,' Hope conceded, her tears continuing to fall. 'You have been very kind to me, Samuel, and I thank you for it, but you are not my father or my brother, or my...'

Husband.

She stopped herself, just before she could say the word.

Hope sniffled, trying to regain her composure. 'As I said,' she concluded quietly, 'it is none of your concern.'

At that moment the door to the carriage swung open once more, causing them both to flinch. Swiftly, Samuel withdrew the hand which had been resting over hers and, despite herself and all that had occurred in those past moments, Hope could not help but feel bereft at the loss of his touch. She watched as Miss Gordon climbed back in, followed in quick order by her brother who, judging by his broad grin, was very satisfied with his findings indeed. The air which blew in behind them was crisp and laced with salt, and Hope found herself wishing she could go outside and take a swift, restorative lungful of it. Right then, she needed something—anything—which might help to get her thoughts in order.

'Well, that was very enlightening,' Mr Gordon began. 'There is a ball each month at the assembly rooms, and the place has a card room, which suits me very well. And the theatre has a performance of *As You Like It* every evening, although it is finishing its run very soon so we must be quick to catch that one.'

'But that is not the most interesting thing we learned,' Miss Gordon interjected. 'Brother, tell them what we heard about the previous play.'

Hope felt her heart begin to beat faster as Mr Gordon leaned forward conspiratorially.

'Oh, yes,' he said. '*The School for Scandal*—one of my favourites. Apparently, an actress went missing on its pen-ultimate night in town. Disappeared right after the show, it seems. No one's seen or heard anything from her since.'

'Really?' Samuel asked, furrowing his brow. 'The poor woman. I do hope she's not come to any harm.'

'I dare say that actresses absconding from the stage is not all that uncommon,' Mr Gordon scoffed. 'Such is the sort of life that many of them lead—or so I hear. Courtesans at best and harlots at worst, in many cases.'

'All right, Charles,' Samuel replied, making a face. 'I do not think that is a suitable topic of conversation with ladies present.'

By now Hope's heartbeat had grown so fast and so loud that it was a wonder the whole carriage could not hear it. Her cheeks burned as she looked down at her lap once more, wringing her hands together and praying that no one would spot her sheer mortification. Of course these people thought that—didn't everyone? Of course Samuel thought that. Whilst he had not said the words himself, he had not contradicted his friend either. Further confirmation, if it was needed, of exactly why he could never know who and what she really was. Confirmation too of exactly why he could never know just how profoundly true her words had been when she'd told him that she was none of his concern.

Gentlemen like Sir Samuel Liddell concerned themselves with high-born heiresses, not lowly actresses with criminal connections. As the carriage set off for Hayton once more, Hope decided that she would do well to remember that the next time she was tempted to be truthful with him. The truth, she realised, would only injure them both.

Chapter Eleven

Samuel cantered along the coastline on his horse, a salt-laced mist dampening his face to match his mood. He'd gone out a little while earlier with Charles, sensing his friend's characteristic restlessness might be best served by some fresh air. He'd been reluctant to leave Hope, but she had insisted that she would be fine sitting in the small parlour with Miss Gordon, who had no more wished to ride than it appeared she wished to do anything at all. Samuel had thought about protesting, about reminding her of his promise to protect her from the threat she faced, but something about the adamant look in her eye dissuaded him.

'I shall not be gone long, and we shall not venture far,' he'd sworn instead.

Hope joining them, of course, had been out of the question; even if she could countenance straying so far from Hayton Hall, her ankle was not yet strong enough to either ride or walk such a distance.

As he'd headed to the clifftops, Samuel had increasingly found himself wishing that she was there; indeed, that they could ride together, alone. That he could show her the wild and rugged parts of his county, and the sheer remote beauty of places where it was possible to ride for miles without seeing a single soul. He had quickly instructed himself to stop being ridiculous; the lady was convalescing in his home, not visiting for pleasure. His duty was to care for her, not to seek to impress her. Not to seek time alone with her.

Not to interrogate her.

He winced, thinking of their conversation in the carriage, how tense it had become. He'd been wrong to press her about her family, and to call into question the plans she had made. She was right; it was none of his concern what she did, or who she sought help from once she was in London. It was none of his business what had happened in her past, or what her terrible uncle had done to her. His questions had damaged the trust which had been building between them—a delicate trust, he reminded himself, which already rested upon the creaky foundations wrought by his lie about who he was.

Since their drive into Lowhaven, Hope had seemed to withdraw from him, burying her nose in her book every time he so much as glanced at her, and staying firmly by the side of Miss Gordon, whose conversation suddenly seemed to hold a great deal of her interest. Samuel understood her need to keep her distance, and had acted accordingly by keeping his. He knew that he'd crossed a line with his intrusive questions, and that he'd upset her. He'd taken too much of an interest and he was not, as she'd pointed out, her father or her brother, or…

Her husband.

She'd been about to say that, hadn't she?

Samuel stared vacantly out to sea, listening to the waves crashing below and wondering why that word felt so odd to him as it rattled around in his mind. Wondering too exactly why he had grown so interested in what the mysterious

Hope Swynford's tale truly was, and why he felt the heat of anger rise within him at his increasing suspicion that she was all alone in the world, left to face some malevolence which she could not bring herself to name. Anger was not an emotion which came readily to Samuel Liddell, and yet that was how he felt. He could feel it in his racing heart, in his blood as it boiled and coursed through his veins.

He tried not to consider that there might be other feelings at play, other reasons for this visceral physical response. Reasons connected to the sight of her emerald gaze, to the sight of her sitting abed in her shift, her dark hair tumbling in waves over her shoulders. To the feeling of her slight frame nestled in his arms, and the feeling of her slender waist beneath his hands. If she was so adamant that his concerns for her welfare were unwanted, he did not wish to contemplate her horror if she knew how often his mind lingered on thoughts such as those.

'I never had you pegged as the brooding type, Sammy.'

Charles brought his horse to trot alongside Samuel's and gave his friend a mischievous grin. Samuel braced himself for an onslaught of Charles's customary teasing.

'I'm not,' Samuel retorted. 'I believe that the reputation for brooding belongs to my older brother, not me.'

'Well, since you've borrowed his title, I dare say you can borrow his character traits too.'

Inwardly, Samuel groaned at the reminder. His continued deception of Hope was something else which increasingly preyed upon his mind. He would remind himself of why he kept up the pretence, of the need to make Hope feel safe, but that did not stop the lie looming like a spectre over every moment he spent in her company, and over every day that she remained within the sanctuary of Hayton Hall. He'd had the audacity to seek and enjoy her company, to express concern for her and to ask questions about her story, when he was not even being honest with her about who he was. The guilt of it was becoming intolerable.

'Do you know what I think?' Charles continued, undeterred by his friend's silence. 'I think you're a little bit smitten with Miss Hope Swynford. That's why you're pretending to be a baronet, and that's why you won't just admit your folly to her.'

'Nonsense!' Samuel declared, shaking his head.

Charles eyed him suspiciously. 'Is it? She's a pretty young chit, as I'm sure you have not failed to notice. And if the uncle's reckless actions in kidnapping her are anything to go by, I'd say she's wealthy too.'

Samuel bristled at his friend's observation. 'You know that such considerations are no inducement to me, Charles.'

'Which part—her uncommon good looks or her large fortune?' Charles teased.

'Both,' Samuel replied. 'Miss Swynford is in my home under my protection, Charles, not so that I can take advantage of her. That is not my way—you know me well enough to know that.'

Charles nodded. 'You were always a finer gentleman than me. I would be thoroughly dishonourable, if only I was better at it,' he added with a roguish grin.

'Just as long as you are not minded to be dishonourable towards Miss Swynford. The poor lady has been through quite enough,' Samuel lectured him.

'First brooding over the chit, now defensive of the chit—are you quite sure you're not pining for her?' Charles asked.

'Absolutely certain,' Samuel snapped back, although even he could hear his words lacked conviction. Her fortune—

large or otherwise—was of no particular interest to him. Her striking beauty, however...

'We should return to Hayton Hall,' Samuel continued, turning his back to the sea. 'We've neglected Miss Swynford and your sister for quite long enough.'

'I doubt Henrietta will mind,' Charles replied. 'She seems to quite enjoy Miss Swynford's company.' He shook his head in mock disbelief. 'Rich, beautiful, and capable of lifting my sister's sullen spirits. The Sammy I knew on the Continent would have been the first gentleman in the room to try to woo a woman like that.'

Samuel grimaced at his friend's words. The 'Sammy' Charles knew would not have allowed such a woman to believe he was someone he was not. But then, that Samuel had not yet had his pride dented by rejection. That painful experience, he acknowledged yet again, was part of what had driven his deceit. What prevented him from ending it was altogether more complex, and was just as attributable to the potent mix of protectiveness and affection he felt whenever he looked at her as it was to his residual feelings of shame and humiliation whenever he so much as contemplated explaining his lie. But he had to contemplate it, he knew that, even if it risked losing her respect. Even if it meant an end to the way she seemed to regard him, as though he was a knight who had come to her rescue. That was nothing less than he deserved.

If only he could find a way to tell her which would not cause her distress. If only he could be certain that the knowledge that she was not living under the protection of Hayton's baronet wouldn't cause Hope to panic, or to flee back into harm's way. The thought that it might was unbearable, and was another reason why he continued to wrestle with his conscience. And another reason, no doubt, why his blood heated with that overwhelming desire to protect her, to envelop her in his arms and not let go...

Where in damnation had that thought come from?

'I am not wooing anyone,' Samuel replied after a moment. 'And certainly not Miss Swynford. That is a ridiculous idea, given the circumstances.'

Impatiently, he cracked his whip, unable to stomach the sound of his own hollow protests any longer. Unable to abide the maelstrom of whirring thoughts as his honour, his conscience and his pride warred with each other in his mind. Instead, he raced back towards the home of which he was not truly master, to the life and title which were not truly his, and to the woman who, to his great shame, believed him to be in possession of all of it.

'Courtesans...and harlots...'

Hope sat alone in the small parlour, forcing her mind to focus on the book which rested on her lap, to absorb the information contained within Mr Hume's dense prose. Her mind, however, had other ideas, returning continuously to those injurious words which Mr Gordon had uttered. Words which Samuel had not refuted as accurate descriptions of actresses. Words which Hope had been smarting over ever since.

'Courtesans at best and harlots at worst.'

The irony of the insult was not lost on her since she was, without doubt, thoroughly unqualified to be called either. During her time in the theatre she had steadfastly refused to succumb to the easy virtues expected of those in her profession, rebuking many a man for his unwanted advances. Indeed, the only experiences she'd ever had of the opposite sex were in the form of those who'd tried to kiss or to touch her without invitation. She'd never experienced any welcome intimacy; she'd never been embraced by a man who made her heart race or kissed by one who stirred the heat of passion within her. These were feelings which she knew existed—she'd heard enough of the coarse chatter of other actresses, after all—but they were not experiences she'd had for herself.

Indeed, she realised, the closest she'd ever been to a man was when she'd unwittingly fallen into Samuel's arms in the pantry, or when she'd allowed him to carry her down the stairs. Encounters which she found herself replaying in her mind, picking over their details, reliving the feelings such closeness had evoked in her. She'd felt comforted, re-assured, safe, but something else too. The heat of something which she could not find words for, but was there none-theless, rising within her as her eyes met his, as his arms held her momentarily, tantalisingly close. Another irony, she reminded herself, forcing her mind to cease from lin-gering over those memories once more. Regardless of the feelings Samuel's proximity might provoke in her, in every respect that mattered—in status and in wealth—she could not be further apart from him.

Hope sighed heavily, putting the book to one side as finally she admitted defeat. Having grown weary of the Anglo-Saxons and the Normans, she'd jumped ahead, seek-ing diversion in the story of John of Gaunt and Katherine Swynford, which Samuel had briefly yet so tantalisingly re-counted. In this, however, she was ultimately disappointed, finding only the smallest reference to their union, and even then it was to discuss how it was believed to have injured the dignity of the Duke of Lancaster's family. As a learned gentleman, no doubt Mr Hume had little time for mistresses who become wives, Hope had thought wryly. Just as baronets could not be expected to have any regard for actresses.

She fidgeted, kicking off the ill-fitting slippers she wore—another item borrowed from Samuel's cousin—and carefully stretching her legs out across the sumptuous fabric of the sofa. At least this unexpected time alone had afforded her some respite from playing her role of the society heiress. Samuel and Mr Gordon were still out riding, and Miss Gordon had retired to her room some time ago, claiming she was in the grip of yet another headache. She had seemed to suffer from a great many of those of late, excusing herself at least once daily on the insistence that she needed to rest awhile. Several times, Hope had observed her brother's brow furrow as his gaze followed her out of the room. It was a look which spoke of his concern, but it was knowing too.

Hope had spent more time with Miss Gordon these past days, feebly shielding herself from the possibility of further questioning by Samuel. Thankfully, the lady had largely desisted from asking Hope any more leading questions about ancestral homes and the like. Nonetheless, between her frequent headaches, clipped conversation and general aloof air, Hope found the unease she'd experienced when first meeting the lady to be fully vindicated. When it came to Miss Henrietta Gordon, it was clear that there was more going on than met the eye.

Then again, Hope thought, Miss Gordon was not the only one at whom such a charge could be levelled. She might be under no illusion as to exactly what Samuel would think of her if he knew who and what she truly was, but that did not stop her guilt at her deception of him continuing to gnaw at her. Moreover, after the way he'd questioned her as they'd sat together in his carriage in Lowhaven, Hope felt that the risk of him unravelling her story for himself was becoming very real.

If he continued to pick over the vague information she'd offered, if he continued to press her for more detail than she was willing to give, then a gentleman as learned as he was could not fail to grow suspicious, and then what would she do? Tell more lies and hope to assuage his desire for knowledge? Tell him the truth and watch the anger and disappointment cloud his usually cheerful countenance? Neither option held any appeal. She regarded him too highly to deepen the deceit, yet she feared the consequences of honesty—she feared losing his good opinion and she feared hurting him. She cared too much to do that.

She cared too much about him, didn't she? And that was the problem. That was the root of her current predicament. Because, as it turned out, deceiving someone so kind, so open and likeable as Samuel caused her pain, far worse perhaps than any of the injuries she'd sustained mere weeks ago. It made her heart sore, and her stomach ache.

Tentatively, Hope glanced at her ankle as it rested on the sofa. The acute discomfort was gone now, as were the bandages. Indeed, the only evidence of injury which remained was the bruising, which had gradually turned from an angry purple to a deep greyish brown. It was not strong enough to walk far yet and it still hurt if she spent too long on her feet but, to all intents and purposes, it had healed. She had healed. Perhaps, she reasoned now, the answer to her growing set of problems was not to choose between honesty and deceit, but to escape. Hayton Hall was only a temporary sanctuary, after all, offered to her while she convalesced. Well, she had recovered, at least well enough to travel. Perhaps it was time to make arrangements to leave.

The sound of horses cantering up the drive caused her to startle, and out of the window she saw Samuel and Mr Gordon approach. Quickly, she sat up straight, sliding her feet back into the slippers as she composed herself and resumed her role. It would only be for a little while longer, she told herself now. She would speak to Samuel about making arrangements for her journey south as soon as possible. He would remain ignorant of her deception and they would part on good terms. In time, his acquaintance with the enigmatic heiress would become nothing more than a strange, brief interlude in his life. Surely her swift departure was necessary. Surely it was for the best.

Hope picked up her book once more, determined to appear absorbed as, out in the hallway, the rhythm of approaching footsteps rang out. Determined too upon her chosen course and determined above all not to dwell on how the prospect of leaving had made her heart ache even more.

Chapter Twelve

'Is everything all right? Where are the Gordons?'

Hope limped into the dining room, feeling the absence of her walking cane with every tentative step. She'd left it upstairs after dressing for dinner, determined to demonstrate that she was fit enough to walk without it and prove she was well enough to leave Hayton Hall. She had not managed to speak to Samuel about that yet; indeed, she'd barely spoken to him since he'd returned from his ride with Mr Gordon yesterday. He'd seemed unusually subdued last night at dinner and had retired early, and today he'd spent much of his time locked away in his library, ostensibly dealing with estate matters. No doubt he was—as a landowner and a gentleman he would have business which required his attention and could not be expected to entertain guests all the time.

The Gordons, however, had not seemed quite so understanding and, after enduring quite enough of Mr Gordon's fidgeting and Miss Gordon's sullen temperament, Hope had excused herself and spent the remainder of the afternoon resting in her bedchamber. Now she'd returned downstairs at the appointed dining hour to find the house quiet, the table bare, and Samuel hovering beside it, leaning on the back of a chair.

'I thought we could take supper in the library this evening,' he said, offering her a small smile. 'I don't know about you, but I've rather wearied of formal dining of late. Too many courses, too much fuss.'

Hope gave a brisk nod. 'As you wish. Will Mr Gordon and his sister be joining us?'

'Afraid not,' Samuel replied, shaking his head. 'They've decided to go to the theatre. Apparently, it's the very last night for *As You Like It* in Lowhaven and Charles cannot countenance missing it. Miss Gordon seemed less enthused, but has done her duty and accompanied her brother,' he added with a wry smile.

'Did you not wish to go with them?' Hope asked.

'My duty is to remain here, with you,' he replied firmly, giving her a look which reminded her at once of his words in his carriage that day, when he'd spoken of his promise to protect her. When he'd acknowledged the look of fear he'd seen in her eyes.

'There will be other opportunities to go to the theatre,' he continued. 'Now, aren't you going to ask me why we're taking supper in the library and not the parlour?'

The mischievous grin he gave her piqued her interest, and she pushed all thoughts of invented nefarious uncles and all too real and threatening fathers to one side.

'All right,' she replied, raising a smile to match his. 'Why?'

'I thought, since we cannot go to the theatre, we would bring the theatre to us.'

Hope frowned. 'What do you mean by that?'

Samuel chuckled as he walked towards her, taking her by the hand. 'You'll see. Come on.'

The feeling of his gentle fingers holding hers made her thoughts scatter, and willingly she allowed him to lead her out of the dining room and down the hallway to the library. Once inside, she saw that a table had been laid with bread, cold meats and a healthy decanter of red wine set between two glasses. Nearby she spied another, smaller occasional table, bearing several leather-bound books. She turned to Samuel then, raising an expectant eyebrow as she awaited an explanation.

'I know it is a little unorthodox,' he said, relinquishing her hand. 'I can assure you, I don't make a habit of dining in the library, but it seemed like the most suitable place.'

'The most suitable place for what?' she pressed him.

'To read some Shakespeare. And to show you something rather precious, which I think you will appreciate, given your enthusiasm for the theatre.'

Samuel beckoned her over to the smaller table, where carefully he lifted up a very thick and apparently very old brown book. 'Shakespeare's Comedies, Histories and Tragedies,' he said as he passed it to her. 'A collection of his plays, printed in 1623.'

Hope gasped, gently opening the book to see the title page, where the Bard's famous image gazed back at her. 'It's almost two hundred years old,' she marvelled.

Samuel nodded. 'It's also very rare. I believe only seven hundred or so copies were ever printed. And we are fortunate enough to have one of them here, at Hayton.'

'Fortunate indeed,' she mused, still staring in disbelief at the treasure she held in her hands. 'I have never seen anything like it. The only scripts I have seen have been...'

Hope pressed her lips together, remembering herself just in time. Her heart raced at the knowledge of what she had almost unwittingly revealed. She'd felt herself—her real self—bubbling to the surface once more. This was becoming too difficult—to hide in plain sight, to suppress her true identity beneath polite speech, fine clothes and a character with the vaguest of histories. To keep lying to Samuel, to repay his unfailing kindness and generosity with deceit. This, she reminded herself, was exactly why she needed to leave. Perhaps she ought to speak to him about that this evening, if she could find the right moment, the right words...

'Oh, I am sure you must have one or two priceless heirlooms tucked away in a dusty family library somewhere,' Samuel remarked, apparently oblivious to her inner turmoil. 'Perhaps in that ancestral home which you've vowed never to set foot in again,' he added pointedly.

Despite herself, Hope found her mind drifting the several miles across the countryside to Lillybeck, to that damp stone cottage tucked on the hillside. She doubted her father kept so much as a broadside in that barren, cold place.

'Perhaps,' she replied, regretting now that piece of information which Miss Gordon had managed to draw from her at their first meeting. At the time she'd thought it an evasive enough answer; now she suspected Samuel had caught the scent of truth emanating from it. 'Here,' she continued, passing his book back to him and hoping to swiftly change the subject. 'You'd better take this and put it somewhere safe.'

Samuel accepted the book, placing it back on the table as he shook his head in disbelief. 'You are really not going to tell me anything, are you, Hope? About your past, about your life before you stumbled into that woodland that day.'

Unable to bear his consternation, she dropped her gaze, momentarily lost for words. Deep down, she'd known to expect this conversation, ever since that carriage ride. This was why she'd avoided being alone with him, why she'd stuck closely by Miss Gordon's prickly side. But sensing what Samuel wanted to say and knowing how to answer him were two different matters. What could she say that would not cause yet more harm? Lies were damaging, but the truth was damning.

Instead, she lifted her eyes to meet his, trying not to dwell upon how their grey-blue depths seemed to swirl with concern, with sadness. 'I thought we'd come to the library to read Shakespeare, not to talk about me,' she replied obstinately, folding her hands in front of her to stop them from trembling. She glanced over at the larger table, still laden with food. 'Perhaps first we should have some of that bread and meat, before it spoils.'

Samuel walked over to the table, lifting the decanter and pouring two glasses of wine. The only thing which was being spoiled, he thought to himself, was their evening together, and the fault for that was entirely his. He'd set out to make the most of their unexpected time alone, to indulge in something which he believed would interest her, to recapture some of the easy companionship they'd enjoyed before Charles and his sister had arrived. And, most importantly, to grasp the right moment to tell her the truth about himself, to offer his heartfelt apology and hope that she would accept it. To reassure her that whilst she might not have the protection of a baronet, she would always have the protection of Samuel Liddell.

Instead, he'd fallen right back into the same trap and had overstepped the mark with his questions, just as he had that afternoon in the carriage. Her life really was none of his business, he reminded himself, especially when he was still not being honest about his own. The problem was, not knowing the details of her story made his mind run wild, imagining the worst possible scenarios until his need to protect her felt quite overwhelming. He'd never been gripped by feelings like this before—burning, unpredictable emotions which made him feel quite out of kilter.

'Forgive me,' he said, handing her a glass of wine and forcing a smile. 'You are right, of course. We should read some Shakespeare, as I originally proposed. Although not from the 1623 book—I don't think future generations of Liddells would forgive me for that. There is a newer, smaller volume of his works on the table.'

He watched as Hope walked back towards the books he'd fetched out earlier.

'Do you have a particular play in mind?' she asked. 'A favourite, perhaps?'

He shook his head. 'To be honest, I like them all. Why don't we let fate decide? Open the book and see which play finds us.'

Hope did as he suggested, putting her wine glass down before picking up the book and opening it at random. He watched as those emerald eyes briefly scanned the page. 'Oh, goodness,' she said with a wry chuckle. '*Romeo and Juliet.*'

Fate, Samuel thought, was clearly laughing at them. Or at least it was laughing at him, given some of the thoughts about Miss Hope Swynford which his errant mind had entertained of late.

'Goodness indeed,' he replied, his throat growing unfathomably dry. 'The star-crossed lovers in fair Verona—which he never visited, or so I believe.'

'"*Two houses, both alike in dignity, in fair Verona where we lay our scene,*"' Hope recited, apparently from memory, since she was not reading from the book. '"*From ancient grudge break to new mutiny, where civil blood makes civil hands unclean.'''*

Samuel grinned at her. 'Very well remembered. A favourite of yours, perhaps?'

She shrugged, closing the book before retrieving her wine glass and taking a considered sip. 'Not particularly— I have watched it a few times is all. If anything, I find it very disheartening.'

'You find a play about love disheartening?'

'Is it really about love?' she countered. 'Surely it's about the thwarting of love—first by the hatred between two families, and then by death. If anything, Shakespeare is telling us that sometimes love is impossible. Circumstances make it so. Fate makes it so. No matter how much two people want to be together, sometimes there are just too many obstacles. There is too much to keep them apart.'

'All right,' Samuel conceded, relishing the opportunity to debate. 'Although you must surely admit that there is beauty in the play too. The love between Romeo and Juliet is genuine, pure and heartfelt, is it not?'

'Of course it is, but therein lies the tragedy because ultimately it is not enough. It does not even serve to end their families' feuding—it takes them both dying to do that. As I said, disheartening.'

Samuel nodded. Her argument was persuasive and her knowledge impressive. She was more than a theatre enthusiast, he decided. It was very apparent that she was acquainted with at least some of Shakespeare's work inside and out.

'You would have enjoyed some of the dinner parties I attended on the Continent,' he remarked. 'Packed with scholars and intellectuals, brimming with opinions on the best and worst that English literature has to offer.'

He watched as her brow furrowed. 'You're teasing me.'

'Not at all—I am in earnest. Some of the best evenings I had while travelling were spent in the company of such people. Poets, writers, artists, philosophers, or simply avid readers. I think you would have liked talking to them too, and I think a great many of them would have liked talking to you.' He reached out, taking her hand in his. 'This evening with you has reminded me of some very happy times, Hope, and I must thank you for that.'

She nodded obligingly, her expression softening. 'That is kind of you to say,' she replied. 'Alas, I am unlikely to ever find myself moving in such circles, never mind on the Continent.'

'You could travel, Hope, it is not impossible. Now that you are free of your uncle, and as long as you can access the means…'

'Believe me, it is impossible,' she interrupted, refusing to meet his eye. 'My life has been very different to yours, Samuel. You do not understand. You cannot understand.'

'Then explain it to me.' Instinctively, he stepped towards her, still clutching her hand with his. Her fingers felt so small and delicate beneath his touch. 'You can tell me about it, Hope,' he said quietly. 'You can trust me, please believe that.'

'I cannot…' She was shaking her head vehemently now. 'I need to leave. I need to…'

'What do you mean, you need to leave?'

She did not answer, and the fear he saw swirling in her eyes was too much to bear. Before he could think about what he was doing, Samuel stepped forward, pulling her towards him and enveloping her in his arms. Instinct overcame thought as he held her and, to his surprise, she allowed him, her head coming to rest against his chest as her arms looped tentatively around him. The feeling of her warm hands against his back made his blood heat and, before he could stop them, his own hands had reached for the near-black curls of her hair, his fingers running unbidden through them, teasing them from their pins, then diving under them to find the soft skin at the nape of her neck...

Against him she sighed, before looking up at him, her green gaze no longer filled with anguish but something else, something he could not name.

'What is it, Hope?' he whispered. 'Please, tell me.'

She shook her head again but did not break eye contact, nor did she recoil from his embrace. Every sinew of his body was alive with awareness of her petite, alluring form pressed against him, rendering rational, gentlemanly thought impossible. Instinct continued to rule him as he leaned down, his lips gently touching hers. His heart sang as she welcomed his kiss—indeed, she kissed him back hungrily, pulling herself ever closer to him, sending shivers down his spine as she ran her fingers over his broad shoulders then through his hair. She kissed like she spoke about Shakespeare—passionately and with conviction. With her encouragement his own passion grew, sending his lips on a quest to find the soft flesh of her ear, then her neck, then the swell of her breasts which hinted at the neckline of her gown...

Good God, what was he doing? He was meant to be confessing to her, not kissing her!

'I am so sorry,' he blurted, pulling away. 'Forgive me.' He swallowed hard, shaking his head at himself in disbelief. 'I should not have done that. Not when there is so much

I need to say. Hope, I must tell you that I am not who you think I am. I am not…'

His words died in his mouth as the door to Hayton's library burst open. He heard Hope gasp as, like him, her eyes flew to see who had intruded so unexpectedly. He was stunned to see Smithson standing in the doorway, looking uncommonly rumpled, a serious expression etched on his heavily lined face.

'I am sorry to disturb you, sir,' the butler began, sounding a little breathless. Samuel watched as the wily old man's gaze flitted between the two of them, no doubt noting Hope's mussed hair and burning cheeks. 'Really—very sorry.'

'Well, what is it, man?' he demanded, his customarily gentle tongue abandoned. Now really was not the time. Not when he'd just kissed Hope. Not when Hope had just said she was going to leave.

Not when he'd been on the cusp of telling her the truth.

'It's Miss Gordon, sir,' Smithson continued, still regarding them both carefully. 'I'm afraid Mr and Miss Gordon have had to return from the theatre early. Miss Gordon has been taken ill.'

At that moment Samuel could have groaned aloud with frustration. The news about Miss Gordon's health was concerning, but the thought of leaving the unspoken truth hanging between himself and Hope was unbearable. However, there was nothing he could do. Duty called—his duty as Charles's friend, and his duty as Hayton's caretaker master.

'I'm sorry,' he said, turning back to Hope. 'I promise that we will talk soon.'

'Of course,' she agreed, regarding him just long enough for him to see the concern and confusion swirling in her green gaze. Then she turned away from him, striding purposefully towards the door. 'I think we should go and assist Miss Gordon, shouldn't we?'

Chapter Thirteen

'What on earth has happened, Charles?'

Samuel followed Smithson into the small parlour, where the broad frame of his friend loomed large, wringing his hands and pacing tirelessly. His sister, meanwhile, had been laid out on the sofa, her eyes closed as Maddie sat beside her, dabbing her forehead with a cool cloth. Hope, who'd followed behind him, immediately joined Maddie at Miss Gordon's side, tucking the loose tendrils of her dark hair behind her ears as she bent down to examine the patient. Realising he was staring at her, Samuel tore his gaze away and focused again on Charles, trying to force himself to focus on the matter at hand. Trying not to dwell on the memory of her lips pressed against his, of the feeling of her in his arms. Of how those heady, intoxicating moments had brought his guilt rushing to the fore. He'd been so close to telling her, so close to explaining everything…

'The physician has been sent for, sir,' Smithson informed him, answering when it was clear, after a long moment, that Charles would not.

Samuel nodded. 'Thank you, Smithson. Charles,' he said gently, trying again. 'Do you know what happened? Do you know what ails her?'

Charles shook his head, his face growing paler by the moment. 'She was fine until after the interval,' he replied. 'Then she began to behave in the most odd manner, calling out the strangest things, then laughing so much that she did not seem able to stop. People were staring at her like she was mad.' His friend paused, clearly collecting himself. 'I decided we ought to leave and got her back into the carriage. She fell asleep on the ride home and I have not been able to rouse her since. I do not know what the matter is with her, Sammy.'

Samuel glanced down at Miss Gordon. 'Is she feverish?' he asked Maddie.

'No, sir,' the maid answered.

'And she was absolutely fine all day, before you went out?' he asked Charles.

His friend nodded. 'She was her usual self, Sammy, warts and all.'

Samuel shook his head. 'Then I am at a loss. We will have to hope that the physician can offer further insight.'

'If he comes tonight,' Charles replied fretfully, glancing towards the window, which had been shuttered against the darkness outside. 'It is rather late, after all. What can we do in the meantime?'

'Keep her comfortable,' Samuel replied, staring glumly at Miss Gordon, who remained unresponsive. 'And keep watch over her, in case there is any change in her condition.'

His eyes shifted once again from the patient to Hope, who seemed to be observing Miss Gordon closely. He watched as she leaned forward, as though listening for something. Then, to his surprise, she reached over, lifting Miss Gordon's eyelids to open her eyes one at a time, frowning at whatever it was she saw.

'What is it, Miss Swynford?' Samuel asked, stepping towards her.

Gingerly, Hope stood up, turning to face him. Her expression, he noted, remained grave. 'I believe I might know what is wrong with Miss Gordon,' she replied, flashing Charles a wary look. 'If I may speak plainly, Sir Samuel.'

Samuel winced at her use of that blasted title. How he wished he could banish it for good! How he wished he could tell her the truth, here and now. But of course he could not—not in front of Charles and his servants. Not when Miss Gordon was plainly so unwell…

He nodded briskly, pushing his swirling thoughts aside. 'Of course. You may always speak plainly to me, Hope,' he replied, venturing now to use her first name in company and hoping she would do the same. In truth, right now, he was not sure how many more 'Sir Samuels' he could stomach.

'I believe Miss Gordon is suffering the effects of having taken laudanum,' Hope replied quietly. Those emerald eyes of hers met his again for the briefest moment before she turned to address Charles. 'Mr Gordon, I wonder if you can confirm whether your sister has been taking this, perhaps on the advice of your family's physician?'

Something about Hope's tone told Samuel that she suspected Charles was well aware of what was going on.

'No, well, indeed, she may have taken a tincture once or twice…' Charles prevaricated.

'This is important, Charles,' Samuel urged him. 'We cannot help your sister if we do not know what is amiss.'

Charles's eyes seemed to widen like saucers. 'For headaches,' he said after a moment. 'Yes—I remember now. She took laudanum on our doctor's orders, for headaches.'

'Took?' Hope repeated. 'Forgive me, sir, but it seems to

me that your sister continues to take laudanum, presumably for the headaches which, as I'm sure you've also observed, she continues to suffer.' Samuel watched as carefully Hope sat down at Miss Gordon's side once more. 'Her pupils are like pin pricks,' she explained, briefly opening one of the lady's eyes again. 'Her breathing is shallow. And the behaviour you described at the theatre sounds very much like the sort of delirium which laudanum is known to induce. In short, sir, if you check your sister's reticule I believe you will find a bottle of what has poisoned her within it.'

'Poison?' Charles said, aghast.

'Yes—poison,' Hope replied emphatically. 'Laudanum relieves suffering but if she has taken too much then... surely, sir, I don't have to explain to you how dangerous that may be.'

Samuel's mouth fell open at the bluntness of her warning. 'What can be done for her, Hope?' he asked.

'She must be watched over, as you suggested,' Hope replied. 'In my experience, we need to keep her propped up, as she is right now on the sofa. It is better for her breathing and better if...well, if she expels anything. And we should try to rouse her, if we can. Beyond that, we can only await the physician's advice.'

Samuel nodded dumbly, her words still sinking in. Knowing, confident words spoken, as she'd just admitted, from experience. Despite the severity of the situation, Samuel found himself wondering about the nature of those experiences, about what Hope might have faced in her past which had taught her how to handle something as dire and life-threatening as this. He wondered too if it was this very sort of experience that caused Hope to guard the story of her past so closely.

Now, however, was not the time to ask her questions such as that. Giving himself a mental shake, Samuel sprang once again into action.

'You heard Hope,' he said, addressing the room. 'Let us pray that the physician's journey here is swift and without delay. In the meantime, Miss Gordon shall not be left alone for a moment.'

Groggily, Hope opened her eyes, grimacing at the aching she felt in her neck and limbs after being curled up on a chair for goodness knew how long. She looked towards the window, relieved to see daylight hinting at the edges of the shutters, which were still closed to the world outside. It had been an endless night. The physician, it had transpired, had not been at home, having been summoned to an emergency elsewhere, leaving Hope and the others to care for Miss Gordon alone and without guidance.

Having checked his sister's reticule and found a small bottle of laudanum tucked within it, Mr Gordon had at last resigned himself to Hope's diagnosis and placed himself at Miss Gordon's side, insisting that he would watch over her first. They had each taken a turn while the others slept, and now, as she pulled herself upright, she saw Samuel was still at his post, his gaze intent upon the patient. For a moment she simply looked at him, taking in every detail from his dishevelled sand-coloured hair to his rumpled white shirt, long bereft of either a coat or cravat.

Memories of those heated moments in the library came rushing to the fore, her fingers tingling with awareness as though her skin itself could recall the feeling of the fine fabric of his clothes, of the outline of the muscles which hinted at their presence beneath them, of the warm softness of his hair. She felt her face grow hot as her mind lingered on how she had responded to his embrace, how she had kissed him back with reckless abandon. It had been an entirely new, entirely terrifying and entirely thrilling experience—to be held like that, to be touched like that. To be kissed like that.

The abruptness with which he'd ended the embrace had astonished her, but not as much as the tortured, guilt-ridden look on his face as he'd begun to speak of things he ought to say, of not being what she thought he was.

What on earth had he meant by that? That question, and all its possible answers, had circled around her mind throughout the long night. She'd replayed his words over and over, picking through them, searching for clues. He'd told her that he shouldn't have kissed her—why was that? Was he, in fact, a married man? Or was he betrothed, with a fiancée tucked away somewhere? Her face heated again as she recalled the enthusiasm she'd shown for his advances— an enthusiasm which was as mortifying as it was curious, especially if the kiss, for him, had been a grave transgression. An act of infidelity, and something to be regretted.

Of course, she reminded herself, if he had kissed her under false pretences, then he wasn't the only one. Last night the master of Hayton Hall had believed himself to be kissing a runaway heiress, not the penniless daughter of an outlaw.

Samuel had promised that they would talk soon, and certainly they both had much to say. Before that kiss had sent her thoughts and her wits scattering, she'd blurted out her intention to leave—an intention which now seemed more vital than ever. After last night, it was abundantly clear that her feelings for the master of Hayton Hall had grown beyond even her wildest imaginings, and it seemed from his actions that there was some attraction on his part too. An attraction, she reminded herself, which he felt towards Hope Swynford and not Hope Sloane. Extricating herself from this situation, and removing herself and her deceit from his life, was now essential. In that respect, whatever he'd been on the cusp of confessing to her last night surely could not matter.

But, God help her, she ached to know what it was...

'Good morning.'

Hope blinked, her whirring thoughts interrupted as she realised Samuel was looking at her.

'Did you sleep all right?' he asked, offering her a weary smile.

'Not too badly, considering.'

'In hindsight, it perhaps would have been best if you'd retired upstairs,' he mused. 'You are still recovering. It cannot have been good for your ankle, curling up like a cat in that chair.'

'I'm fine,' she assured him, resisting the urge to rub her throbbing foot. 'How is Miss Gordon?' She looked around. 'And where is Mr Gordon?'

'Charles is outside, smoking his pipe—as he does whenever he is vexed.' He glanced back at the patient. 'And Miss Gordon seems to be improving. Her breathing is steadier and she has stirred several times in the past hour. Maddie has just taken away the water and cloths as we agreed they're no longer needed.'

Hope smiled. 'You called her Maddie, not Madeleine,' she observed.

Samuel let out a small chuckle. 'I did. A perceptive and considerate lady once suggested to me that I ought to pay better attention to my servants' wishes, especially when they're in no position to challenge me.'

Hope inclined her head, acknowledging the compliment. 'Poor Maddie must get some rest too,' she reminded him. 'If she has been attending to Miss Gordon all night.'

Samuel nodded. 'I've told Smithson to give her the day off. I've also asked Smithson to arrange for some breakfast to be brought. I thought that if we can wake Miss Gordon, we may be able to get her to eat or drink something. And I do not know about you, but I am famished.'

Hope's stomach growled in agreement, and she remembered that they had never eaten the bread and meat which had been laid out in the library. Events, and passionate embraces, had intervened.

'Has there been any further word from the physician?' she asked, ignoring the heat which had crept into her cheeks once more.

'A message was left for him last night,' Samuel replied. 'I expect he will come today.'

'Good. Hopefully, he will confirm that Miss Gordon will recover well.'

'Hmm.' Samuel's gaze drifted back to the patient and gently he shook his head. 'It's a terrible business,' he said in a hushed voice. 'She could have died last night.'

'Laudanum is a terrible business,' Hope responded grimly.

'You sound as though you speak from experience.'

Those grey-blue eyes held hers once again. Hope could hear the tentative note in his voice, as though he had not been sure if he should broach the subject. But after last night, after seeing how she'd recognised what was wrong with Miss Gordon and taken charge of the situation, she knew he could hardly avoid talking to her about it. She knew too that she could not lie to him; she had offered too vivid a glimpse of the real Hope's life to do that. Only the truth, or at least a version of it, would do now.

'My mother,' she said at last, as evenly as she could manage. 'She began taking it for an ailment, to help with the pain. In doing so, she found that it could take away not just her physical pain but every other pain she felt too, and I think she rather liked the oblivion it offered her. But the rub with laudanum is that the more you take it, the more you need to take to achieve the desired effect. And the higher the dose, the greater the risk. My mother found this out to her great cost. She died a number of years ago, alone on her bed, an empty bottle of her beloved poison by her side.'

'I am so sorry, Hope. That must have been very hard to bear.'

Hope pressed her lips together, hoping Samuel could not sense how hard she was fighting to hold back her tears. 'I spent many nights watching over her, just as we had to do with Miss Gordon. And many days pleading with her to stop taking it. But that need she had to obliterate everything was just too strong.'

'Was there no one who could help? What about your father?'

'My father was the reason for much of her pain,' she replied bitterly, the words slipping out before she could prevent them. She should not have told him that. The last person she should be speaking to Samuel about was her father.

Samuel frowned, and she could see he was trying to make sense of her words. 'You do not have to tell me anything more, Hope,' he said in the end. 'Not if you do not wish to.'

But that was exactly the problem, Hope thought. She

did want to tell him. She wanted to break down and weep and tell him everything—about her mother, her father, her true self. About the childhood spent on that bleak hillside in Lillybeck, about her escape from a forced marriage and a life of crime. About her time on the stage, about those colourful years which had exposed her to so much culture and creativity on the one hand, and wickedness and debauchery on the other. About how her freedom had been snatched from her a second time, and how fate and fortune had conspired to send her into those woods, running for her life. Running, as it had turned out, into Sir Samuel Liddell's life, and into his warm, caring embrace.

An embrace, and a life, which she now had to detach herself from—to protect his feelings and to protect her own. Confiding in him was utterly out of the question; the hole she'd dug herself into with her deceit was now far too deep for that.

'I think that is quite enough misery for one morning,' she replied, forcing a smile as she rose carefully from her seat, ignoring how her sore limbs groaned in protest. 'If you will excuse me, I think I'd like to freshen up before breakfast.'

'Of course.'

Samuel too got to his feet. Hope could feel the heat of his gaze upon her as she walked towards the parlour door. She glanced down, feeling suddenly conscious of the state she was in. Her hair was hanging untidily about her shoulders and her clothes clung to her like a slickened second skin. She needed to wash, to breathe. To put some space between herself and Samuel and all that had been said and done. Perhaps then, she thought, her mind might not linger on the memory of his mouth pressed against hers quite so much.

'Hope? Can we speak again later? After last night…

well, there are some matters we need to discuss.' His voice sounded strained. 'Some things I need to explain.'

She glanced back at him, just briefly. 'Yes, of course.'

Hope hurried out of the room, reeling once more at the prospect of what it was he wanted to tell her, even while she told herself that whatever it was should make no difference to her now. The only thing that really mattered, she reminded herself, was leaving before any more harm could be done.

Chapter Fourteen

Samuel knew that he ought to have been exhausted, and yet he could not sleep. He'd spent the day dealing with the aftermath of the discovery of Miss Gordon's affliction, as Charles had rather euphemistically taken to calling it, in a daze brought on by his own lack of sleep. His turmoil over all that had occurred between him and Hope, and all that he had still to tell her, had conspired with his fatigue to leave him feeling thoroughly out of sorts. His stomach had churned almost incessantly, while every spare moment had been haunted by the confusion lingering in Hope's eyes as he'd uttered those most damning words.

'I must tell you that I am not who you think I am...'

More than once he'd given himself a stern talking-to, reminding himself that he had duties to perform, instructions to issue, and an unwell guest whose care required to be overseen. Miss Gordon had awoken properly by the middle of the morning, and the physician had turned up shortly afterwards. The good doctor had thankfully confirmed that Charles's sister was out of danger but had recommended bed rest and a lengthy abstinence from her tinctures.

Despite her weakened condition, Miss Gordon had protested at that. 'My headaches are severe,' she'd insisted. 'The laudanum is entirely necessary, to manage the pain.'

The physician, to his credit, was unmoved. Samuel had felt sure that Hope would have raised a knowing eyebrow at Miss Gordon's objection, had she been present. She'd gone to her bedchamber to rest after breakfast and he had not seen much of her since, although he knew from Charles's report that she'd spent some of the afternoon sitting with Miss Gordon while Samuel had been attending to estate matters at his desk in the library. She'd made only a brief appearance at dinnertime before retiring early, insisting she was still very tired. No doubt she was, but knowing that hadn't made Samuel crave her company any less. He still needed to speak to her, still needed to tell her the truth about himself. Kissing her had made his confession more vital than ever. And as for that kiss...

The memory of that had driven him to distraction more than once during his waking hours. Then there was her intention to leave and his promise to escort her to London—a promise he intended to keep, even if the thought of it made his heart sink and a lump grow in his throat. But he could hardly do anything else, could he? His duty was, and had always been, to protect her, and he would continue to do so, even after she learned he was merely Samuel Liddell. He would honour his promise, even if she despised him.

Even if he so desperately wanted her to stay.

In the ladies' absence, Samuel had spent the evening with Charles, although neither gentleman seemed to have much to offer by way of conversation. For his part, Charles seemed to be in shock over Miss Gordon's near-demise. He was clearly unwilling to discuss exactly what he knew about the extent of his sister's use of laudanum, although in his customarily clumsy way he did make some interesting admissions when referring to it.

'I suppose I ought to write to Mama and inform her of what has happened,' he'd said at one point. 'Although she will not be pleased. She'd put a lot of faith in Buxton's waters as a cure for my sister's many ills.'

'Many ills?' Samuel had repeated.

'I mean the headaches, of course,' Charles had blustered. 'My sister has for a long time been gravely afflicted. It affects her spirits too, as doubtless you have noticed.'

Samuel had nodded, deciding not to press his friend further but finding himself wondering if Miss Gordon, like Hope's mother, had pains beyond headaches which made the lure of oblivion too great to resist.

Once their brandy glasses were empty and their stilted conversation had all but evaporated, both gentlemen had retired. Since then, Samuel had tossed and turned in bed, unable to settle, and unable to quiet his thoughts. Everything he'd tried to push aside during the daylight hours had come racing to the fore, and now he found himself picking through the details relentlessly.

How delicate she'd felt in his arms, how warm her lips had been against his. How enthusiastically she'd kissed him back. How embracing her had felt so right, when in every sense it had been entirely wrong. Hope had sought sanctuary at Hayton, not seduction by its pretend baronet. How he could countenance kissing her when he was lying to her about the man he was... Well, he knew the answer to that. He couldn't. He could not countenance it at all.

Then there was the glimpse of Hope's past, which Miss Gordon's affliction had unexpectedly drawn from her. The thought of her losing her mother like that made his heart ache for her, even while he felt that now familiar protective urge burning within him at her veiled remark about her father and the pain he'd caused. Between her wicked uncle and the father she could not bring herself to discuss, it was clear that Hope had suffered at the hands of the men in her life. A fact which made Samuel's own deception of her even harder to swallow.

He had to tell her the truth, just as he'd begun to, in the library last night. He had to find a way to explain his actions, despite his fear that she would never be able to forgive him. That she would leave Hayton immediately and never look back.

Of course, leaving was exactly what she intended to do now, in any case! He pressed his fist into his pillow in frustration. It was clear that sleep would continue to elude him for some time yet, and his restlessness had left him hot and sweating beneath his sheets. Throwing off his bedcovers, he lit a candle, resolved to go downstairs and fetch some refreshment. Smithson could always be relied upon to keep the decanter of brandy in the library topped up for him; perhaps another small glass might see him on his way to slumber.

Stealthily, Samuel crept out of his room and along the wide, wood-panelled hallway. The house was silent, the servants having long since retired for the night. Just as well, Samuel thought, since he wore nothing but his drawers. For decency's sake he ought to have at least pulled a shirt on, but the cool air of the old house at night felt like a blessed relief against his bare skin.

Swiftly, he made his way into the library, closing the door so carefully that it barely made a sound. It was only once he was inside that he realised the room already had the dim illumination of a candle. Assuming that a maid had neglected to extinguish it before retiring, Samuel marched towards it furiously, muttering to himself about the risk of fire—in an ancient dwelling like Hayton Hall, filled with wood, the place would surely go up in flames in no time at all. It was only when he reached the table upon which it sat that he realised someone was there—someone who had curled up in one of the tall green wingback chairs which faced away from the door. Someone dressed in only a white linen shift and a shawl, with a book draped across her lap while she sat upright but fast asleep.

Hope.

Samuel swallowed hard, struggling to tear his eyes from the sight of her sleeping, her expression serene, her pink lips near-smiling, her dark hair loose and tumbling about her shoulders. Quietly, he stepped back, deciding to simply blow out the candle for safety's sake and leave her to rest. It was the proper and decent thing to do, especially given his own semi-naked state. Last night he'd all but seduced her in this very room; she did not need to spy him standing before her tonight, leaving little to the imagination in his undergarments.

Leaving was his plan, but fate—and Hayton's old floor—had other ideas. As he stepped away again, one of the wooden boards creaked loudly, betraying his presence, and waking Hope.

She jolted upright, blinking, then stared straight at him. 'Samuel?'

Sir Samuel Liddell in nothing but his drawers was a sight to behold. Even in her sleepy, confused state, Hope could not help but let her eyes rake over the details of him—from the broad shoulders and chest, sculpted by muscles usually buried beneath the finery of a gentleman's attire, to the trail of surprisingly dark hair which meandered down the lower part of his flat stomach and disappeared inside the white cotton.

Her fingers seemed to tingle with the urge to reach out and touch him; she fisted them, willing her mind, and her body, to behave. She had never seen a man looking like this before—at least, not a man she found so attractive. Like their kiss last night, this visceral, physical response was also a new experience for her. But that did not mean she should lose her head to the wanton and desirous thoughts currently racing through her mind.

'Samuel,' she repeated, almost choking on his name. Why was her mouth suddenly so dry? 'Is everything all right?'

He folded his arms across his chest in a manner which was endearingly self-conscious. 'You left a candle burning,' he said. 'I was just going to extinguish it, for safety's sake.'

His rebuke was gentle but clear enough.

'Forgive me,' she replied. 'I did not mean to doze off down here. I could not sleep so I decided to read awhile.' She forced a smile, trying to keep her eyes focused on his, and not the other, tempting parts of him, as she held up the book. 'You have a good selection of Mrs Radcliffe's novels. Have you read them?'

She watched as Samuel shook his head, those arms remaining stubbornly folded. 'Alas, no—gothic fiction is not really to my taste.' He continued to hover awkwardly for a moment, glancing down at himself. 'I should go. I only came down to fetch a brandy. I should not...well, should not be standing in front of you looking like this.'

Despite the fact that the way he looked was making her

heart continue to race, Hope found herself laughing. 'I've seen you now, Samuel, so I dare say the damage is done.'

'You may laugh, but what if Charles or Smithson walked in now and saw us together like this?'

Hope considered this for a moment, then carefully took off her shawl and passed it to him. 'Here,' she said. 'For your modesty. Now you can fetch your brandy.'

Samuel draped the shawl over his broad shoulders. In truth, its fine fabric offered little coverage, and Hope could still spy a great swathe of his bare chest and stomach beneath it. He looked ridiculous, and oddly more appealing than ever.

'Would you like one too?' he asked, holding up the decanter.

Hope nodded. Given her current state, a drop of something strong was perhaps not a bad idea. Although whether it was within brandy's capacity to dampen rampant desire, she had no idea.

'Have you finished reading Mr Hume then?' he asked as he poured two small glasses, handing one of them to her as he sat down in a chair opposite.

'No, but I was not in the mood for history tonight. Escaping into some fiction seemed much more appealing.'

'Too much on your mind?' he asked.

'Indeed,' she agreed, not daring to say more about the exact nature of the thoughts which troubled her. Thoughts about him, thoughts about leaving. Thoughts about all the lies she'd told.

Samuel held up his brandy glass. 'Same,' he replied. 'Hence the need for this.' He paused, taking a considered sip. 'Charles said you sat with Miss Gordon for a little while this afternoon. How was she?'

'In low spirits, if I'm honest. It's plain to see that she

fears the loss of her tinctures. I cannot say I blame her. Ceasing to take laudanum after the body has become accustomed to it can make you very unwell. My mother tried to give it up several times, but after days of fever and sickness she would always return to it.'

'Then we must keep a close eye on her, to ensure that does not happen. Tomorrow I will ask Smithson to ensure Maddie and one or two of the other maids take turns to remain with Miss Gordon throughout her recovery.'

Hope smiled. 'That is a good idea. I will assist them too.'

Samuel let out a long breath, clearly contemplating something. 'Charles seemed to suggest that Miss Gordon's headaches are responsible for her low spirits,' he said after a moment. 'However, I am unsure. He seems very evasive about the entire matter, which makes me suspicious that there's more to his sister's current woes than he's telling me. Has Miss Gordon said anything to you that might shed some light on what is going on?'

Hope shook her head. 'No, but, like you, I think whatever ails her could be due to more than headaches. Between her sombre countenance and cutting remarks, it is not difficult to see that she is deeply unhappy.'

'I suppose it is none of our business,' Samuel mused, before draining his glass. 'I dare say once she's well enough to travel, both Charles and his sister will be on their way. I spent an awkward evening with him earlier—it is abundantly clear this whole sorry episode has left him feeling very uncomfortable. And if I know anything about Charles, it's that his usual response to such feelings is to flee.'

Hope took a gulp of her brandy, steeling herself. 'Perhaps I should go then too,' she said, her heart pounding so hard that the sound of it seemed to echo in her ears. She did her best to ignore it, to remind herself that this was something she had to discuss with him. She had to make plans to leave, no matter how hard, how painful it seemed. 'I am well enough to travel now. Perhaps, if Mr and Miss Gordon would oblige me, I could travel as far as Lancashire with them, and make my own way from there.'

She watched with bated breath as Samuel's brows drew together in concern.

'I promised you that I would escort you to London, Hope.'

'But that was before the Gordons arrived and…' She faltered momentarily, her thoughts scattering as she saw the consternation growing on his handsome face. 'You have done so much for me, Samuel—truly, I am indebted to you. But I do not wish to cause you any more inconvenience, not when there is another possible solution.'

'But once you reach Blackburn, you will still be hundreds of miles from London, and you will be on your own,' he replied, shaking his head. 'Surely that is no solution at all.'

Samuel leaned forward, the shawl slipping from his shoulders and unveiling that magnificent physique once again. Hope swallowed hard, dragging her gaze back up to meet his.

'I do not wish to tell you what to do. Indeed, I am not your father, your brother, or…' He pressed his lips together momentarily. 'Or your husband. Therefore, as you once reminded me, you are not my concern. And yet I am concerned. I'm concerned about you going to London, about this uncle of yours, about you wandering straight back into danger. I'm concerned that there is so much more to your story than I know…'

'Well, that makes two of us,' Hope countered, giving him

a pointed look and trying to ignore how her heart lurched at the thought of how little he did know. How dreadful the truth was. 'Last night you told me that you are not who I believe you to be. What did you mean?'

Even in the dim candlelight his grim expression was unmistakable.

'What I meant was...' He faltered, his blue-grey eyes seeming to darken. For a long moment he pressed his lips together, steeling himself. 'What I meant to tell you was that I have lied to you. Hayton Hall is not my house. Its lands are not my lands. And I am not a baronet.'

In the night-time quiet of the library, Hope heard someone gasp. She presumed it was her own voice she'd heard, but the sound seemed somehow separate, somehow distant, as a maelstrom of sudden spiralling thoughts gripped her. Of all the possible explanations for his words last night, this was the very last one she could have imagined. To learn that he was not Hayton's baronet at all had shocked her and yet, as she sat there, her mouth agape as she regarded him, she realised that was only the beginning of her concerns.

A deathly cold chill crept up her spine as the full ramifications of his deceit flooded through her mind. If he was not a baronet, and if Hayton Hall was not his, then the protection she'd felt and the sanctuary she'd enjoyed was surely no such thing at all. Her father was a ruthless, dangerous man—if Samuel was not the prominent, important gentleman she'd believed him to be, then her father would think nothing of snatching her away from him and, worse still, perhaps even harming Samuel in the process. No matter who Samuel really was, she could not bear the thought that she'd unwittingly endangered him. She shivered, feeling suddenly exposed, as the illusion of her safe hiding place crumbled in the face of Samuel's lies. What if her father was drawing near? What if he'd already found her and was just waiting for the right moment to take her away?

'I am so sorry, Hope,' Samuel continued, clearly grappling with her stunned silence, with the look of horror she doubtless wore upon her face. 'Please understand that I only want to protect you, that I care about you. When I kissed you last night, I…'

'No,' she interrupted him, unable to bear her own thoughts or his words any longer. Unable to countenance hearing that he cared about her when her mere presence in this house might yet lead him into danger. 'That kiss was a mistake—a moment of madness.' She rose from her seat, hurrying now towards the door. 'I must leave Hayton as soon as possible. I must speak to Mr Gordon tomorrow.'

Hope hurried out of the library before Samuel could spy the tears which had begun to gather in her eyes. Tears of shock, tears of terror—tears which acknowledged that the safe haven she'd put so much faith in lay in ruins, and the protection she'd believed Samuel had given her had turned to dust.

Chapter Fifteen

'A moment of madness.'

Samuel replayed those words over and over in his mind as he sat at his desk, trying and hopelessly failing to concentrate on working through the pile of papers in front of him. He'd been like this for a couple of days now, attempting to bury himself in the business of running the Liddell estate, to avoid everything and everyone as much as he reasonably could. Mostly, all he'd managed to do, however, was revisit that night-time encounter with Hope again and again, picking over its details while he licked his wounds.

The sight of her sitting in the library, ashen-faced, eyes wide with horror as he confessed the truth seemed to have etched itself indelibly on his brain. He'd expected her to be shocked, angry even, but the fact that she'd appeared so appalled, so offended by the idea that he was neither a landowner nor a baronet, had devastated him. And then there were those words she'd uttered as she'd retreated from him, rejecting his affection for her so emphatically that he felt as though his heart had been trampled on all over again.

That kiss was a mistake—a moment of madness.

All he'd said was that he cared for her, and yet now that

she knew who he truly was she could not even countenance that.

Samuel groaned, burying his head in his hands. How could he have got it so wrong, how could he have so gravely misunderstood a woman's feelings for a second time? In the summer he'd wrongly interpreted Charlotte's flirtatiousness as genuine interest in him, and now he'd allowed himself to imagine that the way Hope had kissed him back might have been an expression of her affection for him. Perhaps it had—but it was an affection which had been easily extinguished as soon as she'd discovered that it held no promise of becoming Lady Liddell.

Of course, she would have known there was no prospect of that if he'd been truthful with her from the beginning. In that respect, Samuel knew he only had himself to blame for her evident disappointment in who and what he really was. He deserved every bit of her dismay, her ire, her swift retreat from his affections. He deserved to feel humiliated.

If only he had explained who he was straight away. If only he hadn't kissed her. If only holding her in his arms like that hadn't felt so perfect. If only he hadn't lost his head in that moment of madness in the library, then he wouldn't be on the cusp of losing his heart now too. Because he was, wasn't he? That was why Hope's rejection of him hurt so much.

And now she was going to leave him. She was going to step into Charles Gordon's carriage and never look back. It was the prospect of that, Samuel realised, which hurt most of all.

Despite being preoccupied by his sister's woes, Charles had not failed to notice that something was amiss between Samuel and Hope.

'Trouble in paradise, Sammy?' he'd asked after knocking on the library door yesterday and trying to coax Samuel out for some tea.

Miserably, Samuel had informed his friend that Hope now knew that he was not Hayton's baronet, and that she had not taken the news well. He had not been able to bring himself to talk about that kiss, or the way she'd rejected him—the wound that had inflicted was still too raw to be confided to anyone. But he had told Charles that Hope now intended to leave, and that she wished to enlist his help to do so—if she hadn't already.

'She'd talked of leaving before now, and no doubt learning the truth about me has made her more desperate to do so,' he'd finished with a heavy sigh. 'I've made a terrible mess of this, Charles. I have only myself to blame.'

His friend had sat down at the other side of his desk, an uncharacteristically serious expression on his face. 'Miss Swynford hasn't said anything to me about leaving,' he replied. 'Perhaps she's had a change of heart?'

'Somehow, I doubt that.'

'Well, even if she hasn't, do you not think you should talk to her about it, rather than skulking around in here? I'm not blind, Sammy. I've seen the way you look at her. You cannot possibly want her to leave. Why don't you just tell her how you feel?'

Samuel had winced at the thought of it. He'd tried to speak to her about his feelings once, he'd told her that he cared for her, and look where that had got him.

'So, I am correct then?' Charles had continued, taking his friend's silence as acquiescence. 'You are smitten with the chit?'

'I care very much about her,' Samuel had begun, his

voice sounding odd and strangled, even to himself. 'I want to protect her. I want to help...'

'Then I would suggest that you talk to her,' Charles had concluded as he rose from his seat. 'You've told her the truth about yourself, Sammy, but perhaps it's time for a bit more honesty. All cards on the table, so to speak.'

Charles's words rattled around Samuel's head as he tried once again to apply himself to his work. In the end he pushed his papers aside, frustrated. Samuel was more accustomed to being on the receiving end of Charles's teasing than he was to being the recipient of his advice. But for all that he was boisterous and more than a little ungovernable at times, his friend's heart was usually in the right place. Perhaps, Samuel considered, his advice was worth heeding. Perhaps he should try to talk to Hope, to explain himself properly. Certainly, it would be better than sitting at his desk feeling sorry for himself.

Surely it couldn't do any more harm. Could it?

Resolved to act rather than dwell any further on it, Samuel leapt out of his seat and hurried out of the room in search of Hope. He strode along the hallway, contemplating where she might be. Often she spent the afternoons sitting with Miss Gordon; if that were the case, he could hardly go bursting in. Perhaps he ought to find Maddie first, and request that she ask Hope to join him in the small parlour...

The sound of soft laughter coming from that very room reached his ears just as he placed his first footstep upon the stairs. Followed by two voices—a woman's and a man's—deep in conversation. Furrowing his brow, Samuel drew closer to the door, then turned the doorknob and walked in.

Hope's wide-eyed expression was what struck him first, as though his sudden intrusion had alarmed her. He watched as her lips parted in surprise, her teacup suspended in mid-air. Across from her sat Charles, that usual broad smile of his illuminating his face as he rose from the comfort of the sofa.

'Ah! Finally dragged yourself away from all that work, have you, Sammy?' Charles greeted him. 'Come and join us for some tea.'

Despite his friend's beckoning, Samuel found that he could not move. Instead, he seemed frozen to the spot, his gaze flitting between the pair of them, taking in the cosy scene. The teapot on the table, the small plate of neatly arranged slices of cake at its side. The way their conversation, and Hope's laughter, had ceased the moment he'd walked in...

'Sammy?' Charles prompted, frowning now.

But still Samuel could not answer. He could only look at the scene before him and think how it reminded him of the events of the summer, when another woman had decided he was not good enough for her and had sought out his older, titled brother instead. Charles might not be titled, but he was the heir to a tradesman's fortune—a better and wealthier prospect, to be sure. As he met Hope's eyes once more, holding her astonished gaze, his blood heated with an intolerable jealousy as it dawned on him that she knew this. That, having learned the truth of who Samuel was, she'd found him lacking and had set her sights far higher.

Just like Charlotte had.

'I think that I will go and get some air.'

Hope watched, aghast, as Mr Gordon made his excuses and hurried out of the parlour. Little wonder, she thought. The tension in the room was so thick that she doubted a knife could cut through it. Near to the door stood Samuel, his expression severe, his usually merry blue-grey eyes uncharacteristically stormy. Something was amiss, but she was at a loss to understand exactly what.

Since that last meeting with Samuel in the library late at night, and since learning who he really was, she'd managed largely to avoid him. She'd spent her time grappling with the turmoil his deception had caused, placing it with that gnawing guilt of knowing that she continued to deceive him. She could not possibly have done anything to offend him. Indeed, if anyone ought to be angry right now, it was her, wasn't it?

'Well, are you going to sit down and join me?' she asked, gesturing towards the chair which Charles had recently vacated.

'I wasn't aware you and Charles took tea together in the afternoons,' he said, ignoring her question.

She frowned. 'We don't usually. However, I wanted to speak to him about travelling with him and Miss Gordon to Blackburn. I believe I told you I would do so, the last time we spoke properly.'

He seemed to bristle at her reference to that ill-fated conversation. 'I see,' he replied, giving her a brittle nod. 'And what did Charles say?'

'He assured me that once they'd made firm plans for their departure, I would be included in them,' she replied.

In truth, Mr Gordon had been a good deal more non-committal than that, professing a lack of certainty over when his sister would be fit to travel. Certainly, he would not wish to name a date, or so he'd told her. Indeed, he'd confided to her that he'd made the grave mistake of mentioning their return to Shawdale to Miss Gordon and she'd reacted terribly. He would have to tread carefully from now on, he'd said, which meant that Hope would simply have to wait. He'd changed the subject then, trying his best to amuse her, to occupy her with lighter topics of conversation. In response she'd smiled and feigned laughter in all the right places, whilst quietly wondering what on earth she was going to do. The longer she remained at Hayton Hall, the longer she risked bringing danger to its door. Not that she even knew who that door, and this house, actually belonged to…

'You both certainly looked very at ease in each other's company,' Samuel observed, snapping her out of her thoughts. 'Given that you were merely discussing travel plans.'

Hope felt the heat of indignation rise in her chest at his insinuation. 'What are you suggesting, Samuel?' she asked, getting to her feet and marching towards him as she challenged him to spell it out.

'I'm suggesting that the two of you seem to be getting along very well. Perhaps that is why you are so keen to travel to Blackburn with him and his sister…'

'Oh, for heaven's sake!' Hope threw up her hands in despair. She stood merely a foot away from him now, her hands planted on her hips as she glared up at him. 'That is completely ridiculous. I've no romantic interest in your friend, Samuel. None whatsoever! I must leave Hayton because my injuries have healed and it is time to do so.'

And because he'd lied to her, she reminded herself quietly. Because she could no longer trust that he was able to protect her, or indeed himself, from the malevolent men who sought her. And because she continued to lie to him too.

Samuel stared at her, unmoved. 'Charles has much to recommend him,' he began again. 'He is extraordinarily wealthy, for a start, although he has no title, which I dare say is the paramount consideration...'

'Not to me!' Hope prodded an angry finger against his chest. Why was he being so insufferable? Where on earth had all this talk of her and Mr Gordon come from?

Touching him, it transpired, was to be her downfall. Almost as soon as she had tapped that finger against the fine fabric of his shirt, her hand seemed to develop a will of its own, her fingers splaying out across his chest, the gesture dissolving from one of fury into one of tenderness. She felt her breath catch in her throat as beneath her hand she sensed his heart beating faster. She looked up at him, her eyes locking with his as he raised his hand, capturing her chin beneath his delicate touch as their lips drew closer.

The kiss which followed was as explosive as it was brief. Hope wasn't sure who deepened it first, such was the speed with which instinct and desire overcame them both. She pressed herself against him, her hands roaming and revelling in the promise of that masculine, athletic physique, hinted at beneath his fine clothes. For his part, Samuel seemed to have absolutely lost control too, his lips firm and hungry against hers, his hands similarly seeking out the curve of her breasts, her waist, her bottom. Then, somewhere within the recesses of her mind, a voice emerged, the one reminding her of his deceit, and of her own. Of the danger of falling for a man she could not have, a man who would be utterly horrified to know who and what she really was. A man she had to leave behind.

'Enough,' she breathed, stepping away from him, breaking the spell.

She hurried out of the parlour, reeling at what had just occurred. One moment they'd been arguing, the next they'd been kissing—how had that happened? How could she lurch from being in the grip of guilt and anger one moment to melting into his arms the next? She made her way up the stairs as quickly as she could, frantically straightening her hair and her gown as she determined to put a safe distance between her and Samuel.

Perhaps she would go and sit with Miss Gordon for a while. She'd passed many an hour at her bedside of late, relieving either Maddie or one of the other maids of their duties for a while, and finding a sort of refuge in the woman's prolonged silences as she either slept or stared vacantly towards the window. Occasionally, Miss Gordon would reach over and tentatively pat her hand, or offer her an appreciative nod of acknowledgement. It was plain to see that the lady's low spirits persisted, although she had said nothing to Hope about the reasons for her continued malaise. For all her suspicions that at the root of the lady's ills lay something more than headaches, Hope had not attempted to press the matter. After all, she knew as well as anyone what it was like to have things about herself that she was unwilling or unable to discuss. She had a veritable list of them, growing day by day.

Topping that list was her hopeless attraction to a man who had lied to her about who he was. A man who'd just as good as accused her of pursuing his friend! A man who did not even know her real name.

Hope drew a deep breath, composing herself as she reached Miss Gordon's door and knocked gently. It would do no good to torture herself with such thoughts yet again.

'Maddie?' Hope called softly through the door, frowning that as yet the maid had not come to answer her knock. Usually, Maddie took her turn to care for Miss Gordon in the afternoon, and was always a committed presence at the lady's bedside, just as she had been while Hope had convalesced.

Hope listened for several moments, surprised that she could hear no sound coming from within. Maddie must have been called away, but what of Miss Gordon—was she sleeping? Or had she taken ill once more? Hope's mind returned to her conversation with Mr Gordon, to his words about his sister's reaction to the prospect of returning home. What if she'd had one of her little bottles hidden away and had sought oblivion from it the moment her brother's back was turned?

Gripped by a wave of panic, Hope pushed open Miss Gordon's door and rushed inside. Her eyes darted frantically about, her heart thudding ever harder as she spied the room's damning details one by one: the empty, unmade bed; the pile of clothes abandoned on the floor; the large chest, all of its drawers wide open, as though someone had been looking for something in a hurry.

Hope heard herself gasp.

As though someone had left in a hurry.

But how? When? And where had she gone?

Hope rushed out of the door, her recently healed ankle throbbing in protest as she began to run along the landing and back towards the stairs. 'Samuel! Mr Gordon!' she cried as loud as she could. 'I need your help. I think Miss Gordon is missing!'

Chapter Sixteen

Samuel stared out of the window of his carriage, watching as the wind swirled the fallen leaves into a frenzy of red, yellow and brown at the side of the road. At least the rain had ceased for now, making the search for Miss Gordon easier. A short interview with a very tearful Maddie had established that the maid had left her charge to attend to some clothing upon which Miss Gordon had spilled her soup, giving the lady ample time to make her escape.

'I am so sorry, sir,' the maid had wept. 'I should have returned right away, but Miss Gordon was very concerned about the stain. She said it was her favourite shawl and that it was so fine, no lye could be used upon it. She insisted that I supervise the laundry maid myself while she cleaned it.'

Samuel had tried to comfort poor Maddie, reassuring her that she was only doing what the lady had asked. It was clear that the prolonged dismissal of Maddie by Miss Gordon had been deliberate, to allow her to get away unseen. It was clear too that she had not been missing for very long, and therefore could not have gone very far. Samuel had proposed searching for her in Hayton village, since it was only a short distance away and if she'd followed the road she'd have likely ended up there. Since the quickest way to search was on horseback, he'd informed Charles that he would ask his groom to ready two of his fastest beasts.

Charles, however, had hesitated, his gaze shifting back and forth between Samuel and Hope. 'I think we need Miss Swynford to come with us,' he'd said. 'My sister seems to like you, Miss Swynford. If—when—we find her, we stand a better chance of her returning with us if Miss Swynford is there to speak with her. And besides, we must take a carriage in any case. We can hardly throw dear Henrietta across the back of one of our horses, can we?'

Samuel had been forced to concede that his friend's logic was sound. For her part, Hope had insisted that she wished to help rather than sit in the parlour waiting for news, and the determined expression on her face was such that Samuel had not dared contradict her. And so, with reluctance and a few cautionary words about Hope remaining inside the carriage and out of sight, Samuel had agreed. An agreement which had left him in exactly the position he found himself now, sitting across from Hope in his carriage as it rumbled along the road towards Lowhaven. Charles had also insisted that he should ride ahead, leaving Samuel and Hope to follow together. For all his evident concern about his sister's welfare, Samuel could not help but wonder if his friend had contrived to throw them both into close confines.

They'd gone to Hayton first, and in the sleepy village where not much went unnoticed they'd quickly learned that a young lady matching Miss Gordon's description had pleaded her way on to the back of a local harness-maker's cart bound for Lowhaven docks. Samuel had made the enquiries while Hope had remained quietly in the carriage.

Indeed, since leaving Hayton Hall she had not uttered a word, apparently preferring to gaze silently out of the window or at the floor—at anything apart from him. Not that he could blame her, he thought glumly. Given his behaviour of late—deceiving her, reacting jealously to the sight of her sitting with Charles, not to mention losing his head and kissing her again—he wouldn't want to speak to him either.

He knew he ought to say something, to offer a proper explanation for what he'd said and done, for why he'd lied to her. Yet now, sitting in her presence, he found himself struggling to formulate the words. His feelings, he realised, were like those swirling leaves outside the carriage window—utterly all over the place, and completely at the mercy of a stronger, higher force. He clasped his hands tightly together, as though praying for some divine intervention, some guidance out of the mess he'd created. Some way to assuage the myriad of feelings which continued to assail him—the hopeless attraction to Hope, the burning desire to protect her. The sorrow and guilt which his deception of her had provoked. The humiliation and hurt of knowing that the real Samuel was once again not good enough for a woman he'd begun to care for.

As the rugged countryside finally fell away and the humble cottages on the periphery of Lowhaven beckoned, his unspoken turmoil finally bubbled over.

'I am so sorry, Hope,' he began. 'I know this is a terrible time to talk about this, while Miss Gordon is missing, but I have to say something. I…'

His words faltered as she looked at him squarely, those emerald eyes steely and challenging. 'Which part are you sorry for, Samuel?' she asked him. 'The part where you let me believe you were a baronet, that I was living in your home, or the part where you accused me of dallying with your friend?'

He flinched at her caustic tone. 'I didn't say you were dallying with Charles. I…' He shook his head at himself as another wave of shame gripped him. Shame at allowing jealousy to get the better of him. Shame at how he'd allowed his wounded pride to rule him so often of late.

That stern stare of hers was unrelenting. 'But you did suggest that, how did you put it, we were getting along very well, and that Mr Gordon's extraordinary wealth might be of paramount interest to me.'

Samuel grimaced to hear his words repeated back to him. To hear how cold, how mercenary they sounded. To realise just how much he'd let his hurt and humiliation poison his thoughts.

'You were right—I was being ridiculous, suggesting that you and Charles had formed an attachment.' He drew a deep breath, trying to order his thoughts, to swallow his damnable pride. 'In truth, Hope, I am sorry for all of it. For everything. For what I said about you and Charles. For leading you to think that Hayton Hall, its lands and the title that goes with it, was all mine. It was wrong of me. Indeed, it was unforgivable.'

'How on earth did you manage to pretend to have a grand house and a title?'

Hope continued to hold his sorrowful gaze as she finally gave voice to a question which had been swirling around her mind. Once she'd managed to quell her initial panic at learning she was likely not as safe as she'd thought, questions about the practicalities of Samuel's deception had plagued her. It was unfathomable—all these weeks at Hayton Hall, cared for by the man she believed to be its master. Convalescing in one of his rooms, being attended to by his servants, dining with him, enjoying tea with him in his parlour. How could none of that have been real? How on earth did someone pretend to have a grand house, to have a title? How could they have guests and servants in that house who all believed that to be the truth?

'Who are you, Samuel?' she continued, her questions flowing freely now. 'What are you—are you Hayton's tenant?'

'Not quite.' His tone was unmistakably grim as he stared down towards his boots. 'Hayton Hall is my home—at least, it is my family home and it is where I have lived since returning from my travels on the Continent. However, I am my father's second son. My elder brother, Sir Isaac Liddell, is the master of Hayton Hall and its estate. He married recently—eloped, in fact—and is travelling in Scotland with his new bride. I am caring for the estate in his absence.'

Hope frowned, her thoughts still racing. 'But the servants all call you Sir Samuel...'

'They do—because I instructed them to.' He paused, grimacing. 'As you once reminded me when you rebuked me for calling my maid Madeleine, masters and servants are not equals. Please do not blame them for deceiving you; they had no choice in the matter.'

'And Mr and Miss Gordon—what do they know of this? Have you been deceiving them too?' This question had circled her mind earlier, while she'd enjoyed tea with Mr Gordon. She'd wondered what he knew, if he was being deceived too. If she ought to say something...

Samuel's expression grew increasingly pained. 'No—Charles and his sister know exactly who and what I am. When they arrived unexpectedly at Hayton Hall, I begged them to play along with the lie. They agreed, although it's clear Charles thinks I'm an utter blockhead and of course he's absolutely right.' He looked up then, his grey-blue eyes sorrowful and heavy with regret. 'Please do not blame them either. I am so sorry, Hope. The fault for this deceit is entirely mine.'

For several moments, Hope simply stared at him, stunned by the extent of his deceit, a thousand thoughts whirling around her mind. Samuel had lied to her about who he was, and he'd involved everyone else in his deception too. The thought of Smithson, Maddie, and the Gordons all being privy to the lie made her feel foolish, gullible even. But then, how could she possibly have known any different? She—the real Hope—knew nothing of gentlemen, titles and grand estates.

That was another thing, she reminded herself yet again. Samuel was not the only one of them who was lying about who he was. Like him, she was not what she had appeared to be. Hope searched Samuel's handsome face, her mind racing with memories of their weeks together. Memories of cosy afternoons in the parlour, of candlelit dinners, of their meeting of minds over Shakespeare's plays. Memories of his embrace, of his kisses. Throughout all of this time, had they come to know each other at all? Or were they each only familiar with the role that the other was playing?

And if she did not know the real him, then who had she been in danger of losing her heart to?

'Why?' she said quietly. 'Why did you lie to me?'

She watched as Samuel dragged his hands down his face. 'Please believe me when I say that I did not intend to lie to you,' he began. 'The day after I found you in the woods, when we spoke properly for the first time, it was clear you'd assumed I was the baronet, that the estate was mine and…

and I could not find the words to correct you. The way you looked at me, like I was someone important...' He paused, shaking his head at himself. 'To my eternal discredit, my foolish pride got the better of me. I vowed I would tell you the truth, but then you told me how safe and protected you felt with me, how fortunate you'd been to find yourself in the home of a baronet. I couldn't bear to take away that feeling from you, to allow you to feel anything less than completely safe. I know it was wrong, but I decided then that I would keep up the pretence.'

'So why tell me at all?' she asked. 'Why did you decide to tell me the truth, that night in the library?'

She watched as he appeared to wrestle with her question. 'As I said that night, I care about you and, besides, after I kissed you, I knew I had to say something.'

Hope felt her cheeks colour at the memory of that first kiss. That was one thing he had not apologised for, she noted. Not that she was sorry for it either. Nor could she find it within herself to regret the way their passions had spilled over in the parlour earlier...

Her thoughts were interrupted by the sharp sound of the carriage door clicking open. Cold air raced in, laced with a spicy sweetness as the scents of rum, cocoa and coffee all mingled. Hope jolted. Until that moment, she had not even realised that they'd stopped. Had not even noticed the bustle and noise of Lowhaven's docks as they sat in the midst of them. She looked up to see Mr Gordon peering in at them.

'If we're going to find Henrietta, we'd best make haste,' Mr Gordon said, his gaze flitting between them both.

Samuel nodded. Hope saw how he swallowed hard, as though collecting himself, before he turned back to address her. 'Will you be all right here?' he asked.

'Of course,' she replied in the most reassuring voice she could muster. 'Please, just find Miss Gordon and bring her to the carriage. Tell her not to worry, that I am waiting here for her.'

Briefly, Samuel seemed to hesitate, as though there was something else he wished to say. If there was, then he decided to keep his own counsel, instead offering her a brisk nod before disembarking. Involuntarily, Hope shuddered as the carriage door slammed shut behind him, feeling a final blast of that cool, pungent air before she was cut off from the outside world once more. She fiddled with the large bonnet she wore to shield her face, before peering tentatively out of the window. From this vantage point she could see Samuel and Mr Gordon begin their enquiries, doubtless describing Miss Gordon to dockworkers and passers-by in the hope that someone might have seen her.

Hope sighed heavily, collapsing back in her seat. She wished that she could be out searching too, rather than stuck inside with only her spiralling thoughts for company. However, that was utterly out of the question. Lowhaven docks might as well be a lion's den. As a centre of trade, they crawled with associates of her father—people who might recognise her even disguised in a fine dress and wide-brimmed bonnet. As she'd learned to her great cost that night at Lowhaven's theatre, her years of absence had not left her quite so unrecognisable as she'd hoped. As much as she wanted to help, she could not run the risk. So instead she sat there, feeling useless, as she stewed over Samuel's lie and his explanation. An explanation which she had still to fully digest.

An explanation which left her with absolutely no idea how she should feel.

On the one hand, she still felt the joint sting of betrayal and anger as potently as ever, and on the other hand, she was acutely aware of the irony of feeling upset at all. Samuel had lied about who he was, but so had she, albeit it for very different reasons. Hope had deceived Samuel to protect herself—in a weakened state, riddled with injuries, and in the home of an unknown gentleman, she had done what was necessary to conceal an identity which, for all she knew, would have meant her being handed straight back to her father.

Samuel had lied to her to…what, exactly? Impress her? Or at least to impress the woman he thought she was— wealthy and well-bred. The thought of that made her groan aloud. How mortified he would be if he knew that he'd dragged his servants and his friends into a complex web of deceit to impress a mere actress and outlaw's daughter.

What a terrible mess.

Then there was his confession that he'd kept up the pretence to make her feel safe. Her heart had ached when he'd spoken of how he couldn't bear the thought of her feeling unprotected. After all, it was undeniable, wasn't it? She had believed in the sanctuary that a titled man and his grand home could offer her. Yet no matter how good and pure his intentions had been, his actions had ultimately fallen far short of being honourable and that was enough to make her question her judgement of him.

Weeks ago, she'd put her faith in a gentleman who'd been unfailingly kind and gentle, who'd seemed so decent and honest. It was Samuel's good nature, and her growing closeness to him, which had made her own deception harder to maintain, which had tempted her to share the truth of her situation with him. Now she wondered if she'd been wrong in her assessment of him. If he could lie to her so effortlessly, perhaps he would cast her out just as easily if he knew who she really was. If he knew she was no genteel heiress at all.

Hope huffed a breath, looking out of the window once more. Both Samuel and Mr Gordon had slipped out of sight now. In vain, Hope searched for them, her eyes skimming frantically over a busy scene of cargo, men and masts. Then, amongst the chaos of the quayside, a figure caught Hope's eye. A tall woman wearing a deep red cape, the hood pulled up to conceal her face. She seemed agitated, darting around and approaching men at random, seemingly asking them something, because each in turn shook his head at her. Miss Gordon—it had to be.

Hope searched again, trying to see either Samuel or Mr Gordon, but neither gentleman appeared to be near. Desperation burned in her gut and her heart raced. Leaving the carriage was an enormous risk, but so was leaving a vulnerable woman wandering alone around a port.

She had to act now.

With a deep breath, Hope pushed open the door of the carriage, hurrying towards the red-caped woman and praying that she was indeed Henrietta Gordon. Praying too that no one on that quayside would recognise the face of Hope Sloane beneath all her borrowed finery, because if they did she would be in serious trouble.

Chapter Seventeen

The scream Miss Gordon let out was like nothing Samuel had ever heard in his life. Even above the din of the port it rang out, a high-pitched yet feral, guttural sound. Part-banshee, part-bear. Across the quayside he saw her, a spectre of chaos in her dishevelled red cape, her arms flapping wildly, her hood falling down to reveal a veritable bird's nest of dark hair. Yet it was neither the sight of her nor the sound she made which horrified him the most. It was the smaller woman standing in front of her, clad in cream, her wide-brimmed bonnet insufficient to shield her face from all the attention which Miss Gordon's scene was drawing. Hope.

Samuel dashed towards her, his heart racing and his hackles slowly rising. What on earth was she thinking, leaving the carriage? After all these weeks in hiding, why would she put herself in such danger?

As he drew nearer, he saw Charles had joined them now, his gestures suggesting he was trying, and failing, to calm his sister down. If anything, the sight of her brother seemed to make Miss Gordon more hysterical. Samuel ran faster, his agitation growing at the woman's relentless cries. They needed to get her away from here. And, more to the point, he needed to get Hope back in that carriage and back to the safety of Hayton Hall.

'Oh, Sammy, thank goodness!' Charles called out as, finally, Samuel reached them. 'Is there a physician nearby? I think we're going to have to call upon the man and ask him to attend. Henrietta is unwell.'

Unwell? That was an understatement. Samuel's gaze shifted from Miss Gordon to Hope, who stood in front of her, speaking softly and calmly, trying her best to reassure her. It seemed to work as slowly the woman's wailing abated, replaced by quieter sobs. Around them he could sense the onlookers circling, their collective breath bated as they watched the scene unfold.

'We need to get you away from here, Hope,' Samuel said, not answering Charles. His thoughts were consumed now with only this—making sure Hope remained safe. 'Now.'

Hope glanced up at him, her green eyes challenging, her jaw set hard. 'I must help Miss Gordon,' she insisted. 'Besides, I dare say the damage has already been done.'

In breach of his usual calm temperament, Samuel felt his temper flare. How could she be so flippant about the threat she still faced? How could she be so obstinate when she was in such clear danger? For several moments he stared at her, her choice of words stinging him as though he'd been struck across his cheek. Words which could easily refer to more than her recognition, her discovery out here. The damage had indeed been done—by him, weeks ago, when he'd lied to her about who he was.

'Please, Hope,' he replied, swallowing down the fire which had risen in his throat. 'Please, go back to the carriage.'

'Not without Miss Gordon,' she replied, her voice quiet

but firm. 'I am not yours to command, Samuel. I am not your sister, or your wife.'

Samuel blinked at her, those words ringing in his ears and whirling around his mind.

'I am not...your wife.'

But what if she was—at least for now, in this moment? Would a new name and a husband be sufficient to throw any malevolent onlookers off the scent? Or, if she was recognised, would the news that she'd wed protect her, if it reached the ears of those who sought her?

No, he told himself, he could not countenance pretending that Hope was his wife, not under any circumstances. He'd quite finished with the business of telling lies, even for good and noble reasons. Even if he rather liked the idea of hearing the words *Mrs Liddell* fall from his lips...

Before he could say anything further, however, Hope turned away from him and back to Charles's sister, who stood trembling and sobbing quietly at her side. 'Come now, Miss Gordon,' she said softly as she took the lady tentatively by the arm. 'Let us return home. A little tea and cake, that's what you need. Then you will feel much better.'

It was hard to discern whether Hope's gentle words had the desired effect on Miss Gordon or whether she'd simply exhausted herself but, either way, Charles's sister submitted to Hope's coaxing without complaint. The audience which had gathered began to fall away as the four of them walked back towards the carriage, apparently losing interest now that it was clear that the scene Miss Gordon had made was over.

Inwardly, Samuel breathed a sigh of relief. Perhaps all would be well, after all. Perhaps no one there had known Hope for who she really was; perhaps word of her presence in the docks today would not reach her uncle's ears. Perhaps no damage had been done.

Except the damage he'd caused by lying to Hope, he thought glumly. He was not sure if that could ever be repaired.

Charles strode up beside Samuel, emitting a heavy sigh. 'Thank goodness that is over. I suppose I should be grateful that Henrietta's hysterics were witnessed here and not in Blackburn. The damage to her reputation there would have been irrevocable. At least here, no one is likely to know us.'

Samuel gave his friend a stern look. 'Frankly, Charles, I am more concerned about someone here recognising Hope, and about the danger that would place her in,' he replied, his voice hushed.

'Ah—of course. Indeed, Henrietta and I owe Miss Swynford an enormous debt for intercepting her like that, despite the risk to herself.' Charles gave Samuel a pointed look. 'Miss Swynford did not look delighted by your efforts to steer her away from danger, however,' he whispered. 'It's clear she's still angry with you. I presume you did not heed my advice about laying all your cards on the table.'

Samuel grimaced, watching Hope as she clambered into the carriage beside Miss Gordon a short distance away. This was a conversation he was not prepared to have—especially when Charles was partly correct. In the carriage, he'd begun to explain himself, but he'd not laid his cards on the table; he'd thrown them up in the air, leaving them to land wherever they might and leaving Hope to make of them what she would. And, of course, he kept one card hidden away—the one which told of the events of the summer, of his pain and humiliation. Of the hope he'd begun to harbour that, no matter who he really was, Hope might care for him too.

'As you said, Charles, you owe Hope a considerable debt for her actions today. I think you can begin by explaining exactly what is amiss with your sister, the moment we return to Hayton.'

'Ah…yes, of course,' Charles replied, looking suitably chastened.

Samuel strode towards his carriage, his heart sinking when he climbed in and saw how steadfastly Hope avoided his eye as she sat beside Miss Gordon. After all that had happened today, Samuel was not sure what tortured him more—the irrevocable damage that his lies had caused between Hope and him, or the uncomfortable, unexpected knowledge that he'd rather liked the idea he'd fleetingly entertained, of calling her his wife.

Throughout the journey home, it was this latter thought which his mind kept returning to. Along with another thought—that even if by some miracle a woman like her would have ever considered him, his deceit now meant that she would never trust him again, never mind consider marrying him.

Hope sat quietly opposite Samuel, sipping her tea and wishing she was a million miles away as they waited for Mr Gordon to join them. Samuel had asked her to come to the parlour almost the moment they'd arrived back at Hayton and put the ashen-faced Miss Gordon safely into Maddie's care.

'Charles is going to explain everything,' he'd said, leaning close and speaking in a hushed voice. 'After what you did for his sister today, he owes that explanation to you most of all.'

Hope had nodded obligingly, a flustered heat growing in her cheeks at her awareness of his proximity. 'Of course,' she'd replied, unable to bring herself to meet his eye.

In truth, she'd wanted to slip away into her room, to put some distance between herself and everything that had happened today. Between herself and Samuel, and that maelstrom of emotions she felt whenever she so much as glanced at him. Her confusion, her upset, and her anger. Her niggling worry that she should not trust him, even as she wished with every fibre of her being that she could. Nonetheless, she was still curious to hear what Mr Gordon had to say about his sister's behaviour. It was, it seemed, a day for honesty—from everyone else, at least.

What a strange day it had been. A strange and dangerous day. As Mr Gordon hurried in, looking flustered, Hope tried not to dwell on just how risky her actions at the docks had been. Neither did she allow herself to consider the sheer horror on Samuel's face at the sight of her standing with Miss Gordon in the midst of the gathering crowd. How tinged with fear his words had been as he'd pleaded with her to return to the carriage. How he'd once again sought to honour that solemn promise he'd made to her weeks ago, to keep her safe.

Samuel rose from his seat, interrupting her thoughts. 'Well, Charles?' he prompted. 'How is Miss Gordon?'

Mr Gordon gave a curt nod. 'She is resting.' His gaze flitted between Hope and Samuel, his agitation evident. 'I hope that you appreciate that what I am about to tell you must be treated with the utmost discretion...'

'Of course,' Samuel replied. 'I am not one to meddle in

the affairs of others, Charles. But this is my family's home and until my brother returns I am its master. I have a duty to know what goes on under Hayton's roof but, more importantly, as your friend I am concerned. Your sister's behaviour today was as alarming as it was reckless. It cannot be left unexplained.'

Mr Gordon gave his friend a pained look. 'I know,' he said in a tight, strangled voice. 'God, Sammy, if only you knew...' He paused, pressing his lips together in a clear effort to collect himself.

'Take your time, Mr Gordon,' Hope interjected, leaning forward and gesturing for him to sit. It was hard to see this usually jovial giant of a man so evidently perturbed. 'Did Miss Gordon go to the port today to try to procure more laudanum? I did see her talking to some of the men around the docks.'

Mr Gordon let out a bitter laugh as he slumped down in a chair. 'Worse than that, I'm afraid, Miss Swynford. It turns out that she was trying to buy herself passage on a ship.'

'A ship?' Samuel repeated. 'What ship? Going where?'

'Any ship, going anywhere,' Mr Gordon replied. 'Ireland, the Isle of Man, the Caribbean—it appears my sister cares not. Such is the strength of her desire not to return to Shawdale that she is willing to go anywhere in the world on any vessel which will take her.'

Hope's mouth fell open. The sea was a dangerous, often lawless place; she knew from bitter experience just what sort of rapscallions sailed its rough tides. A woman like Miss Gordon would have no idea if she was throwing herself upon the mercy of legitimate merchants or a crew engaged in far more nefarious activities. As desperate as Hope had been to escape her father's clutches—not once but twice now—she'd never even contemplated going to sea. Whatever had led Miss Gordon in that dark and potentially deadly direction must have been grave indeed.

'What happened to your sister, sir?' she asked.

Mr Gordon drew a deep, shuddering breath. 'She fell in love, Miss Swynford. A love which my parents forbade. That love is at the root of all that ails her.'

Hope listened as Mr Gordon finally told his sister's sorry tale. Several years earlier, he explained, his sister had become involved with a worker in one of their father's calico printworks. The young man had been about her age, and was known to be decent and hardworking. Miss Gordon, it seemed, had fallen head over heels in love with him, and by all accounts those feelings were reciprocated as the young man had proposed marriage. The pair had planned to run away and elope. However, before they could do so, word of their relationship and their plans reached Miss Gordon's father's ears. Mr Gordon senior had reacted furiously, effectively locking Miss Gordon away in Shawdale and dismissing the young man from his employment. Unable to find work because of the scandal, the young man had been forced to leave Blackburn, and Miss Gordon's heart had been broken. She'd not been the same since.

'I left for the Continent not long after the scandal broke. I hoped by the time I returned that Henrietta would have recovered from it. Unfortunately, she was worse than ever,' Mr Gordon concluded. 'She complained constantly of headaches, chest pains, stomach pains—pains of every sort. She was given laudanum by our physician but, as you know, that has only made matters worse. I've tried everything to help her, getting her away from Shawdale as much as I can. That was why I took her to Buxton to take the waters, and why I jumped at your invitation to come here. But I fear now that she is lost—if no longer to her tinctures, then to her despair.'

'Oh, dear, Charles,' Samuel said. 'You never breathed a word of any of this during our travels.'

'I confess, I was content to be far from my family's woes,' he replied glumly. 'I proved very capable of putting it all out of my mind.'

Hope, meanwhile, found herself overcome with sympathy for the lady who lay in bed upstairs. Little wonder that she was so prickly, so sombre, so prone to drowning her sorrows in the bottom of a laudanum bottle.

'Poor Miss Gordon,' she interjected, shaking her head sadly. 'To have been denied love like that… Really, could they not just have been allowed to marry?'

'What?' Mr Gordon just about leapt out of his seat. 'I am sorry for Henrietta's pain, Miss Swynford, but are you honestly proposing that my father should have consented to the match? With one of his workers?'

Hope felt her hackles begin to rise. 'I am proposing that Miss Gordon should have been permitted happiness, sir,' she replied, standing too. 'I am proposing that she should have been allowed to make her own choice.'

'Are you really?' he scoffed. 'Well, I suppose that having an uncle who tries to sell you off to anyone willing to split the proceeds would affect your judgement on these matters.'

'Come now, Charles,' Samuel intervened, getting to his feet now and standing close beside her. 'That isn't fair on Hope…'

'I'm merely pointing out that your mysterious heiress here might be as embittered by her experiences as my sister is. Not that any of us know much about what those ex-

periences were. Indeed, Miss Swynford, it is odd that you
have so much to say about my sister's story, and so little to
say about your own.'

Hope's heart sank like a stone at Mr Gordon's pointed
observation. The truth, as ever, bubbled not far from the
surface.

'You are right,' she said, changing tack. 'I have said too
much. It is not fair to discuss this when your sister is not
present to talk about it herself. Indeed, with hindsight, I
should have liked to have heard her story in her own words
rather than yours, sir.'

Mr Gordon's nostrils flared. 'I suppose you think her
wicked family has deprived her of those too,' he replied.
'Just as you clearly think we deprived her of the chance to
marry so far beneath her.'

Hope sighed, wishing now that she'd held her tongue. It
was clear that she'd provoked Mr Gordon and he was spoil-
ing for a fight. She glanced at Samuel, noticing how he
remained at her side, watching his friend carefully, every
muscle in his body apparently tense. She knew she ought
to back down, apologise meekly and extricate herself from
this conversation. And yet, as she stood here, she felt the
fire of indignation burning in her gut. Indignation for that
young man and indignation for herself, her true self, and
the way others looked down upon them when their rank in
life was nothing more than an accident of birth. Who they
were—who they truly were—was a matter of words and
deeds, not wealth and titles.

'I just… I find it sad that people are considered above
or beneath each other at all,' she said in the end. 'Surely,
we love who we love and that should be all that matters.
You said yourself that this young man was hardworking

and decent, yet such traits meant nothing because he was not wealthy and therefore your sister marrying him would be viewed as an embarrassment or a scandal. Never mind that it might have made her happy.'

'Outrageous, revolutionary nonsense.' Mr Gordon's face grew a rather unbecoming shade of scarlet as he turned to address Samuel. 'Are you going to tolerate such talk under your roof, Sammy? Or are you going to tell us that you'd quite happily wed one of Hayton's servants?'

Hope watched as Samuel studied his friend, his expression unreadable. 'As a gentleman, I'd never presume to tell you your business, Charles. However, as your friend I sincerely hope that you and your family can find a way to ease Miss Gordon's suffering.' His blue-grey eyes shifted from Mr Gordon to Hope, growing serious as they locked with hers. 'If you are asking me my personal opinion, then I am sympathetic to Miss Swynford's view. I wish to marry for love, and nothing else. Frankly, I do not care if the lady in question is a maid or a marquess's daughter.'

'And yet, until recently you were pretending to be a baronet,' Mr Gordon countered.

Still Samuel held Hope's gaze, his eyes at once searching and sincere. She was in no doubt that his words, whatever they would be, were meant for her.

'I was,' he said after a moment, 'because even I, for all the many advantages life has bestowed upon me, know what it is like to be looked upon as less than someone else. To have the wind knocked so thoroughly from your sails that you wonder if your pride will ever recover. However, that is no excuse. I should never have deceived you, Hope, and I am deeply, sincerely sorry that I did.'

The hurt and the shame which clouded his expression

was palpable. Before she could stop herself, before she could remember that Mr Gordon was still in the room, Hope reached out and took Samuel's hand in hers. Surprise flickered across his handsome features in response to her touch, before melting into such an affectionate smile that it caught Hope thoroughly off-guard even while it seemed to warm every part of her. She wanted to place her trust in Samuel, and she wanted to understand the nature of what pained him. Of who or what had cut him down and caused him to feel so thoroughly diminished.

In spite of everything, she realised, she wanted his affection. She wanted Samuel to look at Hope Sloane the way he'd just looked at Hope Swynford. And above all she wanted to find the strength to tell him the truth.

Chapter Eighteen

Hope sat in front of the mirror, watching her reflection with a soft gaze as Maddie brushed her hair, teasing the tangles out of her curls with a look of pained apology. She had retired early, excusing herself not long after dinner and retreating to her bedchamber to wash and to change for bed. After the day's events, she doubted she would sleep easily, but at least the night-time hours alone would give her time to think. And goodness, did she need to think.

She understood now that Samuel's lie had been born of some painful, unspoken experience and not simply a desire to impress her or to make her feel safe. She wondered about the nature of that experience, about who would look at a gentleman who was so kind, so caring, so jovial, so undeniably handsome and draw the conclusion that he was not good enough. Whoever they were, they were wrong. If she could muster the courage, Hope would tell him so.

Courage. That was something she was going to need in abundance, if she was going to also admit the truth about herself. If she was going to find the words to explain why she'd deceived him, not only when she'd first arrived at Hayton but for all the weeks since. She had to hope that he would understand, that he could forgive her. At the same time, she had to acknowledge that telling the truth was the right thing to do, even if he could not. She owed him that much for his protection, for his generosity. For the affection he clearly had for her. She could not countenance allowing that affection to be directed towards a woman who did not exist for a moment longer. She cared about him too deeply to do that.

Nonetheless, the very real prospect of losing that affection, of watching it disappear along with the character of the enigmatic heiress which she'd inhabited for so many weeks was terrifying.

'I suppose it's all been a lot to take in,' Maddie said, meeting Hope's eye in the mirror and no doubt noting the pensive expression on her face. 'I do hope you're not too cross with Mr Liddell. He isn't a bad sort, I promise you.'

Hope acknowledged the remark with a tight smile. Hayton's servants had now been released from the obligation to keep up their caretaker master's pretence and, unsurprisingly, Maddie seemed relieved. Hope had rebuffed her attempts at an apology earlier, insisting that she had nothing to apologise for when all she'd been doing was following orders.

'I just wish I knew why he told you that he was the baronet,' Maddie continued to muse as she began to plait Hope's hair. 'It's not like he's ever appeared envious of his brother for inheriting all of this. No, I'd say he's always seemed quite content to be his own man, and his brother's heir, of course. Although I dare say he won't be the heir for much longer, now that Sir Isaac has wed again.'

'Again?' Hope asked, giving the maid a quizzical look. She knew that the true master of Hayton Hall was travelling with his bride, but she did not know that this recent elopement was not the baronet's first trip down the aisle.

Maddie nodded. 'That's right. Oh, my mistress, God rest her soul, was such a wonderful lady. So beautiful and so elegant. I remember the first time I saw her, I thought she looked like a princess. How I loved to help her dress! She had the best taste in gowns, although I don't need to tell you that, do I?' Maddie added, grinning at her.

'What do you mean by that?' Hope asked, furrowing her brow.

Hope watched as the maid's smile slipped from her face, her eyes widening in horror as realisation dawned.

'Forgive me,' she said quietly. 'I should not have said that. I just assumed that Mr Liddell had told you everything.'

Hope stared at Maddie's reflection, following her gaze as it slowly crept towards the mirror image behind them. When her eyes came to rest upon the bed, and the cream dress which lay discarded upon it, the penny finally dropped. The wardrobe he'd so easily produced for her—of course. He'd lied about that too.

'There was never a cousin, was there?' Hope asked quietly. 'There was never a trousseau, or a set of dresses left behind.'

Maddie shook her head sadly. 'I hope now you understand my reluctance to alter them for you,' she replied in little more than a whisper.

'Of course,' Hope replied grimly as she turned around and took her by the hand. 'You were being loyal to your mistress. You didn't decide to offer me her dresses—Mr Liddell did. And besides, for all your reluctance, you did take up a few of them for me.'

'Well, of course—you needed something proper to wear,' she said, blinking back her tears. 'And of course you should have worn them. But I think Mr Liddell ought to have told you who they'd belonged to.'

Hope bit her lip, the heat of her own tears stinging as they threatened to fall. What a fool she was! A gullible, thoroughly humiliated fool. To think she'd been sitting there, wanting to trust Samuel again, recognising that he'd been hurt and wanting to understand the painful experience which had led him to make such an error of judgement in deceiving her. To think she'd been agonising over going to him and confessing all, matching his honesty with her own, when all along he was still lying to her!

And why lie about the dresses? What possible reason could he have for spinning her a yarn about a cousin and letting her put on a dead woman's clothes without her knowledge? Was he laughing at her, or could he simply not help himself? Perhaps she really had misjudged him. Perhaps he was not the decent gentleman she'd believed him to be, after all.

Perhaps she was finally seeing the real Samuel Liddell. A serial liar.

Hope leapt out of her seat and hurried towards the door. 'Excuse me, Maddie,' she said. 'I think I need to have a word with Mr Liddell.'

'But…but he's retired for the night. And you're only wearing your shift!' Maddie called after her, aghast.

Hope, however, was not listening. She was already half-way along the hallway and hurrying towards a heavy oak door, beyond which lay the bedchamber of Hayton Hall's pretend baronet.

* * *

The sight of Hope standing in his doorway, feet bare, wearing only a shift, made Samuel sit bolt upright in bed. He blinked—once, then twice—convinced he must be dreaming. Convinced that he must have fallen asleep over the book he'd been trying his best to distract himself with after such an eventful, fraught day. A day in which they'd learned the truth about Miss Gordon, and he'd unfathomably allowed Hope to glimpse the hurtful, humiliating truth about him. A day in which Hope had taken hold of his hand and looked at him with such affection, such understanding. A look he hadn't deserved. A look which had occupied his mind ever since.

As Hope marched towards his bedside, however, her dainty feet stomping on the wooden floor, he realised that he was indeed awake. She really was here, in his room. And apparently, if the fierce expression on her face was anything to go by, she was very angry. Now there was a look he really did deserve to see from her.

'You lied to me!'

Samuel threw the bedsheets back, remembering just a moment too late that he wore naught but his drawers. Self-consciously, defensively, he folded his arms across his chest as he got to his feet and stood in front of her. She stared up at him, her green eyes wild and challenging, her plait half loosened in her fury, leaving several curls of dark hair to make their bid for freedom. He found himself overcome with a momentary urge to undo the rest of it, to run his hands through that lovely hair. Resisting temptation, he clamped his hand harder against his chest. Given her anger, any such move would be seriously unwise.

'You lied to me,' she said again, quieter this time.

'Yes—I know I did, and you've every right to be angry with me. I should never have told you that I was a baronet.'

'I'm not talking about that,' she replied pointedly. 'I'm talking about the dresses. The ones which belonged to your brother's dead wife. The ones I've been wearing.'

'Oh—yes. That.' Damn. His thoughts had been so pre-occupied with his enormous lie, he'd omitted to confess to the smaller one he'd also told. 'I'm sorry, Hope. I should have explained to you about the dresses.'

To his surprise, her face began to crumple, those earlier flashes of anger slowly replaced by the glint of tears as they formed in her eyes.

'Why would you lie about some dresses?' she asked, stepping back and turning away from him. 'Why would you lie about who they belonged to?'

He let out a heavy sigh, unfolding his arms and rubbing his brow wearily. 'If I'd told you the truth about poor Rosalind, then because I'd let you believe I was the baronet, I'd have had to pretend she'd been my wife. I couldn't do that—it was bad enough that I'd claimed my brother's title; I couldn't lay false claim to his wife and his grief as well.' He stepped tentatively towards her, though her back remained turned to him. 'Besides, you needed something to wear. I thought it was better for you to think that those clothes had come from a well-attired cousin who did not miss them rather than a lady who'd lived and died in this house. In my own foolish way, I was trying to make you feel at ease.'

'Surely that was my decision—whether to wear those dresses or not,' she countered, still not turning around.

'And if you had known, would you have worn them?' he asked.

'Yes. No. I don't know.'

He stepped closer again. 'I know I've acted badly, but it was never with mal-intent. Please believe that.'

He watched as her shoulders sagged. When, finally, she turned around, he was alarmed to see that tears streamed down her face. 'This is all such a mess,' she sobbed. 'So many lies. Do we even know each other at all?'

'Of course we do.'

The sudden urge to reassure her overtook him and, before he could stop himself, he pulled her into his arms. She didn't resist. Indeed, just as she had the last time they'd embraced like this, she tucked her head against his chest. Unlike the last time, however, she wore only a thin under-garment and he was naked from the waist up. The sheer intimacy of the moment meant that tender feelings quickly gave way to more carnal thoughts—thoughts he worked hard to suppress as he forced himself to focus on all that he still had to say.

'You do know me, Hope,' he said, softly running his hand over her hair. 'The man you've seen, the man you've taken tea with, the man you've discussed books and theatre with— that man is me. Calling myself a baronet and all the lies which sprang from that—it was all just costuming. All just foolish window-dressing by a man who, when you wandered into his life that evening in the woods, was feeling more than a little lonely and sorry for himself.'

'You said earlier that you knew what it was like to be looked upon as less than someone else,' she murmured. 'What did you mean by that?'

Samuel felt his breath catch in his throat. He'd been expecting that question ever since his remark in the parlour earlier, but that didn't make the events of the summer any easier to speak about. For a moment he pressed his lips together, composing himself. Resolving finally to be entirely truthful, and to hell with the consequences.

'There was a lady in whose company I spent some time this summer,' he began. 'Her name was Charlotte Pearson. We seemed to get on well, and I thought—hoped, really— that it would progress to a courtship. However, Miss Pearson was very clear with me that she did not wish to continue our connection, and it quickly became apparent that she favoured my brother over me, on account of his title and estate.'

She glanced up at him, aghast. 'This woman is now your sister-in-law?'

Despite himself, Samuel laughed. 'Thankfully, no— Charlotte was never likely to succeed with Isaac. He only had eyes for Miss Louisa Conrad, who is now Lady Liddell.'

Hope leaned her head against his chest once more. 'Did you…did you love Charlotte? Did she break your heart?'

He drew a deep breath. 'I didn't love her, though I was more than a little captivated by her, at the time. And whilst she didn't break my heart, she did hurt me, and she certainly wounded my pride. I'd never been made to feel that way before, as though I was so unworthy.' He shook his head, remembering Charlotte's words. 'She spoke as though my affection for her was offensive—she even told me that things might have been different if I had been my brother.'

'Oh, Samuel…'

'I don't deserve your sympathy, Hope,' he said, interrupting her. 'Not after I've lied to you. But the damnable fact of the matter is that when you looked at me and thought you saw a titled gentleman with a grand house, I couldn't bring myself to contradict you. I liked to impress you, and I liked the way you looked at me. I couldn't bear to see your disappointment when you learned what I really am. And when I realised that it was the house and the title which made you feel so protected, telling you the truth felt completely impossible.'

'But you did tell me, in the end.'

'I did, but not soon enough. I should have told you right away. Indeed, I should never have lied at all.'

'Painful experiences make us do all kinds of things to protect ourselves,' she said, her voice almost a whisper.

He sighed into her dark curls. 'They do, but that is no excuse. I am so sincerely sorry, Hope. I'm not a man who is accustomed to telling lies, please believe that. Please believe me also when I say that if you cannot forgive me, I understand. It is enough for me to know that you will leave Hayton knowing who I really am, because the truth is, Hope, I care for you. When I kissed you in the library that evening, it was not a moment of madness for me. It was an admission of my feelings for you—feelings I had no right to feel, given I was deceiving you, but feelings which had grown nonetheless. Feelings which made telling you the truth about myself even harder. A cruel irony, but no more than I deserve.'

Hope looked up at him then, her emerald eyes still watering as they searched his. He became aware once more of her hands resting against his bare chest, of the warmth of skin on skin, of the feeling of her alluring form pressed against him. Of the proximity of his bed behind them, and the less than gentlemanly thoughts laying siege to his mind.

His heartfelt words surrendered to lust-filled passion as he captured her lips with his own, lifting one of his hands to brush her cheek whilst the other remained steadfast on the curve of her waist. His heart sang as Hope responded in kind, her mouth greeting his while her hands left the confines of his chest to explore his stomach, his arms, his back. He shivered at her touch, fighting himself to maintain control. He would not allow this to go too far. He would not take her to his bed.

Not unless she became his wife first.

The sudden thought astonished him, but not as much as Hope's swift action in breaking their embrace.

'No,' she breathed, stepping back from him. 'We must stop.'

He nodded, swallowing hard as he struggled to regain his composure. 'Of course. I'm sorry. I promise I have no intention of ruining you.'

If he'd hoped his words would be reassuring, he was to be deeply disappointed. Instead, he watched as her face crumpled once more, tears spilling unabated down her cheeks.

'Oh, Samuel, this is all such a mess,' she said, pacing about the floor.

He frowned. That was the second time tonight that she'd uttered those words. His heart began to pound in his chest as it dawned on him that all the obvious affection and ardour he had for her might not be enough. She might never be able to forgive him, to overcome the lies he'd told…

'I know the damage my lies have caused between us, but…'

'You're not the only one of us who has lied about who they are,' she sobbed. 'You cannot care for me, Samuel, and you could not ruin me, even if you tried.'

'What on earth do you mean?'

Finally, she stopped pacing. When she spoke again it was in a voice which sounded quite altered and which was laced, he was astonished to note, with a distinctly local accent.

'I am not an heiress. I am not wealthy. I have no uncle

and no inheritance,' she said. 'My name is not Hope Swynford, it is Hope Sloane. I am an actress and the daughter of an outlaw. I am unruinable. I am the lowest of the low.'

Chapter Nineteen

Hope had never believed that telling Samuel the truth would be in any way cathartic but, even so, she was wholly unprepared for the depth of the shame which possessed her as she told the sordid story of her life. She watched the expressions of shock then horror cloud his handsome features as finally she unmasked herself, shedding Hope Swynford like a second skin and allowing Hope Sloane to walk free.

She told him about her childhood on that bleak Lilly-beck hillside, about the lack of food and warmth, about how, one by one, her siblings had perished until she'd been the only one left. About how her father had sought to solve their problems through a life of crime, allowing life on the wrong side of the law to corrupt him so thoroughly, whilst her mother had tried to drown her sorrows in a bottle of laudanum. That part of Hope Swynford's story, she said grimly, had been true.

She told him about her mother's death, how it had left her at the mercy of her father's cruelty and callousness, and how he'd tried to force her into marrying one of his associates. Despite herself, and despite knowing how unsavoury Samuel would doubtless find it, she could not help but speak fondly of running away and joining a theatre com-

pany. Those few years of freedom, she told him, had been
the making of her, and for all the danger and vice which
lurked at the periphery of such work, she'd been happy for
the first time in her life.

Her lighter tone dissipated when she reached the final
chapter of her tale: the story of her return to Cumberland,
of her kidnap and her father's second attempt at forcing a
marriage on her. She barely managed to utter the words
as she spoke of how depraved he'd become, how sinister,
how hateful. How ready he had been to condemn her to a
life with a man who, she knew, had the same blackened
soul as him.

'I've spent my life living on my wits, and when fortune
smiled upon me for long enough to allow me to escape a
second time I took the chance and I fled. I had nothing but
the costume I'd been wearing the night that my father and
his men snatched me from the theatre in Lowhaven. Nothing but that and my sheer determination to live my life on
my own terms, and not his.'

'And then you found Hayton, and me,' Samuel added
sombrely, slumping down on his bed with a look of unmistakable disbelief. 'So you're the actress Charles mentioned that day in Lowhaven. The one who went missing
on the penultimate night of…' He shook his head, apparently struggling to remember.

'*The School for Scandal*,' Hope confirmed with a grim
nod. 'I was playing Lady Teazle. Hence the beautiful gown
I was wearing the night you found me in the woods.' She
regarded him carefully, trying to ignore the tears which
pricked at the corners of her eyes. 'You have to understand,
Samuel, that I did not know you—I did not know if you
were good or bad, if you knew my father or not. My father

supplies his wares to many of the big houses across Cumberland, and has more than a few landowners and magistrates in his back pocket. For all I knew, telling you my true identity and story would have led me straight back into his clutches. So when I realised that my clothes had led you to make certain assumptions about me, I decided to play along. I created Hope Swynford and her story to protect myself.'

'Well, you are a consummate actress.' His grey-blue eyes were wide with dismay. 'Never for a moment did I think you could be anything other than a gentleman's daughter with an enthusiasm for the theatre. You certainly had me fooled.'

'Just as you fooled me into believing you were a baronet.'

'Fair point.' He offered her a grim smile as he got to his feet again. 'You were right—this is a real mess.'

She felt her lip tremble at his observation. 'Like you, once I'd begun my deception I found it so hard to end it, even when I suspected that you would have no idea who Jeremiah Sloane is and, even if you did, I knew you were too good a man to give me up to him.' She shook her head at herself, tears still threatening to overwhelm her. 'You said before that you liked the way I looked at you. Well, I liked the way you looked at me too. In truth, I felt ashamed of who I really was. I thought you'd be horrified if you knew who you'd allowed into your home. Gentlemen like you have nothing to do with low-born actresses with wicked outlaw fathers. The only time a woman like me encounters gentlemen is in the theatre, and believe me when I say that they are often anything but gentlemanly then.'

She watched as he flinched at her implication, and she realised then that she'd said far more than she should. It was bad enough that she'd spoken so frankly about the poverty and criminality which ran through her past like a poison, but to then confront Samuel with the sheer seediness and, at times, outright depravity of what she'd been exposed to off-stage and after dark—that was beyond the pale. Worse still, Samuel might believe that she'd been a willing participant in such behaviour—that she was, as Mr Gordon had once said of actresses, little more than a harlot.

'What I mean to say is…' she began, now filled with the sudden urge to explain herself.

'No—I understand,' he interjected, shaking his head again. 'Believe me, I know exactly what some gentlemen are capable of. But surely you know me well enough to know that I would not…' He strode towards her, and her heart sank as she saw him reach out a hand to touch her before retracting it. Of course, he'd thought better of it. He always would now. He shook his head, as though he was trying and failing to find the right words. 'I cannot imagine what you've had to endure…'

The look of horror which was etched in those wide, blue-grey eyes made Hope feel sick as it dawned on her that he was, indeed, trying to imagine it.

'I'm not a harlot,' she said quietly. 'I was never any man's mistress either. I'd run away from my father because he'd tried to trade me like contraband, and I didn't escape his clutches just so that I could sell myself to the highest bidder. I was determined that my life would be my own.'

'But that didn't stop well-dressed drunken wastrels trying their luck,' Samuel pondered.

Hope smiled bleakly at his observation. 'Quite. And some not so well-dressed wastrels, at times.'

An awkward silence descended between them as Hope waited for Samuel to say something—anything—more. But his words, if he had any, did not come. Instead, he simply stood before her, blinking, his sheer mortification and consternation etched on his face. His entire demeanour, from his wooden posture to the distance he'd placed between them, telling her that everything had changed. That what she truly was had shocked and appalled him, such that he might never recover. Such that he would never care for her again. Indeed, that he likely regretted ever saying that he did.

'It is late,' she said in the end, stepping towards the door. 'I should go.'

Samuel stared at her from across the room, but made no move to follow her. 'Yes, of course,' he said after a moment.

He conceded defeat easily—perhaps, Hope considered, too easily. He crossed his arms over his bare chest, and Hope's fingers tingled with the memory of exploring that part of him a short time ago. A profound sense of loss gripped her as it dawned on her that she'd never touch that skin again, that there would be no more embraces. The chasm wrought between them by the truth was simply too great. Looking at his astonished expression, Hope could see that Samuel knew this too. He knew that he could never look at Hope the actress the way he'd looked at Hope the heiress. There had been too much deceit on both their parts. Too many lies. At least now they both knew that.

'Goodnight, Samuel.'

Then, before he could utter a word in reply, she hurried out of his room. It was only when she reached her own and saw that Maddie had left that she allowed herself to weep in earnest—for all that had happened, and for all that could never be.

They'd both been lying. As he tossed and turned in bed, unable to sleep, Samuel's mind kept returning to that thought.

They'd both told stories, and they'd both had their reasons for keeping the truth from one another—some better reasons than others, but reasons nonetheless.

Hope's reasons, he knew, had been a matter of survival. Had he been in her position in those woods weeks ago, had he been injured and vulnerable and taken into a stranger's home, he might well have invented a tale about himself too. Hearing her confess the dreadful details of her past had been hard enough, but realising that it was shame which had motivated her to keep up the pretence of being Hope Swynford had been unbearable.

His heart had broken for her as she'd stood there and told him that she was ashamed of who she was and, in turn, he'd felt ashamed of himself too. Ashamed of the way he'd allowed his own wounded pride and misguided sense of honour to get the better of him, to lead him to pretend to be more than he was. Little wonder she'd felt unable to tell him her real story—between the baronetcy and the big estate, he must have seemed utterly intimidating. The bitter irony of this was not lost on him. In keeping up the pretence, he'd sought to make her feel safe and protected. Instead, he'd unwittingly placed a barrier between them.

If only he had been honest from the outset, he might have seemed more approachable.

Perhaps.

On the other hand, as she'd told him, in her experience, gentlemen were not to be trusted. His stomach had lurched at her remark about the so-called gentlemen at the theatre, at her implication as to how they'd often behaved. He'd desperately wanted to show her that he was not like them, that his affection for her was heartfelt and genuine, and that it endured—whether she was a wealthy heiress or an actress without a penny to her name. He'd wanted to gather her into his arms and kiss all her feelings of shame away, and yet he had stopped himself. He had held back from her.

Why? Because, despite those familiar tender, protective feelings he had for her, he'd realised he had to tread carefully. The last thing he wanted her to conclude was that he was just another rich rapscallion, seeking to take advantage of her. So he'd kept his hands to himself, and when she'd wanted to, he'd let her go, even when so much remained unsaid.

Such as telling her that she was still the Hope he'd come to know and care for, whether her surname was Swynford or Sloane, and whether her father was a gentleman or a common criminal. Whether she spent her life in drawing rooms playing cards or on the stage playing roles. Such as reminding her that her pretend heiress, just like his pretend baronet, had been a mere costume, that it did not alter who either of them were underneath.

The Hope who'd been on the run from her invented nefarious uncle was the same Hope who'd escaped the clutches of a very real, very wicked father—a woman who loved to read, whose knowledge of Shakespeare was second to none. A woman who'd lost her mother, and whose own pain had made her alert to and empathetic towards the suffering of others. A brave woman, and one who, he now knew, had carved out a life for herself, escaping the clutches of those who'd sought to drag her down not once, but twice. If anything, her runaway heiress story—a story which, notwithstanding the wicked uncle, had implied a certain amount of wealth and status—had meant that he'd not been able to fully appreciate the sheer amount of hardship and wretchedness which she'd overcome.

He did now.

He did, and the strength of feeling that knowledge provoked in him was overwhelming. As he lay in bed, sleep still eluding him, he realised that he wanted to protect her from all of it. From her father's cruelty, from a forced marriage, from men leering at her in the theatre. From cold, damp cottages and poverty and hunger. Weeks ago, he'd offered her sanctuary in his family home; now, he knew, he wanted to offer her love and security, with him. Because he did love her—he understood that now, and knowing that truth had done nothing to diminish how he felt about her. If anything, he loved and admired her more than ever. To him, she was beautiful and she was perfect, and honestly, the way she spoke in that soft local tongue had the ability to drive him wild. He wanted to hear that voice to the end of his days.

He would tell her so, he decided, squeezing his eyes shut. In the morning.

The indigo light of the autumn dawn bathed Hayton's gardens as Hope stepped out of the door at the rear of the house. She breathed in deeply, allowing the cold air to refresh her as the wind teased the shrubbery and tangled the branches of the tall trees in the woods beyond, warning of an unsettled day ahead. How fitting, since it had been a restless night. Hope had not slept a wink, her room growing more stifling and her thoughts more relentless as the hours wore on. Eventually she had felt the need to escape, and so she'd slipped on a day dress and shawl—or rather, as she now knew, Rosalind's dress and shawl—then put on her boots and wandered outside for some air.

She walked slowly along the path, acutely aware of

how heavy her weary limbs felt, and how her swollen eyes pricked and throbbed after so many hours of crying. For the first time in her life, she found herself at a loss. No matter what life had thrown at her, she'd always been able to formulate a plan or, at the very least, to take what she'd been given and run with it—sometimes literally. Now, she realised, she'd simply no idea what to do. No idea where she was going. Not to London—now that she was no longer Hope Swynford, there was no need for that. Back to Richmond? Back to her life in the theatre? Was that even possible? She didn't know.

All she did know was that the truth had changed everything, that Samuel would never look at her in the same way again. Her time at Hayton, her time with him in this blissful, peaceful sanctuary, was coming to an end.

The sound of stones crunching underfoot was the first clue that she wasn't alone. It was a clue which came too late, since by the time she realised a hand had already been clapped over her mouth, stifling any attempt she might have made to scream. The hand was dirty, coarse and all too familiar, as was the cold sting of the knife which was pressed against her throat.

'Time to go home, my lady,' he said mockingly, hissing the words into her ear.

Finally, after all these weeks of searching, he'd found her.

Chapter Twenty

She'd left him.

Samuel pulled on the riding coat which Smithson had handed to him, that same handful of words circling around his mind over and over again. She'd left him. The shame, the pain and the guilt she'd so clearly felt about all that she'd confessed last night had been too much for her to bear. And he, to his eternal damnation, had been thoroughly inadequate in the face of it, failing to comfort her, to properly reassure her. To tell her that none of it changed what he felt for her. Instead, he'd simply stood by as she'd walked out of his bedchamber and now out of his life.

She'd left him, and now he might never see her again.

Now, because of his hesitation, she was wandering the countryside, alone and vulnerable. God forbid she should end up injured again or, worse, find herself a captive of her father once more. If some dreadful fate befell her, it would be all his fault.

She'd left him, and now he had to find her. He had to make amends.

'She could be anywhere by now. This will be like searching for a needle in a haystack.'

Next to him, Charles gave voice to Samuel's niggling

fears as he fiddled with his top hat. Outside, the grooms were readying two horses as fast as they could, after Samuel had all but press-ganged his friend into assisting him in his search for Hope. In the sheer panic he felt following Maddie's revelation that Hope was nowhere to be found, Samuel had appraised his maid, his butler and Charles of what Hope had revealed last night. All three had expressed their surprise. Like Samuel, they appeared to have harboured no suspicions that she'd been anything other than what she'd said she was.

'We have to try, Charles,' Samuel implored him. 'I cannot just sit here, knowing that Hope could be in danger. What if her father finds her?'

'But where should we even begin to look?' Charles countered. 'We don't know where she's going. Try not to fret, Sammy, I dare say she can look after herself. Women like her are…'

'What do you mean, women like her?' Samuel almost growled the question.

Charles held up a hand in protest. 'I mean no offence, of course. All I mean to say is that she's hardly lived a sheltered life. Surely she's proven just how resourceful she is, considering how well she's pulled the wool over your eyes for all these weeks.'

'And surely you can see that she had her reasons.' Samuel wished the grooms would hurry up, so that he could end this conversation. So that he could begin his search.

'I can see that given the chance and the talent required to pull it off, any base-born woman would pretend to be a princess if it meant ensnaring a wealthy gentleman.' Charles fiddled with his collar in front of the mirror, his reflection shooting Samuel a pointed look.

'That isn't why Hope deceived me,' Samuel replied, bristling. 'She lied to protect herself. If either one of us could be accused of lying to impress the other, then it is me. I know what you think of her, Charles, now that you know she's an actress without a penny to her name…'

'It doesn't matter what I think, Sammy,' Charles replied, turning around. 'I'm not the one who is besotted with Hope Swynford or Sloane or whoever she is.' He raised a knowing eyebrow. 'Or perhaps this is something more than infatuation?' he added searchingly.

Samuel shrugged, having neither the will to deny his feelings nor the desire to elaborate upon them. What he felt for Hope had gone beyond mere infatuation, but Charles did not need to know that. The only person in the world who needed to know the depth of what he felt was Hope herself. If he found her.

When he found her.

'Richmond,' he said after a moment, answering Charles's earlier question. 'Her theatre company came from Richmond. Perhaps that is where she is hoping to return to now. It would make sense, wouldn't it?'

'You want to go all the way to Richmond?' Charles stared at him, incredulous. 'That is several days of hard riding across the dales.'

Samuel put up a hand in protest. 'I'm saying that is the direction we should head in,' he said. 'It would appear that Hope is travelling on foot and, whilst she has recovered from her injuries, her ankle in particular will still be delicate. She will not be moving quickly. On horseback we stand a good chance of catching up with her.'

'If we can correctly guess the route she has taken,' Charles pointed out.

'To find her way there, she will surely have to follow the roads,' Samuel replied with a confidence he did not feel. He glanced towards the door impatiently. Where in damnation were those grooms with their horses? The longer they delayed, the further Hope would have travelled from Hayton, and the harder it would be to find her...

'Excuse me, sir.'

The soft, wavering voice of Maddie interrupted Samuel's spiralling thoughts. He spun around to see the maid standing in the middle of the hallway, tears spilling down her cheeks, clutching a delicate swathe of cream fabric in her hands. She held it up towards him, revealing that it was in fact a shawl. His heart lurched in recognition—it had belonged to Rosalind, and had been one of the items he'd given Hope to wear.

'I found this in the garden,' she explained, her bottom lip trembling. 'I was attending to Miss Gordon when she spotted it out of the window, stuck to one of the shrubs.'

'So she has fled via the woods then, and lost this on her way,' Charles interjected.

Maddie shook her head. 'I'm not sure about that, sir. You see, when I went outside to retrieve it, I noticed that the stones covering the path have been disturbed as though...as though there may have been a struggle. As though someone has been dragged along.' She turned her gaze to Samuel, looking at him imploringly. 'Oh, sir, what if her father has taken her? What if he's found her after all these weeks?'

Samuel's heart seemed to sink like a stone into the pit of his stomach. He'd been so wrapped up in the events of last night, so consumed by his own shortcomings in the face of her revelations, that he'd neglected to remember the danger Hope was in. The danger she'd always been in.

She had not run away from him at all. She'd been taken.

'I fear this is all my fault.' A faint voice crept into the brief silence which had descended in the hall, and Samuel glanced up to see a pale and frail Miss Gordon making her way gingerly down the stairs. Immediately, Maddie stepped forward to help her, but the lady waved the maid away.

'I don't quite see how any of this is your responsibility, Henrietta,' Charles said.

Samuel watched as a small frown gathered between Miss Gordon's dark eyes. 'That day at the docks in Lowhaven, when I…when Miss Sloane, as Maddie tells me she is in fact called…when Miss Sloane left the carriage to intercept me, she must have been recognised. If I had not gone there that day, then this might not have happened.'

'Miss Sloane's father is a common criminal, sister,' Charles replied. 'I dare say he would have gone to any lengths to locate her. I am quite certain this is not your doing.'

Miss Gordon put up her hand. 'From what I hear, her father is a smuggler, amongst other things. The notion that she was not recognised by someone at that port is therefore laughable. No, brother, I must take responsibility for the consequences of my actions.' She turned to Samuel. 'I implore you, Mr Liddell, please find her and bring her safely back to Hayton. Whoever she is matters not a jot. She has been good and kind to me, even when I have not deserved it.'

Samuel gave her a solemn nod. 'You have my word,' he replied. 'At least now we know where we need to look for her, and it is much closer to home than Richmond.'

'Where?' Charles asked, frowning.

'An isolated hamlet called Lillybeck, a few miles north of here,' Samuel said, stepping along the hallway towards the library, the semblance of a plan starting to form in his mind. 'But first I'm going to fetch a couple of pistols. If we're going to get Hope away from that villain of a man once and for all, then I dare say we ought to be armed.'

Hope's eyes flickered open, and for several moments she struggled to fathom where she was. Her head was pounding, and she felt sick and dizzy as she tried to focus on her surroundings. Before she'd awoken she'd been dreaming—she could recall that much. She'd been in Samuel's bedchamber, just as she had been when she'd confessed to who she truly was, except that in her dream, Samuel had not appeared frozen in horror, and she had not left. Instead, he'd told her that he loved her, he'd taken her in his arms and embraced her, before taking her to his bed, where she'd spent many hours wrapped up in his crisp white sheets. Wrapped up in him.

It had been a wanton, desirous dream, and one which ought to have brought a blush to her cheeks at the remembrance of it. Instead, as her blurry vision and sleep-addled mind finally gave way to clear and grim reality, she felt the colour drain from her face. Having relished her dream, she'd now awoken to a nightmare.

'Welcome back, my lady. Sorry about the sore head. You weren't for co-operating so I'd no choice but to knock you out cold.'

Hope blinked, trying to force her eyes to focus. 'How did I get...'

'Here?' Jeremiah Sloane finished her question for her. 'In a cart, lass. Roddy's cart. You remember Roddy, don't you?'

Hope grimaced at the memory of her father's long-standing accomplice. His had been one of the few faces she'd recognised that fateful night outside the theatre in Lowhaven, all those weeks ago. Now she thought about it, it had been his cart in which she'd been conveyed, bound and gagged, to her father's cottage that time too.

Jeremiah Sloane sat across the table from her, his customary mug of his strong brew clutched in his hand. Around them the cottage was dim and damp, the light of a single tallow candle doing little to ward off either the shadows or the creeping chill.

Gripped by panic, Hope tried to move, only to realise that she'd been tied to the chair upon which she sat, her hands and feet tightly bound.

'Oh, aye, I wasn't taking any chances this time,' he said, his eyes narrowed at her even as he chuckled. He took a long drink from his mug before wiping his mouth with the back of his filthy hand. 'Hayton Hall then, eh? You did well for yourself there, lass. And, judging by the look of you, you've not been working as a scullery maid neither. Aye, quite the lady. George will love that. He likes nothing better than to spoil fine things.'

'Still intent upon marrying me to one of your disgusting associates, then?' she asked, trying to ignore the bile which rose in her throat.

Her father simply shrugged. 'Marry you, not marry you—George can do as he sees fit. It's naught to me what happens to you, not after all the trouble you've caused.'

Hope stared at him. 'What on earth are you talking about? I've done nothing to you, Pa. Nothing at all.'

She tried her best not to flinch as Jeremiah Sloane launched himself towards her. 'Done nothing, have you?' he repeated, his face mere inches from hers. 'You cost me dearly is what you've done.' He slumped back down in his chair, reaching immediately for his mug and taking another large gulp of its potent contents. 'If only you'd wed five years ago when I arranged it, then all this unpleasantness could have been avoided. Instead, you ran away, and I had to pick up the pieces. Malky was not happy, you know. He'd taken quite a shine to you, so much so that he'd agreed to write off my debt to him as soon as you'd wed. Instead... well, as I said, you cost me dearly.'

'Malky?' Hope repeated, grimacing as her head continued to pound. Five years ago, her father had kept her in the dark about exactly who she was to wed, and she had fled before she'd had chance to find out. She did not recall anyone called Malky, although apparently he'd known her. 'Who is he?'

'Was,' her father corrected her, before draining the contents of his mug. 'He lived on the Isle of Man, traded from there. Died a couple of years back—drowned at sea during a storm. Always a risk-taker was Malky. He wasn't the worst sort, though. A better man than George, to be sure. The man's a beast.'

'A beast you're forcing me to wed,' she goaded him.

Jeremiah Sloane slammed his mug on the table. 'And for that you have only yourself to blame! Unpaid debts don't go away, my lass. They grow and grow. Things started to get desperate, and I had to pay Malky somehow so...'

'So you borrowed from Peter to pay Paul,' Hope said, the penny finally dropping. 'And kept on borrowing, from the sounds of it.'

'Aye, except these men aren't the apostles. In George's case, more like the Devil himself.'

'And let me guess, when word reached you that I'd been

spotted in Lowhaven theatre, you saw a chance to settle your debts for good this time. You offered me up on a plate to this George and he was willing to take me instead of payment, just like that?'

Her father shook his head. 'No, George insisted on seeing you first. A man like that wants to know what he's getting. I knew he'd want you though, the moment he saw you on stage.' He smiled bitterly. 'You got your mother's good looks, after all.'

Hope shivered at the thought of that beastly man surveying her like a prize heifer at a market. 'I'm not goods to be bartered and traded,' she said quietly. 'How could you, Pa? Your own daughter?'

'Sold yourself, though, didn't you?' he retorted, not answering her question. He filled his mug again, then took a self-satisfied sip. 'I wonder what fine clothes like that cost you, Hope? What price the master of Hayton Hall put on dressing you up and letting you parade around his grand house and gardens like a duchess? He must have thought all his Christmases had come at once. An actress? No better than a bawd.'

Hope felt the heat of indignation rise in her chest as she strained against the ropes which bound her. 'Samuel is not like that!' she snapped. 'He has been faultlessly kind to me and never asked for anything in return.'

An amused smile crept slowly over Jeremiah Sloane's face, showing off an incomplete set of brown teeth. 'Samuel is it, eh? You really did get your feet well under his plentiful table. He certainly kept you well hidden. A shame you got careless and went wandering about the port with your fancy gentleman.' He began to chuckle, although quickly it gave way to a terrible hacking cough.

Hope felt a solitary tear trickle down her face and wished with all her heart that she could swipe the evidence away. The last thing she wanted her cold and callous father to see was how much his words hurt her, or how much she cared for Samuel. She was all too aware how capable he was of using even the merest hint of emotion against her and turning it into a weakness to exploit. So she bit her tongue, forcing herself to remain silent rather than letting him know how wrong his sordid view of her relationship with Samuel was. Rather than telling him exactly what sort of gentleman she'd been living with, or just how blessed she felt to have spent time in his company.

Because truly, she thought now, Samuel had been a blessing, and not just when he'd come to her rescue that night in the woods. He'd been a blessing every day since, treating her with a kindness and gentleness she'd never before known. He'd welcomed her into his life and whilst he had lied about having a title, in every respect that mattered he'd shown her who he was. He was a considerate, thoughtful man who was interested in the world, and interested in her, listening to her and talking to her as an equal.

But of course, she reminded herself, she had been pretending to be his equal. The truth of her lowly birth had brought an end to that and, with it, an end to his affection for her. Perhaps, she reasoned, that was what had really brought tears to her eyes, and not her father's insults.

Perhaps she was crying for the loss of a future she'd almost fooled herself into thinking she could have. A future with Samuel. A future where he loved her and she loved him.

Because if she was honest with herself, that was what she felt. She did love him. But that love was as futile as it was unwanted. Samuel could never love her—that much had been plain in his horrified gaze and his distant demeanour last night. No doubt her disappearance from Hayton would come as something of a relief, marking the end of an embarrassing episode in his life when he'd been fooled into caring for an actress and an outlaw's daughter.

'Pity you won't find life with George quite so comfortable,' Jeremiah Sloane continued to taunt her, his fit of coughing abating. 'I sent Roddy to tell him that you're here. Word is that he's in Lowhaven finishing a job, so I dare say it won't take him long to come for you. If you know what's good for you, you'll wipe that sour look off your face and try your damnedest not to provoke him. He's been in a foul temper since you ran away as it is.'

He began to cough again, uncontrollably this time, forcing him to rummage in the pocket of his breeches and fish out a filthy rag with which to stifle the rasping, barking sound. From her restrained position Hope could do nothing but watch and, as she did, she began to study the man, to really look at him as though she might be laying eyes on him for the first time. As a girl she'd been terrified of his ferocity, of his temper, of the power she believed his life of crime had granted him. Now, watching him, she saw an ageing man, his skin sallow, his dirty clothes hanging from his emaciated frame, his would-be handkerchief bloodstained and betraying the illness which gripped him. She saw a man who was no longer in control, whose fate rested in the hands of monsters like George. She saw what all the years of corruption and vice had wrought, saw how it had hollowed him from the inside out.

'You're afraid of George, aren't you?' Now it was her turn to goad him. 'I used to think you weren't afraid of anything—not even the gallows. But now I see there's a lot that frightens you.'

'There's a lot that should frighten you too,' he snapped, breathless, before draining his second mug as though his life depended upon it. As though the potent contents could cure whatever canker had taken hold in his lungs. 'You'd just better hope that George sees fit to make you his wife, because otherwise I dare say he'll take whatever innocence you have left then drown you in the Eden river.'

The stark threat was like a punch in the gut. Unable to bear the sight or sound of her father any longer, Hope looked away, her eyes drifting towards the little window and her thoughts wandering across the rugged countryside to Hayton Hall. To afternoons drinking tea in the parlour, and to gentle promenades in the gardens. To conversations about Hume and Shakespeare. To passionate kisses in the library, in the parlour, in his bedchamber. To the feeling of being safe and cared for. To the happiest weeks of her life.

And, above all, to the man she loved and who, she felt certain, she would never see again.

Chapter Twenty-One

'Should we not alert the local constable?'

Samuel shook his head at Charles's question as they made their way along the rough track which led to the cottage where Hope's father lived. Information about the precise whereabouts of Jeremiah Sloane's abode had been difficult to come by. No one living in the scattered collection of low stone dwellings which made up the hamlet of Lillybeck seemed particularly willing to acknowledge that they knew the man, much less part with the details of where he might be found.

The offer of a few coins, however, had sufficiently loosened tongues, leading Samuel and Charles to an isolated spot on the very fringes of an already remote community. Although Lillybeck lay only miles from Hayton, it was far enough beyond Liddell land for Samuel to feel quite unfamiliar with this corner of Cumberland. Quite simply, it was a place he'd never had reason to travel to—until now. His scant knowledge of the area made him feel decidedly uncomfortable, as did the warning he'd received from the frail old man who'd taken Samuel's bribe for information. A warning which now rang in his ears.

'Have a care, sir. From what I hear Sloane is sickening,

but I dare say he's still a dangerous man. Whatever your business is with him, if you know what's good for you, you'll keep one hand on your pistol.'

Samuel had thanked the man for his advice, before enquiring if he knew anything about Jeremiah Sloane's daughter. 'Perhaps you've seen her recently,' he'd probed. 'I heard that she'd returned to Lillybeck.'

'If she has then I pity the poor lass,' the man had replied, shaking his head sadly. 'She ran away from him years ago—no one knew where she went. If she's come back then I doubt it'll have been willingly.'

Samuel shuddered at everything those words implied before glancing at Charles, who looked at him expectantly. 'No constables,' he said, finally answering his friend's question. 'From what Hope said, her father supplies his wares to some of the so-called great and good around these parts. If he's got magistrates in his pocket, then he's likely got a few constables in there too. I think we have to proceed without the help of the law, for now at least.'

'I don't like the sound of that,' Charles replied.

'Neither do I. But needs must.'

'So, what is the plan, Sammy?'

Samuel let out a long breath as he drew his horse to a halt. They were near the cottage, although now that he'd laid his eyes on it, Samuel felt that calling it a cottage afforded it too grand a title. It was a crumbling, ramshackle place, barely fit to house livestock, never mind people. Around it the grass grew tall, its days as grazing pasture for sheep clearly a distant memory. Near the rough track on which they now stood, lay the detritus of what would have once been needed to run a small farm: the rotting wood of abandoned carts, the remnants of broken fences and pieces of scythes and other tools, long since forgotten. The whole place reeked of neglect and decay. Samuel swallowed hard as his gaze wandered towards the tiny windows of the cottage. He prayed to God that Hope was indeed inside, and that she was unharmed.

'We leave the horses here,' he said, dismounting and leading the creature to a nearby tree, before tethering him carefully to its thick trunk. 'We approach quietly on foot and try to get a look inside the cottage first. We need to assess exactly what we're dealing with.'

Charles nodded his agreement, and together they crept towards the decrepit building, using the tall grass to shield them. If the situation had not been so grave, Samuel would have found the sight of the pair of them laughable. Well clad in fine riding coats and Hessian boots and sneaking towards a place which was the rural equivalent of the slum houses found in larger towns and cities, they looked just about as out of place as it was possible to be. As he tiptoed along, it struck Samuel again just how acutely aware Hope must have been of the difference between their worlds. The poverty and hardship she had known stood in such sharp contrast to the sumptuous comfort of his life at Hayton Hall.

A fresh wave of guilt washed over him. His life, and by extension the life he'd offered her these past weeks, must have seemed utterly intimidating. She must have spent every day feeling like a fish out of water. Little wonder she'd struggled to bring herself to tell him about it. Little wonder she'd felt the need to pretend to be someone else.

Well, there would be no more pretending now, on either of their parts. When he reached a little window, he made a silent vow. He would find her and bring her safely back to

Hayton, and he would offer her a life, with him, for ever.
A life they would share and build together.

He just had to find her first.

'I can't see her,' Charles whispered as he peered tentatively through the window. 'The place is deathly quiet. I
don't like it.'

Samuel found himself bristling at his friend's poor
choice of words, before taking a look for himself. Sure
enough, Charles was right—even in the dim light of the
single-room dwelling it was evident that Hope was not inside. He cast his eyes around, taking in the simple, sparse
furnishings, the bare stone walls, the last remnants of a
single tallow candle, left burning in the middle of a table.
Someone had been there, and not so very long ago from
the looks of it.

'If this place is anything to go by, I'd say crime doesn't
always pay,' Charles whispered. 'I always thought smug-
gling was a lucrative trade, but it seems not.'

'It's a cut-throat enterprise,' Samuel replied. 'Some win
and some lose. It looks like Jeremiah Sloane has been on
the losing side for some time. Hope said he runs some illicit stills from nearby caves too. However, that old man
told us that his health is failing. Perhaps his business has
been failing at the same time.'

Out the corner of his eye, Samuel caught sight of something, like a flicker of movement on the ground. 'What's
that?' he hissed. 'See there—behind the table? It looks like
a boot.' He squinted, trying to peer through the gloom and
murk to see more clearly. 'I think it's…it's moving. Someone is in there, lying on the ground.'

Instinctively, he darted away from the window, rounding
the cottage and heading towards its single wooden door. If

it was Hope and she was bound or, God forbid, injured, then there was no time to lose. He'd detected no other signs of life within. If she was alone, then he had to rescue her before her father returned. He had to get her away from this dreadful place—now.

'I think it is a boot,' Charles hissed, scurrying behind him. 'But Sammy, it might not be...'

Charles's words were cut short by the loud thump of Samuel's boot as it made contact with the door, followed by the brittle crack of the old wood as it gave way feebly to his force. Samuel hurried inside, Charles still following him, to be confronted by a scene which made them both gasp loudly. Beside the table, a man was lying on the floor, groaning softly, his limbs twitching and his eyes rolling as he seemed to drift in and out of consciousness.

Samuel bent down, his gaze immediately drawn to the large bloodstain which was growing across the man's filthy shirt. 'It looks as though he's been shot,' he called, looking over his shoulder at Charles, who lingered behind, looking distinctly pale about the face.

'Should I send for a physician?' Charles asked.

Samuel looked back at the man. He suspected there was no time for that—the man was in all likelihood mortally wounded and would be dead by the time a physician arrived. However, Samuel decided, they had to at least try.

'Yes,' he began. 'Perhaps ask that old man...'

'No...' The man's voice was raspy but insistent. 'I'm done for.'

'Are you Jeremiah Sloane?' Samuel asked, his shock at the scene he'd uncovered abating, and the urgency of finding Hope gripping him once more. 'Where is your daughter? You must tell me, man. Tell me now!'

A sliver of a smile appeared on the man's weathered face. 'You must be Samuel,' he croaked. 'She really must have been like a harlot between your sheets if you want her back.'

Samuel felt the heat of indignation rise in his chest at such a remark—uttered by her father, no less. The man really was the lowest of the low. It was a mystery to him how such a person could have sired such a lovely, brave and intelligent daughter.

'Where is she?' he repeated, through gritted teeth this time. Samuel was not a man to allow his temper to get the better of him but, even so, he could feel himself close to losing it.

Jeremiah Sloane coughed weakly, causing blood to bubble up and trickle down the side of his cheek. 'George has her,' he wheezed, his eyes rolling again. 'They've gone north.'

'North?' Samuel repeated, his heart lurching as all that those words implied became clear. 'You mean to Gretna? To wed her?' he asked. Hope had never named him, but he realised George must be the terrible forced fiancé she'd described.

'Doubt…he'll…do that.'

Jeremiah Sloane's breathing grew laboured now, and Samuel realised they were almost out of time. If Hope's father would not part with his knowledge before slipping away to meet his maker, then their chance of finding Hope might be lost. She might be lost to him, and that was a thought he truly could not bear.

'Then where?' he prompted, hearing the desperation in his own voice as he shook the man by his shoulders in an effort to rouse him one final time. 'Damn it, tell me!'

'Rockcliffe.'

The word was a whisper, barely audible. Jeremiah Sloane

choked again, then let out one more whistling, agonising breath. His bloodied body grew still and limp, his grey, leathery face freezing in a contorted expression, eyes wide, lips parted in an O shape, as though death had come as a shock. As though, perhaps, he'd glimpsed something on the other side that he had not wanted to see. A gruesome testament to a lifetime of wickedness, law-breaking and cruelty, indeed.

Samuel got to his feet, turning away from the grim scene at last. 'Let's fetch the horses,' he said to Charles, hurrying towards the door. 'You must find the local constable. It's clear Jeremiah Sloane has been murdered, and we have a duty to report it. Do that, then return to Hayton, to your sister.'

'I thought you said not to involve constables, that Sloane had the law in his pocket around these parts?' Charles asked, frowning.

'Then if that's the case, hopefully they will be motivated to bring the killer to justice,' Samuel quipped. He sighed heavily. 'Honestly, I don't know, Charles. I only know that we must report what we have found here, immediately. To do otherwise might bring the law's suspicions down upon us.'

Charles grimaced. 'All right, point taken. And what will you do?'

'I must ride for Rockcliffe at once.'

'But where the devil is Rockcliffe?' Charles asked him, following behind. 'And who is this George her father spoke of, anyway?'

'A monster, Charles,' Samuel replied, recalling again Hope's words about the man her father had tried to force her to marry. Shuddering, he glanced back into the gloom of the cottage. 'One monster is dead, and now Hope is in the clutches of another. I must follow the road north, find Rockcliffe and this George, then I will find her. There is no time to lose!'

Samuel ran along the uneven track and back towards his horse, the same silent prayer circling around in his mind.

Please God, let me find Hope, he prayed. *Let her be safe and well. Let her come home with me, so that these malevolent men might never try to harm her again.*

Hope winced as the cart jolted on the road, the sudden movement making her already pounding head ache all the more. Despite herself, she let out a sob, partly at the pain and partly at the shock of it all. Tears ran unabated down her cheeks as her mind replayed all that she'd witnessed once again.

The way George had waltzed into the cottage so casually, as if he owned the place. How he'd licked his lips when he'd looked at her, an unmistakably greedy look lingering in his dark eyes. The way her father had scurried over to him like a beggar asking for his supper, pleading for reassurances that his debt was now settled. How George had refused to answer him, laughing and shoving him out of the way as he'd marched over to claim his prize. The way her father had begun to wail and yell like a man overcome by the realisation that he could never win. How that screaming had caused something in George to snap. How George's cheeks had flushed with anger, a cloud gathering over the already foreboding features of his angular face before he swiftly drew his pistol, took his aim, and fired.

How Hope had watched as her father tumbled quietly to the ground, his desperate wailing replaced by the soft moans of a man whose life was ebbing away.

When they'd left the cottage, Jeremiah Sloane had still lived—just. As George had untied her from the chair, unbound her feet and hands and dragged her away, Hope had been gripped by the most overpowering urge to run to her father's side. To remain with him in his final moments. To not let him die alone. It was strange. After all he'd done to her, Jeremiah Sloane deserved neither her concern nor her care, and yet both feelings had plagued her. His cruelty and callousness were unforgivable, but in the end the brute he'd become had been subsumed by an even greater monster—a leviathan who'd enfeebled him, who'd preyed on his weaknesses as age, debt and misfortune consumed him bit by bit. She would not mourn her father but, inexplicably, she realised that she did pity him. Better that, she supposed, than pitying herself. She would not surrender to such feelings. At least, not yet.

'Stop weeping, or else I'll give you something to weep about.' The monster spoke without even looking at her, his eyes intent upon the road ahead. He sat close by her side on the bench at the front of the cart, his hands firm upon the reins of the single horse which pulled them along. He'd left her feet unbound but had tethered one of her wrists to the cart, subtly enough that it would not be noticed by anyone else on the road, but firmly enough to ensure she had no chance of getting away. Not that she had any intention of trying to leap on to the road and run—she'd already seen what a good shot he was, and any such attempt to flee would undoubtedly be answered by a bullet from his pistol.

Hope straightened herself, fighting back the last vestiges of her tears. He was right; she did need to stop weeping. The options for escape, she knew, were vanishingly small as it was, and would certainly be undetectable if she was too busy crying.

'You already did—you killed my father,' she retorted, mustering a feistiness she did not truly feel. Better that, she decided, than allowing him to sense her fear.

'Ha!' He glanced at her, baring his yellow teeth and grinning in amusement. 'I've done you a favour there, trust me.' He reached out, placing his hand upon her knee and giving it a firm squeeze. 'Do as you're told, and you'll have a better life with me than you ever did with him.'

Even through the fabric of her dress, the feeling of his fingers made her skin crawl. Hope shivered, partly at his unwanted touch and partly at the cold which seeped increasingly into her bones. She wore only the plain blue day dress which she'd been wearing when her father had snatched her from Hayton Hall, and although its sleeves were long, its fine fabric was insufficient against the autumn chill. She was sure she'd been wearing a shawl in Hayton's gardens too, but when she'd awoken at her father's cottage it had been nowhere to be seen. Obstinately, Hope stiffened—against the monster's touch, and against the cold. She would not allow this man to detect even a hint of her discomfort, lest he perceive it as a weakness to exploit.

'And what does this better life entail?' she asked him. She gave him a haughty look, once again masking her fear as her father's warning about being drowned in the river rang in her ears. 'Because I had a perfectly good one, without my father and without you.'

'Which life would that be?' Briefly, he took his eyes off the road, looking at her with a gaze so dark it appeared almost black under the gloom of the surrounding trees. 'The one you spent on stage, or the one you spent at Hayton Hall, playing the harlot for its master?'

Hope scowled at him—better that than allowing the fresh tears which pricked in the corners of her eyes to fall. When her father had made similar insinuations, she'd protested. Now, she decided, she would hold her tongue. Allowing this dangerous, evil man to know anything about Samuel, about how much she'd adored her short time with him or about how much she cared for him, could put him in danger, and she would not be able to live with herself if anything happened to him. Better to let George believe that she'd spent these past weeks being ill-used than letting him know she'd spent them falling in love. A love, she reminded herself, which was lost to her now, even though she would feel it deeply to the end of her days.

'My life in the theatre, of course,' she lied, meeting his eye. 'A life in which I did no man's bidding.'

'Aye, well, you'll do my bidding now,' George snarled at her.

'As what?' Hope challenged him, although she hardly dared to ask. 'Your wife, or your harlot?'

George returned his eyes to the road. 'I've not decided,' he said coldly. 'But, either way, you'll be running contraband and having my bairns, Hope. That's what I've got planned for you.'

Hope looked away, biting her lip so hard that she might draw blood. All the pity she'd fleetingly felt for her father simply disappeared as she faced up to the sort of life the man had condemned her to, and in its place her anger grew. She'd spent her formative years living with a man who used fear, threats and sometimes violence to get his own way, and she was damned if she was going to spend the remainder of her life with another such man. She was damned if she was going to be forced into committing crimes or going to bed with a man who repulsed her. Frankly, she decided, she'd rather he did just drown her in the river and have done with it.

But first, she vowed, she would defy him every step of the way. She would use every opportunity she got trying to regain her freedom. Starting right now. Hope wiggled her bound wrist, straining against the rope, carefully trying to tease it loose without him noticing. She would bide her time, she would play the hand she'd been dealt, and when the right moment came along she would seize it—just as she always did.

Chapter Twenty-Two

Hope grimaced as George directed the horse to slow down and turn into the courtyard of a coaching inn. She'd long since lost any sense of where they were or how long they had been travelling. She knew from the scant details George had offered that he was taking her north, and since he'd admitted he had not decided whether or not he planned to wed her, she presumed they were not going directly to Gretna—a small mercy which she was thankful for. She also knew that the farm from which George ran his nefarious operations was somewhere near the Scottish border, not far from the Solway Firth, where the rivers Esk and Eden meandered out to sea. She had to assume, therefore, that that was where they were headed.

Realising that, however, served only to make Hope begin to panic. Despite her best efforts, she'd had little success in loosening the rope which bound her to the cart, and with each passing mile she felt the weight of her fate bearing down upon her. If she could not escape now, while it was just the two of them on the road, what chance did she stand once she'd arrived at his farm, no doubt living under the watchful eye of his many criminal accomplices? She had other, more immediate concerns too, such as what George had planned once darkness fell. Surely, he could not hope to travel all the way to the border today; they would have to stop somewhere tonight. At this, Hope shuddered—the thought of spending the night anywhere with that monster, and all that such a night might entail, did not bear thinking about. Which was why, when he turned into the coaching inn, she felt her heart sink.

'Why are we stopping here?' she asked, trying her best to sound curious rather than fearful.

'Because I need a drink, and so does the horse.' He glanced at her, a knowing smirk spreading across his face. 'Sorry to disappoint you, Hope, but I don't plan to take a room here for the night. I know you've been used to living like a duchess as Hayton's harlot, but you'll have to make do with a straw bed tonight—unless we forgo that and sleep under the stars,' he added, giving her an unpleasant wink.

'And where is this bed of straw, exactly?' Hope asked. If she could draw some specific information from him, she might better understand where she was. Information which she needed, if the opportunity ever arrived for her to make a bid for freedom.

'A friend's cottage,' he snapped. 'That's all you need to know.'

Hope suppressed a sigh as the horse drew to a halt in the courtyard and George climbed down from the cart. He was never going to tell her anything useful; he was far too cunning for that. She glanced down at her wrist, which was red and raw-looking from all the wriggling she'd done in a vain effort to free herself. Sitting next to him, she had not dared use her free hand to try to remove the shackle; to do so would have surely drawn his attention. However, if he left her to fetch a drink...

'I'll remain on the cart,' she said quickly. 'I can keep an eye on the horse while the stable boys attend to him.'

George began to laugh, walking round to her as he shook his head. 'You must think I'm stupid.'

'No, I'm just not thirsty, that's all.' A lie, of course. She was thirsty, hungry, tired, terrified—all of it. She was running out of options, running out of opportunities. If she was honest with herself, she was beginning to despair.

'I don't care what you are,' he said through gritted teeth. 'You're not leaving my sight.'

He untied the rope, liberating her poor sore wrist—another small mercy, she supposed, although likely useless to her whilst ever she remained under his watchful eye. Unceremoniously, he hauled her down from the cart, all but dragging her along as he approached two wide-eyed stable boys and handed them some coins to attend to the horse. His thirst for beer clearly growing, he hurried her around towards a small kitchen at the rear of the inn, coins again crossing palms—this time those of the innkeeper, who looked at Hope with some concern when he observed George's rough handling of her. However, he said nothing, instead wordlessly pointing them both through a weather-beaten wooden door and into a humble room, where they found a table laden with bread and beer mugs and a handful of other travellers crowded around it. Several male faces glanced up briefly to see who had joined them, before returning to regard their fare once more.

'Here. Sit.'

George pushed her towards a wooden stool, forcing her to sit down. He remained close at her side, still standing as he grabbed a hunk of bread and a mug and ate and drank as though he'd had no sustenance for years. Hope tried hard to ignore her dry mouth and empty, groaning stomach;

she'd sworn she was not thirsty and, besides, she would take nothing that he'd paid for. As her father had learned to his cost, this was not the sort of man you wanted to owe a debt to. This was the sort of man who would always want something in return.

Unlike Samuel. Generous and decent Samuel, who had wanted nothing from her. Kind and loving Samuel, who had given her so much more than sanctuary. If only she really had been Hope Swynford. If only she really had been a gentleman's daughter and an heiress. Then, perhaps…

She did not realise that she was crying until one of the other travellers, an older, stocky man with a round, kindly face, remarked upon it.

'Now then, lass, I'm sure it's not so bad,' the man said, offering her a small smile. She watched as he glanced warily at George, who was still devouring his bread and beer. 'Do you want to eat something? There's plenty to be had.'

'She doesn't want anything,' George snapped, his mouth full.

Hope watched as the man's keen gaze continued to flit between them both, as though he was trying to work something out, and a seed of an idea began to grow in her mind. She raised her sore, rope-marked wrist above the table, giving it a rub so that he could clearly see the marks upon it.

'I'm afraid I'm not very keen on plain bread and beer,' she said softly, putting on her Hope Swynford voice as she eased back into character. 'I much prefer tea and cake, you see. Two of the very best things in life, I can assure you.'

Next to her, she sensed George cease chewing. One by one, each pair of eyes around the table seemed to settle upon her captor, and for several moments no one moved.

'I dare say they are, miss,' the older man said, although

he barely tore his gaze from George. 'But those are things you'll find in the parlour, not the back kitchen. Perhaps if you went in there, you'd find something more suited to your tastes.'

'Don't you dare move.'

George gripped her arm so tightly that it made her cry out, and stools scraped in unison against the stone floor as several of the men rose to their feet.

'What is this man to you, miss?' the older man asked, his kindly expression long gone as his eyes blazed thunderously at George. 'Are you in need of some assistance?'

At that moment Hope saw her chance, and she seized it with both hands. 'This man has kidnapped me!' she cried out, getting to her feet. 'He has stolen me away and means to marry me at Gretna against my will so that he can steal my inheritance. He is a villain and a scoundrel!'

Together, the men rounded on George. Apparently startled by what was unfolding, he took several steps back, his eyes wide with something which almost resembled fear. As the men drew nearer, Hope moved away, finally out of George's grasp. What happened next was as confusing as it was alarming—a frantic scramble of limbs as punches were thrown and angry, expletive-ridden words were exchanged between George and the men. At one point George launched forward, clattering into the table and sending bread and beer flying about the room. For several moments Hope simply stood there, frozen, until three simple words spoken by the kindly older man brought her back to her senses.

'Run, miss. Run!'

Of course—there was nothing else for it. Without another moment's hesitation, Hope hurried towards the door, and towards her freedom. Towards her life, towards the unknown. Towards whatever lay ahead of her. This was it, she realised—she would not get a better chance. Indeed, she would likely get no other chances at all.

Quickly, Hope turned the knob on the door, poised to flee. Then a gunshot rang out.

Samuel was a good number of miles into his journey before he realised that he hadn't quite thought this through. Rockcliffe, he had managed to ascertain, lay to the northwest of Carlisle—reaching it within the day would be pushing the endurance of both himself and his horse, especially at the speed he'd so far travelled. He had indeed been riding hard; his best chance of finding Hope was to catch up with her and her abductor on the road, although how likely he was to manage this, he did not know. He'd no idea by what means this man was taking Hope away with him, and therefore how many miles they would manage to cover before darkness fell. He prayed it was by old horse and rickety cart—the more elderly and ramshackle, the better.

Unfortunately, despite covering a good number of miles of road and making brief enquiries at every inn on the way, so far there'd been no sign of either Hope or the dreadful George, and riding so fast was quickly wearying his horse. Stopping to rest was the last thing he wanted to do, but as he rode towards the latest coaching inn he realised it was a necessity. The poor animal needed water and sustenance at the very least, and if he was honest with himself, so did he. He'd barely eaten or drunk anything that day, such had been his complete preoccupation with finding Hope. With a heavy sigh, he turned his horse into the inn's courtyard, catching the eye of a young stable boy and giving him a beckoning nod. Perhaps, he reasoned, it would be best to change the poor creature while he was here.

Samuel climbed down from his saddle and the boy walked forward. He glanced around briefly, suddenly struck by how eerily quiet the inn was. It was not so much that there were no carriages or coaches—indeed, he could count several, sitting stationary at the far end of the courtyard. It was more that there were no people standing outside—no ladies or gentlemen hovering, waiting to depart, no carriages being readied, and no drivers checking their horses or the position of their passengers' luggage. It was, without doubt, very strange.

'Where is everyone?' Samuel asked the stable boy who, it struck him now, looked a deathly shade of white.

'Most are in the parlour, sir.' The boy's voice was barely a whisper. 'A few have gone behind the stables. They dare not come out.'

Samuel frowned. 'Why?'

'There was a sound like a gunshot. It came from the rear kitchen not so long ago.' The boy paused, swallowing hard. 'The master went to see what was afoot and…and there's a man in there, sir, waving his pistol about. Says anyone who comes in will get their brains blown out. The master's sent for the constable and says everyone's to stay hid—except us, on account of the horses we've to attend to, but everyone else.' The boy looked at the horse, reaching out to give him a gentle stroke. 'You could go, sir. He's tired but the next inn's only a few miles away. He could manage it at a trot.'

Samuel pressed his lips together, absorbing the details of the boy's story. Could this murderous and unpredictable man be the one he was looking for?

'This man you mentioned—do you know if there is a lady travelling with him?' he asked.

'Aye, sir, although if I had to guess, I'd say she's not come with him willingly. Poor lady was shackled to the cart when they got here. The master reckons he's taken her from a fine house somewhere. Says the man's trying to hide it, leaving her looking grubby and without a bonnet, but there's no mistaking that her dress is quality.'

'And the lady, what does she look like?' Samuel tried to remain focused on ascertaining the facts but, despite himself, he felt his fists curl. The thought of any woman being so mistreated made him angry, and the idea that it might be Hope was frankly unbearable.

The boy frowned, apparently recalling. 'Small. Dark hair, all matted and hanging loose like she's been in the wars. But very pretty—meaning no impertinence, of course, sir. Just an observation.'

Any lingering doubt in Samuel's mind was immediately blown away by the boy's description. It was Hope, he told himself, his heart beginning to race. She was here, and she was locked in a room with a madman wielding a pistol. A room, and a man, he had to now work to free her from.

Samuel gave the boy a nod and a tight smile before pressing a shilling into his palm. 'Be good to my horse,' he said. 'Hopefully, this won't take too long.'

'But sir, you can't surely...'

Samuel did not hear the rest of the boy's protest. He was too preoccupied, creeping towards the kitchen which sat at the back of the inn. As he reached the building he ducked down, tentatively edging towards the single small window which offered the only view into the room, and to understanding what was happening inside. Cautiously, he peeked in, surveying the scene swiftly from a low position and praying he would not be noticed.

Immediately he spied Hope, the sight of her making his heart fleetingly lift, before the gravity of the situation she was in made his pulse begin to race with trepidation. She was perched on a stool, her eyes cast down and shoulders slumped in an expression of utter defeat. Near to her was a man with sharp features, pacing to and fro, waving a pistol around menacingly. George—it had to be. On the other side of the room, furthest from the door, stood a handful of men, all looking glum, their hands raised in surrender. Samuel frowned. Clearly, something had happened to provoke this potentially deadly scene, but he was damned if he could discern exactly what.

No matter. All that counted now was rescuing Hope from George's grasp, and ensuring no one else was hurt in the process. Samuel reached into his pocket, placing a careful hand upon his pistol. On the one hand, he felt relieved at having the presence of mind to come armed; on the other, he felt alarmed at the prospect of having to use his weapon. No matter, he told himself. He could not afford to deliberate on this; even a moment's hesitation could prove costly. He would do whatever it took to rescue Hope. If that meant aiming his pistol at her captor and pulling the trigger, then so be it.

He continued to watch at the window as George's pacing slowed and he came to a halt with his back to the door. This was his chance, Samuel realised. He had to act—quickly and decisively. He had to take a leaf out of Hope's book and live on his wits.

It was this thought which spurred him on as he hurried towards the door, launching himself at it with such force as to render turning the doorknob entirely unnecessary. He was aware of a deep, guttural roar coming from the depths of his throat as the door gave way, a sound which was so ungentlemanly and so unlike him that it would have taken him by surprise, had he not been so thoroughly consumed by his mission. Out of the corner of his eye, he saw Hope leap to her feet.

'Samuel? Samuel!' she breathed, part-question and part-affirmation.

A shocked-looking George turned. As Samuel threw himself towards the man he saw him move to raise his pistol but, mercifully, he was not quite quick enough. Overwhelming him with the element of surprise combined with sheer brute force, Samuel wrestled George to the ground, holding him with his face and stomach pressed to the floor while he tried to get the pistol out of his grasp. But his adversary was not about to give up so easily. He flailed about, yelling obscenities as he tried to fight back with a considerable strength of his own.

Thankfully, around him, Samuel sensed the reinforcements begin to assemble. The cluster of men whom George had been holding at gunpoint now sprang into action, several of them joining Samuel in pinning George to the ground, while another, burly man managed at last to prise the pistol from George's firm grip.

Disarmed and overwhelmed, George finally seemed to concede defeat, his limbs growing still, his breathing rapid and exhausted. For several moments Samuel and a couple of his assistants continued to hold him down, apparently not quite daring to move. One of the other men ran outside, returning swiftly with a couple of lengths of rope and offering them to Samuel.

'The stable boys say that the constable is on his way,'

the man said. 'We can use this to restrain him until he gets here.'

'I'll do that.' The burly man grabbed hold of the rope. 'It'll be my pleasure to shackle him like he shackled that poor miss over there, judging by the state of her wrist. You go and attend to her, sir. She's had quite the ordeal.'

Samuel nodded obligingly before hauling himself to his feet. He heard George groan as the burly man took over, holding him down with his considerable weight while tightly binding his hands behind his back.

'You must have been very worried about her,' the man continued. 'Is she your sister, or...?'

But Samuel was not listening. Indeed, his attention was no longer on the burly man, or on Hope's abductor, at all. Instead, his gaze had wandered across the room, towards the woman who stood there, frozen with shock, her dress filthy, her long dark curls mussed, her face drained of all colour. She lifted those emerald eyes to meet his and his heart stirred, just as it had the first time she'd gazed up at him from the floor of her bedchamber, all those weeks ago. Perhaps it had been love even then—it was hard to say. All he knew for certain was that he loved her now.

Wordlessly, Samuel strode towards her, reaching out and enveloping her in his arms. She melted into his embrace, clinging to him tightly as though she too had feared that she might never see him again. For several moments he simply held her, running his fingers gently over the knotted tendrils of her hair. Then she stirred, lifting her chin to gaze up at him, meeting his eyes with a look which spoke of tenderness, of admiration, of affection. Of love. A look which told him everything. He leaned down, his lips capturing hers in affirmation as he poured his heart and soul into that kiss. Everything she felt, he sought to show her, he felt too.

Behind them, an amused voice intruded. 'Not your sister, then,' the burly man said.

Against Hope's lips, Samuel smiled. 'No,' he murmured, breaking the kiss to see that Hope was smiling too. 'Not my sister,' he said, caressing her cheek as he gazed intently into her eyes. 'But I hope, one day soon, she will be my wife.'

Chapter Twenty-Three

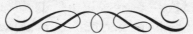

Hope collapsed on the bed, completely exhausted. Outside, the afternoon had given way to evening, the sky darkening rapidly as heavy drops of rain began to fall. Given the coming night, the change in the weather and their weariness, not to mention that of Samuel's poor horse, Samuel had suggested that they should remain at the inn overnight before travelling back to Hayton Hall the next day. Hope had nodded her agreement; indeed, in her shocked state, nodding was all she seemed able to do. Samuel appeared to sense this, and with a reassuring smile he'd taken charge, requesting everything from rooms and food to a bathtub and some clean clothes. Once the constable had arrived and George had been taken away, Samuel had escorted her upstairs before leaving her to wash and change with the assistance of a maid he'd managed to secure for her.

'It's all over now, Hope,' he'd said, cupping her cheek with his hand. 'You're perfectly safe. I will just be downstairs in the parlour and will check on you in a little while.'

Now, lying on the bed and listening to the soft crackle of a small fire burning in the hearth, Hope pressed her eyes shut, replaying his words in her mind. She was perfectly safe, and it was all thanks to him. Samuel Liddell had been her rescuer, not once but twice. Weeks ago, he'd saved her from probable death in the woodland near his home, and today he'd saved her from a fate worse than death—a life spent with George. He'd ridden across the country to find her, and put himself in harm's way to save her from George's awful clutches. Then he'd taken her in his arms and he'd kissed her—a kiss which had told her in no uncertain terms that he loved her, before speaking words which left her in no doubt that he meant to ask her to be his wife.

But how could he mean to marry her, when she'd lied to him about who she was? How could he, a wealthy gentleman, want to wed a low-born actress and the daughter of an outlaw?

A knock at the door caused her eyes to fly open and her heart to race. Her head might know that she was safe, but it was clear it would take some time before her fight-or-flight instincts realised that too. Hope forced herself to take a deep, calming breath. More than likely, it was the maid returning, having left a short while ago to take the bathtub away.

'Come in,' she called out, pulling herself upright. She glanced at the plate of food the maid had left for her, a veritable platter of cheese, cold meats and bread which she'd barely begun to pick at. Her stomach, it seemed, hadn't realised that she was safe either, if the way it continued to lurch was anything to go by.

To her surprise, however, it was not the maid's face she saw peering round the door, but Samuel's. He smiled at her somewhat sheepishly. 'Sorry—the maid said you were dressed,' he said. 'But I will go if you're resting.'

'No, it's all right. Please, Samuel, come in.' She offered a smile to mirror his. 'I doubt I will manage to sleep anyway.'

Samuel slipped inside the room, closing the door softly behind him. 'It doesn't look like you've managed to eat much either,' he observed, nodding towards the almost full plate. He pulled a chair up to the bedside before sitting down next to her. 'How are you feeling?'

'Like I've been hit over the head, kidnapped and shackled, so, all in all, I think I have had better days,' she replied.

'What? He hit you over the head?' Immediately, Samuel leapt to his feet, gently brushing her still-damp hair back from her forehead and looking for signs of injury.

The feeling of his fingers against her scalp did strange things to her insides. 'My father did,' she explained. 'Apparently I wasn't a very cooperative kidnap victim so it was all he could do to silence me.'

'You were unconscious? I will summon a physician at once.'

'Samuel—' gently, she captured his hand with her own, lowering it and bringing it to rest at her side '—I will live. I do feel somewhat better after bathing and putting on clean clothes.' She smoothed her other hand over the skirt of a grey dress which felt about two sizes too big for her.

Samuel raked his eyes over her attire. 'Ah—yes. I'm afraid it was all the innkeeper's wife had to offer.'

She grinned at him. 'It is fine. I have grown accustomed to borrowed clothes.'

Samuel shook his head in embarrassment. 'Please, do not remind me.' He squeezed her hand ever so gently. 'When we return to Hayton, Hope, we shall visit a dressmaker in Lowhaven and you shall have a complete wardrobe of your own—I promise you that. And, despite your protestations, I am going to have a physician attend to you before we travel. I cannot believe your father did that to his own daughter.'

She felt her smile fade. 'George shot him—my father. He shot him, just before he took me away. He will be dead by now.'

Samuel nodded gravely. 'I'm afraid he is,' he replied. 'I went with Charles to his cottage, to look for you. He was near death when we got there. He just about managed to tell us where George was taking you before he...before he passed.'

For a long moment Hope pressed her lips together, putting her feelings in order. Holding back her tears. She would not weep for that man—not after all that he had done.

'At least he told you that,' she said in the end. 'And at least he did not die alone.'

'Oh, Hope.' Samuel slid on to the bed beside her, wrapping his arm around her shoulder and drawing her near. 'You really are a remarkable woman, do you know that? Truly remarkable. The life you've lived...the things you must have seen...'

'My life has been no worse than the lives of many men and women across England, Samuel,' she countered softly. 'Most people's experience of life is closer to mine than it is to yours. Not everyone grows up with a free trader for a father, but most know something of hardship.'

He nodded. 'You're right. It reminds me that I am fortunate but also...well, very sheltered. I have not had to be brave like you.'

She chuckled. 'I wouldn't say that. Just hours ago you wrestled a pistol-wielding madman to the ground, or have you forgotten about that already?'

He pulled her closer, placing a kiss on the top of her head. 'Oh, I haven't forgotten. That was probably the bravest and the best thing I have ever done.'

'Probably the most reckless too. You could have been killed.'

'I confess I wasn't really thinking about that. When I saw you through that kitchen window, all I could think about was getting you away from that monster and back with me.'

She looked up at him then, meeting those lovely grey-blue eyes. 'I'm glad you did, Samuel. I'm glad you found me.'

'I almost didn't.' His expression grew serious. 'When I first realised you were gone, I thought you'd left of your own accord, that after our conversation the night before you'd decided to leave. I wouldn't have blamed you if you had. You poured out your story to me and, instead of comforting you, I held back. I hesitated. Then I let you leave without saying all that there was to say.' He shook his head at himself. 'It was unforgivable.'

'No, it's not. It must have come as a shock to learn that the person you'd welcomed into your house wasn't who she said she was at all.' She paused, swallowing hard. Preparing herself for complete honesty. Preparing herself to face up to what she'd seen in his eyes that night. 'It must have been disappointing too, to learn that I am so far beneath you in status. Indeed, you'd have every right to be angry with me.'

'I cannot deny that it came as a shock, but I'm not angry, and certainly not disappointed. You hid your true identity for very good reasons, Hope—reasons far better than the foolish ones I had for borrowing my brother's title. Indeed, you're the one who ought to be angry with me. As for disappointment, surely you know me well enough by now to understand that neither wealth nor connections are of much interest to me. It is companionship, it is the meeting of like minds, it is love—those are the things I want.

Besides, you do yourself a disservice to speak about yourself in such a way.'

'I'm an actress, Samuel,' she reminded him. 'No better than a courtesan or a harlot, as I recall your friend Mr Gordon once saying. And, even worse than that, I'm the daughter of a criminal. I doubt it's possible to have a more dubious background than that.'

He caressed her cheek, lifting her chin gently and placing a brief, soft kiss upon her lips—a kiss which, despite their heavy conversation, left her wanting more. 'You're a beautiful, intelligent, strong and resourceful woman,' he replied. 'You are admirable, Hope—truly. You have survived everything that life has thrown at you. Indeed, against all the odds, I'd say you've flourished. You are clever and you are cultured and you are brave. That is what I should have said to you when you told me your story.'

She raised her eyebrows at him, trying to ignore how her heart sang at his words. She would not get carried away, no matter how sincere his sentiments sounded to her ears. 'So why didn't you?' she asked.

He sighed. 'Partly because I felt ashamed of myself. If I hadn't been so busy pretending that I was a baronet with a big estate then perhaps you'd have found me more approachable. Perhaps you would have told me the truth sooner.'

She smiled sadly. 'I doubt that very much, Samuel, although I do wish I had.' She frowned, searching his gaze. 'You said that was part of the reason. What was the other part?'

Samuel breathed out an embarrassed chuckle. 'The other part was the fact that we were in my bedchamber, late at night and only half-clad. You'd made some remarks about how gentlemen had treated you in the past, about what they had expected, and…and I did not want you to think I was just another gentleman seeking to take advantage of you.'

'You would never have done that,' she replied. 'You've always been impeccably good and decent towards me.'

Samuel nodded. 'Nonetheless, Hope, I was still a man standing in his bedchamber with a beautiful woman. Believe me, it took all my self-restraint not to kiss you or take you into my bed.'

Such loaded words made her cheeks colour, as did the realisation that she wished he had. She tried to suppress the thought, reminding herself that there were a hundred other matters they ought to be discussing. How he couldn't possibly wish to marry a base-born actress being top of the list.

Before she could say another word, however, Samuel sat upright and released her from his embrace. 'I should probably leave you to rest. We can talk more tomorrow. You need to sleep if you're going to be fit for the ride back to Hayton.'

'Don't.' She touched him lightly on the arm. 'Stay awhile—please. I know I am safe here but I'd rather not be alone.'

For good measure she shuffled over, patting the sheets where they lay over the space she'd made. She watched Samuel hesitate, his gaze switching contemplatively between the bed and her. He was a gentleman to a fault— a true, proper gentleman. That was one of the things she loved about him. It was also one of the reasons why she knew that in the cold light of day, when the dust had settled on the chaos and terror of today, he would realise that he could not marry her. If, indeed, he had not realised that already. After all, he had not broached the subject again. Hope pushed the thought from her mind; there was little point in dwelling upon that now. Samuel was right—she needed to sleep and, whether it was wise or not, she wanted to have him by her side.

After several moments of deliberation, something apparently made up Samuel's mind. 'All right,' he said, sliding back on to the bed beside her and taking her into his arms once more. 'I will stay, just until you fall asleep.' He kissed the top of her head as she nestled under his chin. 'I love you, Hope.'

'I love you too, Samuel.'

Hope closed her eyes, overcome by the comfort and reassurance she found in this intimacy, as well as the myriad of other, less familiar feelings she felt stirring within her. But even as she relished his warm embrace, her doubts and her fears continued to niggle at her. He loved her and she loved him, and yet she feared that would not be enough. She would not be enough and, sooner or later, Samuel would come to his senses and see that whilst Hope Swynford could have been his wife, Hope Sloane never could.

Chapter Twenty-Four

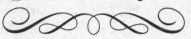

The ride back to Hayton was torture, almost as much as the previous night had been. The feeling of Hope sitting on his horse, nestled against him, continually reminded Samuel of their night spent in the bed at that inn. Indeed, it had been a full night. Despite his insistence that he would leave once she fell asleep, he had fallen asleep too and had remained there, holding her in his arms, until the first hints of the sleepy autumn dawn slipped through the thin fabric of the curtains which hung at the small window.

Nothing improper had happened, of course—they had both been far too exhausted for that and, besides, he was a gentleman. But still, the experience of waking beside her, of feeling her warm, petite form pressed against him, of burying his nose in those dark curls while he kissed her good morning had been overpowering. It was more than lust—although God only knew he had felt plenty of that. It was a sense of rightness, of belonging. A sense that if he was fortunate to spend every morning waking like that, with Hope in his arms, then at the end of his life he would die a happy man.

It was love, but then he knew that. He'd known that for some time. Now, as he caught first sight of Hayton Hall's castle-like roofscape, he knew he needed to make things formal. To ask, in the proper way, the vital question. In the aftermath of Hope's rescue and George's apprehension, he'd blurted out his intentions in the heat of the moment, and yet he had not actually asked her.

Last night he'd gone to her room intent upon proposing, but one look at her pale, weary, worried face was all he'd needed to understand that it was not the right time. It had been clear to him that Hope needed to talk about what was on her mind—her ordeal and the death of her father, not to mention her clear and persistent worries about what Samuel thought of her, now that he knew the truth. What she'd needed from him, he'd quickly realised, was comfort and reassurance. Proposals, he'd decided, could wait.

Although, he realised now, not for much longer. He wanted her to know that his intentions were serious and sincere. And he desperately wanted to know whether she would accept him or whether, in the cold light of a dismal, damp autumn day, she would decide that she wanted to return to Richmond and to the stage. To that life she had so admirably carved for herself against all the odds.

His horse drew to a gentle halt outside the grand front entrance to Hayton Hall, prompting a flurry of activity from all directions. Samuel was vaguely aware of the simultaneous approach of his groom, his guests and two of his household servants as he climbed down, before reaching up to assist Hope. Gently, he lifted her down, once again overcome by the feeling of holding her in his arms, the heightened awareness combined with those more desirous emotions which were absolutely not appropriate with so many people nearby. As he drew her level with him, Hope's eyes met his and he gave her a smile—one which she returned with just as much affection as he hoped his would convey. A good sign, if ever he wished for one.

Composing himself, Samuel turned to greet the assembling welcome party. He would ask her soon, he told himself. He would find the right moment, and until then he would simply have to be patient.

'Well done, Sammy,' Charles declared, patting him on the back. 'You've brought her back. I do hope there was no harm done, Miss Swyn—Miss Sloane,' he corrected himself swiftly as he turned to Hope.

Samuel watched as Hope nodded, a look of uncertainty momentarily clouding those lovely green eyes as she regarded his friend. 'I am quite well, thank you, Mr Gordon, all things considered. Samuel tells me that you went with him as far as Lillybeck, to look for me. I am grateful to you. I know what you must think of me, now that you know who I really am...'

'Ah, yes. I'm afraid that in the past I have been far too adept at judging books by their covers, Miss Sloane,' Charles replied, a deep blush rising from beneath his collar. 'Such opining will cease henceforth. As a rather spirited young lady once informed me, I'd do well to pay more attention to the character of my acquaintances rather than other, more avaricious considerations.'

Samuel smiled at his friend's words which, for all his embarrassment, were clearly heartfelt. Beneath that boisterous personality and propensity for outright snobbery lurked a good heart. Hope, meanwhile, inclined her head politely, the ghost of a smile playing upon her lips. 'I am glad of it,' she replied. 'Especially if you intend to extend such generosity beyond your own acquaintances and consider, perhaps, those of your sister's acquaintance by the same standard?'

Charles's beetroot visage was all the confirmation that was needed that Hope's message had indeed hit the mark. Samuel could have kissed her out of sheer admiration for the way that, despite her own ordeal and exhaustion, she did not miss the opportunity to champion Miss Gordon's lovelorn cause. Instead, he reached for her hand, threading his fingers through hers and giving them a squeeze in solidarity.

Miss Gordon, meanwhile, hovered beside her brother, looking somewhere between relieved and chastened. 'I owe you an apology, Miss Sloane,' she began, her lip trembling. 'If I had not run away to the docks, you might never...'

Hope shook her head. 'It was my choice to join the search for you, and to get out of the carriage when I saw you,' she insisted, touching Miss Gordon delicately on the arm. 'You have nothing to reproach yourself for. My father was determined to find me—if he hadn't then, he would have eventually. At least it is all over now.'

The brave smile Hope gave Miss Gordon made Samuel's heart lurch for her, and he squeezed her hand again before releasing it as Hope hurried towards Maddie. He watched as the maid gathered Hope into her arms, letting out a few heartfelt sobs of relief as she whispered words that Samuel could not quite hear.

Next to them, Smithson hovered, endearingly trying and failing to remain composed as he clasped his hands behind his back and grinned from ear to ear. Samuel could not help but think about the wily old butler's warning to him all those weeks ago, about lies and the way they could all too easily get out of hand. How right the man had been, although Samuel suspected that even the ever-perceptive

Smithson could not have predicted where Samuel and Hope's deceptions would have led them. Nor could he have known, that evening when he'd lectured Samuel on being truthful, just how close to the surface the truth had always bubbled between them and how, despite the disguises they'd worn, they'd come to know and understand each other's true characters nonetheless.

He knew the essence of her, and she of him. Everything else, as he'd once told her, was simply window-dressing. He could only hope and pray that she would agree. That she would consent to becoming his wife. As Maddie released Hope from her embrace he stepped forward, offering Hope his arm. He could bear the wait no longer—he had to ask her. The right moment, such as it was, could be created as well as found.

'Hope, would you mind joining me in the gardens for a few moments?' he asked her. 'There is something I'd like to discuss with you, then we can freshen up and dine.'

Hope's eyes widened briefly, before she nodded her assent. 'Of course.'

Samuel walked with her to Hayton's sprawling rear gardens, his heart hammering in his chest. The right moment could indeed be created, he told himself and, despite his nerves, this felt right. Hope deserved to be asked for her hand properly; she deserved to know just how sincere and honourable his intentions were. She deserved to know just how much he loved her. There would be no more secrets between them, and certainly no more lies.

They drew to a halt on the footpath, the earthy, damp smell of the surrounding shrubbery heavy in the air. Samuel drew a deep breath, hurriedly collecting his thoughts as he settled upon what he would say. He'd never proposed marriage before—he had to do it correctly, had to find the right way to express himself...

Before Samuel could utter a word, however, Hope relinquished his arm and turned to face him. 'If this is about what I said to Mr Gordon, about his sister's acquaintances, I was only trying to...'

Samuel placed a gentle finger over her lips, smiling at her. 'I know what you were trying to do, and I think Charles understood too. But this is not about Charles, or his sister's romantic entanglements,' he replied quietly. 'This is about us.'

She furrowed her brow, then looked away. 'It's all right, Samuel,' she began. 'You don't have to explain yourself. I understand well enough that whatever this is between us cannot go on. You are a gentleman, whereas I am an actress and a...'

'You are the woman I love, Hope,' he replied, still smiling. 'And you love me—you told me so, only last night. Surely that is all there is to understand.'

She nodded. 'I do love you, Samuel, but what if love is not enough? What if the circumstances make it impossible? What if there are simply too many obstacles?'

He gave her a knowing look. 'Like Romeo and Juliet?' he asked, recalling her words in the library that night when they'd discussed Shakespeare. That night when they'd first kissed. That night when everything had changed.

'Yes—like Romeo and Juliet,' she replied.

'But, unlike Shakespeare's lovers, the only obstacles for us are ones we make ourselves. And for me, Hope, there are no obstacles. When I look at you, I see a woman I cannot fail to admire. You are not shameful, you are remarkable. Being an actress has not made you a scandal or a harlot—it has made you a talented woman with a passion for the theatre, not to mention a knowledge of the Bard which is second to none. I love you, Hope, and I believe with all my heart that love is enough.' He took hold of her hand. 'As a clever lady I know once told a friend of mine, we love who we love and that should be all that matters.'

He watched as she pressed her lips together momentarily, suppressing a smile at hearing her own words quoted back at her. She regarded him carefully. 'Are you sure that it isn't Hope Swynford you've fallen for? How can you be sure you're not in love with a character?'

'How can you be certain you don't love Sir Samuel the baronet and not Samuel Liddell, the title-less younger brother?' he countered.

'Because they are the same...' she began. He watched with delight as a wry smile crept on to her face. 'All right—point taken.'

He held those lovely emerald eyes with his own. 'The night that you told me your story, you said you'd allowed me to care for a woman who doesn't exist, but that simply isn't true. Hope Swynford might be a character, but she is also you. Calling yourself Hope Swynford rather than Hope Sloane and an heiress rather than an actress didn't change who you are, Hope, and even while you kept your true story from me and everyone else at Hayton, it was always there, wasn't it? Indeed, I would venture to suggest that a sheltered heiress would have been far less likely to astutely point out the unfairness of me not heeding my maid's wish to be called Maddie, or to recognise and empathise with Miss Gordon's difficulties. Only you, the real you, could have done those things. I'm not in love with a character. I'm in love with you. Marry me, Hope.'

Her eyes widened and she searched his gaze, clearly

disbelieving. 'When you spoke of marriage at the inn, I thought it was only because of the situation—that it was the stress and the relief talking. Never did I imagine that you could be serious.'

'I have never been more serious,' he replied. 'Do me the honour of becoming my wife, Hope, and make me the happiest man alive.'

Samuel held his breath for what felt like an eternity, watching her as she seemed to consider his proposal. Then, to his sheer relief and utter joy, she leapt forward, throwing her arms around his neck and pulling him close to her. He responded in kind, wrapping his arms around her waist and vowing in that moment to never let go. To make her the happiest woman that ever lived. To build a life together, one filled with laughter and adventure, with family and fun. With afternoons sipping tea and eating cake in the parlour, surrounded by all the children they would have, and evenings out at the theatre or spent cosily inside, savouring the finest bottle of Bordeaux and poring over a good book. With nights curled up together, and mornings waking to each other's embrace. A comfortable, contented life which consigned hardship and heartache to the past.

He buried his nose in the thick curls of her dark hair, breathing her in, imagining the years stretching before them, filled with promise. Then he realised that he had not yet heard her answer.

'So, is that a yes, then?' he ventured, whispering the words in her ear.

Hope gazed up at him, an irrepressible grin illuminating her face. The best and most wonderful smile he'd ever seen. The smile he wanted to see until the end of his days.

She reached up, placing the briefest, loveliest kiss upon

his lips. 'It's a yes,' she replied, her mouth still close to his, inviting him to kiss her back.

Which he did, of course—thoroughly, and with wild abandon.

Epilogue

February 1819

'*If music be the food of love, play on...*'

Hope settled into her seat as the curtain went up, the many candles which illuminated the stage casting their bright glow over the darkened theatre. From her position in the box at Lowhaven's Theatre Royal she could see Duke Orsino strutting around, musing about his unrequited love for Countess Olivia. Next to her, Samuel reached out and took hold of her hand, giving it a tender squeeze. The irony of them enjoying a performance of Shakespeare's *Twelfth Night* together was not lost on him either. Indeed, he'd flashed her one of his amused smiles when he'd told her that the play was coming to town just after Christmas, pulling her close to him as he'd informed her that he planned to reserve seats.

'People in disguise, falling in love,' he'd remarked, kissing the top of her head. 'The Bard could have written that one for us, couldn't he? We must go and see it.'

Hope had laughed at that, reminding him that they went to see virtually everything that Lowhaven's theatre had to offer, a habit which would doubtless become fixed now that they had settled into their own home on the edge of town. They'd moved at the beginning of the new year, after spending the Christmas season at Hayton Hall with Isaac and Louisa. Hayton's real baronet had returned from Scotland with his wife in November, their travels brought finally to an end by the worsening weather and Louisa's delicate health.

The brooding older brother had been stunned to discover that in his absence his younger sibling had not only fallen in love, but had wed. Hope had observed Isaac's astonished expression as Samuel recounted the extraordinary tale, from their first meeting to their marriage in a private ceremony by common licence in Hayton's ancient, humble church, witnessed only by the Gordons.

The return of Sir Isaac Liddell had thrown Hope into turmoil, and her old fears about her base-born status and dubious past had briefly resurfaced. As Samuel's older brother and the head of his family had regarded her carefully during their introduction, she'd found herself fretting, convinced that he'd be horrified about their union. As it turned out, she need not have worried. Despite his serious demeanour and brusque manner, Isaac was a kind soul who'd welcomed her into the family without hesitation. When he'd learned about her lowly origins and her life on stage, he had not even flinched. Instead, he'd seemed to perceive her discomfort and had done his utmost to assuage it.

'You're a veritable woman of the world, Hope,' he'd remarked kindly, regarding Samuel with affection in his keen blue eyes. 'And therefore perfect for my brother, since he has seen so much of it.'

Recalling the memory, Hope smiled. Isaac and Louisa had joined them at the theatre this evening, although they planned to return to Hayton in their carriage as soon as the final curtain fell. Another thing Hope had quickly come to understand was just how besotted Hayton's baronet was with his lovely wife, and just how protective—even more so since they'd discovered that the fatigue and sickness which had been troubling Louisa did in fact have an altogether happy cause.

Hope glanced at Louisa. Even in the dim light she could make out the serene expression on her face, one hand resting firmly on her swollen belly as she watched the play. The baby's arrival was expected in the early summer. God willing, Hayton Hall would have an heir, and the Liddell brothers would greet the next generation of their family.

Although, Hope increasingly suspected, the child would not be the sole member of that generation for very long—not if her own morning queasiness and absent courses were anything to go by. It was a suspicion she'd not yet shared with Samuel, but with each passing day she felt more sure of it, more excited, and more anxious. Tonight, she was bursting to tell him the happy news, especially since it had already been a day for it. Earlier that day she'd received a letter from Henrietta Gordon, telling her that she was no longer Miss Gordon at all. Last autumn Mr Gordon and his sister had departed from Hayton on a mission to reunite Miss Gordon with her lost love. It was a mission which had taken them to the burgeoning mills of Manchester to find the man in question, and a mission which had ultimately succeeded.

Moved by the depth of their daughter's misery and their desperation to cure her of it, the Gordon parents had finally accepted the match. A wedding had followed, and the newlyweds had now settled back in Blackburn, where the new

Mrs Smith was, in her own words, blissfully happy. Her husband, she wrote, had secured a job alongside her father, and although it was early days, he was proving himself extremely capable in all that he did.

Hope had studied the letter several times, shaking her head in disbelief at such an incredible tale, committed to paper in the hurried hand of a woman who was clearly delirious with joy at the surprising turn her life had taken. It was a feeling which Hope recognised immediately, since it was one she knew only too well.

'If this were played upon a stage now, I could condemn it as an improbable fiction...'

Hope smiled at the familiar famous line in the Bard's play, a line which could just as easily apply to her own life of late as it did to a story written more than two centuries ago. A year ago she'd been a travelling actress, on the run from a terrible past. Now, here she was, sitting in one of the best seats in the theatre, married to the most wonderful man and probably expecting his child. Improbable—indeed, it was improbable. So improbable that sometimes she had to pinch herself to be certain she was not dreaming.

Perhaps Samuel was right. *Twelfth Night* could have been written for them.

On stage, disguises were dispensed with as, at last, all was revealed. In the faint candlelight Samuel's gaze caught her own and held it, even as all around them the crowd grew noisier, chuckling and murmuring in excitable anticipation. They were, for a moment, in their own little world, one of mutual affection and shared understanding. One which, Hope considered, was worthy of one last revelation of her own. Gently, she lifted Samuel's hand, bringing it to rest upon her stomach, and nodded slowly. She watched as those blue-grey eyes of his widened, and his mouth fell open in surprise.

Then he leapt to his feet, pulled her into his arms and embraced her as the final curtain fell to rapturous applause.

* * * * *

COMING SOON!

We really hope you enjoyed reading this book.
If you're looking for more romance
be sure to head to the shops when
new books are available on

Thursday 26th September

MILLS & BOON

FOUR BRAND NEW STORIES FROM
MILLS & BOON MODERN

The same great stories you love,
a stylish new look!

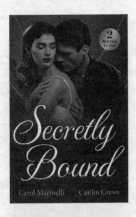

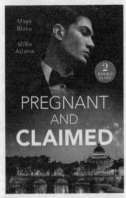

OUT NOW

MILLS & BOON

afterglow BOOKS

Afterglow Books is a trend-led, trope-filled list of books with diverse, authentic and relatable characters, a wide array of voices and representations, plus real world trials and tribulations. Featuring all the tropes you could possibly want (think small-town settings, fake relationships, grumpy vs sunshine, enemies to lovers) and all with a generous dose of spice in every story.

♪ @millsandboonuk

📷 @millsandboonuk

afterglowbooks.co.uk

#AfterglowBooks

For all the latest book news, exclusive content and giveaways scan the QR code below to sign up to the Afterglow newsletter:

SCAN ME

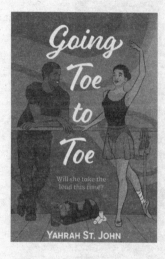

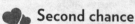
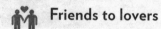
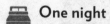

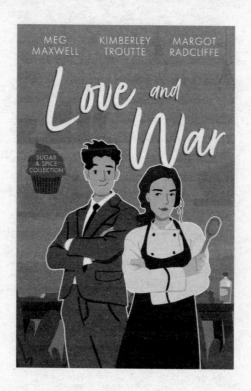

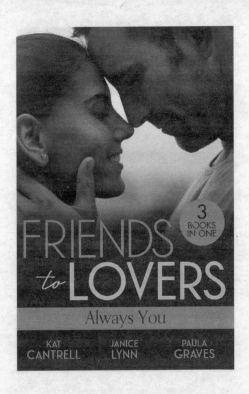

MILLS & BOON

THE HEART OF ROMANCE

A ROMANCE FOR EVERY READER

MODERN
Prepare to be swept off your feet by sophisticated, sexy and seductive heroes, in some of the world's most glamourous and romantic locations, where power and passion collide.

HISTORICAL
Escape with historical heroes from time gone by. Whether your passion is for wicked Regency Rakes, muscled Vikings or rugged Highlanders, awaken the romance of the past.

MEDICAL
Set your pulse racing with dedicated, delectable doctors in the high-pressure world of medicine, where emotions run high and passion, comfort and love are the best medicine.

True Love
Celebrate true love with tender stories of heartfelt romance, from the rush of falling in love to the joy a new baby can bring, and a focus on the emotional heart of a relationship.

HEROES
The excitement of a gripping thriller, with intense romance at its heart. Resourceful, true-to-life women and strong, fearless men face danger and desire - a killer combination!

From showing up to glowing up, these characters are on the path to leading their best lives and finding romance along the way – with plenty of sizzling spice!

To see which titles are coming soon, please visit

millsandboon.co.uk/nextmonth

GET YOUR ROMANCE FIX!

Get the latest romance news,
exclusive author interviews, story
extracts and much more!

blog.millsandboon.co.uk

MILLS & BOON
MODERN
Power and Passion

Prepare to be swept off your feet by sophisticated, sexy and seductive heroes, in some of the world's most glamorous and romantic locations, where power and passion collide.